T0044413

THE
DOWN DAYS

THE
DOWN DAYS

- A NOVEL -

ILZE HUGO

SKYBOUND BOOKS / GALLERY BOOKS

NEW YORK   LONDON   TORONTO   SYDNEY   NEW DELHI

Skybound Books
Gallery Books
An Imprint of Simon & Schuster, Inc.
1230 Avenue of the Americas
New York, NY 10020

This book is a work of fiction. Any references to historical events,
real people, or real places are used fictitiously. Other names, characters,
places, and events are products of the author's imagination, and any
resemblance to actual events or places or persons,
living or dead, is entirely coincidental.

Copyright © 2020 by Ilze Hugo

All rights reserved, including the right to reproduce this book
or portions thereof in any form whatsoever. For information, address
Gallery Books Subsidiary Rights Department,
1230 Avenue of the Americas, New York, NY 10020.

First Skybound Books/Gallery Books hardcover edition May 2020

Skybound Books is a registered trademark owned by Skybound, LLC.

GALLERY BOOKS and colophon are registered trademarks
of Simon & Schuster, Inc.

For information about special discounts for bulk purchases,
please contact Simon & Schuster Special Sales at 1-866-506-1949
or business@simonandschuster.com.

The Simon & Schuster Speakers Bureau can bring authors
to your live event. For more information or to book an event,
contact the Simon & Schuster Speakers Bureau at 1-866-248-3049
or visit our website at www.simonspeakers.com.

Interior design by Michelle Marchese

Manufactured in the United States of America

1   3   5   7   9   10   8   6   4   2

Library of Congress Cataloging-in-Publication Data is available.

ISBN 978-1-9821-2154-9
ISBN 978-1-9821-2153-2 (ebook)

To the ghosts of Cape Town's
past, present, and future.

THE
DOWN DAYS

MONDAY

THE DAILY TRUTH

WE REMEMBER

By Lawyer Tshabalala

It started with a tremor, small and unassuming, as these things generally do, my broe. Just a few words on page seven (by yours truly) about three tween girls stuck in a giggle loop.

The school called in a bunch of experts, who gave the thing a fancy label. And this put the parents' worries to rest. Because who doesn't like a good label to help them sleep at night?

Mass psychogenic illness. Also known as mass hysteria. Just a couple of tweens with their hormones running riot. Nothing to worry about.

It had happened once before. In the sixties, in Tanzania. Remember the Tanganyika laughter epidemic? And that story turned out fine. No need to panic, run tests, stick needles into anyone.

The experts took the Tanganyika epidemic as a blueprint and or-dered the girls to be isolated from their peers. So, the school sent the girls home to ride out this wave of runaway emotion somewhere else. Case closed, problem solved, job well done.

Only thing was, it didn't work. The girls didn't stop laughing.

Four days passed and the girls were burning fevers now. Struggling to breathe, eat, sleep. One by one they were rushed to the emergency room. Test after test was run while they lay shackled to their beds to stop them from falling off. Fed through tubes, attached to breathing apparatuses, and monitored around the clock.

Seventeen days. One day longer than the worst of the cases reported in the Tanzanian epidemic. And the girls were still laughing. Eyes tearing, voices broken, mouths salivating like mutts, faces contorted in the most horrific grins, knees jerking, arms flailing, bodies forever convulsing like crash test dummies.

Meanwhile, the "joke" was catching. The girls' families started laughing first, then their friends, their coworkers. The nurse with the heart tattoo on her ankle who came in quick to change the IV drip. The car guard holding out his hand for tips.

At first the guys upstairs clung to the mass hysteria diagnosis and tried to stem the tide by closing all channels of information. Lawyers were hired to file DMCAs to stop people from streaming all those YouTube clips or posting images in their feeds on social media. This was the Information Age, after all, and the tide couldn't be turned. So, the government pulled rank, imitated their chums in China, and orchestrated a total web blackout. Our city became data dark. But like Adam and Eve, we couldn't go back after tasting from the tree. Social media addicts were up in arms, their trigger fingers were itching and twitching, and a new kind of violence, dubbed "withdrawal rage," swept the masses. Addicts would snap and bring out their fists for as much as a skew look in a queue, and violence stats soared.

And along the way, more and more people were cracking up. It's psychological, it has to be, the experts proclaimed: an extreme response to Third World stressors.

But the girls, the ones the Laughter had chosen first, were now showing other symptoms, too. Their bones disintegrating, their organs turning into soup. And this thing, this mass collective joke, was blowing up in everyone's faces, with laughter resonating on every street corner, and death following suit.

Today, exactly seven years on, we remember the day that changed our sick city forever. Dorothy, Jennilee, and Andiswa: may you rest in peace. Along with every single soul who followed after. And God, Allah, Vishnu, the government, our ancestors (or whoever we choose to believe in) help us. May we one day find a cure for this curse.

SANS

Sans was a weasel. A wheeler. A dealer. A scavenging DIY schemer. A once sweet arrow-on-the-narrow turned small-fry ponyjacker, and now also a proper, serious, eye-on-the-prize pony dealer. As a pony man—the best, mind you, in this Sick City—he made a living dealing in real, 100 percent human hair, which a network of street kids and a convent of swindling sisters procured for him by all manner of means. It was the Down Days, sure, and Sick City was worse off than most, but chicks still dug their weaves, and a full head of hair cost a pretty penny.

It had been seven years since the Laughter turned the tip of Africa topsy-turvy. And Sans was doing fine. That was, until he met his unicorn.

He was wasting away his morning in Greenmarket Square playing cards with a bunch of dead collectors. On most days this patch of cobbled earth was a petri dish of industry, but today the air was dissonantly quiet and the traders who called these stones home looked bored and forlorn as they leaned against tables or sat around on plastic crates. It was one of those faux-sham-phony-bogus charlatan days that life sometimes coughed up: when every soul on the planet seemed down and out—like today wasn't a wise day to get out of bed and face the world—and the streets felt like a film set after most of the cast and crew had gone home.

But this particular set was as old as the city itself. Before the Down Days, the square was a heaving mass of bodies and colorful stalls, with migrants pressing curios from all across Africa on fat-walleted tourists with fanny packs bulging over Gore-Tex shorts. Long before that, barefooted slaves hawked fruit and veg on these same smooth stones.

The city's tourists had long since gone the way of the quagga, and the slaves, well, their bones salted the earth underneath these same streets. But the vendors remained, now hawking or bartering everything from petrol, Jik, and paraffin to chicken feet. One stall was doing a roaring trade in cooler boxes packed with survivors' blood. Their sales pitch went that the blood was rife with antibodies that could cure the Laughter. Another vendor was charging his customers' cell phones using some kind of contraption that he powered by pedaling like a madman on an exercise bike. If you had enough cash, most traders also delivered. That way, those rich saps who hadn't flown the coop before the borders closed could wait out the Down Days without coming into contact with another breathing, sweating soul.

Sans was chucking cards onto the hood of a car. It was the middle of May, although you wouldn't think it. The sun was searing hot and his mask was soaked in sweat. But he was winning—so he didn't care—when he saw her. His unicorn. One strand of strong virgin hair uncurling from the scarf fashioned over her scalp. Perfect arms tattooed with dark freckles like a map of the Milky Way. Real-girl hips. And those eyes—one green, one brown.

She walked right up to him and asked him for the time. A seemingly innocent question requiring a seemingly straightforward answer. If only he could have foreseen the path this meeting would take, traced the conjecture with a pen, connecting the dots, maybe everything would have turned out fine. But he couldn't. So he gave the answer that any man without sufficient foreknowledge of his imminent future would say.

Three words.

"Quarter past eight."

And with this, his troubles started.

FAITH

Faith September sat waiting behind the wheel, staring through the windshield. Outside the wind was playing tennis with an empty crisps packet. A mottled seagull dipped and dived, trying to nip at it.

As the number one driver for the Hanover Lazy Boys Corpse Collection Association, Faith spent her shifts on the streets of Sick City. Her guardjie and general sidekick, Ash, was a stringy white boy with a mullet who was in the habit of spinning tall tales and called his 9mm his baby.

In her life before the Down Days, Faith drove a minibus taxi. A tough job, with pay-as-you-go—or as many fares as you can load—wages. Time was money, every second wasted was a fare lost, and passengers had to be squeezed in fast and tight, skin on skin, like Tetris blocks. This led to some hairy driving to make ends meet and lots of name-calling from pissed-off passengers and motorists who didn't understand the challenges of the job and would scream and moan and call minibus drivers all sorts of names, like *bastards, lunatics, cowboys,* and *cockroaches*.

Then the Down Days came, and many taxi companies expanded their business into the epidemic industry, pimping their minibuses to move coffins instead of customers. As it turned out, the dead paid better than the living (and never complained about sharing seats) and this cockroach was now quite literally living the high life with a skyscraping pad perched above the ocean in Clifton and a full tank of petrol whenever she needed it.

That wasn't to say her life was all roses, though. Carting the dead around was backbreaking work and distraught mourners would often throw things, scream at her, chase her away, or call her all sorts of names, like *grim* or *vulture* or *hyena*. But Faith had come to accept that grief wasn't rational and couldn't be argued with, so she just put her head down and got on with it. That said, sometimes there was respect, too. Every now and again a stranger would stop her in the street, call her Charon (after the mythical ferryman who carried souls over the River Styx), and give her a brown coin as a token of appreciation for the work that she did.

Ash was at the market, hunting for air freshener and taking his own sweet time. A girl, no more than a child, crossed the street, pushing a rusted trolley. The girl tugged at the ears of her cutesy teddy bear medical mask, the trolley's wheels going *squee-squee* as they rolled over the tar. Startled, the gull fled upwards, leaving the crisps packet behind. As the girl lifted the trolley up and onto the pavement and disappeared into the folds of the Company's Garden, Faith stroked the bruise above her right eye. The damn thing was tender as hell and throbbing like techno.

Earlier that morning, while playing cards in the square, they'd been called to the home of a preacher who had promised his congregation that he would raise their dead. "Just wait four days," the sanguine pastor had apparently proclaimed, "and your loved ones will rise and walk among you again."

Four days had turned into four weeks.

The cops were called when the neighbors started complaining about the smell. So they raided the preacher's house and found grinner upon grinner stacked next to the TV set. When Faith and Ash came in to load the smiling corpses, the congregation was fuming and a riot was brewing.

The smell of the mob: fear, rage, adrenaline, sweat.

Stones were thrown (hence the ugly purple bruise), along with a couple of eggs. The cops retaliated with tear gas.

When they finally had all the grinners packed in the van and Faith started the engine, her back killing her, Ash began retching, just barely making it out the window. "Sorry, boss," he'd said. "It's the gas, it always does this to me."

After leaving the coroner, they could still smell the sick, so Faith sent Ash to the market for air freshener. She opened her window a crack. In the rearview mirror she studied the file of rusting metal carcasses lining the shoulders of the road: car upon deserted car whose owners had flown the coop, kicked the bucket, or couldn't afford the skyrocketing price of petrol and opted to skateboard, cycle, hail one of the few remaining minibus taxis catering to the living, or use their feet instead. Some of the windshields were shattered, others thick with dirt and dust on which a hundred and one fingers had left their mark. "Wash me," "Johannes was here," "Cindy & Tamatie foreva." Bright spray-painted imagery adorned others. A kid in a black hoodie was squatting on the roof of a beat-up Mazda, touching up the teeth of an image of a spotted hyena with a yellow spray can. The hyena was flashing its fangs, cold black eyes staring heavenward. The kid's sunshine-yellow mask had a laughing cartoon mouth painted on it; a brave choice if she'd ever seen one. These days, folks were mobbed or rounded up by the Veeps—the Virus Patrol—for much less.

On the radio, the city's only remaining nongovernment-affiliated station, run by a passionate group of volunteers, had an interview on with some woman from some organization. Faith didn't catch the name—Citizens Against Something-Something-Something. She was being interviewed by the station's husky-voiced midmorning presenter, Sandy B.

"It's atrocious, simply atrocious," the woman was saying. Her voice grated. "These kids need guidance. It's simply unacceptable to have an army of orphans running amok. Children need parents, authority figures, discipline. And when normal family systems break down, the government needs to step in and provide us with a solution."

"But," Sandy B. interjected, "we've all heard about the current state of these facilities. The government-run orphanages are filled way beyond their capacity. The system is failing these kids. So surely—"

"The system, any system, is darn well still preferable to the situation we have on our hands right now. I mean, every darn day this city is turning more and more into *Lord of the Flies*, what with these little hooligans on every street corner. Right this morning I caught one going to the bathroom on my daisies! My daisies, for goodness sake! Those bleeding-heart liberals who are moaning and groaning that the current welfare system is legalized child slavery should take their rose-colored glasses off and face facts. I mean, what about education? Who is teaching these street rats to read and write? Give it ten years and we'll be thrown right back into the Middle Ages, with all these children, now adults, running the country when they can't even spell. No. I say round up the little trolley-pushing tsotsis."

"But new reports indicate the situation is temporary. That the French have developed a vaccine that should be in production quite soon. Following this, more schools will be opening their doors again and—"

"Please! Do you really believe that? Open your eyes! The West doesn't care about us. They've closed their borders and left us here to rot. No. Something has to be done, come hell or high water. I say the government has to do its job, keep rounding them up and carting them off or else—"

Faith reached over and changed the station. The boy on the roof of the car put his spray can down and started fiddling with his phone. Then he slid off the bonnet and disappeared down a side street, passing a pair of kids busking on the curb. Kid number one was shaking a tin can to the beat while kid two was drawing dollar signs with a Sharpie onto the other's free arm. The song their lips were churning was a hot ticket for busking street kids all over the city, although they never seemed to learn more than the first verse, which they belted out in sing-scream until folks plead-paid them to stop. These two were different, though. They seemed to know the words.

Faith reached for the knob and turned the radio down to listen:

> *We are traveling in the footsteps*
> *Of those who've gone before*
> *But we'll all be reunited*
> *On a new and sunlit shore.*

Oh when the saints go marching in
When the saints go marching in
Oh Lord, I want to be in that number
When the saints go marching in.

And when the sun refuse to shine
And when the sun refuse to shine
Oh Lord, I want to be in that number
When the saints go marching in.

When the moon turns red with blood
When the moon turns red with blood
Oh Lord, I want to be in that number
When the saints go marching in.

Faith thought back to all those grinners this morning, stacked next to the TV set. How desperate those families must have been, to believe a crazy charlatan like that, saying he can raise the dead? She got it, though. Wanting to believe in something. She got it more than anyone. What with loading up grinners day after day, taking them away. Then there was that stupid suit. That canary-yellow cage. The way people stared at her when she was wearing it. Stepping back or averting their eyes when she walked past. As if she were death itself.

Not like any of this was new. Sick City had been delivered from the loins of the sick from the start. That's what her mother had always said. That illness did more than sticks and stones to build and break this city's bones. Scurvy was why the West first came to the Cape and brought slaves to these shores. Disease was behind the first seeds of seg-regation, too—the perfect excuse to give voice to silent prejudices. Way before the horrors of District Six, when the bubonic plague had raged through these streets, the homes of those deemed unwhite and unclean were razed to the ground. Their inhabitants chased to tented quaran-tine camps on the barren, sand-swept Cape Flats. If your skin was lily white, your home was merely disinfected and you were free to come and go as you pleased. If it wasn't, you needed a plague pass to travel.

No, none of this was new. The cradle of humankind was also the cradle of guns and germs and death. All those little red flags on the map the color of blood. The soil here was thick with bones. This had always been a city shaped by germs. These streets were birthed by disease. And one day, it would be destroyed by it.

But not yet.

For now, most people are still getting by. Chins up, as Ash liked to say. Chins up. Where the hell was that kid anyway?

TOMORROW

Tomorrow was at the market, feeling up avocados. Pressing her fingers into each green skin to see which one would give. Finding the perfect candidate, she turned around towards her purse, which was resting in the belly of the rusted trolley where her baby brother, Elliot, was playing with an empty coffee tin.

These days the prices at the local supermarket were a punch line to some kind of bad joke, with most of the shelves standing empty, gathering dust. Queues for what was left stretched around the block. So Tomorrow preferred to do her shopping here, in the Company's Garden.

The city's green lung was a relic of Sick City's days as a Dutch East India Company colony, when greens were planted to save passing sailors from scurvy. As if history was folding in on itself, the Down Days had led the locals to digging out almost all the pretty flower beds to plant vegetables again.

"How about this weather, né?" said the fruit vendor while adjusting her headscarf, dotted with fat little sausage dogs. "The wind's being a right banshee today. I can't stand it. And have you seen the mountain? All wrapped up in its shroud. Old Van Hunks and the Devil must be smoking up a storm again."

"Yes, auntie, they sure must be."

Van Hunks. The name made her think of her dad, who used to tell her the myth as a bedtime story: about this pirate called Van Hunks who used to live on the slopes of Devil's Peak back when Sick City was still called the Cape of Good Hope. Van Hunks lived for his pipe. Every day he'd sit on top of the mountain, blowing smoke rings and watching the ships sail by in the bay. One day a stranger approached him there and challenged him to a smoke-off. Van Hunks said yes, and for three days, Van Hunks and the stranger puffed without rest. Day four, they were smoking up a storm when a gust of wind blew the stranger's hat off, revealing the grooved and twisted horns of the devil himself. A sight like this would have had many a man choking on his own black smoke. But Van Hunks wasn't deterred. He just kept puffing. And he still is, they say.

On days when the mountain is swathed in fog, the old folk know it's just Van Hunks and the devil, still up there, smoking. Tongues smarting, lungs burning, neither ready to admit defeat.

Some say their duel has been going on for so long that they've developed a strange kinship. Together they huddle, spines curved into frowns like old men's backs tend to do, watching the empty harbor that has long since stopped sheltering ships and the bodies going about their lives below, while the smoke billows from the bowls of their pipes. Never interfering, just watching. Watching and puffing and packing their pipes on repeat.

"So what do you have for me today, sweetie?" the fruit vendor asked.

Tomorrow bent double to retrieve the bag tucked away underneath one of her brother's plump legs. Zipped it open and retrieved five glass jars. "For your pickles."

"What about the eggs?" the vendor asked, her brow knotting into a frown.

"Sorry. Not today. A mongoose got into my hens."

The lines above the vendor's threaded eyebrows smoothed out. "Not what I was hoping for. But we can work with it. Here." Her hands reached across the table. In each cup of flesh rested one green potbellied fruit. "Take two."

The girl scooped up each ripe avocado and placed them in the trolley next to Elliot. "Thank you. I'll do better next time."

The vendor smiled, one hand tugging at the hem of her glove. "You have a good day now, you hear? And cover up that poor boy, will you? Or next thing you know, he'll be blown away with the wind."

Tomorrow grinned, happy as a Cheshire cat that the woman had noticed the boy. Elliot was a funny kid, quiet, in his own world, easy to overlook. He tended to slip through the cracks and this worried her sometimes.

"Yes, thank you, auntie, I will. See you next week."

"As-Salaam-Alaikum, my kind."

"Wa-Alaikum-Salaam."

The girl and her baby brother headed up through the garden's old aviary, which was now a thriving chicken coop. "Cluck-cluck-cluck," prattled the toddler, pointing a finger at the fat hens as they dug in the dirt. A loud bang cut through the air as the city's daily med cannon fired, frightening the hens and the boy, who emitted a loud howl. Tomorrow kissed the boy on his head, gave his cheek a quick pinch. "There now, my sweets, no need to cry. Look, look! A squirrel. Let's follow him. Come!" The boy swallowed his howls, pointed gleefully at the squirrel, and the girl pushed the trolley farther.

At the far end of the garden was the steps of the Iziko South African Museum. The old colonial edifice loomed over them like a goliath's wedding cake. Slathers of white icing framed the yellow walls.

After the tourists had left, and the museum's funding had dried up, the artifact-stacked rooms became an informal mass garage sale, where locals bartered for odds and ends, from toothpaste and chlorine to homemade toilet paper and fried pigeon sosaties. A year ago, the World Food Programme and other international-aid programs had used the museum as a base to distribute food, formula, and rations. But suspicion, fueled by the endless pick of crackpot and not-so-crackpot conspiracy theories that bred like rabbits in these kinds of times—that the Laughter was a plot by either the government or the nebulous "West"—had resulted in mob-led beatings and the odd sjambokking of aid workers. Many of them had since given up on the cause and left. The wall to the left of the entrance was scarred with paint from a previous protest turned violent. STOP POISONING OUR CHILDREN! DEATH TO ALL IMPERIALISTS! the bloodred-painted letters proclaimed. Next to the exclamation point, a queue was forming in front of the museum's red medmachine. On the other side of the big brown museum doors, a government cleaner in a puffy Tyvek suit was spraying the ground with bleach.

"Come, my little penguin," Tomorrow cooed into the trolley. The boy looked up, blew a raspberry, and went to work again, banging the coffee tin like a drum. The girl lifted him out of his metal cage, slung him across her hip, tin and all, and pulled the trolley up the stairs behind them, grunting with the effort. She fiddled around in her bag till she found the two plastic medpasses, and the two children waited patiently in the queue for their turn to get checked. Then the big brown museum doors swallowed them with a gulp.

Inside, spread out underneath the suspended ribs of a giant southern right whale skeleton, the museum was a trickle of activity. Below the leviathan's broken umbrella of bones, a motley straggle of figures milled about between the tables strewn with things while the dead presided over proceedings from the safety of their glass coffins, their black pretend-eyes betraying nothing. The air had a chill, and the trolley bar felt cool in Tomorrow's palm. TRY SOMETHING NEW TODAY, read the ad prattle on the bar.

The girl tugged at the beanie on her brother's head, pulling it down to cover his ears. He gurgled at her as she pushed past a snarling taxidermied gorilla balancing on its hind legs. Someone had thought it funny to dress the poor animal in a yellow health-worker suit, complete with goggles, gloves, and mask. The new garb made the creature look more embarrassed than fierce, but the stuffed monster still left Tomorrow ill at ease.

She pushed harder; the trolley rolled faster. A funny-looking guy with a mullet squeezed past her, gripping a can of purple air freshener. What a weird thing to spend your money on. Who had the cash to spare to make sure their farts smelled nice? Why couldn't he rather spare a rand or two for her, instead of spraying it away into the toilet bowl?

"What a cute kid." A woman stopped to bend down and pat Elliot's head. There was a tattoo on her wrist. A snake curling around a stick. Her bottle-red hair needed a wash.

Tomorrow gave the woman a quick nod (polite smiles were pointless now that everyone wore masks) and forged on, past cabinet after cabinet of forgotten yesterdays. Rows of frozen corpses that, although already dead much longer than she'd been alive, still seemed ready to pounce.

A family of foodists stopped her to peddle their sales pitch, which was all about eating like a monk and humming a lot in order to live into your hundreds. They were handing out little pink pamphlets and selling all sorts of weird supplements in little hand-labeled bottles, from organic bee pollen to caterpillar fungus to colostrum from preservative-free moms.

Tomorrow found the stall she was looking for squeezed in between a tall Sikh selling paraffin and a muthi stall whose youthful proprietor was singing to himself underneath a nylon clothesline strung with dried black cats, anaconda skins, herbs, hippo tails, and horse legs.

While the bug-eyed vendor gossiped with another customer—something about a mutual acquaintance who had recently gone full hermit from the paranoia, only leaving his apartment once a week to throw out the trash—she picked up a bag of sugar. Looked at the price. It wasn't cheap. But it was her birthday and it had been ages since she'd last baked anything for the two of them. "Feast when you feast and fast when you fast," her dad had always said when he was still around.

Decision made, she turned towards the trolley to tell Elliot about the cake and how she was going to decorate it. Red—she'd use red icing, his favorite color. Sure, it would look a bit garish, but . . .

There had been a street magician who stood on a wooden box outside their house sometimes—their old house, that was—and bartered coin tricks for whatever you had to give. He also sold Ziploc bags of Ethiopian coffee beans, which his wife would roast in a pan at her feet, then grind, steep, pour for you into a small blue cup, and sprinkle with salt. But his passion was coin tricks. She knew by the smile he tried to suppress each time a kid would gasp or their mother drop a slack-jawed chin when they gave him a rand and he turned it over in his hand, blew on his palm, and then opened it with a quick flutter of his fingers like a startled dove—and the coin was gone.

Tomorrow used to love watching him, hoping for a glimpse of the vanishing coin that would betray his act. But she never did spot it—the man was too quick.

She would think of him afterwards, when she replayed this moment in her brain. Remembered her cold shock, the optimist in her convincing herself that the empty trolley was a silly trick, a sleight of the brain. A joke. That someone must have picked Elliot up to coo at him. They'd gone for a quick walk to show him the fluffed-up rabbits curled into the corners of their cages down the aisle, but they'd bring him right back.

They would. Sure they would. Any second now.

Any.

Second.

Now.

SANS

After Sans had given her the time, he invited the girl for a drink. She suggested this café around the corner, just down the street from his flat. A sign in the window said the place was open twenty-four hours. He made a mental note.

They sat at a table in the back. The waiter brought two beers. Sans couldn't put a finger on it, but there was something about this chick. She was dressed kind of weirdly, with her hair tied up tightly underneath a doek, except for that one strand. He couldn't see much of it, but what he did see, he liked.

Her lips were bare, no mask in sight. Maybe it was in her bag? Maybe she'd forgotten to put it on? Maybe he should say something? He slid his eyes underneath the table. No, she didn't have a bag. A girl without a mask was a recipe for trouble, all right. But Sans had never been one to shy away from trouble, and he wasn't about to start today.

The girl wasn't much of a talker, but that was okay because it meant there was more time to drink. So he ordered another round. The speakers were slinging out some seriously sweet tunes. When the Bullitts started with "Run & Hide," and Jay Electronica dropped that verse about the future being uncertain, with the wizard just a man inside the booth behind a curtain, he kissed her. At first, her lips pursed tight and she pulled away. Then she started kissing him right back. One thing led to another and before he could catch himself, he'd invited her up to his flat. The power was working so he put the kettle on. Waited for the click. They stood in the orange sunlit glare of his tiny kitchen. Her fingers played the wayward strand like a violin.

"Show me your hair," he said as he passed her the cup.

"Why?" she asked.

"Just 'cause." She put down the tea. He hoisted himself onto the cold counter with his palms and watched while her fingers fiddled with her headscarf. The strands fell. He was so stunned, he almost let go of his cup.

LUCKY

ucky was standing on the roof of the car, touching up the hyena's teeth, when he got the text. He put the spray can down and slid his phone out of his pocket. It was Sans. Something had come up and he wasn't able to make his regular drop tonight. Would Lucky pretty please help a brother out? Lucky sure would. The drop in question was a big deal—think a shitload of ponies and then some. Strange, though—it wasn't like his boss to ask for help. Maybe it meant the guy really trusted him. Trust was lit. Trust meant more work and more work meant more cash for spray cans—his next piece was already forming in his mind, a big fat pigeon smoking a big fat blunt. He'd paint it on the bleach-white walls of that ugly-ass Sanitation Church in Long Street. A risk, sure, but so damn totally worth it. Those white-robed crazies with their scrubbed-raw hands wouldn't know what the hell had hit them.

FAITH

Speak of the devil. The thud of the passenger door broke Faith's spell. Ash climbed into the seat, one hand holding a can in a dubious shade of purple.

"Lavender. You know I hate lavender."

"Take it or leave it. They were all out of that pine-cone stuff you like. Besides, do you know how expensive this stuff is these days? Daylight robbery, man! We're talking almost half my rent!"

"Since when have you ever paid rent?"

Ash shrugged. Faith grabbed the air freshener out of his hands and started shaking it. "You read today's *Truth*?" she said, pressing the nozzle and changing the topic.

"No," coughed Ash, pulling his T-shirt over his mouth. "Why?"

"Don't be so dramatic," she said, rolling her eyes. "New rumor is it's the Yanks' fault that we're dying all over the place."

"The Yanks? Last time it was the Russians. Before that, the story was that it was those guys, the Mallemaians, who wanted to cleanse the Rainbow Nation—wash all the colors out."

"No. That's yesterday's news. New word on the street is that it's the Yanks. That they shipped the Laughter in through vaccine drives. Said it was vaccines for polio and measles they were giving us—for free, from the goodness of their big red-white-and-blue hearts—but that was just a cover-up. 'Cause it's way cheaper and quicker to stick their needles

into us way down here in Africa than into rats or monkeys in their
fancy labs—which could take years of testing and jumping through
legal hoops. If the vaccines worked, these big pharma snakes could go
into production much faster and make fat wads of cash by selling them
to the US military. The plan, they say, was to use them on soldiers who
would go into war zones and spread the Laughter. All the while being
vaccinated against it themselves. Pretty clever, right? Wouldn't be surprised if our own government was in on it, too—giving those in power
the opportunity to cordon off Sick City and invoke martial law."

"Don't know," said Ash. "Sounds a bit out there to me. Pandemics
happen. They've always happened. Nature is cruel. Don't know why
people always feel the need to blame someone for them." He pulled
his T-shirt down a notch. "Truth be told, I liked your ergot poisoning theory best. Good old Saint Anthony's fire. Caught from ingesting
ergot-infested grain. Made sense, sounded kind of logical, fit most of
the symptoms, except for the viral part. No nefarious fairy-tale villains
in sight. Besides, I've never liked rye bread anyway. Yuck."

"Ha, ha. Tease me all you want," she said, turning the key in the ignition. "I mean, who knows what the truth really is. But I'll tell you one
thing—no way I'm reporting it if I ever fall sick. Not me. I'd rather go
on the run. The stories you hear about the things that happen in those
quarantine holes . . . No, I don't trust the system one bit. Not anymore."

"Please. Are you even hearing yourself, woman? Last time I checked,
we—me and you—we *are* the system. And all this paranoia and fear-
mongering only make our job, and the job of every single poor damn
health worker in this city—who are putting their lives on the line to help
everyone, I might add—harder!"

She was about to protest when someone knocked on Ash's window.
The window was fogged up from the cold and still covered in egg from
this morning. As Ash wiped at the dirty, eggy glass, it made her think
of those little yellow lotto scratch cards. When had she last seen one
of those? But his rubbing didn't reveal any cherries, dollars, or treasure
chests, just a bleary-eyed uniform stroking his stubble, holding a fat
rubber baton with which he was doing all that bloody knocking.

Ash rolled down the window. "Morning, Officer."

"Morning," said the uniform. "Can I see your medpasses, please?"

"Sure," said Ash, who never missed a beat. Just stuck his hand into the glove compartment, scrabbled around, then handed his pass over through the open window.

Faith searched her pants pockets for her own plastic card. A familiar panic flooded her body like muscle memory, slowing down her limbs, folding her fingers into invisible knots. *Breathe, don't laugh, breathe. It's here somewhere. It has to be . . .*

There. Found it. "Here you go, Officer," she said, stretching across Ash, swallowing down the nervous giggles, trying her best to keep her face blank.

The uniform twisted his brow into a frown and studied the pair of plastic rectangles. He swiped both cards through the box he wore on his belt and waited for the strip at the top of the screen to do its thing.

"Everything hunky-dory over there, Officer?" said Ash, all clown-ish and chipper, like the whole scene was one fat joke. But Faith had known him long enough to read behind his cool veneer. The kid had a tell, a habit of using ridiculous phrases like "hunky-dory" when he was on edge. Inside Ash's head, she knew, his brain was sweating buckets. Just like hers.

The uniform's brow relaxed. Black gloves passed the plastic passes back through the window. "Have a nice day."

It was over.

Another med check ticked off.

Another day still in the clear.

TOMORROW

Tomorrow's eyes scanned the stalls; her neck jerked left, right.
She spun around like a top.

Nothing.

A mistake.

It had to be.

Just a mistake.

"My brother. Did you see him?" The sugar vendor was too busy gossiping to hear her.

The room seemed to be swelling, the colors swimming together like wet paint. Surely there hadn't been this many people here before? Where did they all come from? So many faces. All blank.

She started counting to calm herself. Just like her dad had taught her. *One, two, three . . .*

This wasn't real. Wasn't happening.

Four, five . . .

Her skull felt electric. Like she was swimming in a packet of popping candy.

Six, seven . . .

Her chest a voodoo doll—something there stabbed, stabbed, stabbed. Wasn't she too young to have a heart attack?

Eight, nine . . .

Her legs. She noticed they were running. Running on autopilot.

Ten.

"Hey!" shouted the vendor, noticing her at last. But Tomorrow's ears were tuned to another frequency.

Rounding a corner, she tripped over a black pug. The little dog yelped and its owner yelled at her, but she didn't look back. Her legs were the only part of her body that seemed to be working right. So she kept running. Room after room. Underneath dangling skeletons. Past giant squids and strange nameless creatures with dead eyes made of glass. She kept running. Kept running. Didn't dare think.

When she couldn't find Elliot between the stalls, she headed towards the door. The broken EXIT sign had long since lost its glow, but the letters still led the way and all she could do was follow.

As she reached the threshold, a hand grabbed her shirt from behind.

"Gotcha!" The hand's owner was wearing a red beret, a basketball shirt, and a pair of dirty Nikes. The other hand held a chain that was, quite disturbingly, attached to a very alive, mercifully muzzled hyena.

"Hey! Watch it!" she started, then registered her fingers still clutching the sugar. "No. No. It's not what you think! I mean, I wasn't stealing. I . . . My brother . . . he's gone."

The security guard bent down, put a hand on the girl's shoulder. "Okay, okay, slow down. Try to breathe. Tell me what the problem is."

He tugged at the chain in his fist and the hyena bared its teeth.

Tomorrow's whole body recoiled.

"Don't mind Jamis. He only bites on command. So if you tell the truth, everything will turn out just fine. But if you lie, Jamis won't be smiling so nicely anymore."

The girl batted at the wayward curls hijacking her eyes. She knew it would be useless to run. So she forced her voice to be as steady as possible. "My brother. He was in the trolley. He's only a baby. Someone— someone must have taken him. Please."

The security guard's face softened. He held out his hand for the sugar and she gave it to him. "Let's return this and then we can go to the control room. They still have some cameras there. We can see if we can find something on the security feeds. If you're lying to me, I'll be able to see that on there, too. Come, Jamis."

Inside the small room it smelled like incense and stale smoke. The guard, who said his name was Ateri, replayed the footage on a black-and-white screen while the hyena lay on the cement floor, its head resting on its inwardly folded paws. The angle of the camera was wrong, so they couldn't make out much, but it did show a woman with long hair hovering near Tomorrow's trolley, then her body, or the back of it, making its way to the door. The woman kind of maybe looked like the same one who'd patted Elliot's head earlier, but Tomorrow couldn't be sure.

"So what now?" she asked the security guard, her voice small.

"We call the police. Don't know what good that will do, but I can get fired if I don't follow the rules."

Tomorrow's body crumpled inwards like a crushed paper cup. She could feel the guard watching her. "Your parents. Where are they?" he asked.

She kept her eyes on the floor.

"Relax," the guard tried again. "I'm not the Veeps. I just work here. You don't have to be afraid of me. I'm trying to help."

Of course you'd say that, the girl thought. But she kept her mouth shut.

"They're dea—I mean, succumbed? Your mother and father?"

Her mouth stayed shut, but her eyes looked up. *Kind eyes*, she thought to herself. He had kind eyes. That had to count for something, right?

"I've lost some, too," the guard said, taking the eye contact as confirmation. "I know what it's like."

"I . . . I'm all he's got."

"When did it happen? Your parents. When did they succumb?"

"Three months ago. But we're doing really well, we are. I had . . . I have a job. I'm taking care of my brother just fine. We don't need anyone."

The guard leaned over, touched her shoulder. "Listen, I get it. I don't trust the men upstairs, either. Who does? I mean, I've heard about those new state-run orphanages, too, putting kids into abandoned buildings like pilchards and throwing away the key. Not enough staff, not enough food to go around—sure doesn't sound like somewhere I'd want my girl locked up. But we have to phone the police. Besides, maybe those dogs can tug on their government leashes and do something good for a change, find him."

The hyena licked his stubby paws.

"I could leave, before they arrive. You could tell them everything."

"But how would they contact you if they found him?"

The room was quiet for a while. Jamis sighed and rolled onto his side.

"Hey, what if I had a guardian?"

"Sure, but how—"

Tomorrow shot up from the chair. The thin plastic legs buckled under the force of the sudden movement. It toppled over and clattered onto the floor, causing Jamis to sit up and giggle. The sound made her throat clog up and her runaway heart lose the plot. It was the sound of death itself. But she tried her best to brush the fear away. "Can you give me fifteen minutes?" she asked.

Outside in the street she found a car guard leaning against the wall. "Hey, brother, you haven't seen anyone come past with a kid in their arms in the last while, have you?"

"Don't think so, girly. It's been quiet all morning. Why?"

"Slow day?"

"Jissis. You have no idea," said the car guard. "What with the fuel shortages, the price of petrol, and everyone dying all over the place, it's like no one drives anymore. Look at these wrecks."

"Tell me about it."

"My motjie says I'm being an idiot, that I should hang up my yellow vest and go into the blood-hawking business. But I've never had a head for sales, you know, and I've been working this same corner for ten years now. It's my life. Other guys just do it for the cash, but I've come to love this spot. And I'm good at it. Jirre, I've got a smile like the grille of a newly polished Ferrari, makes the customers feel all nice and happy. And my eyes, they're like a hawk's. I can spot a screwdriver or a crowbar from here to Grassy Park. It's a calling. The yellow vest is my life. You can't give up a calling like that just because business is drying up. No. You lift up your chin and keep at it. So I stand here, come rain or shine or this blerrie mal wind. When money gets short, I grease my lungs with some karate water and I bring on the Pavarotti for small change. But I keep standing here. Seven days a week. *Stand here and they will come.* That's what I always say to myself. *Stand here and they will come.*"

"I feel for you. These are dark days for sure. Hey, maybe I can help. Want to make some easy money? All you have to do is pretend to be my dad for a while."

Briefing the car guard, whose name was Johannes, took less than fifteen minutes. Tomorrow didn't want to waste any more time—Elliot could be halfway across the city by now.

She got back to the room with Johannes in tow. Ateri was drinking the last dregs of a Coke, slurping at the straw, while the hyena lay on the floor, watching cartoons on an ancient iPad.

"You can call the cops now," she said.

They sat. They waited. Watched TV with the mottled beast. Johannes was starting to get antsy.

"Think about the extra cash," the girl reminded him. "You've already waited this long. Don't say no to some extra change in your pocket now. You told me yourself the pickings are slim and you need the money. Besides, this is such an easy way to make it."

"I don't know. I don't want to get into trouble."

"It's just a bit of acting. It's not against the law. Did Idris Elba get thrown in jail for kicking butt in that new Star Wars flick? No, he didn't. He got paid lots of dollars, didn't he?"

"It's not quite the same bag of chips, is it? This is Sick City. Not some galaxy far, far away."

"Sure it is. Sure it is. Hey, just stay a few minutes longer. Please. I'll make it worth your while. Promise."

So Johannes stayed. And three whole hours later, the cops came. Well, one of them anyway. A cutout cliché of a cop with a broom of a moustache that poked out above his government-issue mask, the space between his eyebrows lined with several thick exclamation marks. The moustache looked pretty freaked to see a hyena in the room. But he tried to keep cool.

There were only two chairs in the tiny office, and Tomorrow and Johannes were sitting on them, so the moustache took a seat on the edge of the desk that was farthest from Jamis while the hulking security guard leaned against the wall.

"Terrible weather we're having today," said the moustache.

"Sure," said the security guard. "The wind's being a real howler."

Neither Tomorrow nor Johannes said anything. The car guard was sweating with stage fright. He looked like he was about to pass out. The hyena kept his eyes on the ancient iPad.

"So, Mr. Pretorius . . ."

Tomorrow squeezed Johannes's hand in what she hoped was encouragement. She needed this guy to stay calm. Play his part. Elliot was out there, scared, alone.

She and Elliot had been glued at the hip since their mother succumbed. This was the longest they'd been apart, ever, and her whole body was aching for him.

"Mr. Pretorius," the moustache tried again. "I was asking you a question."

"Huh?"

"My dad's hard of hearing. Lost his hearing in one eardrum during a march pre-1994. One of the boere fired a gun too close to his ear. Been a bit deaf since." Her real dad's story—she'd read somewhere that the best way to lie was by telling half-truths.

"I see. And where is your wife today, Mr. Pretorius?"

"Uh, she—"

"What does it matter? We have to find Elliot. My baby brother is God knows where with whomever doing God knows whatever to him and we are standing here chatting about the weather."

"Yes, yes, miss. I understand your concern, but this is procedure. We have to follow procedure, you see, and—"

For the first time in her life, Tomorrow felt like punching someone. "Look around you, dammit! She's dead. His wife's dead. Like everyone else in this stupid city."

The moustache kept his eyes on Johannes like Tomorrow was invisible, a ghost. "Your son. What is his name again?"

"Andre. His name's Andre."

"Elliot," Tomorrow corrected him. "Elliot Pretorius. Andre is his nickname."

"That's an odd nickname, isn't it?"

At his post against the wall, the security guard shifted uncomfortably. "How about this weather?" he said. But no one heard him.

"So what?" said Tomorrow. "What if it's an odd nickname? What's it to you?"

Moustache crossed his legs. The trickle above his brows deepened into a raging river. "Miss, would you mind giving your dad and me some time to chat without interrupting? This is a conversation for grown-ups."

Tomorrow's eyes spat fire.

"So, Mr. Pretorius," the moustache continued, "where were you when your son was allegedly taken?"

"Allegedly? What do you mean allegedly?" said Tomorrow.

Moustache didn't bat a lid. Just kept his eyes glued on fake dad's.

"I was outside," said fake dad.

"He was waiting for me," said Tomorrow. "He doesn't like to shop. Crowds make him claustrophobic."

"Mr. Pretorius?"

"What she said."

"I see," said the moustache and scribbled something in his notebook. "So why didn't you see the woman exiting the building, then?"

"I—"

"Where were you standing exactly, Mr. Pretorius?"

"He was in the street. He was waiting for us outside on the pavement in Victoria Street."

"Ah. So the alleged suspect fled along Government Avenue."

"Not necessarily. My dad, he's not very observant. He daydreams. They could have walked right past him and he wouldn't have noticed a thing."

The exclamation marks on the cop's brow deepened.

"I see. Anything else? Do you have a description of the woman?"

"She had red hair, I think," said Tomorrow. "Bright bottle red."

"You think?"

"No . . . I know. I'm sure of it. She had bright red hair. Yes." *The woman from the footage has to be the same woman who bent down to coo at Elliot. They looked so alike. Yes.* She was almost, just about, a hundred percent sure of it.

"We have some security footage of the incident, but it doesn't reveal much. I can show it to you if you like," said the security guard.

"That would be great, thanks. But let's wait until after my interview with Mr. Pretorius. Anything else?"

No one in the room that smelt of sweat now said anything. Johannes kept his eyes on the ground.

"Well, we'll need a recent photo," said the moustache.

"I have one on my phone. I can forward it to you." Tomorrow saw her brother's brown curls in her mind's eye, phantom-felt his cheek resting against her collarbone. It took everything she had not to bawl.

"And a contact number."

"Here, you can have mine. Johannes, I mean Dad, works during the day. It's better if you phone me."

"I see. And what line of work are you in, Mr. Pretorius?"

"Why is that important?" said Tomorrow.

"Well, it is possible that the kidnapping could have been related to your line of business, Mr. Pretorius."

She threw her hands up, clenched them, shook them like they were crawling with bugs. This was hopeless. The cop was an idiot.

"We can't exclude any leads at this stage," the moustache tried again. "So please, what do you do?"

"This is a waste of time. You're wasting time." She was ready to pounce now. Ready to tear that thick, fat moustache right off his fat face. The hyena lifted his chin, glared at the cop, gave a snigger. Moustache tried to act cool, but his hands were trembling.

"Calm down, daughter of mine. The man's only trying to do his job," said Johannes, falling into his role at last. "I'm a car guard, sir. Surely there isn't a connection?"

"Probably not," said the moustache. "But you can never be sure."

"Of course. Any other questions, sir?"

"Not at this time."

"When do you think you'll have something? Find Elliot?" Tomorrow tried her best to keep her voice calm. Feign some respect.

Moustache didn't look at her. Kept his eyes on her fake dad as he spoke. "Well, we're understaffed at the moment, as you well know.

And kidnapping isn't a priority matter anymore. As you might understand, a healthy city is paramount in the current political climate, and
catching defectors takes up most of our resources at present. But we'll
do our best."

"Your best? Your best!" She was readying to pounce again, but the
car guard jumped the gun.

"Thank you. Please excuse my meisiekind. We appreciate all your
help."

When the moustache was done, and her fake dad had been given a
talking-to, Tomorrow found the bathroom, entered the cubicle, and
vomited. She had paid Johannes with her mother's wedding ring. He
wasn't too happy about it—he was expecting cash. But it was real gold
and she was sure that he could pawn it somewhere.

Her stomach empty, she slid down onto the floor, legs hugging her
chin. She was trying, she really was, but she couldn't keep up the act
anymore. *Be strong*, she told herself. *Don't be a baby, don't break down
now. Don't* . . .

- 9 -

SANS

She was lying on his bed, her virgin hair slung across the pillow, the tips plunging off the edge of the bed like a thousand tiny anchors. Sans couldn't believe what he was seeing. Hair of this quality, color, and length was the stuff of fairy tales. Thick, strong strands that cascaded down to her hips and seemed to change color—from black to blue to indigo, purple, gray, and back to black. He watched, mesmerized, each unicorn strand worth a rand—a new phone or a pair of sneakers. He had a rule about not eating where you're sleeping, but he'd never been more tempted to break it. His fingers were aching for a cut.

He was sitting there, pondering the gleaming glory all spread out on his pillow, limp and vulnerable, when the city's daily med cannon rang through the corridors, announcing the time at 12:00 p.m. sharp. In the old days, pre-Laughter, the city's big noon kaboom was nothing more than a cute colonial curio from a time when cannons were used to signal the time to the ships in the bay. Now it was a signal of a different kind. Sans headed into the hallway where a few other residents were already lined up, thumbs at the ready in front of the red machine.

When the Down Days first came knocking, the government relied on cell phone apps for med screenings. But the apps were too easily hacked, generators were in short supply, and daily load-shedding meant the average guy on the street's phone was always out of juice. So these clunky machines—dubbed *postboxes* by their users—popped up all over the city.

Two heads in front of Sans, a mother was consoling her crying kid, who was begging her to let him skip his check.

"I'm sorry, little bear," she said. "But we have to. You know we do."

"But what if the siren goes off and they come and cart me off to that place where they took Uncle Alfred and I never see you again?" His mother bent down and hugged him to her breast as the boy's sobs grew louder, his whole body shaking with the force of his fear.

"It's going to be okay," cooed his mother. "I promise. Look, do you have your thermometer with you? It's in your pocket, right? Take it out."

The boy did as he was told. "Let's take your temp, quick. If it's all fine, we'll know it's safe to stick your pass in the slot."

Sans waited for the trembling kid to take his turn. When his own turn came, he slid his medpass into the slot.

There was a low hum and a thin ray of light washed over his body. *"Body temperature scan slightly elevated. Please continue to level two."*

Shit. That wasn't good.

Trying to stay calm, he stuck his thumb into the oval hole at the top of the postbox, and waited for the familiar sting. A high-pitched ping followed. Sans pulled out his thumb and stuck it into his mouth to suck away the blood. *"DNA scan complete. Congratulations. White blood count acceptable. Please proceed,"* whined the uptight voice from inside the yellow box. He rolled up his sleeve and stuck his arm into the slot. Pressed a button and waited for the needle to do its thing.

"Injection complete. Thank you. A healthy city is a happy city," sang the voice inside the machine before spitting out his pass.

When he got back to his flat, his unicorn was still there.

"What about you?" he asked her.

"What about me?"

"Aren't you going to get checked?"

The girl didn't say anything, just stared out the window and down into the street where Johannes, the car guard, was perched on a crate in front of that Asian girly den (the one where those pretty Cape Flats "geisha" girls were always sitting in rows in the fluorescent-lit foyer, hoping for walk-ins). Johannes was belting out his usual brand of mashup Manenberg opera while jingling a tin can with loose change.

"Hayi, wena, do you want to play with fire? You know what will happen if you get caught without an updated medpass. You get thrown on the Island."

"The Island?" she said lazily, as if they were talking about palm trees and sandy beaches. Outside the window, Johannes had stopped singing and was chatting to some girl with crazy curls.

"Forget about it," he said, dipping his fingers into her hair. The strands seemed to writhe, like something alive, moving and coiling around his fingertips. Like a Klimt mermaid she seemed to him, all hair and foreboding.

"I want you to wash my feet with it," he murmured, kissing her roots.

"What?"

"Never mind. Forget about it."

He walked her to the gate, where a kid in gumboots, her long purple braids tied up in a knot, was laying into the buttons on the intercom like she was giving them CPR. "Hey, Sans," said the kid.

"Hey, Kholeka. Here for me?"

"Nah, delivering some lip porn to the guy at number eleven. That new game is still on the Mouse's download list. Will drop it off in next week's package, 'kay?"

The Mouse, aka Mickey Mouse, was the city's biggest data dealer, slinging hard drives filled with the latest international movies, series, music, even phone apps and educational material, all sorts of digital shit. Technically illegal, the system worked better if you didn't know the source, and the guy was a hermit, a ghost. Only his runners knew where he lived and they were paid a mint to keep their traps shut.

"You haven't told me your name," he told his unicorn as they pushed past the little button-whacker into the street.

"Whatever you want it to be," she said, all coy and syrup sweet.

"Ha. Cute. But no, really."

"That which we call a rose . . ." she teased. "But really. You would only forget it, wouldn't you?"

"What about some digits, then?"

She gave him a quick, quizzical look.

"Your phone number."

Her finger pointed down. "Your shoe. It's untied."

He stooped down to make the knot.

A few steps in front of him on the pavement, a mother with a boxy fringe was hunched over, chiding her two twin boys, her hands gripping the necks of their T-shirts. "Akin, you stop that right this minute. No laughing outside the house. How many times have I told you? Do you want the Veeps to pick you up and lock you away? You, too, Shafiek. Wipe that smirk off your face right now—don't think I can't see it behind your mask."

"But, Mom. He tickled me."

His eyes trailed the trio stomping off towards the mountain. When he turned his head back, his unicorn was gone. He'd fallen for the oldest trick in the book. She might as well have said, "It's not me, it's you." In a way, he wished she had.

LUCKY

Lucky was on his way to make the drop when it started raining. He was running a few hours early, in any case, so he ducked into the new therapy bar on the corner to escape the downpour. He'd heard the doormen were lax, and to be fair, he was dying to see what all the fuss was about.

The place was crowded with rowdy peeps pressed together like Pringles. On a stage lined with thick rope, a man in a suit was beating up the Easter Bunny, sweat pouring off fake fur.

Sick City's newest chain of therapy bars was proving to be beyond popular, with three new venues expected to open soon. The concept was simple: this was a fight club for the frustrated, a strange new cure for the dangerous levels of anger and violence that had been building in the city. The Days getting you down? Come beat someone up in a nice, safe, legal way.

For a rand or two, you got three minutes in the ring with someone dressed as the president, the taxman, Jesus, Santa, your boss, your wife, your boyfriend, neighbor, the Pope. A live punching bag on which to take out your rage. Pay extra and the game could be rigged in your favor.

Of course, there were precautions that needed to be taken. Civilian fighters had to be kitted out in scrubs and gloves and goggles. The bar's own fighters could bare their skin, but had to undergo rigorous daily med tests before getting into the ring.

Before the therapy bars, mob violence was getting intense. Lucky once watched his neighbor, a kid of about fourteen, being necklaced by an angry mob because the senile old bag at the end of the street had accused him of stealing a butternut. A *butternut*.

The crowd had doused him with petrol and lit the match. Then a local preacher used his one good Sunday jacket to put out the fire. No one helped him. Not even Lucky.

Afterwards, Lucky read an interview with the kid's mother in the *Daily Truth*—where she kept repeating over and over how it was all some huge, sick misunderstanding. How he was a good kid, her boy, no skollie, would never steal anything—the boy didn't even have a nickname.

Lucky still had nightmares about it. Not because of the necklacing—he'd seen guys being necklaced more times than he cared to remember—but because he'd known the kid. Had played soccer with him to pass the time more than once. And still, he'd stood there. Rooted to the spot like some stupid statue dripping in pigeon shit. While the flames leapt higher. Didn't even blink.

Things were better now, thanks to the therapy bars. Don't have money for a ticket into the ring? No problem. If you went to your local clinic, chatted to the nurses there, they'd give you a government-sponsored coupon equal to one free session. There was a limit to how many coupons you could pick up in a month. If you were extra pissed about something, you had to fork out. But it was pricey, so you had to be pretty loaded. Lucky had heard there was this guy called the Mouse who lived underground somewhere in some kind of secret apartheid bomb shelter or something who could hook you up with fake coupons cheap-cheap or in exchange for all sorts of shady favors.

He was standing in a corner of the bar, hustling for cigarettes, when the redhead came up to him and offered him a drag. Van Hunks, his favorite brand. He hadn't been able to get hold of a single entjie, let alone a Van Hunks, in months. He inhaled the smoke slowly, savoring the smooth warm sensation as it slid down into his lungs. The redhead started chatting to him about the match. She looked familiar, but he couldn't place her face. With one thing leading to another, the talk soon shifted to sharing a pipe: "If you're into that sort of thing?"

Lucky sure was, but it was getting late and Major was waiting. He thought of Sans and how pissed he'd be if he found out that Lucky had missed the drop. His boss usually made the drops himself, but today something had come up. The way Sans had acted when Lucky came to pick up the cash around noon—the way he stood outside the door and didn't want Lucky to come into his flat—made Lucky figure that there was a girl involved. There always was, wasn't there?

Lucky squeezed the strap of his backpack with his fist. Thirty ponies at 3,000 rands a pony. That was an unholy amount of money to be carrying around—he'd better stop screwing around and get to the sisters quick.

"Go straight there and back. Don't mess around. Don't even stop to tie your shoelaces," Sans had said before giving him the cash.

But the woman kept sing-saying in her syrupy voice, "Just one hit," until Lucky finally said, "Let's make it quick," and followed her into the back seat of her car, where she locked the door and took the thing out of her handbag.

"What kind of a pipe is that?" he asked.

"A magic pipe," her honey voice cooed. That was about all Lucky remembered before things turned black.

11

TOMORROW

When Tomorrow arrived back at the house, the fingers holding the key were dancing their own crazy dance and couldn't find the keyhole. After she finally got the door open, she dropped her bag and headed into the kitchen, where yesterday's dishes were stacked like skyscrapers. Somehow her body found a chair. But her mind wasn't there. She didn't even register the speck of brown mouse scuttling past her toes and the gray cat scrambling after it. Just sat there. Sat there. Thinking about everything and nothing.

Someone had left a copy of the *Daily Truth* on the kitchen table. Tomorrow didn't care for the *Truth*. Her mother had called it a conspiracy rag, full of grand schemes and cheap shots. But now she leafed through it to forget. Thumbed the pages. Tried to read. But the sentences were swimming. For a moment, she considered paging straight to the classifieds—she had to find a new job fast before rent day came around—but she was too worried and stressed to even think about that now, so she stuck to reading the articles instead. Most of page two was an ad for a traditional healer. "Mama Lily: Want to change your miserable life? Through my strong ancestors all is possible. Laughter charms and cures, cheating lover, love binding, bad luck with relationships, tokoloshe, enemies, witches, curses, banishing evil, dream interpretations, business and family affairs, strange happenings and many more. I also work on penis size. All guaranteed results." Below that there was an ad for a doomsday cult, and squeezed in next to that was an article on how the Laughter was first designed to be some kind of Malthusian population-control experiment. Tomorrow didn't know what a Malthusian was, but it sounded like a supervillain in a comic book. *What a load of crap*, she thought, and switched to the back page to read the cartoons instead. But she couldn't concentrate. Her thoughts kept reversing back to the market; her brain kept trying to find Elliot's face in the crowd.

There was a noise coming from the sink. The tap was dripping. She hadn't noticed it before. Water was *p-p-plopp*ing into the basin like a heartbeat. Like a pulse. What a waste. She really needed to stand up and close the thing. She was willing her limbs to work when she noticed the *Truth* again. At the back of her mind something tickled. A memory, a thought, an idea . . .

She turned a page.

Then another.

And another.

Until she found what she was looking for.

There, next to the ad for the sangoma, another ad, smaller, so small that only her subconscious had seemed to register it the first time around. "Need help? From lost kittens to life crises, contact F. September. Truthologist. Patternologist. Private Detective. Pro Bono." Just that. And a number.

She pulled her phone out of her pocket. Four bars. A miracle. A sign.

She had to dial the number three times before she got it right. Her brain felt muddled and wired at the same time, out of step. Third time was the charm. It was ringing.

Ringing.

Ringing . . .

"Hi, this is Faith September."

Finally. "Hi. I'm calling about your ad in—"

"I can't come to the phone right now, but leave a message straight after the beep."

12

PIPER

Tamatie stacked the bottles of Jik into a pyramid. "Showmanship is the secret to great salesmanship," his dad had always preached. That, and an eye for the details. Tamatie's eyes were locked in on a detail right now: the slim, flaming redhead getting out of the van across the street. Something about the woman wasn't quite right. Not her bra size or the mess of her half-dyed, wet red hair. Something else. That felt off. He had a sense for these things. And that fox was trouble. He was sure of it.

It was getting dark, the rain was pouring down the sides of the stall's plastic tarp ceiling, and the cold made his phantom arm ache.

Tamatie adjusted one pillar in his pyramid and looked up towards the van again. The woman was still standing there, in the rain, in front of the bar. It had been twenty minutes now. Her eyes darted up and down the street while she scratched her neck and hands like they itched. Was she waiting for someone?

The woman fiddled with her mask and Tamatie wondered what her mouth looked like. It had been so long since he'd seen a real, live, female mouth. Was it small and sleek and prim, with the lips turned up a smidge at the tips? Or full and thick with a prominent cupid's bow and a nice plump and curvy bottom? And the color? Plain Jane nude or nice and rosy? Soft and smooth to the touch or slightly chapped? Did she have dimples when she smiled? There was a lot of lip porn doing the rounds, what with everyone all covered up in masks now, but Tamatie wasn't the type to trawl the web for cheap chops. Every now and again he did stop to wonder, though, 'cause who didn't appreciate a good lip . . .

The street was at a slope, and Tamatie's stall was uphill from where the redhead was standing, giving him a good view of the stain of black roots that flowered from her crown.

With his attention diverted, his eyes and mind not on the job, the pyramid started teetering dangerously. One palm shot out to quell the impending cave-in, but he was too late. Plastic collided with pavement. Tamatie picked up the tumbled bottles, placed them on the table, and began to stack from scratch, focusing again on the task at hand.

Piper pulled the sleeve of her shirt down over her tattoo. She hated it now, reminding her of another time, when she was another person with a different life, a profession that might have been honorable. She scanned the street for what felt like the hundredth time. In the distance, she could hear multiple sirens wailing in stereo, the soundtrack to the city. A dead taxi growled past with the windows rolled down. The mullet-headed guardjie had his hand on the roof, his palm tapping to the beat of some kasi tune she didn't recognize. Her own soundtrack was playing the Velvet Underground. She could hear Lou Reed's voice at the back of her mind as she stood on the corner, scratching at her neck. *I'm waiting for my man.*

Tonight her man was late. And it was getting to her. Piper walked to the back of the van. It was a "company car," and Major only let it out of his sight on Mondays—the old caretaker would be wondering where she'd gotten to with it by now. She rested her hand against the back window and peeked in through the gap in the curtain. She could just about make out the two little lumps lying there in the dark. They seemed to be sleeping again, which was a relief. Earplugs. She couldn't believe she'd forgotten the earplugs. The one from this morning had been a real earache. All that screaming and shouting and banging was enough to make anyone go mad.

Piper swiveled around, straightened her back, and tried to wipe the rain out of her eyes—"A good posture in life is half the battle won," her mother was always harping on—and started pulling at her sleeves again. Across the street a Jik vendor was giving her the stink eye. *Such a bad place for a meet*, she thought to herself again, annoyed from scratch, but her man had insisted.

Her nails were raking the tattoo, her skin was itching something fierce, and it triggered the same old memories of the day she got the infernal thing, how her mother had cried, the future looking so bright. Perfect little Piper. That was her. Always climbing higher. Burning brighter. Prefect in high school. Captain of the hockey team. Straight A's in high school. Then med school just because she could, not because she had any real interest in medicine, but because she was smart enough to get in, because it was what was expected of her. The plan was to become a surgeon. She had the hands, the drive, and the brain for it. During her second year as an undergrad, she'd read a book by Oliver Sacks, whose words were poetry to her. He made medicine sound like art. It made her think about the brain. Really think. About how much people still don't understand about how it functions. This was terra incognita. With so much still uncharted, unmapped.

For the first time since starting med school, Piper saw being a doctor as more than an achievement, another gold star to add to the list. Was that what having a vocation meant? If so, she had one. She decided to specialize in neurology. The future seemed sure, everything falling into place.

Then the Down Days descended and all her friends from med school were either hopping on planes to leave the country or signing up to help. Perfect little Piper felt like she needed to lend a hand, too. That it was expected of her. If she had to be totally honest, a part of her was also fascinated by the drama of it all. What was that expression about watching car crashes? How you knew you had to turn away, that you shouldn't look, but you just couldn't help yourself. This was something like that. But instead of just one crash, it was a tsunami-style freeway pileup stretching all the way from here to . . . everywhere.

The virus was also unlike anything anyone in the medical community had seen. Another untamed frontier. An opportunity to break new ground. Make a name for herself. Excel. As if there was this chart tattooed onto her brain, like the one her mom taped above her bed as a child, and she was always working out ways to add more mental stars. Her whole life up to then had been about toeing the line and racking up stars. So of course she packed a suitcase and signed up, got stationed at the Green Point Sanatorium.

Things were good at first. Exciting, even. But as the days wore on, every little thing she saw pecked away at her. So many corpses: women, men, children, babies . . . Parents separated from their daughters, sons. The pain of telling a six-year-old boy that his entire family had succumbed and were now lying forgotten under a sheet, soaked in their own blood, vomit, piss. Wanting to hug the crying boy, but not being able to because of the yellow suit.

The fear she saw in her patients' eyes every day when she approached them in her mask and gloves and goggles like a giant yellow Teletubby to usher them into the examination room. The way they acted like she was some kind of monster, a demon, a tokoloshe.

As the sickness spread, her family and friends (the ones who hadn't already fled) started making excuses not to see her. "I'm wearing protection," she'd say. "No need to be scared; I miss you, let's meet up." But they'd just smiled politely, saying, "It isn't that. I'm just busy, that's all. Next week, let's make a plan, or the week after that."

The other volunteers weren't always too friendly, either. Packed together in the same tented quarters twenty-four seven, sharing the same tiny kitchen, sleeping in dormitories, touching and feeling and breathing on each other day in and day out. What if the woman with the red-rimmed glasses snoring in the bunk next to you, or eating her apple alongside you in the cafeteria, hadn't been careful that day when she was taping up her suit? What if she had been distracted, thinking about her daughter, whom she missed so much all the way in London, and slipped up? She could be standing there, trying not to smile too much while you told her your favorite joke (the one about the married couple who go to the drive-in), but inside her skin the Laughter was already starting to pull the strings and you were next.

Soon the nightmares came. She'd wake up in the middle of the night sweating, the anxiety burning through her body and mind like a virus.

In her head she'd be screaming, but like an actress in a jerky silent film, no sound coming out. *Get a grip on yourself, don't be such a cliché*, she'd tell herself while lying there alone, trapped within her own mind. Then she'd look down at the tattoo on her wrist, trying to make out the black lines in the dark, and swear at God and Asclepius and whomever else would listen, while the bodies next to her snored and stirred and farted.

It started out with plain old codeine (Ngoma, Captain Cody, or Purple Rain, as some of her codeine-head patients called it). A swig here, a swig there, straight from the bottle, just to take the edge off.

After a while, she needed more, and moved on to fentanyl. Just a little at first. You prescribe fentanyl to a patient, but instead of giving them the whole needle, you inject a little into yourself. Share the fun.

She knew what she was doing but after a while she didn't care. As the need grew, she'd pocket syringes when it was her turn to restock the pharmacy, swap whole needles with dirty, empty ones that she filled with saline. Then the sharing of needles gave her hep C, which she ended up passing on to a few of the patients. Maybe more than a few. But she couldn't stop and people were dying left, right, and center anyway, so no one was noticing. At least not at first.

When they finally did, Piper's whole perfect world folded in on itself.

Things were different now. Her new profession didn't come with an oath to do no harm. Hell, the meaning of that word was ambiguous anyway. Take *euthanasia*, for one. The way she figured, she was doing the little street rats she was scooping up a favor. Sure, her technique lacked a certain finesse, the way she had to drug them and grab them. But they were out cold for most of it, and when they woke up they were sent to a better place. A win-win as far as she was concerned.

She was making a difference, making the world a better place. One day someone would thank her. Track her down, maybe even make a TV documentary about her. Once this was all over and everyone had gained some perspective.

Yes. They'd thank her. Give her some kind of medal, they would. She was sure of it.

MAJOR

The Sisters of Godiva House of Holy Hair stood behind a graffiti-clad brick wall in Sea Point. Gulls swooped above the garden shrine where ponytails strung up to dry whipped in the wind.

Under the shaded courtyard awning, the sisters sat in cross-legged rows from 8:00 a.m. to 3:00 p.m. each day, their bald heads wrapped in blue turbans, electric razors in hand while devotees queued, ready to offer up hair in exchange for health.

The sisters washed the hair in basins of tepid water, then tied it tightly into ponies before cutting and shaving each head. The younger sisters kneeled alongside with baskets, taking the ponies away to be sorted and strung in the wind to dry. Each strand was a unique DNA fingerprint, a piece of soul awaiting a holy, ritual burial. Give but one pony, they said, and you and your loved ones might be spared for another year or two, the Laughter kept at bay.

Major had been working at the convent for thirty years, since back when it used to be a boarding house for single girls run by the St. Mary's convent. These days his employers were more airy-fairy. The sisters with their blue turbans, colorful saris, and bindis were an odd bunch compared to the nuns in their penguin robes. But in the end, the job remained the same: trim the hedges, water the flowers, sweep the hallways. Keep your head down, don't ask too many questions, keep nosy visitors away.

Tonight the ponyjacker was late. To pass the time, Major unlocked the convent's processing room. The high-ceilinged hall with its scratched and faded wooden floors where the sisters sat each day testing each braid's virginity, then weighing and sorting them while gossiping in a mishmash of languages with the radio blaring, was eerily quiet.

The caretaker walked through the silence, past the long metal tables piled with pyramids of human hair in every texture and color, to turn on the radio. Sitting down on the sofa by the window, he took out the rolled-up copy of the *Daily Truth* that was wedged in his back pocket and shifted his attention to the sports section. He picked up the mug of cold tea off the table next to the couch, took a sip, put it down again, marveling for a moment at the nice little coffee table he'd recently fashioned using some old books he found in Mother Superior's library. He was quite proud of his makeshift table. The books were just gathering dust in there anyway, so he'd rescued some of the heavier ones, stacked them on top of each other, and thrown a sarong on top. Now he had somewhere to put his teacup while he read. He was smart like that, he liked to think. Always coming up with clever hacks like these to make life easier.

When the clock struck nine and the ponyjacker still hadn't turned up, Major picked up the phone and called Sans. There was no answer but that wasn't unusual—with an increasing number of cell phone towers giving up the ghost, it could be a mission to find a signal. Major was lucky that the convent was in a signal-friendly zone, but not everyone had the same good fortune. In Sans's section of the city, having a phone meant daily treks up the stairs of the old Absa building with the rest of your neighbors to check messages and make calls, with some prick at the top charging R2 a pop to let you onto the roof. Lucky for Major, Sans was a man who lived for his phone. Network coverage meant business and business meant money.

An hour later he had a text from Sans, saying he'd sent one of his kids to do the drop tonight. Looked like the little street rat had stood him up, but no worries, just wait a sec, he'd be right over to sort things out and make the drop himself.

- 14 -

SANS

The moon hung cold and white in the sky like a blind eye when Sans reached the convent. Hunching his neck, he pulled the hood of his jacket farther down to cover his face. As the rain pelted down, he thought back to the first time he came here. The perfectly manicured garden was a wreck. Weeds sprouting every which way. White paint peeling off the walls in chunks like a melting iceberg. But now the place looked properly pious. Hair extensions were big business these days and the sisters were doing a roaring trade. Back in the day, folks used to get most of their 'dos from India, Russia, and Vietnam. In Venezuela, too, gangs had been cashing in on ponyjacking for years. But now that the borders were shut, Sick City was warm for the hair trade, too, with pony gangs like Sans's sweeping the streets for tails.

Train stations used to be easy pickings for the ponyjackers. You walked through the cars, checked the heads, and took your pick. If the train was full enough, you could risk it, get the job done right there and then. But mostly it was a waiting game. You followed when she got off at her station. Hoping for an empty street. A broken streetlight. A two-man operation—one guy to hold the knife in front, for show, the other to tie a ponytail and snip. Virgin hair that had never seen the inside of a bottle of L'Oréal paid best. Thick, shiny, straight hair got first prize. But a good head of dreads could also get a mint.

Nowadays, getting hold of ponies was easier. In Pollsmoor, prison warders traded prisoners their locks for smokes. Coroners were getting in on the pony game, too, phoning him if a good head of hair found its way onto their slabs. But the lion's share came from the sisters. Sure, there were downsides—you had to fork out cash to make cash, and the sisters weren't cheap—but the risks were low, the merchandise came prechecked, cleaned and sorted, and, best of all, you didn't have to scrounge around, living from pony to pony all the time. You just picked them up in bulk each week.

"Good to see you, brother," said the caretaker when Sans showed up. He held out his jerseyed elbow and Sans brushed it with his. The Down Days being what they were, handshakes were a thing of the past. Sick City's new ritual greeting was deemed much safer. "What happened to your kid?"

Sans had no idea, but he wasn't about to tell Major that. "The flu," he lied, wiping the rain from his eyes with one palm. He tugged at his wet jacket and shed it like skin, then threw the thing over a chair by the door where it lay in a dripping heap.

"Not the bugger of all bugs, I hope?" Major asked, handing Sans a towel that used to be red at some point, but was now more of a dirty faded pink.

Sans pulled it through his leaking hair. "Nah. Nothing that serious. Baby flu. Sneezes and sniffles. He'll be on the job again before the weekend. Anyway, how's your nephew?"

"Good, good," said Major, and ushered him into the processing hall.

"Happy as Larry with that job you hooked him up with. His mother's not too charmed, though, seeing that it's not totally aboveboard and all—blue-collar. But I keep reminding her that it's the end times now and the apocalypse is not a place for prudes, right? You have to adapt or die."

"Damn right, guy. Damn right. Talking about adaptation, rumor is that the government has started growing dope now—what with the medicine shortages and everyone bartering for meds in the *Truth* and social media. Earmarked an area on Table Mountain for it. They're busy taking out the fynbos. Prepping the soil as we speak. Using the grinners as fertilizer. Which will surely help with all the smog from those bloody cremation factories. Anyway, apparently they're thinking of legalizing a few other illicit substances, too. Your nephew's little business included."

"Really? My sister will be over the moon if that happens. Such a stickler for the rules, she is. And for keeping up appearances. I keep telling her that way of thinking is for better times and other people. Only rich people can afford to live by the rules now. But every argument I make she has a blasted Bible verse to counter with. You can't argue with Jesus, she says. Well, I'd love to bloody phone Jesus up and ask him how I'm supposed to stay on the straight and narrow road if the whole fucking thing is turning into one big blasted pothole the size of bloody Kimberley. Does Jesus have a hoverboard I could borrow to navigate the thing? No. Didn't bloody think so."

While he was talking, Major was laying out this week's sample bags on an empty table. Sans opened one up. Took out a strand with one gloved hand. Checked for variations in color. Sniffed for chemical odors. Ran his fingers up and down each strand to check for cuticles. Normally, running his hands through all these ponies would give him one hell of a rush, but today he felt nothing. Couldn't help looking at all the hair spread out before him and thinking how none of it even remotely compared to the locks that had draped his bed only a few hours ago. Although it felt like years already. How did that work?

He felt numb and sad and out of whack, like a junkie who had chased the perfect high and could never go back. But it wasn't the same thing, though, was it? He would see her again, right? He would chase that high again. Touch it. Skim it. Breathe it. It would be all right.

Sans pushed the girl to the back of his mind, took out his lighter, and set the tips alight. Watching as they turned to ash. Burning with white smoke. White was good; it meant the follicles were totally human. The synthetic stuff would have melted like the Wicked Witch, and the smoke would have been much darker.

He stuck his fingers in his shirt pocket and took out a small plastic bottle of neutralizing shampoo, applied it to the strands to check for added chemicals. After making sure each sample was properly virginal (you could never be too careful, even with longstanding suppliers—he'd caught more than a few trying to cut the merchandise with synthetic hair to stretch stock), he gave Major the go-ahead. The caretaker unpacked the rest of the merchandise, carefully weighed each pony, placed it in a clear plastic bag, and packed it into a cardboard box.

"You got the cash?"

Sans held his breath to think. Blew out. "I'm a little short this week. You know how it goes. Nothing serious. Stick me until the end of the week?"

"How much?"

"Ninety thou?"

"Sho. That's not chump change, is it? Don't know if Mother will be too happy."

"Major," said Sans, putting a hand on the caretaker's shoulder and squeezing in a way that he hoped was brotherly. "How long have we known each other?"

"Ten years or so, I guess," said the caretaker, shifting from one foot to the other while fingering the rolled-up copy of the *Daily Truth* that had found its way into his back pocket again.

"That sounds about right . . . And Major?"

"Uh-huh?"

"When have I not been good for it?"

The caretaker took out the creased tabloid from his back pocket and drummed one rolled-up end against his open palm while chewing his bottom lip.

"Um"—Major cleared his throat, a nervous tic he'd been stuck with since his teens—"I'd love to give it to you brother, in the aid of good customer relations and all that. I mean, you've been real good to me these last couple of years. To Mother, too. Don't think I don't know it. I mean, it's easy to forget, but this place used to be a real shithole before you approached us with your little business plan. But Mother's a real shrew when it comes to money. And a total stickler for the rules, too. You know that. She'll never fall for it. I'm sure you can rustle something up quick, right? You're a man of means and ways, right? We can just postpone the pickup to later this week?"

"Yes, sure," said Sans, trying to act cool. "Come to think of it, I know a guy who owes me. Let me sort it."

"You sure, brother?"

"Positive."

"Why so glum?" the caretaker asked, packing away the ponies again. "Don't think I haven't noticed: you've been skulking around with your tail between your legs since you arrived. You sure we're cool about this money thing?"

"Totally. I told you—I know a guy."

"Then what?"

"Ag . . ." Sans fingered the bag filled with freshly dug up ponies.

"I know the feeling, brother. I sure do. Want some moonshine? It's the best medicine, you know. Kills germs and girl troubles like nothing else."

15

FAITH

Like its neighbors, house thirteen teetered against the cliffs above the ocean. Most of these glass mansions used to be holiday hangouts for filthy-rich foreigners—investment bankers, movie stars, and the like—who came here in the summer to escape the snow. Now they were home to everyone else.

Faith opened the front door and made her way up the spiral concrete staircase. (The lift hadn't worked since before she'd moved in.) At her floor, she passed room after room where bodies were packed together like measuring cups. A cavernous guest bathroom housed a family of six—with dishes cramming the ceramic his-and-hers sinks and a double-bed mattress hugging the floor of the glass shower, shirts and socks strung on a piece of rope across its chrome taps. On a table next to the toilet bowl, she counted four half-empty coffee cups. A trio of baby crocodiles, their jaws open, tails swaying, tiny claws splayed apart like Chinese fans, swam in the big oval bath. Cute. The head of the family was a traditional healer who made extra cash selling them as muthi for a whopping six thou a pop. Folks forked out to bathe in the critters' blood, which was supposed to give you fat stacks of good luck. Faith didn't really believe in all that muthi stuff, but she liked to keep an open mind.

The lounge, with an ocean view like you wouldn't believe, was now a dormitory where bedrolls in every color lay stacked in rows like a marching band. So, too, the master bedroom. The walk-in closet served as another apartment for a trio of Zimbabwean blood hawkers Faith played soccer with sometimes.

In another room, a pool table with a mattress on top served as a bed while three toddlers played with toy cars underneath it. Someone had painted a road onto the marble floor with pink spray paint and the little moppets were birring and beeping their cars while navigating the painted bends, with lots of crashing and banging along the way. A couple of green plastic soldiers lay on their backs in a neat line next to the road, and a little white minivan seemed to be the most popular toy of the day. An argument was brewing amongst the trio. "Mine! Mine!" the youngest, a boy, was shouting while hugging the van to his chest.

"No! I'm the dead collector," his sister, about four or so, scolded. "You can be my guardjie."

"No, you're the guardjie!" screamed the boy. Faith saw him stomp off to find his mother, who was peeling potatoes in one corner while her eldest stood behind her, braiding her hair.

Faith turned a corner and came to a hallway. Its floor was all glass. And below it, rows and rows of fancy cars. Serious petrolhead stuff. Lamborghinis, Porsches, Jaguars, you name it. The kids upstairs had come up with all sorts of schemes for breaking in there over the years, but no luck yet. The owner had gone all Pollsmoor on his babies before he fled. Installed the kind of security system you only see in prisons and bank vaults. Battling the vertigo, Faith put one foot on the glass. Then another, and so on. Like that crazy French tightrope walker she'd once watched a documentary about, who'd balanced his way one foot at a time across the Twin Towers in New York. One last step and she'd reached the other side. Her fists slackened. Shoulders unwound.

At last. Standing in front of her door, she was digging in her bag for her keys when the door across the way opened and her neighbor, Ateri, emerged. He was hugging a bucket full of laundry to his chest. He lifted his face in a nod and she tried not to stare at the thick pink scar that wormed its way down from his eyes to his jawline, twisting sideways as he smiled. Behind him, Faith glimpsed Jamis, his hyena, sitting stoically in front of the TV set. Her next-door neighbor wasn't much of a talker, but she'd spent more than a few hot summer evenings with him over the last few years, drinking quarts on the roof, the hyena always close by, often resting his head on Ateri's knee while they talked. Ateri had a big thing for stand-up comedy—he had all these banned DVDs in his room with hours of stand-up sets on them, and sometimes he'd invite Faith out with him to this seriously dodgy, illegal comedy spot in town. In a city with a prohibition on Laughter, this was a dangerous hobby—some might call it downright stupid—but Ateri had a passion he couldn't shake, and with a job like hers, Faith was always desperate to let off steam.

When the Laughter first hit Africa and its southern tip was still considered a safe zone, Ateri and Jamis had traveled all the way from Nigeria—on foot and hitching rides whenever they could find them. (Most people didn't warm easily to riding shotgun with a hyena.) Back home in Nigeria, Ateri and his brothers had made a living in the family trade as Gadawan Kura—hyena handlers—entertaining crowds with tricks for Nigerian naira. Bystanders would gape as Jamis spun around on his hind legs and jumped into Ateri's arms. A strange way to make a living, sure, but Ateri was born into it. When he was a baby, still weaning, his mother would feed him the traditional medicine of their trade, potions to protect him from harm from the animals they lived with. Now his brothers, his wife, and his daughter were nothing but memories and ash in a shoebox under his bed.

Inside her apartment, Faith felt around for a candle to light and a match to light it. Cupping the flickering flame with her other hand, she carried it to the kitchenette. The fridge was empty and silent, but there was a half-full bottle of warm, flat beer standing in the sink. She picked it up, brought it to her lips, then carried it across to the chair by the window—one of those floor-to-ceiling affairs, all waves and no walls, so big it made her feel small, inconsequential, strangely safe.

The day she'd found this place had felt like winning the lottery. The ad wasn't very descriptive. Just two or three lines. Its poster, a retired chemistry teacher, if she remembered correctly, hadn't been one for words. There were no photos, either. But she went to have a look anyway. Call it a hunch. When she crossed all those cars and stepped in here the first time her head had felt like it might just explode. The place was massive. The rich stockbroker who'd owned the place pre-Laughter had built a special wing for his teenage daughter and pulled out all the stops. There was a mini-kitchen with a built-in stove. A Godzilla-sized bathroom with a freestanding bath. Marble floors. And the view. That ocean view. To make your jaw dislocate.

Faith took the *Daily Truth* out of her backpack, opened it with care. Her fingers stroked the sooty newsprint like it breathed. The first page carried an article about a solar war brewing between the residents of Woodstock and Salt River. Each neighborhood's solar panels were controlled by rival gangs, and the gangsters were always trying to find new ways to tip the scales in their favor on the city's energy stock exchange. Now members of the Woodstock Boys had gone and blown up some inverters at a solar farm in an abandoned garment factory in Salt River. Two young boys, who were playing inside the factory at the time, were killed. The Salt side was rioting. They wanted their babies' killers brought to justice. A Woodstock neighborhood watch member, who did not want to be named, said the suburb was holding its collective breath, fearing a bloodbath, and a family member of one of the slain boys, who also did not want to be named, told the *Truth* that a war was brewing and that "those Salt River bandiete had better watch their backs."

There was an anniversary spread about the Laughter on the second page. And underneath that an article on chimeras—human–animal hybrids the government was said to be breeding in their labs to experiment on in the hopes of finding a cure for the Laughter. The reporter claimed he had a source who'd been into one of these places. And that the creatures caged up in there went against all the laws of nature. Sentient sheep, intelligent rats . . .

She turned another page. Scanned through the classifieds.

Under services, there was an ad for a "freelance sin-eater, part-time ghost buster. Call Fred 078 555 5679." Faith knew the guy in the ad, but not well. Just on a "Hello, how's the weather?" kind of basis. She was always running into him on the job. They tended to end up at the same death scenes.

Fred Mostert specialized in a kind of old-school Western magic that was passed down from father to son. Apparently his great-grandfather had brought it with him when he'd arrived here by ship from the old country, wherever that was. Faith didn't know much about it except for what Fred had told her in his odd, circular way, but the way she understood it, the dying paid him to absolve their sins on their deathbeds, and he did this by eating them (the sins, not the people). He also ate the sins of those already dead, he said. She wasn't quite sure how that part worked, but anyway, he was a sweetie, Fred. Always polite. Always keen for some small talk. Ash didn't care for him much. Called him the Oaf, the Fat Guy, Jabba the Hutt, or the Joke. Said he was a charlatan. That he should be ashamed of himself, making money from other people's sorrows like that. Secretly, Faith thought that was the pot calling the kettle black, but she'd never say it to his face. When it came to some things, it was best to keep your mouth clamped. Pick your battles and whatnot.

Next to Fred's ad, in the BARTERING section, there was an ad offering fresh food and other grocery goods (meat, milk, coffee, toothpaste, etc.) for hair, provided it was virgin and of good quality, twenty-five centimeters or longer. And below that someone was looking for secondhand therapy-bar costumes: "The bloodier, the better. Call Andy. After hours only."

It made her think of Lawyer. She wondered if he was still angry with her. Should she call him? Maybe not. Faith hadn't always been a fan of the *Truth*. Thought it was a bunch of sensationalist nonsense once. Some of Lawyer's stories, they seemed downright crazy, didn't they? But a lot had happened in the last seven years. She'd seen things. Things she couldn't always explain away. Then she'd read this quote by John Lennon. Lawyer had shown it to her when they'd just met and things were still pink between them. (You know, the color of a freshly healed wound after the scab had fallen off?) "I believe in everything until it's disproved." But it was the other thing that he was to have said that stayed with her the most: "So, I believe in fairies, the myths, dragons. It all exists, even if it's in your mind. Who's to say that dreams and nightmares aren't as real as the here and now?"

"That's the thing about the *Daily Truth*," Lawyer had told her that night when she'd first brought him up here and they were looking out into the black sky over the ocean, with the waves muttering in the distance. He'd been freelancing at the *Truth* for a few years already. "The *Truth* entertains all these possibilities. You know that saying about innocent until proven guilty? That's how we see it at the *Truth*. Everything's possible until disproved. We keep an open mind. Because the world is stranger than most people care to admit and the truth is never as cut-and-dried as people want it to be. Nowadays it's all science and facts and logic. People are scared. So they keep their blinkers on. But think about all the weird stuff, the stuff dubbed crazy conspiracy theories in the past, that have since been proven to be true as the truth."

"Like what?" she'd asked.

"Like the Tuskegee syphilis experiments, Project MK-Ultra, the Nayiran testimony, Operation Paperclip, Operation Mockingbird, the FBI poisoning alcohol during Prohibition, Project Muizenberg, the Manhattan Project . . . Hell, Faith, take Galileo. When he told folks the Earth revolved around the sun, everyone thought the guy was a quack."

Faith took another sip of beer, thought about phoning Lawyer again, wondering if the stupid dolt had managed to get himself killed yet, then decided against it. Let sleeping dogs lie and all that. Putting down the now-empty beer bottle, she curled her feet up into a knot and watched the waves breaking on the black shore in a loop, running everything she'd just read through her head. Moving the data from mental compartment to mental compartment until she found a fit. She had a thing for finding patterns, like some people were drawn to singing in the shower or dropping bad puns. It was a compulsion. She couldn't help herself. Apophenia. That's what the psychologists called it. The word for people who saw patterns in random data. An error in cognition. A flaw.

But it wasn't. Not always. And she wasn't crazy, either. It wasn't like she went around every day seeing the face of the Virgin Mary in her morning toast. It was different than that. Different because sometimes, more than sometimes, she turned out to be right. Like that time. The time when her someone and her little someone else . . .

Her dad was a toymaker. Wooden stuff that he'd sell at markets mostly, as well as a few brick-and-mortar shops and online. But his real passion was puzzle boxes. He'd spend months designing them. Basing them on traditional Costa Rican, Japanese, Turkish, Moroccan, Chinese, Indian, or Polish designs. Complicated affairs, requiring up to sixty-five moves to open, some complete with wooden gears, levers, and interlocking moving parts, which he'd sell to collectors online.

But it wasn't just toys. Everything was a puzzle to him. "There's a solution for everything, sweet pea," he liked to tell her. "If you can't find it, just adjust your angle."

So every day Faith read the *Truth*, adjusting her angle, and sometimes she'd see them. The patterns. Connecting across the pages like constellations. Like star maps. Some of these patterns she'd seen had really helped people. Like the time she'd figured out that a series of seemingly unrelated articles in the *Truth* about the unsolved murders of young women were connected—the work of a serial killer. Thanks to her efforts, the psycho had been caught and now spent his days behind bars. Thanks to the SAPS detective, too, who hadn't dismissed her as a loon when she called him about her suspicions. Case closed. They'd had a heated fling that fizzled out fast. But there were no hard feelings. They were still in touch. Every few months he dropped by with a six-pack and a batch of cold cases for her to pore over, hoping she would see something, connect the dots.

Lately, the cases had become weirder, as more and more people resorted to all sorts of ingenious and quite often downright illegal ways to make ends meet. Like a recent case she helped with—very Walter White—of a murdered orthodontist whose wife was convinced he was a stand-up guy. So vanilla, she'd told Faith, that he'd never even smoked a single cigarette in his life. After he died, it came out that nobody cared about having a perfect smile anymore, what with having to wear masks and all, so he'd become a laughing gas dealer on the side and was murdered by a rival drug lord because of a territorial dispute.

The way Faith figured, the masks people wore these days weren't just physical. And there were many of them. Somedays it felt to her like there wasn't a single true soul left. Like every single person in this town was just a series of masks over masks over masks with nothing real left underneath. Not that there was anything anybody could do about it anymore. She couldn't help wonder how much of who people were and who they became was really up to them? It was like the Laughter had flipped a switch. Even if you didn't catch it, it changed you. Remade everyone. Faith couldn't even remember who she was before all this . . .

16

SANS

He hadn't always been a ponyjacker. There was a time, not too long ago, when Sans lived a shiny life safely ensconced in white electric-fenced walls and parental arms. His parents were serious, upstanding types with perfect teeth who sipped Malbec and talked politics and art at the dinner table. When he was a kid, his mother had a heavy book on Italian Renaissance art that gathered dust, wedged in between a potted plant and a Dogon fertility statue on a wooden side table next to the couch. While his parents where napping on Sundays and the house was quiet except for the *tick-tock-tick-tock* of the wall clock, he would kick off his shoes, climb onto the couch, extract the book from its dusty tomb, and marvel at the half-naked women watching him from beyond the pages, with nothing to cover their bits but a hand or a strand of golden hair. The locks themselves seemed magical—suspended in blue air, they dipped and twirled and tugged like marionette strings.

After twelve mostly uneventful years at school, Sans went on to university on the slopes of the mountain to major in art history. For a while, all was good and well and bright and prosperous—there was even a girl, talk of marriage and mortgages. Until he lost the girl to greener pastures and graduated from that ivy-clad haven to realize that the whole world was suddenly going pear-shaped, and on top of all that, art historians had a hard time finding jobs in this new, dying reality.

He got the ponyjacking idea while chatting to this chick one day about how difficult it was to get good weaves now that the borders were shut. A plan took shape. He'd always been blessed with a tenuous and pliable take on morality, and hustling seemed an easier way to pay the bills than writing cover letters and buying new ties for fantasy job interviews, all while trying to feign normalcy on double dates where everyone pretended everything was the same-same but different, spewing small talk about lame TV shows while wielding silver forks with latex gloves and trying to eat with their masks on. (The swankier joints handed out fans, packaged in paper pockets like chopsticks, to hold to your lips as you chewed.)

Now his electric-fenced youth was nothing but a fuzzy memory. A coat that no longer fit. Most days Sans could barely remember any of it. Like a dream unraveling at the edges upon waking.

His story up to now was a cliché, but that was fine. Sans had never met a cliché he didn't like. Rags to riches, riches to rags—he was the kind of guy who appreciated the poetry of a well-trodden path.

Talking about clichés, he couldn't believe he'd trusted Lucky with all that cash. What had he been thinking? He had been thinking with his pants, that's what. And for what? The damn cherry went and pulled a disappearing act anyway.

He was stepping through the convent's gate into the dark. It was 3:15 a.m., the Devil's Hour, as his grandma used to call it. The air smelled of salt. The night was quiet. Just him, the road, and a lone wino leaning against a streetlight, hugging his date for the night, a small bottle of hooch that, guessing by the way the guy was swaying, packed one hell of a punch.

Sans was walking along the empty pavement, cursing Lucky, the little rat, when he thought he saw something out of the corner of his eye. Stopping, he turned his head, and there she was. His unicorn. Just standing there, watching him. Her inky Klimt tresses glinting in the moonlight. Her eyes blank.

He was about to talk to her when something brushed his arm. Breathed against his neck. Without thinking, his hand moved to his pants pocket, where he kept his knife.

"Hey! Easy there, my laanie. Spare a few rands for some bread?" It was the wino. Holding out a cupped hand.

When Sans turned his head back, his unicorn was gone.

"Did you see that?" he asked the wino.

"See what, my laanie?"

"The girl. The girl with the hair. She was standing right there."

The wino frowned. Pulled his cupped hand back. "No girls here, my laanie. I'll have what you're smoking, please."

What the . . . ? Was the guy shitting him? He could have sworn he just saw . . . What kind of garage hooch did that cheapskate of a caretaker slip him? Or was he seeing things now, too? No. Fuck it. Today wasn't the day to turn into his mother. He had no time for cracking up. He needed to focus. Find Lucky. *Lucky, where are you, you little bastard?*

After walking for what felt like forever, he turned right, towards the Bo-Kaap, where rows and rows of candy-colored cottages lined up like dominoes on the slopes of Lion's Head. The cottages, built as rentals for freed slaves and artisans back when the city was still just a speck, stood tightly packed together like rows of rainbow-hued Lego blocks against the cobbled streets.

He climbed the white steps to the shocking pink cottage where most of his street kids lived. The ones whose parents had caught the Joke. Empty houses weren't too hard to come by now, provided you had the right connections, and it was easy enough for a guy like him, with means and ways (who didn't mind getting his hands dirty), to procure this one when the owner, a friend of a friend of a friend, kicked the bucket a year ago. The place needed some TLC, but it was nice enough, and better than living in an underpass.

He knocked on the door.

A young guttersnipe with a thick mop of blond curls opened it. "Elliot? Are you here about Elliot?" she asked, all swirls and spunk.

"Who's Elliot?"

"Never mind," said the guttersnipe, her face falling.

"And who are you, for that matter?"

"Seeing as you are at *my* door . . . after you," the guttersnipe shot back. She raised her brows, and the curls coiled across her eyes in metronomic clumps.

"Sans," said Sans. "You're new?"

"Oh," said the girl. "Sorry. I didn't know." Her suicidal locks coiled from twelve to six again. "It's Tomorrow."

She brushed the hair from her eyes. Sans noticed they were red and swollen. The kid must be high as a kite.

"What's tomorrow?"

"It's my name. Like in the day after today."

Sans just stared at her crazy hair as it did its thing.

"I moved in last week. With Elliot. He's my brother . . ." The sentence trailed off, the word *brother* petering out in a kind of croak. Then she steadied herself and her pointy chin came back up. "Lucky said it was okay, that you wouldn't mind. That a lot of space had opened up recently."

Another lock clocked in at six. Sans studied its arc . . .

"Hey?" the hair's girl said.

"I heard you. Yes. Where was I? Lucky. I'm looking for Lucky. Is he here?"

"No. I haven't seen him since this morning."

"Any ideas where he might be holing up?"

"No."

"You sure you're not fucking with me, kid?" said Sans, resting one hand on the wooden doorframe. "I won't find the little bastard hiding in there if I step in to have a look?" He took a step towards her, pushed his body over the threshold. Her breath stunk of sleep. But she didn't flinch.

"Whatever," was all she said. "Do what you need to do."

He was about to push past her into the house, when he stopped. Her eyes. Her fucking eyes. Those big manga peepers. And the way they seemed to glaze over. They were spooking him. Making him think of earlier. Those gleaming black hole eyes he saw on the street. Why was he feeling so paranoid? What the hell was in Major's hooch? Fuck this. He needed to get the hell out of here. Needed to think. "Just tell Lucky to call me when he turns up, okay? He has something of mine and I'd like to get it back."

The girl nodded. Sans started down the steps.

"Hey," she called. "Your leg?"

"Yeah, it's fine. Old injury. Shark attack. Real big one, too. Great white. Just get Lucky to call me, okay?"

He turned around to go again. Then swiveled back. "I can cut it for you, you know."

"What?"

"Your hair. It keeps falling over your eyes. Doesn't it drive you mad?"

The kid didn't say anything. Just stared at him.

"Just think about it, okay?"

The girl nodded, but her black-hole eyes didn't even blink. Sans suppressed a shiver. Looking into those dark, dead eyes, he suddenly came face-to-face with the realization that if he couldn't find the kid soon—and more important—the money, he was going to end up with his own black hole of a bullet hole in his cold, dead forehead. *Dammit, Lucky. Where the hell are you?*

17

LUCKY

When Lucky woke up, he was lying in a black metal box. His wrists were tucked behind his back, tied together with something cold and plastic. Cable ties? The box was moving; he could hear cars, and honking. *What the hell?*

Then it clicked. A van. The woman he'd been talking to outside the therapy bar had thrown him in the back of a van. But why? It didn't make any sense.

His head felt heavy and muddled—like an old forgotten storeroom, packed to the rafters, in need of a good scrub. His left temple throbbed.

A soft groan at the back of his neck made him jerk. He inched his body around and there she was. A girl. Tied up like he was. Older than Lucky, by maybe a year. With braided hair snaking across her forehead, eyes, and lips.

"What the . . . You okay?"

The girl nodded. "My name's Lerato," she whispered, her voice barely audible. "Yours?"

"Lucky."

"Ha. Think we could use some right about now."

He looked at her, his face a question mark.

The corners of her mouth crept into the beginnings of a lopsided smile. "Some luck."

Lucky's wrists ached. "How long have you been in here?"

"Hours, I don't know. Since before you came. I could hear you and her talking up in the front earlier. Saw when she chucked you back here, too."

"My head. It doesn't feel right."

"She drugged us with something. That pipe thing she was carrying around with her—did she show it to you, too? At least it takes the edge off. I'm not half as freaked out about this as I should be. Which is one small blessing, I guess."

TUESDAY

18

THE DAILY TRUTH

OPINION

IT'S RAINING CASH

You don't have to win the lotto to get rich quick. Just stand outside without an umbrella, writes Lawyer Tshabalala

Something strange happened in Bree Street yesterday. I mean, even stranger than usual, people. "Just after 5:00 p.m. and Sick City was shutting shop when, fluttering down from heaven to touch our brows, Madiba's face rained down on us," tells street vendor Tamatie Johnson.

But this wasn't the Second Coming, folks. Notes. Hundreds of notes. Cold hard cash falling from the sky. And not small change, either. Not greens, reds, or blues, my broe, but bright, flaming orange ones.

The bizarre incident brought the city to a standstill, as everyone and their mother ran in front of trucks, bicycles, skateboards, goats, cows, and carts to catch Madiba's smiling face.

"The wind was howling, and I was on my way to work when all these notes started pouring from the sky. Like magic. Or a reality TV show or something," said Sick City resident Terrence Baadjies.

"It's God's work. It has to be," a local pastor on the scene named Oupa Ndlovu proclaimed. Another bystander, who didn't want to be named, said if it was indeed the Almighty who was responsible for this, why didn't He make it rain food rather than money as she was tired of the constant grocery shortages and block-long supermarket queues? To this, Oupa responded, quite rightly, that money was the lightest resource, wasn't it, and nobody wanted potatoes falling on them now, did they?

Now, readers, I'm not religious much, but I did go to Sunday School once. Anyone remember that parable about the bree weg and the smal weg (the wide road and the narrow road)? Wasn't the wide road supposed to be lined with all the money and the girls? With a nice and toasty bonfire waiting for us at the end? Matthew 7:13–14, "For wide is the gate, and broad is the way, that leadeth to destruction, and many there be which go in thereat: Because strait is the gate, and narrow is the way, which leadeth unto life, and few there be that find it." So, if this was indeed the Big Guy's work, He sure has a bang-up sense of humor, right?

That made me wonder what the end-timers were saying about all this cash raining down, on Bree Street, nogal. So, I left a message with a spokesperson for the Church of the Four Horsemen in Adderley Street, but so far, no comments. But I'll keep you posted, brothers and sisters, I sure will.

Someone else did have something to say, though. When the *Truth* contacted her for a soundbite, well-known Sick City sangoma Mama Lily had another angle. She said the notes were a sign that the ancestors were finally favoring the city again—that they'd finally forgiven us and that the falling rands were a taste of better things to come.

Well, we can only hope, my dear readers. We can only hope.

19

SANS

He left the street rat with the crazy hair and made his way down into the belly of the city. A halo of red dawn fire was circling the sky. In Long Street, sleeping shapes, mummified in blankets from head to toe, lined the pavement. A volunteer health worker in a plastic suit was doing the rounds, checking for pulses. The blue-haired, dreadlocked dead collector, whom Sans played cards with in Greenmarket Square, was waiting in her van across the street. Her guardjie, a mouthy kid with a mullet, was resting his head on the dashboard with his eyes closed, snatches of sound escaping from his headphones through the open window and into the cold morning air. Sans nodded to the dead collector and she lifted a finger to her brow in recognition.

A young boy was herding cows across the tar, funneling the brown beasts in a solemn procession through the rows of abandoned cars to greener pastures (the rugby fields of a nearby abandoned high school, he guessed). Sans could barely remember the time when these streets didn't know cows or dead collectors. He thought about those American apocalyptic films he saw as a kid. Vicious viruses sweeping nations and the world coming to an end with a bang and a crash. One day you're going about your business, greasing the hamster wheel as a midlevel salesman in a pencil factory, and the next day everything is at a stand-still. In a blink you've turned into some kind of gun-packing Rambo who trawls the countryside fending off cannibals and living off fried rats. But that's not how things tended to turn out in the real world. No bangs here. Things just kind of fizzled out slowly until the past felt like a hazy fairy tale that had happened to somebody else.

The big brown beasts trundled past. He couldn't quite figure how everything could feel so wrong and yet so right at the same time, ever since he'd met that damned cherry. And worse, now he couldn't get her out of his damn head.

What he should be worrying about was Lucky and the missing bag of cash, but all he could think about was the feel of the cold green linoleum on his palms as she dropped her shiny black anchors right into his cold beating heart. The way the strands seemed to change their hue as her body moved under the lamplight. Just the thought of it was enough to drive a man to drink. Not that he needed an excuse anyway—he hadn't exactly had a sober night now, had he? Why hadn't he just gotten her damn number, he asked himself for the hundredth time. Hell, even her name would have been a start.

As he watched the red dawn spread, it reminded him of a song his mother used to listen to. For some reason that Sans could never quite figure, his mother seemed to own only one record, which she played over and over, while cooking or puttering around the house, until the lyrics of the songs and the singer's deep, terrifying voice engraved itself onto his young, pliable brain.

He could hear it now, as he walked. The voice. Singing about love being this burning, fiery thing. *"And it burns, burns, burns. The ring of fire . . ."*

20

FAITH

Six a.m. Dawn patrol and the streetlights still glowing in the smog like mutant fireflies. This was the hour when the city's health workers swept the streets for corpses. The council preferred it this way, bright and early before the rest of the world woke up. Leaving the dead to lie in the street after sunrise was bad for morale, and a PR nightmare to boot.

Faith was sipping at the hot coffee from her flask, one hand scrubbing the fog-glazed windows with the sleeve of her shirt, when she saw him through the windshield, walking down the road with his hands in his pockets. The ponyjacker with the limp. Pony Boy gave her a nod as he strode past and she lifted an index finger to her brow in return. The guy was a weird one. Faith had a boyfriend once, a sportscaster who became a total stuck record when he'd had too much to drink, always finding a way to bring the subject back to his one true love—Arsenal Football Club. That's what Pony Boy was like. A complete one-track road. Married to the job. He had this look he gave girls. Even some guys. Like they were all nothing more than hair on legs to him.

Ash was resting his head on the dashboard, headphones around his neck, groaning to himself. She could only catch a word here and there, his usual early morning skit about "unethical working conditions," "corporate slavery, man," and "the big fat effing zombie machine."

"Oh, hush, what do you know?" Faith piped in. "You wouldn't know a tie if it bit you on the ass. Here." She leaned over, one hand groping underneath the seat, and pulled out a can of Coke. "This will make it all better. Promise."

"I see. *Qu'ils mangent de la brioche.* Let them eat cake."

Faith rolled her eyes.

"Sugar, I mean. It's morphine for the masses, you know."

"Shut up and drink the hexed thing."

He half-smiled, popped the ring, took a few sips. Then his head jerked upright like a jack-in-the-box.

"Better?"

"Much. Much, much. Thank God for sugar. Bring on the cake!" He rolled down his window, took a deep breath. "Ahh, beautiful morning . . ."

"*The living is easy,*" purred Faith, like a diva. Ash had a thing for old-school tunes like these. Ella, Eartha, Nina, Frank, the works. He was full of contradictions like that. Always walking around dressed like that guy, Ninja, from Die Antwoord, or the ghost of Tupac himself. With this moer-me face one second and grinning like a mad fool the next. Anyway, the vintage tunes had rubbed off on her over the years. Their roots were entwining like an old married couple. It was something they shared now. Hazards of the job and all that.

"*Fish are jumping,*" crooned Ash. "But seriously now . . ." He cleared his throat and spat a thick blob of phlegm out the window. "Back to the sugar thing. I miss Reese's Pieces, man. Don't you miss Reese's Pieces? It won't be long now until this whole Laughter thing gets sorted out and the borders are open again. First thing I'm doing when they open the borders is going online and ordering me some."

"What are you talking about?"

"Reese's Pieces. You used to get them here when I was a kid. Like Smarties, but with a tummy full of peanut butter."

"No. I mean about the borders opening up."

"I'm sure you've read about it. The *Sick City Gazette* says the US have developed a vaccine. They're getting ready to ship it in as we speak. The French are also close to a cure, so either way we'll be rid of this quarantine nonsense soon."

"Ag . . ."

"Ag what, Miss Paranoia? You don't believe it? You're going to give me another conspiracy lecture, aren't you? Okay, spit it out."

"Fine. You're right. I don't believe it. The bullshit about the vaccines. It's all a front. There's no such thing as a free lunch. Never has been. They're just trying to gather intel. The *Daily Truth* says the head of the Young Militants is hiding out somewhere in Grassy Park. And they're just up to the same crafty shit again, that's what."

"What do you mean, *again*?"

"Don't you know? Have you been living under a rock? Vaccines were how they got to Osama bin Laden back in the day, that's what."

"Before my time. Way before my time. I was just a kid then."

"Well, let me fill you in. It was seriously dodgy stuff. The CIA organized a fake vaccine drive and got a bunch of health workers to put on their best Mother Teresa faces and smoke the motherfucker out. They put up posters advertising free hepatitis B vaccinations to the masses, but actually they were collecting DNA in a scheme to find bin Laden through his family. Crafty fuckers."

"No ways, man. That sounds like some serious conspiracy-nut stuff right there. You should really stop reading that rag of yours. The *Truth* is warping your brain. Besides, even if you're right, don't you ever think about the consequences of spreading these kinds of stories? Of feeding anti-vax paranoia like this? People could die. Real people. Someone's mother, father . . . someone's kid."

"But it happened! Was all over the news back then. In all the papers, on TV, too! The government didn't even deny it. Just kept mum. That's as good as confessing, IMHO."

"Yes. Right. Let's say I believe you and leave it at that. Agree to disagree and all that. Truce?"

Faith pulled a face. Sighed. She thought back to a conversation she'd had with Lawyer a while back. About how there was no point in trying to convince people of something if they'd made their minds up. "Truth is," he'd said, lying there on her bed with his arms folded under his head, "it doesn't help if you show people the truth. They're only going to ignore it and believe whatever they want to anyway. Even reasonable-seeming people are completely irrational when it comes to this—it's like we can't help ourselves. I read this article once saying that researchers have found that people get a dopamine rush when their beliefs are confirmed. That feeling validated makes us happy. Crazy, right? No wonder people don't want to change what they believe. My biggest wish for the world is that people could stop pontificating. Dogmatize, sermonize, moralize. These are all swear words in my book."

"Truce," she told Ash, and looked out the window, one finger absentmindedly stroking the bruise above her eye.

It was quiet in the car for a while. The boy sipped the black sugary liquid in silence and Faith watched the world wake up outside the car window. The mummified sidewalk sleepers hatching from their cocoons, one by one, like moths. The bleary-eyed vendors pushing their trolleys laden with goods towards Greenmarket Square. In her side mirror, she watched the ponyjacker with the limp ducking into an all-night coffee bar down the street.

"Hey," said Ash. "That was that weirdo ponyjacker, did you see him? What do you think was up with him yesterday?"

"What do you mean?"

"He was acting like a total straitjacket. Didn't you notice? Oh, wait. You didn't. You were off in one corner reading that conspiracy tabloid again."

"What are you talking about?"

"You were getting your *Daily Truth* fix on."

Faith rolled her eyes, like they did in the movies. Ash always made her roll her eyes sooner or later.

"Anyway," Ash said, "so we were all standing there, playing cards. And that guy, Sans, was on a roll. Winning, you know? But sweating buckets, which was kind of weird, because it really wasn't all that warm. Then all of a bloody sudden, he looks up from the game, says 'Quarter past eight,' mumbles something about a drink, drops his cards right there on the boot of the car, and takes off. Just like that. Didn't even say goodbye. Weird, huh? You think he's caught the Joke?"

"Nah, I'm sure he's not sick. I mean, the postboxes would have picked it up, wouldn't they? And he wasn't laughing, was he?"

"No. Not even a giggle. He was serious as serious itself. But still, it was weird."

"Poor guy. Maybe someone close to him succumbed. Grief affects us all in different ways, I suppose."

"Ag, please, man. Why do you always have to go sounding like a fortune cookie and spoiling a perfectly juicy story? Everyone's a 'poor guy' to you, aren't they, you little bleeding heart. Except when it comes to relationships. Then your empathy seems to go right out the door."

"Seriously. You're bringing that up again?" Faith dug her nails into her thighs. She and Ash had had a two-day fling a year ago. A silly thing, really, a mistake, even by her standards. Truth be told, there was a fifteen-year age gap between them. Positively a chasm. And the kid still couldn't let it go. Seemed to take the whole thing personally. Didn't get it. Any of it. So there was no point in explaining. Thing was, the way she saw it, the Down Days didn't just bring death and plummeting interest rates. It drew some kind of invisible line in the sand. They were all halved somehow.

Faith's heart now was a coin with two sides. There was a Then side, a Now side, and a skinny, grooved slither in between. Her Then side was more conventional, believed in the institution of marriage, even monogamy. There was a someone back Then. He was her everything. And that was good. Very good. Until his insides turned to mush and the ground swallowed him up and all Faith was left with was raw, raw pain. Her Now side knew that the secret to all those happy endings in fairy tales was that they ended in the middle and skipped all the long, drawn-out excruciating bits towards the real end, that matrimony was a bitch and that this particular world wasn't made for monogamy. That this was a don't-think-just-do-it-and-suck-the-marrow-out-of-life kind of world they were living in. And that . . . that was fine.

Ash was different. He was younger. His Then side was smaller, his heart shaped differently. He didn't remember much from before—beyond the taste of chocolate, soda, chips. She envied him for that. He had his own demons, his own line to deal with, sure, but at least his heart wasn't a coin with a groove in the middle like a tear that would never quite heal, always itching and puckering and raw to the touch. Yes, she envied—sometimes even hated—him for that.

There was a hole in her black tights. A pebble of smooth skin peeked through the gap. Faith stuck her finger into the hole and tugged at the loose threads lining the fleshy stone. Focusing on the feel of the thread, she fed the tear. Trying to breathe. Calm down. "I'm sorry. But we've been through this, Ash. You know my feelings on monogamy . . . Are you really still angry?"

"Nah. Guess not." The boy ran a hand through his ratty hair, flicked the strands back. "Buried with the fishes. Water under whatever water is supposed to go under and all that. Fuck it. Seems the space suits are packing up. Doesn't look like there are any grinners to load. But let's check with the suit in charge and go get another coffee somewhere. I'm buying."

21

SANS

After the night he'd just had, he wasn't quite ready to go to sleep. The all-night café down the street from his apartment was empty, save for a doe-eyed couple by the window and an old man with a beard that was threaded with soup. A sign behind the bar announced that the café now catered to foodists (ASK YOUR WAITER FOR MORE INFO). Sans opted for a table in the corner, next to the wall. In restaurants, as in life, he preferred skirting the edges.

As he waited, he spent his time toying with the salt shaker and studying the wall where framed photographs and newspaper clippings skimmed the cracks in the plaster. For a moment he wondered about all the bodies that had sat there before him, watched over by the yellowing photographs, their fancy frames matted with dust.

"Morning," said the waiter, breaking his trance. "Can I get you anything?"

"A coffee. With something extra in it. Double whiskey, or whatever else strong you've got."

"Hey. This isn't the Ritz. No whiskey here. Moonshine okay?"

"Sure. Why not."

"Coming right up."

Sans watched the waiter retreat, scuffling away to the kitchen with his bedhead hair, the thin line of beard that hugged his chin like a noose. The torn jeans pocket from which a dirty dishcloth wilted. Then he turned his attention to the café wall. Next to a sepia-tinted print of the café circa 1902 hung rows and rows of copies of archive photographs and portraits and prints. His eyes scanned the images of faces long forgotten, and for a moment he imagined his face one day gracing a wall like this, a hundred years from now. The span of one's whole life reduced to décor. A depressing thought. Rows and rows of somber, bleached faces, standing stiff like action figures. He wondered what stories they would tell if someone could listen.

The bedhead appeared with the coffee, ruining his trance once again by plonking the cup onto the table. Black liquid pooled into the saucer. Sans was soaking up the spilt coffee with a serviette when his pocket vibrated. He looked down at the light blinking on his cell. Like those blinking red lights on bombs in movies seconds before they exploded.

"Where's the bathroom?" he asked the bedhead waiter, who was busy washing a table to his right.

"Through the kitchen." The waiter pointed his dirty dishcloth towards a red door half-hidden behind a jungle of a potted palm tree, its green fingers splayed this way and that. "Hey, man. You're limping. You okay?"

"What? Oh. It's nothing. Fell off my bike and sprained my ankle."

On the toilet door was an ad for rum. He pushed the door open and stepped into the tiled cube. He was standing in front of the urinal, looking at the wall, where a mosaic of grubby flyers fought for attention. One of them, an A5 square, stood out from the fray. "Money problems? Lost love? Phone Fred 078 555 5679."

Double jackpot. Two birds with one stone. What were the chances? He'd never phoned one of these things before—they were all a bunch of scams, weren't they? Promising the desperate everything they wanted: girls, money, health, abortions, big penises. But man, for the first time in his life, he was feeling pretty desperate. That blinking red light on his cell hadn't been good news. A message from those lovely Korean business partners of his. Wanting to know where their ponies were. Sounding pretty pissed.

That's what you get for trusting people, he told himself. *A missing bag of cash and a couple of angry Koreans, who are known to own some pretty big guns, breathing down your neck.* Rumor had it that one of the local enforcers his bosses liked to employ was a member of the 27s—a real fierce fuck with a bleeding dagger tattooed onto each cheek and GOOD LUCK BITCH etched onto his forehead. He'd heard the guy liked to play with his victims first, that he would continue doing all sorts of creative things to your body for days until the pain got so unbearable that most people just begged him to shoot them. *Nice.* If he cleaned out all his savings, he'd still be at least fifty thou short. Screwed. *Lucky. Where are you, you little fuck?*

22

PIPER

Piper unclasped the padlock and the heavy garage door swung heavenward. It sighed as it swung, letting out the dark. She parked the van inside and walked across the grass glitter-bombed with morning dew. Past the empty courtyard swirling with smog. To the wooden door.

Piper pressed her knuckles against the grain, all gnarled and knotted like her junkie veins. Footsteps hammered down the narrow stairs. Major opened the door. He fiddled with the belt of his dressing gown.

"Delivery," she said.

"You're late," said Major, rubbing the sleep from his eyes. "You were supposed to drop the van off last night."

"I had some errands to run."

"Where is it?"

"In the garage. I tried the door, but someone latched it from the inside again."

"Give me a second to put some pants on."

Piper waited, pulling at the cuticles of one hand with her teeth, rubbing her arms. The caretaker appeared and together they made their way to the garage.

"The package?" asked the caretaker, after pulling at the rope to lower the door. One lone light dangled from the ceiling, throwing a cliché spotlight over his face.

"They woke up a while back," said Piper. "There was shouting and screaming at first, but it's been quiet in there for the last thirty minutes or so. I think they're sleeping."

The caretaker knotted his brows. She could smell stale alcohol on his breath. Piper said nothing.

"You can't keep bringing them in kicking and screaming like that last one. That baby from yesterday morning was a real earache. My eardrums were ringing until noon. Keep at it and next thing the neighbors will start asking questions."

"Yes. I know. Sorry."

"This is a good neighborhood, you know. Nice and clean and quiet. I like it here. I like it very much. But because it's a good neighborhood, and folks want to keep it that way—nice and safe and clean—they get nosy real quickly. A person as much as walks skew around here and they alert the police or the neighborhood watch. They've got those WhatsApp groups that let everyone know if someone as much as farts. That doesn't mean they will come—the police, I mean, when someone phones . . . When do they ever come these days unless you're infected, hey? But still, we don't want to attract any attention. It's bad for business."

The caretaker cleared his throat, then shuffled over to the back of the van. He was wearing flip-flops—black. On each big toe a tuft of fur sprouted like a mini bonsai. "Let's see what you have for us today then, sweetheart. Open it up."

Sweetheart. The word grated.

But Piper bit her tongue, turned around, and did as she was told. (She'd always been the obedient type, a curse of personality that she reflected upon as she fiddled with the lock.) The white doors of the van swung open to reveal the huddled lumps inside.

"Hmm," said Major. He picked up a metal rod that was lying in a corner on the floor and poked one of the lumps, which curled up tighter into itself like a startled millipede. Major dropped the stick. It clattered as it hit the concrete. The millipede flinched, shrank smaller. He picked up the other lump. The girl lump. The one that was still sleeping. And he slung her across one shoulder like she was nothing. The girl lump stirred, whimpered like a puppy. One eye opened, but clamped shut again when it caught Piper looking.

"Keep an eye on that one while I'm gone," said Major and carried the lump up the stairs.

"It's okay. I won't hurt you," Piper whispered to the millipede as the man left through the gnarled door.

The boy uncurled slightly, just enough to lift his head. Turned his face towards her. Frowned. "Don't I know you?"

"No."

For a moment, the garage was deathly quiet, as the millipede's brown eyes searched hers.

"I . . . I remember now," he said, his voice soft.

"Remember what?"

"Wh-where I know you from."

"All right, all right. The therapy bar."

"No," he whispered, "not the therapy bar." He pushed himself up into a sitting position with his hands. "B-b-before that. We met before that. You held my hand."

"What are you talking about? We met yesterday. At the therapy bar. Shared a pipe. I never held your hand."

"Y-yes you did." His face was changing, the fear melting to make way for something else. "At the sanatorium. When my mother succumbed. A year ago."

"You must be confusing me—"

"No. I remember now. You held my hand. You held my hand. You told me everything was going to be okay. That it would t-take time, but that I would heal. You told me I would be okay." His stammer was smoothing out now, his voice becoming stronger, louder, more assured. "The other doctors, they made me sit outside in the corridor. Wouldn't let me in to see her. Then you came. You brought me some tea. Held my hand. Didn't even have your gloves on. Told me that you believed she was in a better place now. And that I would be okay. It was all bullshit, though, wasn't it? Greeting card stuff. But it helped."

"I . . ."

"And now you're here. Where is here? I don't get it. What's going on? Why are my wrists tied up?"

"I'm sorry. I really am."

"Were you abducted, too? Why aren't you tied up? You're going to untie me, too, right? Help me get out." Then he seemed to remember that she was the one who had drugged him.

The millipede was squirming now. The betrayal was eating away at his fear. He was trying to get up, using the wall of the van as support. "*Sorry* doesn't explain this." He held up his bound wrists.

Piper looked away. She folded her arms around her waist like a straitjacket, her fingernails digging into her itching back. She wanted to leave, just go. Find her fucking man who'd stood her up last night and get nice and dull and low and slow and sweet. Float. Far away from this kid with his eyes that stabbed, stabbed, stabbed. To her nothing place, where everything was plasma.

Too late, it was too late. The millipede had straightened out now and was staring at her with his saucer eyes again. "Please. Let me out. Help get me out of here."

A sound in the distance. Like a drumbeat. Growing stronger. Footsteps. Coming down the stairs.

"Please," said the boy again. "Please."

The caretaker entered the garage. He bent down and wrapped his arms around the millipede. Piper's eyes trailed the ground below her feet as Major carried the boy out.

"Please, Doctor," the millipede tried again, but Piper stayed mute.

"It's not going to be okay, is it? You lied to me." The millipede was changing tack. Screaming now. His voice growing louder. Louder. LOUDER. Bouncing off the walls.

"Shut up," said the caretaker, squeezing the millipede tighter with his inked arms. "Shut up. The neighbors. You'll wake the neighbors!"

A hand reached for Lucky's mouth. Tried to clamp it shut. But the boy wasn't scared anymore. He curled his neck back like a cobra. Rammed his head into Major's chin. Didn't stop.

"You said it was going to be okay! You held it! You held my hand!" The screaming carried on all the way up the stairs.

A smack. A whimper. The screaming stopped. And Piper was alone again with the itch she couldn't scratch.

- 23 -

FAITH

They were playing poker on the curb again. The card gods were frowning on Faith. She was losing. But she didn't care. Her head wasn't in it today. She couldn't concentrate. The anniversary was coming up. Of the day when They had . . . you know . . . moved on. Maybe that was why her head was feeling so thick and her heart so dead? Or maybe she was just tired. Tired . . . This job had an expiration date. You could do it for only so long, that's what everyone said. Hanging around dead people all day had a habit of messing with anyone's psyche.

"Hey, lady. Are you playing or swaying?" said Ash.

"What?"

"Come back from la-la land, please. You're acting weirder than that loony jacker did yesterday. The cards aren't going to play themselves."

"Huh?"

"It's your turn!"

"Oh. Sorry. Just a sec."

"What did you get up to last night? Or should I rather ask who did you get up on?"

Muted laughter from the other players. More jibes were sent her way. She was telling them all where to put it when the radio crackled. A callout to some yuppie's house against the mountain; one of those

Victorian numbers just off Kloof Nek. So they folded their hands and went to work.

The house was exactly as she'd visualized it. Gray, Victorian, double story, with broekie lace and the works. Faith parked the van against the curb across from a deserted play park. There was a sign against the fence that read: COVER YOUR HANDS. COVER YOUR MOUTH. DON'T LAUGH. And below that: PUBLIC LAUGHTER IS A CRIME. OFFENDING MINORS WILL BE DETAINED; THEIR PARENTS FINED. The empty swings swayed in the wind in a ghostly kind of way that gave her the creeps and made her think of Then again. How weird to think there was a time when parks like these rang out with the sound of giggling children. A knot formed at the back of her throat. She gulped it back as best she could and pushed at the wrought-iron gate.

At least it wasn't a code red, so she didn't need to wear her suit. She hated wearing the thing. The ugly, uncomfortable waterproof smocks, taped up at the wrists and the ankles, with a double layer of gloves, goggles, shoe covers, leg coverings, and that damn N95 mask she had to put on instead of her regular mask as soon as she got to a scene. A claustrophobic nightmare that made it hard to breathe, forced her to suck in the same recycled breaths on repeat.

Well, at least it wasn't one of those ridiculous space suits you saw in films. With those ventilators that made you sound like Darth Vader himself. Those things just weren't practical in the long run. For starters, most people couldn't stand to be in them for more than twenty minutes. Walking coffins, they were. You could get PTSD just from spending a whole day in that contraption, never mind dealing with the effects of the disease. Add to that they were hellishly expensive, and difficult to come by after the borders closed up. The few still floating around were mostly used as fancy-dress props at therapy bars and such.

Thinking about the stupid suit reminded her—she needed to buy duct tape. She was running out. Only had a month or so of tape left. She'd have to go to the market tomorrow. Sort it out. Best to take Ash along and buy a box or two. There were always issues with stock these days—the vendor she bought from sometimes didn't have stock for weeks.

Ash followed her through the garden towards the porch steps, where two Veeps were chatting to a gangly young paramedic about soccer scores.

"What are we looking at?" Ash asked one of them, a short, round-faced guy with a big, ready smile, which seemed to turn upside down at the question.

"Eish. It's a bad one. Another one of those family suicides. Seems we're getting them all the time now."

They found them in the bedroom. Four plastic cocoons. On the floor. Lying according to size, from large to small, like un-nested Russian dolls. Blood splattered every which way like some kind of fucked-up Rorschach test.

Ash called in one of the patrollers and together they carted the smallest cocoon away. They'd been working together a long time, so he knew the deal. This job, they'd both seen things that would make others hurl their lungs out just thinking about it, but there was one thing Faith still couldn't bear. If the grinners were younger than twelve, she couldn't touch them, just couldn't. Ash had to pick up the slack.

So Ash did that and Faith stayed in the room with the dead. To the left of the biggest cocoon was a mirror. Someone, one of the cocoons probably, had taped a postcard above it. One of those island-vibe snaps with a cheesy palm tree: "Mauritius. Wish you were here."

Yes. That was it. It wasn't just the anniversary. It was time. At age thirty-eight and three months, Faith September was planning her retirement.

SANS

Sans left the café in a foul mood. It wasn't even eight yet, but underneath the gloves his hands were wet with sweat. What the hell was up with this seesawing weather? The back of his hand was itching like a mother. He stuck a finger in one sleeve to scratch, but this only made it worse. For a second, he was tempted to take the damn things off. If you got caught barehanded in the street, the fine was high as fuck. And if you couldn't pay, you were dragged off to the Island or the Flats. Nah, it wasn't worth it—he'd have to suck it up.

Up ahead, they were installing a new billboard: STAY ALIVE. DRINK BLACK HORSE BRANDY. The whole damn city was going up in flames, but these buy-buy eyesores still defiled every street corner, with every brand—from booze to coffee to condensed milk—claiming it could prevent you from catching the Joke. Cleaning products especially were selling like hotcakes. When the Down Days first came swinging, the government hired workers in plastic suits to spray the streets each week. Everyone was told to wash their hands with chlorine, disinfect with bleach. Within six months the shelves at your local shop were filled with new brands, plastic bottle after plastic bottle promising all sorts of miracle properties. Some people took the ads to heart, started cleaning like their salvation depended on it. A few suckers even started drinking diluted bleach, thinking it would cure them from the inside out. A Sanitation Church sprang up, declaring cleanliness to be godliness, redemption more attainable with each wash. Believers scrubbed their hands raw and succumbed all the same, but still the church grew. Today it had a huge zombie flock and headquarters in a shiny building in Long Street.

Despite the heat and his itching skin, Sans was a man on a mission. He was heading to the Absa building, his hood's signal sweet spot. He needed to start phoning everyone in his address book and then some— see if he could find Lucky. His head was down and his feet pounding the pavement. On the day this stretch of sidewalk had been cast, some sucker in a good mood with a need to make a mark had drawn a smiley face in the wet cement, locking the doodle into the pavement for all eternity. Normally, Sans just walked by, but today he looked down at the little gray face, where it lay smiling up at the sky forevermore, and took it personally. Slamming the soles of his sneakers into the smiley, he swore to himself and whoever else could hear. Maybe it was the alcohol fueling his fire, maybe it was the blinking, vibrating messages on his cell, but the honeymoon was really over now and he was feeling pretty pissed. He was sweating, he was angry, he felt like punching someone. But he had no one to punch, so he kept walking. Past pigeons, pimps, crazies, cocksuckers, suits, sinners, and street corner preachers. Sweat stinging his eyes, Rorschach blots blooming in his armpits. What was up with this heat?

He was so deep inside his own head, he didn't notice the pair of street rats angling his way. "Aweh, my laanie," said the eldest kid, grabbing Sans by the elbow, while the younger rat trailed him like a tail. "Got some giggle porn, lip porn, tickle porn, some nice laughing gas for you. Good price today. Turn that frown upside down, ek sê!" While the older kid talked, the younger one kept his eyes on the street, scouting it up and down for virus patrollers.

Normally, Sans was all for supporting young entrepreneurs, but his mood today was black and getting blacker by the minute. "Oh, fuck off before I call the Veeps," he shouted.

"Fokken piemp," muttered the youngest, before the two little hustlers scattered.

Sans kept walking. Walking. Towards the swarm of punters milling about in front of the new downtown therapy bar, jostling to get in.

Wait.

Was that . . . ?

Did he just . . . ?

A glint of his unicorn's smooth black hair. Those fine pert shoulders that jutted back like wings. He pushed himself into the heart of the swarm.

"Hey, guy! Watch it!" he heard someone gripe.

"Asshole," muttered another.

The eye of the crowd smelt like sweat and beer and stale smoke. Limbs pushed and rubbed and poked. Sweat melded with sweat. Sans had this weird feeling that he was going to drown. He arched his neck up high, pushed his elbows out, and spun around. But he couldn't see her anywhere. His unicorn was gone.

Then something weird started happening. Something that blew his brain. The crowd was growing eerily quiet. Like someone was turning the volume down. And the bodies surrounding him were melting away like mist.

What's worse, there was this wet puddle on the ground, like someone had spilt their beer on the pavement. But something wasn't quite right with it.

It was growing. Expanding. Morphing. Into. Something. Someone.

His unicorn? No. Not her, no. This chick was younger, just a barefoot kid, no more than five or six. Then he heard something weird, like waves in the ocean, roaring and rolling and crashing. Seagulls, too. And mixed in with that a strange creaking sound, floorboards maybe. The specter was eyeing him up like Gandhi, finding him wanting, but as he looked at her, her face changed, distorted into fuck knows what. There were flowers growing out of her eyes now, white creepers, and animals, all kinds, climbing out of her nostrils, and strange old buildings, white, miniature, falling out of her mouth and tumbling to the ground like dominoes.

Then the wave came. Washed over him. Not a metaphorical one, but an actual spraying, braying, whirling, roaring, splashing, crashing, wet, angry wave. A cold ocean monster with snaking wet tendrils that slammed him to the floor in pain. He was drowning. Sinking, sinking. Into a white. Bright. Blank. Light.

A shot of Technicolor.

A flash of limbs, skirts, sneakers.

He was coming up for air.

Gasping for breath.

A crowd of faces were staring down at him on the sidewalk.

"You okay, dog?" someone asked. A boy in a hoodie, earphones curled around his neck.

"What was that?" someone else said. "Some kind of stroke?"

"No. I . . . I'm fine."

The boy in the hoodie looked at him. Frowned. "My cousin has epilepsy," he said.

"No, really. I'm good."

He pushed his way through the circle of bodies—past a tall guy hugging a blue sports bag and a woman with pink-streaked hair—into the hot, blinding street. He walked away as fast as he could without downright running. Didn't want to look too spooked. But his face felt flushed and his damn hands shook. What a total tit. What the hell was wrong with him? Could it be some kind of response to stress, his money woes messing with his head? Kind of like what had happened to his mother when that guy stepped into her office and shot himself. Or maybe it was the good old evil eye or some bad juju he'd picked up, not that he believed in that stuff.

Sweet mother, it had better not be the Bug.

Somehow, he felt that the whole damn thing came back to that chick. He was doing fine before he met that bloody cherry. That bloody, beautiful cherry. That lay was bad, bad, beautiful luck. Hey, maybe she used some bad muthi on him? Laid a curse on him or worse—slipped a paste of ground-up pigeon hearts into his beer to make him fall in love with her? Whoa. Here he was again, talking about evil eyes and all that, when he didn't believe in that hocus-pocus stuff.

Not only was he running out of time to find Lucky before his suppliers smelt a rat, but he was going all cuckoo's nest to boot. No. There wasn't time to screw around. He had to get his head straight.

Get ahold of yourself, he told himself. *She's just a girl. A girl with perfect Pantene hair. Unicorn hair. But a girl nonetheless. Fuck.*

A few feet in front of him, an informal waste recycler was clattering his trolley over the cracked sidewalk while muttering the same two sentences over and over: "I'm gonna get you, you son of a gun. You mother-effing son of a gun." For a moment Sans imagined what the streets would sound like if everyone else could just get dead already. Would it bring some kind of absolution? Or would he be driven mad by the sound of his own echoing footsteps? The recycler ground his trolley to a halt in front of a mushrooming trash can and started sifting through it. The outside of the can was plastered with some star soccer player's ugly mug. Underneath it, a cheesy government slogan: BE A CHAMP. CHECK YOUR TEMP. Sans's pocket vibrated. Then it vibrated again. He checked the screen. Thirty unread messages.

"I'm gonna get you, you son of a gun. You mother-effing son of a gun," the recycler rattled once more with his head deep inside the maw of the can. With nothing around to plug the cracks, the dam swelling inside Sans burst with a bang. "Shut up! Just shut the hell up, why don't you!" he screamed, balling up an angry fist and kicking the trash can soccer player right on his smug A4 mug.

- 25 -

TOMORROW

At the sound of the front door opening, Tomorrow woke up. She lifted her head from the kitchen table. It was Ayanda, and his new bae. She couldn't remember the little glue-sniffer's name. The pair of them were giggling hysterically, which was totally against the rules but probably didn't mean anything sinister—just that they were wasted. She listened as they made their way down the passage. Heard the key turn in the bedroom lock. The sound of music piping up. "Hold up, they don't love you like I love you," Queen Bey's husky voice crooned through the door.

Tomorrow stood up and stretched. Her foot, which had been tucked underneath her, was heavy and useless with sleep. Her eyelids were thick, and her tongue felt as though it were stuck like sticky tape to the roof of her mouth. She hadn't slept at all the night before, waiting and waiting for the cop to phone and say they'd found Elliot, and then Lucky's boss arriving and surprising her like that, reeking of booze and looking for Lucky and offering to give her a haircut. Where was Lucky anyway?

In the sink she found a semi-clean cup. She filled it with water and slathered some leftover cooking fat onto a bread crust while the radio blabbered in the background. She didn't remember turning it on last night. She half-caught the tail end of a conversation between the DJ and some old lady caller phoning in to moan about the state of things.

"Who wouldn't be afraid of dying?" the woman was saying at a pitch that put Tomorrow's teeth on edge. "With all the online funerals

I've been going to. I mean, it feels like there's one every weekend. It's damn right almost illegal to go to a funeral in person now, thanks to that minister—the one with the poodle hair, I always forget her name, D-something. Not that I want to, mind you, go in person, I mean. Too risky, all those bodies pressed together around one grave.

"Anyway, I've got my good black dress pressed and ready all the time now, because we're going to so many of the darned things. My husband as well, with his shirt, tie, and jacket hanging from the closet door ironed and ready to go. Not pants, though. He doesn't need the suit pants. Says why should he, if no one can see his bottom part with the camera. Anyway, so many funerals. That's if the power's not out and the generator isn't on the fritz . . ." Tomorrow let the sound of her chewing the crust drown out the woman. Her thoughts returned to Elliot.

Detectives always said in movies when children got lost that the first twenty-four hours were crucial. After that, the chances of finding the kid alive . . . She glanced at the clock. Elliot had been missing for twenty-two hours. Another two left. One hundred and twenty minutes. Seven thousand two hundred seconds.

She checked her phone. No bars. She slipped on her sandals, grabbed her keys and phone, and headed to the door. Down the passage, all was quiet. Ayanda and his girlfriend were probably sleeping.

Tomorrow locked the front door and hurtled down the steps. She hurried up the street towards the mountain and Schotsche Kloof. The day was still in diapers, but the suburb's signal sweet spot was already swamped with bodies, all milling around, cells to ears. She cupped her hand over the screen to check for bars. Yes. A whole row of them. No messages from the cops, though. Of course.

She stuck her hand in her hoodie pocket and rooted around for the torn scrap of *Truth* she'd stashed there earlier. Finding it, she unwrapped the wrinkly paper ball and smoothed it out against the wall with her fingers, blackening the tips with ink. *There. That's better.* She read the words out again, whispering it aloud to herself as it were some kind of magical mantra. Or a spell to fix everything.

"F. September. TRUTHOLOGIST."

26

FAITH

The parking lot by the sea was just about empty. While dispatch did their thing, Ash snoring next to her, Faith flattened Tuesday's *Truth* on her lap. She chewed on the back of a pencil as she paged through it. The front page carried an article about money falling from the sky in Bree Street. Two pages on, she found an article about the death of a known drug dealer who had been found murdered on the roof of an abandoned office block in the same street, along with an unidentified teenage male. She circled both articles, folded up the paper, and placed it on the dashboard.

The sky was still gray but the air felt hot and sticky. After yesterday's unseasonal howling gale, which was supposed to clean Sick City out, the weather hadn't improved much. It was turning into a miserable day. She looked towards the lighthouse, where an old woman was hugging a street pole as the wind tore at her skirt. A Good Samaritan was trying to give the windswept woman a hand, but the stubborn old thing was refusing to let go of the pole.

There was a coffee stall across the road. Faith picked up her coat from the floor of the passenger side. It had an Ash-sized footprint on the back. She cursed herself for leaving the coat in stepping position. She put it on, footprint and all, and climbed out of the minibus. She locked the door behind her and headed across the road.

A one-legged man in period costume was leaning against the lighthouse wall. "Lovely day, don't you think?"

"Yes," said Faith.

"Say, I haven't seen you around these parts before."

"That makes two of us. I haven't seen you here before, either."

"Strange," said the man. "But never mind. We've met now. I'm the light-house keeper." The man tipped his old-school hat. "West, Daddy West."

Faith nodded, then walked on and joined the bleary-eyed queue of people waiting for a caffeine fix. A crowd was starting to form around the old woman attached to the pole, who was mouthing them all off, sailor-style.

She was watching the drama unfold from the safety of the queue when she heard her phone pipe up. She couldn't remember when she'd heard it ring last. The stupid thing almost never had a signal (and most people preferred to text now anyways). She fished it out of her bag, fumbled with the sliding mechanism.

"Hello?"

"Are you the truthologist?"

"Sorry?"

"F. September. I'm looking for F. September?" The voice on the other end of the line seemed small, unsure.

"Um . . . yes, this is she."

"I'm calling about the ad you placed in the *Daily Truth*."

Faith had felt a bit stupid when she'd first placed the ad. It was Lawyer's idea. "You have a gift," he told her. "It would be wrong not to use it."

"Why don't I just write for the *Truth*, like you?" She'd laughed.

"You can. But you would hate it, wouldn't you? The truth is too import-ant to you. I mean the real truth. Whatever that means. It's just semantics to me. I don't really care either way. What I do, you see, has nothing to do with the truth. I just give people options. It's up to them to choose what to believe. You can do that, too, sure, and you'll be real good at it, but it won't be enough. Not enough for you. And not enough for your gift."

"There you go again, talking about my hunches like they're some-thing supernatural. There's nothing supernatural about a hunch. It's just dumb luck, really, when I get something right."

"Are you kidding? Dumb luck? That's like saying Ronaldo was just a random guy who happened to kick some balls around for a living! It's not luck. It's your brain. It's wired differently. Everything's a puzzle to you. You have a way of picking things apart and putting them together again. Making connections where others don't."

"Now you're making me sound like some kind of savant. Like Rain Man. Or that guy who memorized the backs of all those cereal boxes."

"Cereal boxes?"

"Never mind."

"Fine. Call it what you want, sister. But the fact is, the world is going tits-up crazy. This city is losing the plot. Weird things are afoot. Strange things. Things I couldn't explain away if I wanted to. The Laughter might turn out to be the least of it. And if there is any truth out there to find, any truth to anything, I can't think of a better person to find it than you, Faith September."

27

SANS

After seeing that crazy trip of a girl-child thing, whatever it was, with the eyes and the flowers and the buildings falling like blocks, who had looked just like his unicorn—and then, as if things couldn't get any worse, passing out like a spaz on the sidewalk—Sans really needed another drink.

So he went back to the café, the all-night, all-day place near his apartment. The booze was cheap and he needed to think.

The door was closed but there was a sign behind the glass in Gothic type: WELCOME TO THE KNIGHT OF THE SAD FACE CAFÉ. WE'RE OPEN. Sans hadn't noticed the café's name before. He wondered what the owner had been smoking to come up with it.

He pulled at the door. Down the street, a guy with a crew cut and a sports bag slung across his shoulder was staring at him. He gave the guy the stink eye and the guy got lost quick.

He chose the same table as before and began doing calculations in his head. He could clean out his piggy bank ten times over and pay a visit to every scumbag who'd ever owed him a cent, but that still wouldn't make him enough cash to stave off his pissed-off gangster chums. He could dust off his knife and go on a ponyjacking spree, sure, but it would take forever to rack up enough quality locks. No. He needed to find Lucky, chop-chop.

The same waiter was still on duty. He brought Sans a spiked coffee that slopped into the saucer. Nice and strong, though. Nice and strong.

Yes. He'd phone and text every single number on his cell, everyone he'd ever done business with. Someone must have seen the kid. Thanks to the quarantine, the city was pretty damn compact. A person couldn't hide out forever. But just in case finding the little backstabbing bastard didn't pan out . . . well, there was another option. A plan B, so to speak. Plan unicorn.

He'd done the math, and hair like that—Holy Grail hair, One Ring to Bind Them hair, Maltese Falcon hair, Deathly Hallows hair, that suitcase in *Pulp Fiction* hair—was worth a mint. If one single average-to-good pony was worth three thousand bucks, then oh, baby, phew, he could easily pay off his suppliers with hair like that. One unicorn pony could do the trick. Fix everything. Yes. He drained his cup, liked the sound of that.

He caught the waiter's eye and ordered another drink. *Lose the coffee this time* was the silent message, instantly received. While he waited, Sans turned his attention to the wall beside his table. Something had caught his eye there earlier and he wanted to get back to it. He scanned the images, one by one, from left to right. A mishmash of copies of archive photos, paintings, drawings, prints. Dates scribbled underneath, like pins in time's moldy corkboard. He spared a thought for each face as his eyes scanned past. Wondered what these sad-faced bastards' lives had been like. What it had felt like for them to die. Where their bones were today and how many times he'd walked over them on his way to here, there, or somewhere else. Were they turning in their unmarked graves at what the world above Sick City's pavements looked like now?

Then—he found it.

Found her.

And the café, its tables, the chairs studded with limbs, the waiter revving up the coffee machine, all went poof. All he could see was that oval shape. The eyes—one green, one brown, even though the drawing was in sepia—the brows, the mouth.

The hair.

Fuck a duck. His unicorn. His chest was hurting something fierce. He noticed he wasn't breathing. So he sucked in some air, took another look. Her face, her hair, but something about the hair wasn't quite right. The artist hadn't done it justice.

How in every-single-damn-deity-in-the-dictionary's name could this be? Was he hallucinating again? Or did his unicorn have a long-dead relative who looked exactly like her? Yeah, yeah, yeah. That must be it.

He took out his phone and snapped a pic of the pic. Noticed there were another five messages blinking. As he lifted his hand to beckon the waiter again, a crazy thought snuck into his brain. His grandmother (his real one, whom he'd met only a few times, long after his real mother had kicked it) was a big believer in communing with your ancestors and all that stuff—what she called the veil between the worlds. Growing up, he hadn't bought it for a second. But he didn't know anymore. In the last year, he'd seen and heard some unbelievable shit. Things that made him feel like his head would break just thinking about it.

For instance, he meets this chick at a bar about a month ago. She's drunk. They're both last-rounders. He's sitting there at the empty bar, watching the roaches climb the walls and this chick starts telling him these tall-ass tales about how the Down Days has brought all sorts of unholy supernatural shit out of the woodwork. That the lines between life and death were thinning and the city was splitting at the seams with spirits trying to commune with the almost dead.

Sans used to be the kind of guy who prided himself on his skepticism. Still was. It was what kept him afloat. But now, well, maybe . . . What if there *was* something to all of those crazy stories?

He turned the thought over in his mind.

Held it up to the light.

Put it down on the table and poked it with a finger.

Nah. What was he thinking? No way. He didn't believe in spirits. At least, not those kinds of spirits.

The waiter stuck his head out from behind the coffee machine and Sans lifted his hand. "Another double."

When his pocket vibrated, his whole body jumped. The cup left his fingers. The shards scattered across the checkered floor like one of his grandmother's bone readings.

"Wait." He called to the waiter, who was already unscrewing the bottle cap, shot glass at the ready. "Why not make it two? Thanks."

28

FAITH

The one-armed bleach seller across the road was building a plastic Tower of Babel. Above his head an LED government sign spouted statistics and soundbites on repeat: "The Laughter is real. Denialists kill with words / Hiding infected family members is a crime / Remember to wash your hands / A healthy city is a happy city. The Laughter is real . . ."

The gray sky had turned to a persistent drizzle, but outside the dirty window of the Knight of the Sad Face Café, the world continued its business as always. A woman was selling apples to an old man in a T-shirt and jogging pants while the baby on her back was making eyes at a stray dog peeing against a lamppost. Two suits were trying to push through a trio of street kids who were jostling them for cash.

The owner of the bar across the road was standing on a ladder, scrubbing his front window while a young boy, his son, perhaps, sat on the bottom rung playing with a wind-up robot, tugging at his red Spider-Man mask. The bar owner yelled something to the boy, who stopped tugging and ran inside.

A hipster with a bird's nest beard rode past the café window on his fixed-gear bicycle. Seeing Faith watching him through the window, he winked, almost smashing into a street kid with wild curls who was speeding past on her skateboard. "Hey, kid!" yelled the hipster, but the kid just flipped him the bird. With a couple of deft moves, she came to a dead stop right outside the café door, picked up the skateboard and yanked the door open. The bell jingled. Drops of rain flew off her hair. She shook her head and looked around. Then she strode past the waiter, who was busy scooping glass shards into a dustpan with an all-purpose cloth, muttering something about drunk pony assholes under his breath, and stopped beside Faith.

"Faith, right? We talked over the phone?"

Faith tried to keep the surprise out of her voice. "Yes, that's right. Pleased to meet you."

They rubbed elbows and the kid propped her skateboard up between the wall and the table and sat down. She was wearing an oversized white T-shirt with the words BLOOD B GONE CLEANING on the front and, in smaller letters, WE DO IT SO YOU DON'T HAVE TO. Faith must have been staring, because the girl pinched the fabric between her fingers, pulling at it so she could read it properly.

"It's a work shirt. We wear it underneath our suits. I'm an aftermath technician. You know, cleaning up all the blood and stuff after someone dies? I mean, off the books. Or at least I was. I kind of just quit. So I thought I'd go and ask at the Sanitation Church, see if they've got anything for me. My housemate talked to this girl who works there and she said they need someone to pour chlorine baths for ritual cleansings. Sounds like a pretty decent gig. With dental and everything. You need to be really clean to work there. Regular tooth-whitening sessions is part of the dress code, which makes absolutely no sense, considering no one sees anyone's teeth anymore anyway, but whatever. I'll have to tie my hair back, too, maybe even cut it, which isn't ideal, but hey."

The girl's hands mimed little explosions as she talked—boxes, grapple hooks, church spires. A peacock spreading its feathers, a bowl, a book, a rock, a gun. Faith felt herself smiling at this strange, animated little creature.

"Sorry," the girl said. "I'm rambling. I guess I'm nervous. I've been told I talk too fast when I'm nervous. I need to find Elliot and I'm motormouthing on and on."

The waiter plopped down two cappuccinos.

"No worries," said Faith, tracing her pinky through the hot foam. "I talk a lot when I'm nervous, too. Say, have you ever thought about trying your hand at data running? You already seem to enjoy skate-boarding. It might be a good fit?"

"Hey, that's true. I never considered it before. But now that you mention it, it sounds lit," the girl said, and Faith noticed her posture slackening.

"Tell me. How old are you, Tomorrow?"

"Fourteen."

"I see. So how old are you really?"

"Hey! I'm short for my age, okay? Anyway, what does my age have to do with anything? Can we get on to business now?"

"You're right. On the phone you said that your brother was abducted from the market in the Company's Garden? The one inside the old museum? That you were shopping for ingredients for your birthday cake?"

"That's right. I was buying some sugar."

"Tell me what happened."

"Hold on," said the kid, knotting her nose into a pretzel. "I have a question first."

"Shoot."

"Your ad says you do this pro bono. That means free, right?"

"Right."

"So what's the catch?"

"No catch."

"Seriously. I mean, what do you want in return? You're not some kind of perv or something?"

"Not a perv. Nope."

"What, then? Why are you doing this?"

"Call it charity."

Frowning, the kid bounced her knee against the underside of the table, setting Faith's coffee cup clattering, spilling brown liquid into the saucer. "Sorry." She clamped her leg down with one palm as if the limb had a life of its own. "No. Not buying it. No such thing as charity. Not really. Next?"

"Fine. Let's call it penance, then. Would that work?"

"Penance for what?"

"Something. Personal. Something that happened a long time ago."

"Something like what?"

"I don't talk about it."

"Why not?"

"I just don't."

The knee started up again. "So you're really, really doing this for free? For real? No bullshit? You're not going to pull a fast one on me later? My dad, when he was alive, dragged me to this thing once, this meeting where these guys in suits and pointy shoes told him he'd won a competition but they just wanted to sell him shares in some crappy seaside bungalow next to a sewage treatment plant. This isn't anything like that, hey?"

"No," Faith said. She leaned forward on her elbows. "It isn't like that. I'm really doing this for free."

"And you're not going to ask for anything back?"

"Not a thing."

"Well."

"Well?"

"Well, you were asking about the market?"

"Yes. Where were you standing when your brother disappeared?"

"I was at the back. You know, next to that muthi stall with all the animal bits strung up like laundry? Looking at buying some sugar."

"And where was your brother?"

"He was in the trolley. Right behind me."

"And then?"

"I turned around for a second and when I turned back he was gone."

"The cameras. There are still a few cameras there, aren't there? Did they pick up anything?"

"Yes. There was a woman. But I couldn't see her face. She bent over Elliot when he was sitting in the trolley. The security guard thinks she took him."

"Which security guard? The one with the hyena?"

"Yes. He was really nice to me. We looked through all the footage together. Talked to some of the stall holders. But no one really saw much. The muthi vendor did remember the woman—said she was quite hot. A real firecracker. But he didn't see her pick up Elliot. Didn't remember Elliot at all, actually."

"That's weird, isn't it?" Faith studied the girl's face. She was half turned away, looking out the window, the leg jigging again.

"I don't know, hey. Maybe he just doesn't like kids."

Faith tried to read her expression. The girl was being defensive, but why? What was there to be defensive about? She was the one who'd called Faith, not the other way around. Did she want her help or not?

"Is there anything else you can tell me about this woman from the video footage?"

"Well, I think I might have seen her before . . . when I was entering the market, I mean. But I'm not sure. There was a woman who said hello to Elliot. Said he was beautiful. I think she might have been the same woman as on the video. Well, I thought so anyway. But the more I think of it, I don't know."

"This woman who said hello to Elliot, what did she look like?"

"Well, she had red hair. Real bright red, like a fire truck."

"Great. That's great. Anything else?"

"She . . . There was this tattoo. She had a tattoo. On her wrist. A snake on a stick, I think."

"Good. That's great. Did she have any other defining features? What color was her skin?"

"White. She was very pale. Now that I think about it, I could see her veins showing through her wrist."

"Was she tall or short?"

"Tall, I think."

"What about her face? What did her face look like?"

"I don't know, I . . . I was distracted. I really didn't get a good look."

"Anything else? Did she have a particular way of walking, for example?"

"Um . . ."

"Close your eyes. Try to picture her."

"I . . . I really can't remember. I'm sorry."

"Don't be sorry. You did good." Faith brushed away a stray dread, and one finger accidentally skimmed the bruise above her eyebrow. She winced. Still tender.

"Hey, what happened there? Are you okay?" the girl asked.

"Ag, hazards of the job, is all. Did you notice anything or anyone else around at the time of the incident? Anything suspicious? Did anyone else talk to you or look at Elliot?" The girl shrugged. She was being downright sullen. Why? She splayed her fingers, gripped the rim of the table, and arched her back against the chair, bending her neck this way and that. Faith noticed that her nails were chewed to the quick, the skin around the edges bracketed with shredded skin and clotted blood.

"There was a guy who almost bumped into me," she finally said. "He had a mullet and was holding a can of air freshener. But I don't think . . ."

"That's good. Is there anything else you remember? Anything at all?"

"No, I don't think so."

"One more thing," said Faith. "Do you have a photo of him? Your brother?"

The kid took out her phone, scrolled down, held it out to her. A chubby little boy with stick-out ears and dimples smiled back at her.

"I gave the mousta—I mean, the cop a copy of this pic as well."

Faith downed the last of her cold coffee and studied the girl. Her chin was up defiantly but it was wobbling and her eyes were bright with unshed tears.

"So do you think you will find him? He's all . . . I mean . . . Just find him, okay?"

Faith was adrift. Above the abyss, the rusting engines, she walked across the dark glass bridge to her front door. Her thoughts were bottomless. Her head was down. Her mind so far away that she didn't even feel the familiar vertigo, the French tightrope fears.

Until.

Something moved at the end of the hallway. A noise, a breath, a cough. Her heart was a ball clogging up her throat. She swallowed the urge to scream.

A trio of shapes materialized out of the darkness. Three silent figures. They must have been standing there all along—she'd just been too preoccupied to see them—waiting for her in the dark. A woman, a man, and

a young girl, around six or so. The man was wearing a bright red tie and
the woman and girl were wearing coats and ankle-length skirts. The girl,
who was looking down at the glass floor while sucking in her lips, was
holding a pack of yellow pamphlets, her delicate fingers clasping them
to her chest like a bridal bouquet. Faith had seen the woman and the girl
before once or twice, working in the house's vegetable garden downstairs
or scooping water from the swimming pool after it had rained. But she'd
never spoken to them before now. Didn't know their names.

"Can we talk to you, sister?" said the man. "Just a minute of your
time, please?"

"We are so excited to share our good fortune with you," said the
woman.

"Now isn't the best time," said Faith, sticking her key into the lock
on her door.

"Please, sister. Five minutes. If you don't like what we say, we will
leave. God's honest truth."

Too tired. She was too tired to fight. So she said fine. The trio came
in and she pointed them towards the couch. Defeated. Resigned to her
fate. They sat in a solemn row, from big to small, hands folded identi-
cally on their laps. The girl's pamphlet stack was balancing precariously
on her knobby knees—one knee pink, the other a purply-yellow-blue
flower.

Faith remained on her feet. "Coffee?" she asked.

"Do you have tea?" said the man. "Rooibos?"

"Yes, sure."

"No milk," said the woman.

She fished some clean cups from the cupboard and arranged them
on a tray. The power was out again. Lucky thing she'd remembered to
pour some boiling water into the thermos this morning. She poured
the water into the cups, scooped some chicory into her own cup,
plopped tea bags into the other three. There was a packet of biscuits in
the cupboard. She hadn't eaten all day, so she opened up the packet and
put it on the tray, too, carried the tray to the couch.

The trio took to the tea. Faith noticed how loose the man's suit hung
on his shoulders. Same with the woman's coat.

"Biscuit?" asked Faith, holding the packet out to the girl.

"Oh, no. No-no," said the girl with a face like a springbok in headlights, looking at her dad, eyes wide.

Faith put down the biscuits and picked up her cup. That was when she saw the toddler slung across the woman's chest. The boy must have been tucked away underneath her coat. Now the coat was unbuttoned. The woman unclipped the sling and put the kid down on the carpet, where he sat *vroom*ing and *brrrroom*ing a toy car up and down the arm of the couch. As Faith's eyes followed the toy's trajectory up the armrest, she noticed the big block letters printed on the pamphlets on the girl's lap— THE TWELVE COMMANDMENTS OF FOODISM—and it all clicked into place. There was a family of foodists sitting in her lounge. Great. Just great.

The man put down his cup and cleared his throat. Faith steeled herself while he ran his fingers through his greased-back hair, straightened his tie, folded his fingers into a teepee, freed the frog from his throat, and began to speak. "I have something exciting to tell you, sister. Something that could save you. Something that could fix everything."

Yes, please, Faith thought. *Bring it on. Save me.*

"We have come here to bring you good news," the man continued. "Have you heard the expression 'You are what you eat'? Well, we are here to tell you today that this is true, sister. Truer than you could have ever thought. Your health, your thoughts, your emotions, every particle and participle of your entire being is influenced by what you eat. By changing what you ingest, you can change everything. By adhering to the twelve food commandments and banishing all that is unholy from your lips, you can reach absolute absolution."

She couldn't deal with this right now. She was tired. So tired. Lead-weights-tied-to-her-soul tired. All she wanted was for the suit to stop talking. For these holier-than-thou crazies to get off her couch. *Don't be an ass*, she chided herself. *Don't be an ass. Keep calm. Carry on.*

Yesterday that would have been easy. She would have feigned interest, tried to keep an open mind, maybe even asked a question or two. But not today. All she could see when she looked at the family of four sitting in her living room were those cocoons. Four in a row, stacked from large to small. *Wish you were here*, at the top.

"What's so unfortunate, sister, so unfortunate, is that if only everyone could have broken free from the shackles of consumerism and become enlightened to these principles from the start, the Laughter would have been banished from the city years ago. It's so unfortunate, so unfortunate, that all those souls had to die because they weren't shown the light. That's why we're here today, sister. To change that. It might have been too late for those poor unfortunate unenlightened souls, but it's not too late for you."

"Really?" She felt a prickle of anger rising beneath her weariness.

"Yes," said the man, dialing up his Kool-Aid grin. He wasn't wearing a mask. Neither was his wife or kids. He was that sure of himself.

"Can it bring the dead back to life?"

"I don't follow?"

"Can following your twelve commandments bring the dead back to life?"

"Of course not, sister. That would be magic, wouldn't it? We don't believe in magic. We follow facts."

"Facts. I see. I get it now. How stupid of me to get confused. Tell me, then, Mister Know-it-all-so-sure-of-yourself-foodist-freak: what's the point?"

The man exhaled slowly, deliberately. He fiddled with his tie, recrossed his legs, cleared his throat again. Turned the cup around in the saucer like a doorknob. "Know what I tell folks who disagree with me, sister? I tell them that's fine, but I'll be the one having the last laugh when I'm celebrating my hundredth birthday and you've already long since succumbed."

Faith put her cup on the tray and stood up. "Not everyone wants to live to be a hundred, you know. If that's your life's purpose, I feel sorry for you, I do. For all of you. Now get out."

The man's jaw dropped. The woman almost spilt her tea. She scooped up the baby and his toy car, while hubby grabbed their daughter by the elbow and started tugging her towards the door.

"Just ignore her, sweet pea," the woman said to her husband, who was looking like he was about to blow. "She's a hopeless case. It's already too late for her. All those postbox meds flushing through her system, coupled with all the preservatives clogging her veins, is getting to her. I think she might be going postal, is what. I've told you what Tillie told me they're saying about the postboxes now, haven't I?"

"Yes, Nora," said the man to his wife. "You are right. That has to be it." Then he turned his attention back to Faith. "Just think about it, sister. But get back to us soon, you hear? You are nearing the precipice. I can feel it."

Faith began herding them through the door in case they decided to give it another go.

"Amen," said the wife.

"Amen," chorused the daughter.

"Car, car, broom, broom, toot, toot," gurgled the son.

"I'm serious," the man said, one hand on the doorjamb. "Wait another week and it could be too late." Then the door blotted out his face.

WEDNESDAY

29

THE DAILY TRUTH

PILL SWITCHEROO
MAKING US CUCKOO?

By Lawyer Tshabalala

Dear Lawyer: What's with all the crazy happening in the city right now? you've asked me. Well, my dear readers, I've searched high and low for an answer, and am chuffed to say I finally have a scoop. News from up the ladder, via a top-secret source, is that the injections distributed via the city's postboxes are thought to be causing mass hallucinations across the city.

But Lawyer, why now? you ask. *Haven't we been dosing up on those little pricks for close to two years already?* Well, turns out we haven't. Not quite. My source says that our dear government recently switched the original postbox meds for a generic version they are getting cheap-cheap from some unlicensed factory in the Eastern Cape, said to be owned and run by the vice president's cousin.

When contacted for comment, the government PR machine said it's all a conspiracy theory, total nonsense, of course—that the injections are all aboveboard with absolutely no side effects whatsoever. Of course, of course . . . Stay tuned for more updates, folks. Over and out.

- 30 -

SANS

Sans was dreaming. A swarm of angry scissors was snipping in his ears. He swatted at them with his hands as they dipped and dived, cutting at his fingers. Blood dripped into the wet grass. He crouched down and started running. The scissors followed, the blades singing *schwee-schwee-schwee* as they bit at the air against his skin. She was there, too, his unicorn, and she was laughing, her hair dancing some kind of crazy jig in the wind to a rapid, pounding, techno soundtrack that would turn out to be the beat of his own heart. The closer he came, the more her hair whipped and swirled and grew, until her body became one with the wind and the strands alone remained. Tugging and reeling upwards into the sky like the strings on a thousand helium balloons, which in turn exploded and morphed into a flock of seagulls that lunged at him in one white blur and started pecking off his face.

He woke up to a racket in the hallway. Someone was pounding on his next-door neighbor's door: "Open up, this is the Virus Patrol! Open up!"

More banging.

"Please, please!" A woman's voice. "He's not sick! It's only the flu, I swear!"

Another voice, a man's: "I'm sorry, ma'am. Someone phoned our tip-off line. We have to take him in to get checked."

A third voice: "It's going to be okay, Primrose. It's going to be okay. I promise. Don't worry. I'll be home soon."

Sans listened as the footsteps passed his door, waited until he couldn't hear any more. When he was sure the coast was clear, he grabbed his jacket and got the hell out of there.

In the hall, the door next to his apartment had a foot-sized hole in it. Through the gap he could hear someone crying softly. He lifted up a finger to the door to knock, thought better of it. He didn't know the woman that well, and besides, what the hell would he say to her anyway.

After washing down some coffee at the Sad Facts Nights Café, with a shot of something for his nerves, Sans found himself in the square as usual. The dead collectors and the other card players hadn't arrived yet, so he milled around, keeping an eye out for his unicorn, hoping for the best, while the dream tugged at the back of his mind like a kite stuck on a fence.

He'd contacted everyone in his address book and then some. Every single goddamn coroner, hustler, rat, and dirty cop. None of them had seen Lucky. Gone to the sanatorium, chatted up one of the nurses there, and bribed her for a patient list. No luck. He'd even gone door to door in Lucky's street, talked to aunties, uncles, kids, bergies, two imams, and a street corner priest. The trio of old grumps who liked to sit and sun themselves outside the barbershop across the street. The glittered and tasseled velvet-masked working girls one street up in their fuck-me boots, synthetic wigs, and elbow-length cabaret gloves, who liked to punt their wares with flair. They hadn't seen a thing, either. They knew the kid, had shared the odd entjie with him. And the occasional joint. But no luck. They hadn't seen him since Monday.

He was running out of ideas. Save for plan B—Plan Unicorn. But that was more of a pipe dream than a plan, wasn't it?

He was sitting on the pavement, watching the vendors reel in their customers with smiles and rhymes, when an idea popped into his head.

He went up to one of the traders, a tall, bald guy who smelled of booze and bleach, took his phone out of his pocket, scrolled to the photo he'd taken in the café, and asked the vendor if he'd seen this girl. Like a cop in one of those crime shows his mom used to watch. But the vendor just shook his head. He approached the chick with the short green braids next, the one who sold cloth nappies and printed masks. She didn't say anything, just stared at him through the curtain of dangling face masks patterned with Hello Kitty and hearts and dinosaurs and flowers and clouds and pandas and bananas and Delibirds and dollar signs and crosses and dots and stripes and Chimchars and shook her head.

So he fished some coins from his pocket, bought a badass number printed with fanged skull teeth, pulled the elastic bands over his ears, as if that was what he'd intended to do in the first place, and sauntered off.

One by one he worked his way through the stalls, tried them all. But no dice. A tall, slender blood hawker with a tattooed forehead and pencil moustache said he could "organize" him someone who looked just like her: "A little bit of Garnier, my broe, maybe some surgery—I know a guy—and you won't know the difference. Cross my fingers."

He was walking back through the maze of stalls when he spotted a guy with a crew cut and a blue sports bag slung across his shoulder, leaning against a street pole reading the *Truth*. The guy looked mighty familiar. He was about to walk up to the guy, talk to him, when he spotted a black thread on the ground. At first he thought it was a stray piece of weave, a lost lock, but the thread was too long. He trailed it with his eyes. The thing was long as fuck. There seemed to be no end to it. So he followed it. Followed the trail of gleaming black thread. Followed it all the way out of the square down a narrow alley to a grate, where it plunged downwards, disappearing into the dark. He tried pulling at the thread, but it didn't budge. And the grate was stuck. Now what? He was about to turn back when he thought he heard a voice, from somewhere down there, calling him. "That which we call a rose," called the voice. "That which we call a rose . . ."

A *hoot* behind his back. Another *hoot*. Make that three. A voice. "Hey, buddy, get out of the road! Can't you see I'm trying to drive here!"

When he looked down again, the thread was gone. And the grate had some disgusting muck on it, puke or something worse.

FAITH

Faith bent her body over the rim of the bath. Something hit her as she opened the tap. A thought—no, a memory. A Then one, from when there was still a someone and a little someone else. A daily pre-bath ritual of delving into the freshly poured water and fishing out a neon zoo of ducks and fish and boats and cups and spotted giraffes before easing herself into the steaming void. She undressed and sank her legs into the rising water, then her back. As she did, she noticed a small yellow bruise on her left thigh. The little someone else used to get bruises like these on his arms and legs. Then there were the scraped knees and little red cuts that she'd patch up with rainbow-colored plasters.

Little mushroom clouds of steam rose up towards the bathroom ceiling. Her thoughts were spiraling backwards fast—down, down, down a slippery rabbit hole that she knew from experience led nowhere good.

She flicked her head sideways, and shooed the memories back. Shifted gears, tried to concentrate on the new freelance gig instead. Went through it all in her head, replayed everything the girl, Tomorrow, had said. The way she figured it, the problem was this: the boy was a no one. A zero. A nothing. A rat. Sick City's growing army of orphans was an embarrassment to everyone. An issue that no one had the resources to deal with right now, let alone the heart. So, they all turned a Stevie Wonder. Or put the blame on the kids themselves.

Why didn't the little street rats just toe the line, single file, to those lovely no-journos-allowed care facilities, they probably asked—if they asked anything. With their guards and barbed-wire up the wazoo. Yes. The kid was an embarrassment. A symbol of a bigger problem. One no one was quite ready to face. As far as the rest of the city was concerned, this beautiful boy with his dimpled cheeks might as well have been invisible. So how did one go about finding an invisible boy?

Invisible boy, invisible boy . . .

Yesterday, after Tomorrow had left and before Faith had gone home and had to deal with the foodists—it had been a very long day—she had already asked around at all the morgues, and no one with the kid's description had popped up on any slabs. So that was a dead end and a blessed one at that.

She'd also visited the museum and asked Ateri to replay the security footage for her, but it didn't reveal much. He was surprised to hear about her freelance gig. They were neighbors, sure, but not close enough for that kind of sharing and caring. Lawyer would say she was embarrassed. Embarrassed that she cared. And maybe he was right. She'd gone around to the back of the market, which was where Tomorrow had said Elliot had been taken, and talked to both the sugar and muthi vendors. Weird thing was, both of them remembered seeing Tomorrow, but neither of them remembered the boy. Even stranger, in the middle of talking to the muthi vendor, asking him about Elliot, the man's phone had rung. As he'd whipped it out of his pocket, she'd noticed the photo of a baby on the screen before he took the call.

"Cute kid," she'd commented when he'd finished talking.

The vendor had given her this monster beam. "My daughter," he'd said. "Six weeks old. She's my whole world now."

"She's gorgeous," Faith had said. "I remember when I had mine I couldn't help but notice cute babies everywhere—like I'd never noticed a single kid going out before, but now they were everywhere. Do you find that, too?"

The vendor had nodded with vigor, smiling like he had a secret. "Totally. I keep seeing kids all over the place."

"Yet you didn't notice the boy. Weird, huh?"

"Come to think about it, that is weird . . ." Then he'd turned his attention to a waiting customer who was asking about the price of the bunches of impepho dangling above Faith's head and she'd moved off, the encounter teasing at the edges of her mind.

She'd also been in contact with her detective ex to check the official status of the Elliot case. He'd promised to call back as soon as he knew anything, but the department was pretty backed up, he'd warned her, so it could take days, if not weeks, before she'd hear anything.

So what was her next step? Sinking farther down into the now-tepid water, Faith pretended she was a PI in a paperback. What would Bosch do? Or Griessel? Or Quinn? Start at the beginning. Follow the breadcrumbs. Start at the start. But she'd already done all that, hadn't she? And the crumbs had blown away.

The water grew cold and the tips of her fingers turned into prunes. What would, what would? Then the answer hit. Obvious. So obvious.

She reeled her body upwards, one arm fishing for the towel.

The Bunny. The damn Bunny would know. Time to suck it up and go say hello.

- 32 -

SANS

Sans was chucking cards onto the boot of a car with his regular bunch of dead collector chums. The only female dead collector, Faith, didn't seem interested in playing today. She was leaning against a street pole, thumbing through that rag of hers again. He'd lost three games in a row already, more fuel to fire his already foul mood, and the chick thumbing through the rag was sommer annoying him.

Her guardjie, the mullet-head with the lame name, saw him looking irritably her way and gave a shrug.

"I don't know why you read that rubbish," Sans called out. "*The Daily Lies*, more like it. And that Lawyer guy?" He made screwy signs with his fingers to his head. "I heard he was locked up in Lentegeur—you know, the mental hospital?"

The guardjie slapped down a card, then dug his greasy glove into a bag of crisps.

"Yes, yes," said Faith, nose still in the folds of the rag. "I've heard it all before and I don't care."

"Crocodiles in the sewers. Mutant rats. Shady men who control the world," Sans tried again. "It's always the same bullshit, isn't it? You do know that it's all bullshit, right?"

"Maybe, maybe not. You shouldn't be so quick to discount every-thing that blows you out of your comfort zone. John Lennon said he believes in everything until it's disproved. He's even been quoted as saying: 'I believe in everything until it's disproved. So I believe in fairies, the myths, dragons. It all exists, even if it's in your mind. Who's to say that dreams and nightmares aren't as real as the here and now?'"

"John Lennon! Really? So, we're quoting a wife beater now, who threw his own firstborn son away like he was trash and cheated on his wife? Or are you going to be telling me now that that's also fake news? One of your alternative facts?"

"Wife beater? What are you talking about?"

"Ah, see. You don't know everything."

The dead collector shrugged, and her blue locks gave a quick bounce. "Whatever. All I'm saying is that there are more things in heaven and earth and all that. So it's best not to jump to conclusions before you're sure you have the whole picture."

Shakespeare. The chick had just quoted Shakespeare, although he doubted the little conspiracy nut knew it herself. What was it with all the cherries in his life quoting Shakespeare suddenly? His mother, God rest her soul, had loved *Hamlet*. Read it to him as a bedtime story. Maybe that was why the line did the trick, or maybe he was just feeling desperate. "Say, talking about more things in heaven and earth . . . Does that rag of yours have a classifieds section?"

"Yes, so?"

"I've got this friend, right?"

"Yes. So what? Is he an unimaginative bastard like you?"

"Ouch!"

"I just tell it like it is."

"So, about my friend," he continued, brushing off the sting. "He needs an expert of some sort. Only he doesn't quite know what kind of expert yet. He's going a bit haywire. Thinks he might be hallucinating and such."

"Sounds like he needs to see a psychologist."

"Yes. That's what I told him. But he's got a hang-up with head doctors. So I was wondering, what would your rag recommend for someone like that?"

"My rag?"

"Your highly respected, quality newspaper, I mean."

She shifted her weight against the pole, closed the rag, and folded her arms. "Fine. There are stories doing the rounds. Stories about spirits."

"Spirits? Barmen mixing alcohol with methanol, you mean, and causing brain damage? That's old news." Sans scratched his head. "I suppose it could be brain damage, mind you, I hadn't thought of that. I mean, that would suck for him, but it's better than being crazy, right?"

"No. Not those kinds of spirits. Dead people. Ghosts."

His eyeballs did a loop. He looked at the mullet-head, but the guy was focused on getting the last bits out of his crisps packet. He couldn't tell whether he was paying any attention to this conversation. "No thank you. No way. No such thing as ghosts. Don't believe in 'em. Never have, never will."

"Me, neither, to tell you the truth," she said, stroking a nasty purple bruise above her left eyebrow. "My guess is guilt."

"Guilt?"

"It can do strange things to a person. And the way I figure it, you're not—I mean your friend's not—exactly choirboy material, is he?"

"Hey, lady, what are you implying?"

"You asked for my opinion. There you have it. By the way, if your friend wants a hand with his conscience, I know a guy."

A snort. "I think my conscience is good, thanks."

"And your friend's?"

"Just dandy."

"Oh, well, that's great, then."

"Maybe my friend's just hitting the bottle too much. It's more likely that."

"Maybe, but . . ."

"What? Spit it out."

"Personally, your 'friend' sounds like he could do with the services of a sin-eater."

"A what?"

All the card players looked up. Even the guardjie.

"Fred Mostert. Big guy. Sin-eater."

The guardjie nodded knowingly, scrunched up the empty packet into a ball, and stuck it into his jacket pocket.

"So you don't know everything, then?" Faith said, tapping her copy of the *Daily Truth* as if that were some kind of oracle. "There's this guy. Hangs out at the Green Point Sanatorium. Bills himself as a kind of all-around Happy Meal of a white-sangoma-ghostbuster-priest-karma-doctor. But his main deal is sin-eating. It's a family trade."

"What the hell is sin-eating, though?"

"He absolves sick people's sins by eating them. Far as I know, some of the European colonists brought the ritual with them when they first set up camp here to plant their veggie garden. Funny to think that planting one pretty little garden ended up causing so much hell, and generations of it at that, don't you think?"

"Like the Garden of Eden."

"Touché. That makes two gardens, then. Best we all lay down our trowels and stop planting gardens right away. Weapons of mass destruction, I tell you."

Sans couldn't be sure, but he thought he detected a small crease around her eyes, a smile brewing underneath the dead collector's mask. Was she just laughing at her own joke, or thawing to him?

"Anyway. I see Fred around now and again—our paths tend to cross. We both spend a lot of time hanging around the dead and the dying. He's a sweetie. You'll find him most days in Green Point, at the sanatorium, although sometimes they chase him away. He's also got fingers in other pies, not always steak and kidney." The crinkle at the eyes again. "Word is that he's legit, the real deal. Either that or he's a hell of a good scam artist."

Sans's guess leaned towards the latter, but something was dawning on him. He did know this guy. Or he'd seen his name somewhere, and recently. "Does he also find lost things? Love? Money?"

"Multiskilled, as they say. But then you have to be, in this city."

Sans didn't like the way she was looking at him.

"Probably penis enlargement, too. Tell your friend."

"Ouch. Funny. But seriously, ghost-eating? I mean, you've got to be shitting me."

"Sin-eating. And fair enough. It sounds kind of ridiculous, doesn't it? But that's all I have. Barring a trip to the psychiatrist. We're living in interesting times, my friend." She poked him in the ribs with the rolled-up rag. "As I said before: Who are we to be the judge of what's ridiculous or not?"

Sans found himself counting her dreads, working out how much they were worth. Pity she'd gone and dyed them blue. She might have been a real cash cow.

The buzz in his pocket made his whole body rock.

"You okay?" asked the dead collector.

"Golden." He swallowed back the bile, his throat burning with sick. "Out of interest's sake. About finding lost money. Do you think—?"

From inside the dead collector's van, a radio crackled. "Sorry. Gotta go. There are grinners waiting. Come on, Ash."

Sans watched them go. Screwed. He was still screwed. Sin-eater his ass. It was his cash he needed—no time to waste on fairy tales. So he went back home. To pour himself a drink. Have a sandwich. Think about his sins. Ponder the merits of the concept of karma.

Was it two, three, maybe four drinks later that he climbed the stairs again to the top of the Absa building to make the call? No one was counting, especially not him, so he couldn't be sure, but his legs felt heavy and the climb to the top felt like a bad case of earworm, as if he were climbing the same stair after stair after stair, over and over on repeat. He was starting to think that he'd succumbed and purgatory was one never-ending Escher painting when he finally reached the roof to phone the bloody guilt-eating, ghost-swallowing, money-whispering whatever-he-was. He punched in the number. The phone rang and rang for what felt like forever. Until it didn't.

"Hello," said the man on the other side.

Wrong number, he wanted to say, then chuck the blinking-message-flashing-piece-of-shit-harbinger-of-doom down the side of the building to scatter into a million plastic pieces down below. But he didn't. Idiot. He said hi.

Later, looking back on all of this and replaying the order of events in his head, he would figure out that this was the moment. The moment when it all went from tits up to tits overboard. If meeting the unicorn was what plunged him into the rabbit hole in the first place, this was the moment his ass hit the other side.

33

FAITH

Faith hadn't yet gotten to page three, what with Pony Boy interrupting her, but if she had, there was something else she might have told him. There was this article in today's *Truth* claiming the injections distributed via the city's postboxes were making some unlucky souls hallucinate.

She read and reread the article with interest. Maybe that was what was wrong with Pony Boy's "friend"? Hadn't Ash told her he'd seen Sans talking to himself the other day? She should probably tell him when she saw him again. Tomorrow. She wouldn't forget. Tomorrow. *Tomorrow. Focus, Faith, focus.*

The therapy bar was packed. Faith pushed through the crowd, squeezing her limbs through the gaps, careful not to touch any arms or hips or hands or ears or shoulders. It made her think of that game they used to play as children at school fairs. There was this curved piece of wire attached to a plank and you had to navigate the bends with a metal loop without the loop touching the wire—otherwise a buzzer would go off. She used to love that game, would always make it right through to the end of the wire to win something, a plastic toy or a piece of candy. Steady hands. She'd had steady hands back then.

She made her way to the edge of the ring where a waitress in a short skirt was waiting around looking bored while balancing a serving tray on her head with a lone beer on top of it. On the other side of the ropes, a good-looking guy in his twenties wearing red overalls adorned with

shiny reflectors (a paramedic, perhaps) was beating up his patsy for the
night, a giant furry teddy bear, who was taking the hits like a champ.

When the teddy took a tumble, Pretty Boy paused for a second,
wiped the sweat from his brow with one gloved hand, and motioned
to the waitress, who unbalanced the tray from the top of her head and
handed him his beer. Pretty Boy took one swig and broke the bottle
against Teddy's head. A buzzer went off and the referee waved a red card.
Pretty Boy just shrugged, took out an R200 note from his pants pocket,
and waved it at the referee, who conferred with the floored bear in a
whisper, then took the money and nodded at Pretty Boy to continue.

"Excuse me," said Faith to the waitress, who was inspecting her
red come-to-bed nails for any imperfections through her transparent
gloves. The waitress looked up at Faith. Her mask had a see-through
slit, to show off her red lips (the same shade as her nails), which she
now puckered into a disapproving pout. "If you need a drink, you'll
have to get it at the bar. I only wait on the patients."

"No. I know. I don't want a drink. I'm looking for someone. One
of your therapists."

"Which one?"

"The Easter Bunny. Is he in tonight?"

"You mean Lawyer? He's not just a bunny, you know. That's just one
of his suits."

"Yes. Sure. Is he working tonight?"

"Why should I tell you?" asked the waitress. Behind her back Pretty
Boy had proceeded to take a running leap from atop the ropes and was
now straddling the bear on all fours while pummeling its furry head with
murder in his pretty blue eyes. The sight made Faith's stomach spin.

She focused her attention back on the waitress. "Why shouldn't
you?" she asked.

The waitress sighed, rolled her eyes like a queen. "Fine. Whatever.
Out back, in the alley by the changing rooms. He's on his break."

The Easter Bunny was leaning against the wall between a scrawny guy
in a Stormtrooper suit, who was sitting on his helmet, nursing a black

eye with an ice pack, and another waitress wearing an even shorter skirt than her colleague inside. He must have been saying something very funny to the Stormtrooper because he was laughing so much he almost dropped his ice pack. (Despite herself, Faith was impressed. These days not a lot of people had the balls to laugh like that.) The waitress just puffed on her cigarette, the milky smoke curling up towards the tar-black sky in lazy question marks. Faith wondered how much tip money she had to make to be able to afford one of those. Or maybe the Stormtrooper had given her one? Word around town was that being a live punching bag paid a mint. Although you could only do it for so long before all those kicks to the head started messing with your brain.

"Lawyer?"

The Easter Bunny dropped his sentence midway and looked up. "Well, look what the cat dragged in." His mask was wrapped around his chin while he smoked and his bare lips turned up into a smile but his eyes didn't follow suit.

"Well, I certainly never expected to see you again," he said later while they stood squeezed together in his dressing room, which was just about bigger than a toilet cubicle. A row of suits hung on hooks against the yellow plasterboard wall—different skins at the ready for him to slip into. Next to the door was an intercom panel that buzzed out your name if a customer selected you from the menu.

"A nice surprise, then?"

"Not exactly," he said, hanging his big bunny head on a hook on the wall.

"Come on. You didn't miss me?"

The Bunny sat down on the cubicle's only chair. *It must be hot inside all that fur,* she thought, as sweat pooled at his eyebrows and along the sides of his ears. "Really? You just up and vanish in the middle of the night, taking my two best T-shirts with you, and then you pop in here weeks—months!—later and ask me if I've missed you? You can't be serious."

"Come on. It's not like we were that serious or anything." Faith ran her fingers though her hair. "You knew I wasn't into that."

The Bunny propped one paw onto the cubicle's tiny dressing table and glared at her. "Into what?"

"Relationships."

"You say it like it's a swear word."

"*Well* . . ."

"Well, hell, Faith, it's not like I thought we were going to grow old together or anything, but three years. Three years! Was it really necessary to vanish without saying a damn word, stealing two perfectly good shirts on top of it?"

"I . . ."

"Yes?"

"I don't know. Probably not."

"I mean, what kind of person breaks up with someone else via Post-it Note?"

"I . . . I don't know." Faith sighed. "What do you want me to say, Lawyer? That I'm an idiot? That I'm sorry?"

"Hmph," the Bunny snorted. "And then some." He folded his arms, leaned back into his chair until its front legs lifted and the back of his head kissed the wall.

"I'm sorry. I really am."

There was a patch of dried blood on his fur, just below the knee. Faith watched him pick at it for a bit. She needed to choose her moment.

"So. Go on. What is it? What do you need?" Lawyer looked up, stared straight at her.

"What makes you think I need something?"

"Do you take me for an idiot? Just because I get beat up for a living doesn't mean I've got shit for brains. Well, at least not yet."

Faith stared up at the costumes on the wall: a doctor's coat, a black cloak (a judge's robe, maybe, or the Grim Reaper's), a yellow health-worker's suit, a policeman's uniform, a proper suit and tie, a bright purple dinosaur. "So what's new at the *Truth*? Anything juicy?"

His frown softened, petered out. "Fine. I'll bite. But just because I miss talking to you about this stuff. I've got some interesting intel on the Laughter. A source who's saying it's a prion disease."

"A what?"

"A prion disease. Don't know much about it. Hell, I almost failed biology. But the way I understand, it's like a neuro-thingymajig thing.

A brain disease. Affects the nervous system. In the fifties, these cannibals in Papua New Guinea—"

"Whoa. Hold on. Cannibals?"

"Yup. Funerary cannibalism. They ate their dead. A way of returning their life force to the community. Sounds kind of romantic, doesn't it? Becoming one with your loved ones and such."

"Ugh. No way, Lawyer."

"To each their own. Point is, you only get it when you eat people. The disease. And get this, Faithie—one of the symptoms is uncontrollable laughter."

"But how does that tie in with us? I mean, it's not like you see brains on the menu at your local takeaway joint."

"According to this source, we've all been eating corpses for years. The whole city has. Brains, too. Ground up into boerewors. All courtesy of one of our leading supermarket chains. What with the skyrocketing price of beef, the goons upstairs started resorting to other sources of protein, like raiding the city's mortuaries. All hush-hush, of course."

"You know I'm a sucker for a good conspiracy theory, but that sounds ridiculous. Too ridiculous even for the likes of me."

"I'm just telling you what I've heard."

"Ja. Whatever. Next, please."

"Next what?"

"Next Laughter theory. That one's over the top. Don't think I'm buying it."

"Whatever. You don't have to believe it. But don't knock it too fast. Stranger things have happened."

"I guess."

"Well," said Lawyer. "Enough chitchat. What is it?"

"What's what?"

"What we've been dancing around this whole time. The reason for your sudden visit. What it is you want."

She looked down, trailed her eyes the length and breadth of his white furry paws. Next to the left one there was a chip in the cement floor. It looked a lot like a broken heart. Then his paw shifted and the heart was gone.

"I'm working on a case. A missing boy. And I've run into a dead end. I was wondering if you'd heard anything."

"Heard anything about what?" he said, sticking his paws behind his neck to fiddle with the zipper of his suit.

"I don't know. Missing children."

"This is Sick City. Children go missing all the time."

"I was hoping for something more specific."

"Well. There is one thing."

"What?"

The Bunny shed his fur, lifted one leg out of his suit. Underneath the fur, he was all skin. "Don't you read my column?"

"You know I do," she said, looking away. "Which one?"

"About the amakhosi gangs. Last week."

"Must have missed it. Tell me?"

"There are rumors floating around." He was scrounging around on the shelf above his head for a T-shirt now.

"What kind of rumors?"

"About kids going missing. I don't know much yet, but I've been doing some digging, and the theory I've been working on is that the city's amakhosi gang kids are being kidnapped by the government and shipped out to war zones across the world—the US mostly, but also Africa—to work as mercenaries for hire."

Amakhosi gangs were a favorite topic for the *Daily Truth*. A subculture of Xhosa teens who ingested a mix of muthi and alcohol in order to become possessed with ancestral spirits. The kids believed the spirits would make them super strong. Like superheroes. The gangs had been around for years, since way before the Laughter arrived, but popularity and numbers had spiked recently. Lawyer interviewed this sociologist about it a while back, who said the whole thing wasn't a supernatural phenomenon, but a social one. He put it all down to the fact that the kids felt dispossessed, powerless. As a reaction to their circumstances, they ingested the amakhosi muthi to feel like they had some kind of power, that they belonged. The sociologist seemed very sure of himself.

"Anyway, Faithie," said Lawyer, "it's all in the column. You should read it. I have a source who says they even recruit here."

"What do you mean, here?"

"Right here. In this therapy bar. That they find kids with a good right hook or whatever and proposition them. The new medic who works here, I think she might be in on it, the recruiting. I've been following her but I haven't seen anything concrete yet. Call it a hunch."

"I'm the one who has hunches, remember?" Faith said. "You're the journalist."

Lawyer smiled. "Yes. Well. But she didn't turn up for work yesterday, nor today, so I'll have to wait and see. Maybe I'm wrong."

Back in the therapy bar the crowd was roaring. Some poor sod in the ring was most probably kissing the floor and they were loving it.

"There's something else," said Faith.

"There always is, isn't there?"

"More blood! More blood!" the crowd chanted from beyond the cubicle's walls.

"A library card. I need a library card."

"You're kidding. You know I can't do that."

"Yes. But you—"

"No buts. You knew how it worked from the start. You have to follow the code. Or you get kicked out. You didn't. So, you got the boot. No, Faith, don't. Don't look at me with those eyes. You had your chance. You screwed it up. Plain. Simple. Done. Dusted. Game over. The end."

"But I had to. It was important."

"It's always important with you, isn't it? That's your problem."

There was a red vanity case on the table next to the door. Lawyer picked it up and held it out to her, like an offering.

She raised her eyebrows. He shrugged. She opened the case. Inside were some bandages, scissors, salves: a medi-kit.

"While you're here you might as well help patch me up."

"Don't you guys have a medic for this sort of thing?"

"I told you. She didn't pitch up tonight. Management hasn't said anything yet, but the rumor around the office is that she caught it. You know, the Great Equalizer. Poor thing. But then, she never was good with keeping her mask on."

They kept silent while she worked. The crowd had piped down. There was always a lull between fights. In the room next door someone was humming something, but Faith couldn't place the tune.

"Ow! Be careful! Didn't your mother teach you how to tie a bandage?"

"Oh, shush. Sit still. Don't be such a manbaby."

"A what?"

"A manbaby."

"Is that even a word?"

"Sure it is." She put the scissors down. "How does that feel? Too tight?"

"Perfect. It feels perfect. Thanks."

"Cool. So. About that card . . ."

"No way. Not this time. You got your privileges revoked. You know that. There are rules."

"But you can talk to him. To the librarian."

Lawyer dropped his chin to his chest. He ran a finger across his stubbled skull while resting his elbows on his thighs. "I don't know . . ."

She bent downwards, dropping her knees to the floor to catch his eye. "Please?"

The Easter Bunny looked into her eyes. His fingers kneading and drumming at his skull.

"I'll color inside the lines this time," she said. "Cross my heart . . ."

34

SANS

The entrance to the Green Point Stadium Quarantine and Disease Control Sanatorium was swarming with visitors clutching flowers and other tokens. The kiosks where soccer fans used to stock up on beer and boerie rolls back when the center was still a stadium now supplied masks and yellow anti-infection suits. The locals called this Limbo, the place where you were brought before being deported to one of the infected zones: the Island, the no-man's-land virus prisons of the Cape Flats, or the breezy upper-middle-class sanatoriums in Kalk Bay.

Sans passed a group of foreign volunteers huddled together in their yellow space-invader suits. Masks around their necks, they were passing a cigarette from hand to hand. Nicotine was getting scarcer by the day—a luxury few locals could afford. The spacemen were jabbering away in French, oblivious to the looks of longing cast their way by the locals. The burning cigarette continued its slow circular journey from one hand to the next. Some of the volunteers had taped photographs of themselves to their chests to make them look less faceless space invader, more human. Although putting away those bloody entjies would probably work better.

He found the reception desk at gate seven. "I'm looking for a guy. Goes by the name of Mostert, I think? I was told he hangs around here sometimes?"

The receptionist looked up from the pages of the *Sick City Gazette* and tapped her fingers on the counter. Her blue tartan gloves had little touchscreen-friendly patches glued to the tips. "Mmm . . . You mean Fred? Sure. The new matron, Abrahamse, has banned him from the wards, but he's still about. I don't know how he gets away with it. Must have the warden in his pocket."

"Where can I find him?"

"There's a coffee stand around the corner. His office, he calls it. Good chance you'll find him there."

"What does he look like?"

"Big guy. Moustache. You won't miss him."

"Thanks." There was a stack of A5 pamphlets on the counter. Sans picked up the top sheet and pulled it closer: DON'T LAUGH, warned the header, in big, bold, capital letters. Then:

Laughing in public is illegal.

If you feel a surge of laughter bubbling up, try these techniques to stifle it:

1. Try thinking of something sad or upsetting.
2. Practice your breathing exercises.
3. Try pursing your lips into an "o" shape while frowning.
4. Induce a coughing fit.
5. Stuff a clean sock or a handkerchief into your mouth to stifle laughter.

If the above techniques fail and you still feel an urge to laugh, take your temperature immediately, then proceed to your nearest medmachine for a more comprehensive test.

Always report any illegal laughter by phoning the city's tip-off line at 0800 11 12 13.

And remember: It's not snitching if you can save a life.

"This is terrible. Who writes these things?" Sans asked the receptionist, crumpling the piece of paper into a ball. "Has every decent propa-

ganda copywriter in this whole damn country kicked the bucket? This is
so bad that I don't know if I should laugh or cry about it." He tossed the
paper ball over the counter into the receptionist's empty wastebasket.

"Rather cry, please," said the receptionist, lowering her spectacles to
throw him a deadpan stare. "Anything but laughing. I just don't have
the energy today for all the extra paperwork."

He grinned at her beneath his mask and turned to go.

"Hold on," said the receptionist. "One more thing. Tell Fred he still
owes me, Cindy, that tenner he borrowed from me last week. If it's not
here by tomorrow morning, as sure as hell is hot and the sky is blue,
I'm charging interest. Make sure you tell him that, too."

Cindy was right. The sin-eater was just where she'd said he would be,
sitting at a plastic table beside the sanatorium's coffee stand, chatting
to a chick in a yellow dress. A queue of jittery bodies snaked from the
table all the way to the door. None of them looked nearly as embarrassed as Sans was to be there.

He watched the queue of crazies, fiddling with their phones or making small talk about the weather—one chick was sitting cross-legged
on the floor, leaning over so far that the top of her head kissed concrete, another guy in a suit and tie was talking to the ceiling. "Shut up,
Margie," said the guy in the suit to the ceiling. "I told you to shut the
hell up!"

He was about to turn around, make a run for it, when his pocket vibrated again. Screwed. If he didn't find Lucky and his money—soon—
he was screwed. Especially if his plan B was a ghost. Fine. Whatever.
One foot in front of the other. Get it over with. Talk to the fat bastard.
It's not like he had anything more to lose. Apart from the last tenuous
dregs of his sanity, perhaps.

When his turn came, he took a step towards the fat man's table.
"Fred? Fred Mostert?"

"Have a seat," said Fred, and pointed to a plastic chair.

Sans sat down.

The fat man lifted his hand and the girl manning the coffee kiosk stirred into motion, spooned some chicory into two paper cups, filled both with hot water, and brought them over. "We're out of milk," she said, as she handed Sans the cup. "Sugar, too, of course." Sans paid her and she left.

"Go on," said the fat man, taking a sip.

Sans had worked out his game plan beforehand. He was going to interrogate the guy first. Even if the blue-dreaded dead collector had sort of vouched for him, he needed to make sure the guy was legit for himself. But now that he was here, staring into the fat guy's bottomless eyes, he couldn't quite get it up. Couldn't remember a single question or line of attack.

The silence grew golden while the fat man just sat there, staring at him, playing with the lid of his coffee cup. Sans wasn't normally one to shy away from a round of eyeball chicken, but there was something about this guy. The way his Pantone blue eyes seemed to stare right through you, gnaw at your innards like some kind of empath vulture.

So he cracked. Spilled his guts like a snitch with a tik problem. Started with his money problems, and worked his way around to the bit about the cherry—that bloody, beautiful cherry—his unicorn. The way she kept popping up and out of his life like some kind of demented jack-in-the-box.

When his story was done, and the tepid cup of instant coffee emptied, the silence shining like a big fat grand prix cup, the guy still didn't speak. Just turned the plastic lid around and around the merry-go-round in his stubby fingers.

Sans's pocket vibrated again.

And again.

Stress and fear bubbled like lava at the back of his tongue. *Bloody fat bastard! Just say something already!* he wanted to shout, then ram the bloody plastic lid down the fat fuck's throat for good measure. But he kept a grip and tried to ease the silence by eyeing his surroundings. At the table next to them, a stubbled guy in a jacket and tie was crying into his Coke. And behind him, a cocky young janitor was chatting up the coffee kiosk girl, who batted her plastic lashes, and curled a black lock (synthetic) around one finger.

"Well, your girlfriend might be right. It might be guilt that's eating you up," said the fat man finally, breaking Sans's trance.

"She's not my girlfriend."

"Is she a girl?"

"Yeah."

"Is she a friend?"

"Kind of."

"Then it's all semantics, isn't it? Anyway, it might be guilt, yes. But there is another option, too."

The guy had an annoying habit. As he talked, he swayed his head from side to side. It reminded Sans of one of those bobblehead toys you find on dashboards.

"Okay," said Sans, wrapping his gloved hands around the cup. "I'm listening."

"Going by the type of things you're seeing, which doesn't sound like your garden-variety spook to me, and the fact that you haven't stopped sweating buckets since you walked in, even though it's a pretty breezy day outside . . . it sounds to me like you've caught the big one."

"The big what?"

"Why, the bug of all bugs, the throw-you-on-the-Island-and-end-your-life-as-you-know-it-big-fucker-that-the-guys-upstairs-will-have-your-neck-for-in-a-jiffy bug, of course." Wobble-bobble went the fat man's head.

"Nah. I've read all the pamphlets, listened to the radio announcements, seen all the billboards. This isn't a symptom. And besides, I don't feel sick."

"That's just what they'd like you to believe. That it's all coughs and keeling over. They don't like to talk about the unlucky donners who get stuck with a bad case of the Eye when the sickness hits. Keeling over seems like a right picnic compared to that. And it causes a heck of a lot of PR problems for the okes upstairs."

"What are you talking about? The Eye? There's nothing wrong with my eyes. Haven't you heard a word I've said?"

"Noooo. You know, the Eye. The second sight. As in channeling your ancestors. Visions and whatnot."

"That again. I should have warned you going in. I'm not into all that stuff. Traditional healing. Sangomas. Whatever. I don't believe in ghosts, either, just for the record."

"Oh? Then what exactly are you doing here, boet? I have a number for a great psychiatrist if you want it."

"No. Please. No head doctors. I don't know why I came here. You're right. Maybe I should go."

"Hold on," said the sin-eater, rocking his head hypnotically. "Don't get your panties in a twist. You don't have to believe me if it kicks you out of your comfort zone too much. Just hear me out before you run away. I know it's all a bit much to take in. I sometimes forget to bring it on slow. I can be too quick to the draw, like Dirty Harry. Too heavy on the ears at the first hear. A lot of my new customers, the voodoo virgins, as I like to call them—not that I do voodoo, you understand, it's just a bit of fun with alliteration—are skeptical in the beginning. And while I can't make you believe, I can tell you this: if you're looking for an expert in this field, if you're looking for the best, you've come to the right place. The dead and dying are my business, boet. Have been since I was a laaitie. Death has always run in my family, one way or another. I would have loved to have a regular job—but I got born into this."

"Yes, yes. I hear you. But how do I know you're the real deal? That you're not making all this stuff up just to screw with me? This city is full of 'healers' who get rich off desperate suckers like myself. Next you're going to tell me you can double my penis size as well."

"You don't know, boet, you don't." The sin-eater grinned as he chucked the empty cup into the bin and stood up. "Look. I'm late for an appointment, but I've got an extra anti-contamination suit in my bag. Might be a bit loose around the waist, but it'll do. Want to come with and help out? After we've sorted out this customer, you can buy me a dop and we can talk about your Eye problems."

"Thanks, but I think I'll pass."

"Suit yourself, but what have you got to lose, right? Seems to me drinking a dop with a mad oke on the off chance of him being able to help is a lot better than having waves slamming you into the pavement willy-nilly."

Sans's pocket vibrated. "What about the money?" he asked.

"What money?"

"When I phoned you, you said you would be able to help me find the money I lost."

"Oh, yes. That. Not nearly as interesting a topic, don't you think? But I suppose it does make the world go 'round. Come along, then."

It was hot in the tented room. The yellow plastic suit squelched as Sans walked towards the bed where the dying guy lay.

"Did you bring the fried chicken and the brandy?" the sin-eater asked the woman in the red mask who was standing at the foot of the bed, choking back tears.

"I did." She picked up a flask with the brandy and a brown paper bag bursting with chicken drumsticks that was on the floor next to her handbag and handed them over. Sans saw that her fingers were trembling. "Will this work?" the woman asked softly. "Will his sins be absolved?"

"My family has been doing this for generations, ma'am."

The sin-eater unpacked the bag, carefully placing a plastic sheet, then the drumsticks, on the sick man's chest, and muttered a quick chant: "I give easement and rest now to thee, dear man. Come not down the lanes or in our meadows. And for thy peace I pawn my own soul. Amen."

After this, he removed his mask, took a swig from the silver flask, then began eating. When every bone was picked clean, he stood silently, rocking his bulk on the balls of his feet. Then he rubbed each gloved finger with a paper serviette. "All done."

"What do we do now?" said the woman in the red mask.

"Now you pay, and then you pray, of course," said the sin-eater, wiping a scrap of chicken from his moustache.

35

FAITH

The bar had been there forever. Well, at least for as long as there were such things as bars around here. The gray-haired barman was pouring last calls to a rowdy crowd of leftovers, who didn't seem quite ready for the walk back to their empty apartments yet. Faith threaded her way into the eye of the storm. Her right hand clasped the card Lawyer had given her. Brown, the size and shape of a credit card. On the back was a stamp with a date. Next to it, a handwritten signature (the librarian's, she presumed).

"What can I get for you?" the aged barman asked. He was slapping the draughts down, the spilt lager pooling into the grooves of the rough-hewn wooden counter. A string of rings hugged his right eyebrow. Another dangled from his left nostril. Faith put her palm on the counter and slipped him the card. "I'd like to borrow a book, please."

The barman raised a ringed eyebrow. "Put that away," he said, grabbing a glass from the stack behind him and swiveling back to pour.

He thumped the draught down on the counter. The white froth danced on the head of the beer like seafoam after a storm. "That will be fifty."

"I—"

"I said fifty, please."

She extracted the money from her purse, counted it, gave it to him.

"Have a seat," said the barman, and like a magician revealing a trick, he fanned his fingers in the direction of an empty table at the back of the bar. "Go on. It's last call, though, so no more after that one, you hear?"

Faith did as she was told. While the space around the counter itself was still a hive alive, this side of the dive bar was emptying out. In the corner next to the jukebox, a woman was dancing on her own with her eyes closed, while a fat tabby cat sitting on a nearby table watched her with his one good yellow eye while licking his fluffy balls. In the other corner a group of guys were playing a drinking game—flicking cents into an empty glass. Above their heads, petals of red paint wilted off the wall.

She nursed her beer, thinking about nothing in particular, until a waiter in a neat bow tie came by and stooped over the table to wipe it with a cloth.

"Busy night?" she said, just making conversation.

"It's always like this now," said the waiter. The hand holding the rag paused for a second. The waiter looked up at Faith. "You know, the way I see it, things were different when I was a kid."

"How so?"

"Well, choices were like Smarties—wot-a-lot-I-got. But nowadays the average fool on the street like me and you, we've only got two."

"Ja? So what are they?" she said, playing along.

"Well, we can either choose to pray or choose to drink. Although the way some of these guys come in here to hug the bottle, you'd think they thought it was the same thing."

"In a way, I guess it is."

The waiter nodded, then turned his chin left and right, as if to check whether anyone in the bar was watching them. But the drinking-game guys' eyes were glued to their coins and the dancing woman's were still squeezed tight. The tabby was the only one paying them any attention, having glanced up from the business of grooming his balls.

The waiter's hand moved to his breast pocket, out of which he produced a crumpled brown packet. Van Hunks, her favorite brand. "Ladies' bathroom. Last cubicle. Now, don't you smoke them all at once."

"I won't. Thank you."

"You have a nice night, okay?" said the waiter, and shuffled off.

Faith flipped open the pack. At the bottom, a small metal object glinted in the dark. She turned the pack upside down, tapped the open end against her palm, and the key dropped down. Then she lifted her head and scanned the room. The tabby looked up, narrowing its yellow eyes in recognition. She nodded to him, blinked (someone once told her that this was a sign of camaraderie in cat language), and stood up.

The bathroom was empty and she walked through the fluorescent glare to the last stall, which had an "Out of order" sign on the door. Underneath it someone had used a marker to scribble "If no one comes back from the future to stop you from doing it, how bad a decision can it be?" in generous, flowy letters. Pondering this wisdom, Faith slid her finger along the top-left edge of the laminated sign to undo the fat wad of Prestik attaching it to the wall. Her fingers did the same with the other three corners. The sign flopped off the door and onto the floor.

In the center of the empty brown space the laminated folio had concealed was the strangest little keyhole. The cover was brass and shaped like an eye, with long lashes curving upwards. And along the edges was a whirl of intricately carved details: sea monsters, minuscule mermaids, and other twirling tiny things.

Faith slipped the key into the hole and turned. The door swung open. Behind it was a cubicle, the same shape and size as the others, only this one didn't have a toilet in it. Just a bare slither of empty space and another door. Next to this door was a doorbell. And above that, a brass plaque that looked like a much more recent addition than the keyhole. Faith read the words engraved on it: WHO CONTROLS THE PAST CONTROLS THE FUTURE. —GEORGE ORWELL. She pressed the bell with her finger. *Ping*. Nothing happened. So she pressed it again, *ping, ping*.

A *click*. A panel in the wooden door slid open a crack to reveal a face. The face was long and narrow, with fleshy lower eyelids that drooped in folds like bunting. And a star map of liver spots from top to chin.

"Yes, yes! Hold your horses," said the face, glaring at her over a pair of egg-shaped glasses.

Faith showed him the card.

"You," said the face.

"Me," said Faith.

"We're almost closing."

"I'll be quick."

"You'd better be," said the face, while the thicket of grooves above its eyebrows rippled.

The door slid back all the way. Behind it were steps leading down a staircase so deeply sloped it almost wasn't a staircase at all. More of a slide.

Faith held onto the polished brass banister, adorned with the same *Where's Wally?* curlicue intricacies as the keyhole cover, and dived downwards.

At the bottom was a boxy room, fringed by red velvet curtains, and right in the middle of the room was a chair. It was a pretty ordinary-looking chair. A disappointment of a thing, really, with black steel legs and a padded seat in run-of-the-mill office blue. Like you would find in a dentist's waiting room or those snaking seat queues at Home Affairs.

"Sit, please," said the face, which was now a body as well. Lean and sinewy like a secretary bird and wearing a red velvet jacket that looked as if it had been made from the same material as the curtains.

Faith did as she was told.

"Do you want to browse the database or make an entry?" asked the secretary bird.

"Browse, please."

"Wait here."

She waited, studying the red curtains, and after a while, the librarian came back holding some gloves and a pair of what looked to Faith like shower caps. The secretary bird glared at her; one hand dangled the gloves in front of her face like a muleta. "I am not much of a fan for second chances, little lady, and there's nothing I hate more in this world than someone disrespecting this library, but Lawyer is a good friend and a fine man, so I made a concession for his sake this once. But you so much as touch a pen or a piece of paper on my watch, and this is the last time you will ever set foot on the Society's premises again. We have these rules for a reason, you hear? There is a code. And it isn't just there for shits and giggles. Understood?"

"Yes, sir."

"Good," he said, passing her the gloves. "Now put these on over yours. And these," he added, passing along the two caps, "are for your feet. Quick-sticks, please, we don't have all night."

She did as she was told and the librarian pushed the curtains aside to reveal a hugger-mugger of interconnected rooms, stitched with heavy tomes and wooden filing cabinets. In one corner, an old and almost obsolete computer stood gathering dust. Above it hung a painting in an elaborate gold frame. From out of this gilded cage a serious young woman surveyed the room, hands folded neatly on her lap.

"Welcome to the secret Library of the Society of the Down," the librarian said theatrically, twirling the fingers on his right hand like a vintage promo girl. Faith could kind of picture him in a sequined leotard. With a feathered headdress, a banner, and red, glittery heels.

"Okay," said the librarian. "So you know the drill. To this side are the shelves—the books on conspiracy theories, alternate histories, as well as official histories that go back all the way to the Middle Ages. Everything under and above the sun."

The man had a strange tic of tapping his palm against his thigh as he talked and Faith found it hard not to stare.

"Over here we have a collection of transcribed oral histories, and over here you will find our filing cabinets," he continued, *tap, tap, tap.* "From what I can recall, you are familiar with these, but let me give you the rundown again so there is absolutely no confusion. These are the main focus of our collection and the main reason for the existence of our little library. Each cabinet contains handwritten histories, some dating as far back as the early 1800s, written by Society members. If something is in a language you don't understand, I can probably translate. We have recently started computerizing some of it, but most of it exists only here in these rooms. And in here . . ." he added, pointing a sinewy finger to his head. "The perks, as they say, of having an almost, just about, but not quite flawless photographic memory. But I digress. Think of these cabinets as one giant collaborative alternative or 'unofficial' history encyclopedia. All written entries are reviewed by myself or one of my colleagues at the Society before they are allowed to enter the system and end up inside one of these"—he gestured towards the filing cabinets—"so don't even think of adding anything without sending it my way first." *Tap, tap, tap.* "Now is there anything in particular you are looking for?"

"Entries about missing kids."

"Ah, kids. Classic search choice. Lots of material. Any particular kids you are interested in, or just your average run-of-the-mill snotter?"

"Um. I'm not sure. Street kids, maybe? No. Maybe I'll just start with run-of-the-mill first and narrow it down as I go."

"Well," said the librarian, "we've had quite a few entries on the topic recently, matter of fact. Start with those?"

"Yes, please."

"As you wish."

She followed the librarian through the maze until he came to a stop. "Here we are. *C*, for *Children*. Enjoy." *Tap, tap, tap.* Then he turned around and left Faith to it.

She watched him walk away and turned her attention back to the cabinet. On the wall next to it was a plaque. WELCOME TO THE SOCIETY OF THE DOWN. PROUDLY A-HISTORY, A-BELIEF, A-REALITY SINCE 1800. FIGHTING OPPRESSION. GIVING A VOICE TO THE VOICELESS. WE BELIEVE EVERYTHING. WE BELIEVE NOTHING. REALITY IS FICTION. FICTION IS TRUTH. WE RECORD EVERYTHING. WE DON'T CHOOSE THE TRUTH.

It made her think back to the day she got kicked out. Lawyer had been livid, pacing up and down the shelves. "How could you, Faith? What you did goes against everything the Society stands for."

"But the kid that died," she'd protested. "We both know it's that virus patroller's fault that he's dead. You were there. We both saw what happened. It wasn't an accident like they said."

"I know. But that's not the point. The point is that you broke in here and censored recorded information to suit your own views. The whole point of the Society and its library is to record everything. We never, *ever* tamper with recorded content just because it doesn't fit our own memories or beliefs. That's our code. It's the only way we know to fight confirmation bias and conservatism bias. You can't charge in here and change facts you don't believe in. You can add to the record, add your point of view, but you can't censor anyone else's. Both sides of the story should be told. It isn't your place to decide what's true, what's right, and then censor the rest. Even if you saw something with your own eyes. That's not what the Society is about."

"But the way they were making it out, they were putting the blame on the kid's dad. Acting like it was his fault. We both know that that isn't true."

"That's why I wrote down both versions. You still don't get it, do you? Face it, Faith. Right and wrong—or what *you* believe is right or wrong—is all-important to you, and that's good. But it's not right for the Society. Your world is white and black. Ours is made up of every shade of gray under the sun."

"But isn't that dangerous? To give people the chance to choose their own truth like it's a flavor of soda? What if they choose wrong? What if they think they have all the facts, but it's actually the wrong ones? Dangerous ones? Like people who believe vaccines cause autism? Aren't you worried about spreading ideas like that, ideas that could be dangerous in the wrong hands? Ideas that could kill?"

"I hear you. But I still believe that history shouldn't just be written by the victor, that information control and censoring is wrong, period, and that all information and opinion should be free to everyone."

"But—"

"No buts. I'm sorry, Faith; I've been told to tell you your card has been revoked."

Coming back to the present moment, Faith pressed her head down, pushed open the creaky cabinet drawer, and started sifting through the catalogue cards inside. *C* for *Children* yielded a wild selection of topics: child trafficking, illegal organ harvesting, muthi murders (the younger the kid, the better the muthi apparently), albino muthi murders, amakhosi gangs, child soldiers, illegal adoption, scientific experiments, child labor (there was a whole section about the use of kids in the wig trade—little hands worked marvels when it came to making false eyelashes), cult recruitment, illegal vaccine testing.

Faith was mulling this all over when something caught the corner of her eye, a light blinking through the fabric of her bag. Her phone, sending through a message from her detective ex at the SAPS. She read it twice. *"Hey Faith. Missing person angle doesn't check out. Elliot Pretorius (1 yrs) succumbed (Laughter) 2 mths ago. Identity theft possibility? False name? Good luck. Beers soon? You're buying."*

Faith stuffed the phone back into her bag and swore to herself. Why would Tomorrow lie to her? It didn't make sense. She prided herself on her ability to read people, could usually smell a lie from here to Maputo. There was something off about the girl's story, sure, but her pain seemed real. So much for the research, then.

She pushed at the drawer to close it. It didn't budge. The hexed thing was stuck. She wrenched it out an inch, then rammed it with her shoulder. The drawer gave a drawn-out squeak like a rat in heat, then thumped its big mouth shut.

The librarian was sitting atop the desk that cradled the computer, head down.

Faith studied the painting of Anna de Koningh that hung above his head. The brushstroke black eyes hypnotized her. Lawyer had told her all about Anna and her lost prophetic diary on her first visit. Always a sucker for a good treasure hunt, Faith had been looking for it on and off since.

She focused her attention back to the librarian. The old man was now drawing something in a red notebook. His knuckles looked swollen and bent. There was a tattoo on the third one to the right. A black circle, with a maze inside it, and a kind of cog or pinwheel shape right in the middle. She'd seen it before. Lawyer had the same tattoo on his upper arm. One of many—which was why she'd never asked him about it.

"What does it mean?" she asked the librarian.

"Why, forty-two, of course."

"No. I mean your tattoo. What does it mean?"

"Ah. It's the strophalos."

"The what?"

"Hecate's maze." The librarian looked up. He seemed surprised. "You do know, don't you?"

"No."

"I see," said the librarian, his lips curling into a little smirk. Faith couldn't figure out if he looked amused, bemused, or just disappointed. She continued to watch him draw for a while, one hand scribbling, the other tapping. He was so focused on the page now, it seemed like he'd forgotten all about her. She cleared her throat: "Shall I let myself out, then?"

The librarian's nose wrinkled a notch, but he didn't look up again. He was drawing something else now. A dog. A hulking canine creature with gaping jaws and large jagged teeth.

"Yes, indeed," he said. "Don't mind me. The door's in the same place it was when you came in."

36

SANS

The bar was stuffed. Limbs lined wall to wall. A smell of sweat and vomit and beer. A fat tabby was picking at its paws underneath a painting of Jan van Riebeeck (or whoever it was). The dead man's dandy mug was obscured by a spray-paint scrawl that read "Screw this guy." Pink doodle horns sprouted from his curls. A pink pitchfork floated in the air behind his shoulder.

Sans and the sin-eater were plonked at a circle-stained booth. Sans was nursing a beer; the sin-eater was on his second glass of brandy and Coke.

"Thanks for the dop, boet," said the sin-eater, knocking back some more karate water. "Sin-eating always leaves a bad taste in my mouth. Makes me thirsty as hell. And this guy's Christmas stocking was packed with a few particularly unsavory morsels."

Sans listened with one ear while watching the bar go by behind the fat man's back. Wait, was that Faith emerging from the bathroom and heading to the door? He pushed his head down, instinctively. Last thing he wanted was for the dead collector to find out that he'd followed her loony-tune advice.

"You know," continued the sin-eater, adjusting his large rear on the leather couch, "I really like this place. Noisy with history. Back when this city was nothing but a little tit-sucker—the Tavern of the Seas—this was the place. There's a reason they called it that, you know. Tavern of the Seas. The whole town wasn't much more than a drive-in—or should we rather say 'sail-in'—dive bar back then. Scores of travelers right off the boat came here to blow off steam and wet their whistles. Right here where we're sitting now. You can almost see them, can't you? Drinking, fighting, making merry, lekker getrek, laughing their asses off . . . Look, that one right there is—"

"Yes. I get it," Sans interrupted. "So what's the deal here, brother? Why haven't you reported me yet?"

"To whom? The fashion police?"

"The what?"

"Those tackies you're wearing. They're not exactly subtle, are they? I mean, gold Nikes? The moment I saw you walk into the cafeteria, I thought, Sho, look at the rims on that one—"

"Hey! What I'm wearing is none of your business. I'm talking about the Veeps."

"Now, why on Earth should I go reporting you to them, then?"

"If I'm infected like you say, I should be deported, right? Locked up. If what you're saying is true, I'm a danger to everyone I come into contact with. I could be killing you by proximity as we speak."

"That's what they say."

"They say it because it's true! I've seen the dead, the dying. Do you think this is all some kind of grand illusion? A joke?"

The sin-eater signaled the waitress and ordered another round. "Oh, yes. A cosmic one. And we're the punch line. But gags aside, let's just say that my profession has gifted me with a unique perspective on life and death and all the rest."

Feeling a migraine brewing, Sans pressed on. "You have a way of talking in circles, don't you? Fine. But what about my money? You said you'd help me find it. And all this shit I've been seeing? This *Eye* business you've been going on about. What's *that* about?"

The waitress brought the drinks and Fred slid Sans another lager. "Drink up. You're going to need to be more lubricated before we get down to the fun stuff."

"What fun stuff? Stop toying with me. Just spit it out."

"As you wish." The fat man cracked his knuckles, fingered his moustache again. "So here's where you're going to need to trust me a little, boet.

Suspension of disbelief and all of that. Sometimes, when the Laughter hits . . . how can I put it . . . it doesn't affect everyone in the same way. Something in some people's makeup, their DNA or whatever you would like to call it, is different from the ordinary oke on the street."

"What do you mean, different?"

"Call it the Nostradamus effect, if you will. You've heard of Nostradamus, right? Sixteenth-century oke who said he could see the future?"

"Sure."

"But I bet you didn't know Nostradamus was an apothecary before he became involved in all that prophecy hoodoo. The guy was working on a cure for the bubonic plague, the Black Death, when his whole bleddie family died of it. Wife, children, the lot. But the lucky bugger survived. He was coming into contact with all these sick okes for work, so logically he should have been first in line. To kick the bucket, I mean. But he didn't catch a bleddie thing. It really messed with his head. On top of all that grief and guilt, he started seeing things, too. Weird, crazy, impossible stuff. Like airplanes. Imagine what he must have thought of that. Giant metal birds of doom that go *vroom*. I guess it really scared the poor bugger."

Jesus, was this guy ever going to get around to finding his money for him?

"Anyway, so Nostradamus went and figured he was immune somehow and that the crazy dreams and the stuff he was seeing were all connected. Became obsessed with figuring out how. Spent every waking hour on it. Invented some kind of pill using his own DNA. And it managed to cure a whole bunch of people. But the aftereffects of his cure drove most of them quite mad, so he got disillusioned, gave up on the whole medicine business, and got more and more into the occult. Began writing down his prophecies. The rest, as they say, is history. Or maybe, I should say, the future. Who knows?"

"Okay. I hear you. But—"

"I'm getting there, hold your horses, boet. So my thinking is that's what's happening with you. You've got the fever but for some reason you didn't get the full-blown disease. And the effect of your body fighting off the infection is that you got stuck with the Eye."

"But if what you're saying is true, why me?"

"Ever heard of the Italian family who couldn't sleep? Generations of the same family coming down with this weird disorder. Some prion disease of the brain caused by a mutation or some such. The insomnia starts sometime after their eighteenth birthday. Gets worse and worse until they croak. Nasty stuff. But I'm digressing."

No shit. Sans took a swig of beer.

"The point is I think you might have a rare genetic mutation of some sort. Ha, you and old Nostradamus might even be related. Wouldn't that be a story, hey, boet?"

Sans watched the fat man nurse his Klippies and Coke and wondered why he was even indulging this lunatic. A week ago he wouldn't have given this guy the time of day. He thought about standing up, leaving. His rational mind knew he should have left the bar hours ago. But something made him stay. Probably the forty-odd messages and missed calls from those damn gangsters. The worst thing was, it was like a part of him was actually starting to believe this nonsense. If that was the case, if he was willing to reach that far, he was clearly more desperate than he realized.

"Listen, boet," said Fred, leaning his meaty elbows on the table, "my connection to the dead. Had it since I was a laaitie. It's kind of a family affliction, as I think I've mentioned, but it doesn't quite work on demand. Think of it as a Twitter feed to the other side. All these tweets coming in all the time, and I can't filter them. Every now and again I hear about one of you guys. A seer who wasn't *born* with the Eye. Way I figure it, you guys seem to pop up every century or so—all connected to pandemics, all starting with a fever."

"So I'm not the only one?"

"Not if we count the dead. I don't know much about the living. Not my area of expertise, as they say."

"And what about the girl? How does she tie into all this?"

"Well, the way I figure, you two are connected. Think of her as your other half from the other side of history. She's got the fever, too—and from the way you said she's dressed, I'm guessing it's smallpox—and while you're sitting over here looking into the past, she's over there glimpsing the future. Make sense?"

"No. Not even remotely."

"Oh, well."

"Suppose what you're saying is even one half of an inch true. I still don't get why me."

"Haven't you been paying attention? Because you both have the Nostradamus gene, boet. Or maybe there's another reason, who knows? I might be an expert on this stuff, but I'm not God himself, you know."

"And the visions? Are they supposed to mean something?"

"Way I figure it, you and your cherry have your wires crossed. It's like there's a webcam in her brain and she's downloading the footage directly into yours in real time. Get my drift?"

Sans plonked his beer down. A volcano of warm foam erupted from the bottle's neck, running down the glass and onto the table. "This is crazy. You're crazy."

"Might be, might be, but this is Sick City. We're all mad here. So, it doesn't really matter now, does it?"

Sans closed his eyes, laid his forehead onto the damp table, and tried to still the spinning room. "Right. So if what you're saying is true—which I'm not saying it is, by the way—would the postboxes pick up anything? Can't I just continue punching in my medpass and see what happens?"

"You could, you could. Maybe you want to risk it, maybe you don't. There's an easy way to solve all this, though, you know."

"What?"

"Don't go all ostrich on me and pretend you haven't figured it out already, boet." The fat man stuck his hand in the pocket of his windbreaker and fiddled around in there, took something out. A pen? No. Fuck.

"I always carry extras. Don't worry. I haven't used this one on myself. It's still nice and new and sealed in plastic, boet."

"No."

The sin-eater raised his eyebrows into triangles.

"Just no."

"Think about it. If you're so sure I'm wrong about all of this, it won't hurt now, will it?" The fat man glanced around to make sure no one was looking, then slid his closed hand across the table. He opened it and they both stared. Sans swatted at the offending thing like a fly. Then, keeping it covered with his palm, he slid the thermometer towards him. He glared at the fat man, who smiled back.

The sin-eater traced the rim of his glass with his index finger until it sang. "Hey, if you want to be Rambo, gamble with death and give yourself up to the Veeps, that's fine with me. And if you need a good sin-eater before you go, you know where to find me."

He was in the safety of the bathroom. Feeling all paranoid android like a junkie. The walk through the dive bar had been a long one, as if all the eyes in the whole damn place were searing into his skin, the mercury monster burning a hole in his pocket, his brain, his heart. To make matters worse, he was hallucinating again. The last stall at the end of the bathroom was morphing in and out of focus like a disco strobe. One moment he'd be seeing the white door of the stall all normal and good and fine; the next it'd be gone and in its place, he'd see a brown door, old, with this brass keyhole in the shape of an eye. An eye. The Eye. Did he have the Eye? Right now he'd rather have his cash back and take his chances. That bloody backstabbing brat of a Lucky.

He grabbed the door of the closest stall and pulled at the handle. After locking himself in, he took the little shitstorm out and struggled with the plastic covering. His fingers felt useless and dumb. Plastic shucked, he stuck the thing into his mouth and sat on the lid of the pot. Waited. For what felt like ages.

Took the thing out.

And looked.

Fuck. Fuckity fuck. He was fucked.

Fortunes measured, he pushed his way through the boozing maelstrom towards the front door. No way was he going back to the table and facing that smug bastard. No damn way. But who was standing there waiting for him, smoking a Van Hunks, when he got outside? The devil himself. As if the fat fuck had known he was going to try to give him the slip.

"Bad news, boet?" asked Fred.

"Screw you."

"Maybe later. Want a cigarette?"

"I don't smoke."

"Not a bad time to start, don't you think?"

They stood there for a while. Inhaling. Exhaling. Nothing else. Until the fat man said, "I know a guy."

"Ja, whatever. We all know a guy."

"Boet, I'm not pissing over your credentials for knowing people. I can see you're the kind of guy who knows your fair share of guys. But seeing that it's only a few hours until the next med cannon, does your guy work through the night?"

Sans glared at him. The fat man just smiled back.

"And what do you get out of this? A cut of whatever I pay this guy?"

The fat man blew a smoke ring into the sky. Sans sighed. His head ached.

"Okay," said Fred. "Let's tango. I'll lead, shall I? A mission with frisson. A drag that lags. A drama-o-rama with really bad karma. A total bleddie nightmare. Nah . . . I'm just kidding. It's going to be a piece of cake."

Fred Mostert, sin-eater, ground the butt of his cigarette under his shoe and led the way to his car.

37

TOMORROW

Tomorrow found herself back at the kitchen table. It was morning again, the second morning since Elliot . . . She was exhausted. Needed to sleep. Really sleep. After meeting with the truthologist, Faith, she'd spent all day yesterday just walking the streets, trying to find Elliot, with this awful, chewing feeling in the pit of her stomach that she should actually be at home, waiting for him there. What if someone had found him and brought him home and she wasn't there to meet them? What if that person gave up and left?

But all the waiting was driving her crazy, so she didn't wait; she walked. All over the city. Everywhere she'd ever been with Elliot, and everywhere she hadn't. Talked to so many people, showed them the picture on her phone, begged them to look, to look again, one last time, to remember something, anything. When she finally got back home her feet were bleeding. So she fell into her bed, chucking her feet-mangling shoes across the room like a pair of missiles. Didn't even remember to eat. But she couldn't sleep. Just lay there. Her brain replaying the same thoughts on repeat.

Now it was morning and she was back, sitting at the same stupid kitchen table. Eyes thick with lack of sleep. Head numb. Feeling small and ineffectual and useless and close to cracking up.

And tired. So, so tired.

She rested her elbows on the kitchen table. One of the table legs tipped under the weight. All it needed was a piece of cardboard underneath it—a corner from a cereal box, that would do it. There was a box of Coco Pops in the pantry. Elliot didn't like Coco Pops. She would go to the pantry and get it. She would. She would make herself some coffee and get it.

Just not right now.

Not right now.

Then she heard it. Soft at first. Then louder.

A knock.

Someone was knocking on the door.

She jumped, and the wonky table shook under her weight. This was it. *Please, please let this be it.*

It was going to be okay, right? It was all going to be okay.

Yes.

Please.

- 38 -

FAITH

A gang of neighborhood kids were chasing a soccer ball around in Tomorrow's street. One wild kick and the ball made a beeline for Faith's chin. She swerved, missed the hit, chided the little posse for not looking where they were aiming, then double-checked the address the girl had given her.

She found the candy-floss cottage at the end of the street and climbed the steps to the front door. The paint on the left side of the doorframe was chipped away, revealing the bare brown skin of the wood underneath where someone had once wedged a screwdriver into the frame. While she knocked on the door, she mulled this trace of Then and thought about the thief who might have dug at that piece of wood, wondered what his name was. Did he have a nickname? And how did the thief's mother sleep? Did she lie awake at night, thinking about how the baby she'd birthed from her belly and nursed for twelve months from her sagging tits, the child she'd washed and bathed and clothed and fed and taught all about God and Jesus and the Bible and how to be good, to say *please* and *thank you* and then some, chose a different path in the end, and there was nothing she or anyone else could do about it?

The door swung open, and there stood Tomorrow, her face a blank scale waiting to be tipped.

"Any news?" said the girl, drawing in a breath and not releasing it.

"Yes. I mean no. Not quite."

"I don't understand." Her features oscillated as the scale tried desperately to steady itself, her hand still on the handle of the open door.

"Me neither. That's why I'm here. You see, I talked to a friend of mine who is on the force."

"And?"

"I . . . I don't quite know what to make of it. He says Elliot . . . He says your brother . . ."

"My brother what?"

"He . . . I don't know how to put it, Tomorrow. There's no easy way of saying this, so I'm just going to spell it out, okay? They're saying he doesn't exist. At least not anymore. They say he has succumbed."

"Those bastards." The scale took a dive towards the floor and the girl's face crumpled. Her hand fell off the door handle and she turned around and retreated into the darkness of the house without saying another word.

Faith hesitated, before following the girl down the narrow corridor to the tiny kitchen at the back. The place was a jumble. Dishes stacked every which way. Flies hovering. Faith batted the air with her hand, then sat at the table. Tomorrow followed suit. "Sorry about the mess. I've been . . . distracted, I guess. And Ayanda doesn't help much with . . . And Lucky's been . . ."

"I understand. Don't worry about it. Really."

"I can put the kettle on if you like? Make some tea?"

"Thanks. But I'm actually good."

"I'll make it for me, then. If you don't mind?"

"Know what? Maybe I'll have a cup."

"Good." The girl fiddled with the kettle. Faith watched her closely as she lifted it off the counter, opened the tap.

"Say, you said you do this pro bono, right?" she asked as she waited for the kettle to fill up.

"Right."

"Are all your cases like that? Free, I mean."

"Most of them, yes."

"What's your day job, then? How do you eat?" She put the kettle onto the element and switched it on.

"I'm a dead collector."

Tomorrow turned her head, looked Faith up and down like she was trying to get a handle on her, like she wasn't quite believing what she'd just heard. Faith was used to this exact look—she'd seen it more times than she cared to remember. There weren't a lot of women in her line of business. "You don't look like a dead collector," Tomorrow finally said.

"What's a dead collector supposed to look like, then?"

"I don't know. Just not like you, I guess."

"Well, truth is, I wasn't always a dead collector. Or a taxi driver, either, for that matter."

"What, then?"

"I designed jewelry."

"That's a leap. What kind of jewelry?"

"Puzzle rings, or gimmal rings, were my specialty. You ever seen a puzzle ring?"

"Nope."

"It's kind of what it sounds like. A ring and a puzzle in one. I'd design all these separate bands—the most complicated ring I ever made had seven separate bands—that you could fit together to form one ring. I'd inscribe secret messages or images on the hidden sections, that the wearer would only be able to see if they took the whole ring apart. People used to love that kind of stuff. The secret stuff."

"Sounds cool. Why did you stop?"

"Something happened. Made me real angry for a while. I couldn't think, couldn't work. Just woke up one day and didn't care for it all anymore. Couldn't be bothered. So I got a job as a taxi driver."

"Why?"

"I don't know. I guess I wanted to do something where I wouldn't have to think too much for a while. Something that would take my mind off things. To just do, you know? Just drive. Not think. The speed was good, too. The crazy driving, the road rage, the mad rush to load enough passengers to pay off the company quota and still make enough money to eat."

"Sounds kind of stressful to me."

"Stressful, yes, but a different kind of stress, a different kind of challenge than before. And different was good. But then the Laughter started revving up, changing things for good, and with all the fuel hikes and shortages, the taxi companies changed strategy and moved into dead collecting. Don't know if you know—you're probably too young—but they made a deal with the government where the guys up top paid the fuel, which meant the taxi companies could stay in business. With the new deal in place, their yields were much higher, so it was a no-brainer for them. And that was it. Here I am."

"But what about all that stuff they say in the news? About all the bloody faction wars that happened after the handover? And all the muthi-jacking that's going on right now? The papers say the market for magical body parts is through the roof and that dead collector vans are hijacked all the time now. Aren't you scared? Do you have to carry a gun?"

"It's regulation, yes. Taxi association rules. But I don't use mine. I'm not one for guns."

"You're not carrying yours now?"

"I keep it locked up in the cubby hole."

"But what if you get jacked?"

"My guardjie handles that side of things. He's pretty good with a gun. Lucky for us it's only happened once."

"And what about the faction wars? Back then? Did you have to fight? Did you shoot anyone?"

"What's with the Twenty Questions?"

"Sorry. I didn't mean to pry. I told you last time I talk too much when I'm nervous."

"No worries."

The kettle clicked. The girl turned her head towards it, reached out her hand.

"Tomorrow?"

"Yes?"

"Why do you think the police are saying those things about Elliot?"

"The police, the police. Who knows about them? Why do they say or do anything these days? They're just there to cart people off to the sanatoriums, aren't they? They don't help anyone. They're just uniforms with their hands cut off, the whole lot of them. Why do they even exist anymore anyway?"

"I hear you. I understand your frustration. But I'm here, aren't I? I'm here to help."

"Yes. You are." Her voice was soft, her face still turned towards the counter.

"Tomorrow."

The girl didn't say anything.

"Look at me, please."

The girl turned around. But her eyes still trailed the floor.

"Please. I'm here. I'm sitting right here. I'm not going anywhere. And I want to help. Do you believe me?"

"I think so. Yes."

"Okay, good, that's good. That's a start. But I can't help if I don't understand. You get that, right?"

The girl kept quiet but her eyes swiveled up to meet Faith's.

"So I need to know. Why are the police saying Elliot is dead?"

"Dead." The girl's voice sounded numb.

"Succumbed, I mean. The police are saying that Elliot caught the Joke and passed away two months ago."

Tomorrow thumped her fist against the counter and Faith jumped, her nerves jangling. Spoons clanged. A cereal box shivered. A plastic cup toppled to the floor, spilling onto the frayed white rug underneath Faith's feet. Yellow liquid branched out between the rug threads in winding rivulets. The pattern the spill was forming reminded Faith of one of those clips in nature documentaries of trees growing in fast-forward. Tomorrow lunged for the cup and swore to herself as her fingers fumbled with the plastic. "I'm not making this up, dammit! I'm not! Elliot really was taken! It's just that . . ." She scooped up the plastic cup and threw it into the sink. Started tinkering with the dirty dishes.

"It's just what?"

"Nothing. They're talking crap, that's all." She started stacking and unstacking cereal bowls like Lego blocks. "You know how they are, don't you? Always making excuses about why they can't seem to help." Her fingers swept over the Lego towers as she spoke. The skinny digits moved through the air in an unsure staccato, as if they couldn't quite figure out what or where to touch first.

"But the records," Faith tried again. "They don't lie. And the records say Elliot is dead. That he succumbed to the Laughter. Months ago."

"Well . . . there's that word again. Dead. Died. Deceased. Got the Joke. Caught the Joke. Succumbed, if you want to be politically correct. I mean, what does it mean, really? It's all relative, isn't it?" A spoon teetered and slipped from the top of one Lego stack, hitting the edge of the sink with a *thunk*. Tomorrow shuddered.

"I'm sorry. I don't think I'm following you," said Faith.

"I mean . . . just because you're dead doesn't mean you don't exist, right?"

"What are you saying? Are you admitting that it's true? That your brother *is* dead? But then why—"

"Dead, dead, dead. I really hate that word, don't you?" Tomorrow scooped up the renegade spoon and plunged it into the dishwater. "In one way, depending on how you look at it, for lack of a better word, I guess, then yes. He's dead."

"Depending on how you look at it?"

"In the way that his body, or what was left of it, succumbed, then was burned and turned into black, black smoke."

"So what is left then, Tomorrow? You're going on in circles. Are we talking about heaven? The afterlife? And what does that have to do with the price of glue? I mean, your brother is dead. So he can't possibly have been stolen."

"'Course he was! Do you think I'm some kind of liar? My baby brother, he's all alone somewhere, scared out of his wits, and you're just sitting here in my kitchen asking stupid questions, not even trying to help!"

"I'm sorry. I'm trying to help. I know how it feels, Tomorrow. I suppose most of us do these days, don't we? Grief. Reality. The truth. The way it twists you up like a dirty dishcloth and wrings you out to dry. How it makes you numb and cold and dead inside. But in so much pain at the same time. Like the pins and needles you feel after sitting on your foot for too long. Numb, but in pain. And you find yourself floating somewhere between pain and nothingness, with nothing to hold on to. And the only way to keep walking, keep breathing, is to find something to hold on to, even if it's something small, something crazy, something impossible."

The girl pulled her fingers out of the dishwater, wiped them on her wrinkled skirt, and sat down across the table from Faith. "That's a real good speech. And I get it. I do. But that's not what's going on here." She sighed. Combed her fingers through her wayward hair. "But you seem to care. You seem to want to help. So I'll try to spell it out. If it means so darn much to you."

"Yes. Yes, please. I really do want to help."

"That woman. The one in the market. With the tattoo. She didn't take Elliot's body. Yes. If you really have to know, if you have to make it your business, then yes, yes, yes. That particular part of him has been gone a while already. But the rest of him, the real him, is still here. Was here, at least. With me. And that woman—she took him. She stole my brother's ghost."

39

PIPER

The boy. The boy, the boy, the boy.

He was killing her.

He was all she could think about now. When she closed her eyes, she saw his face. When she looked in the mirror, she heard him scream.

Truth is . . . The truth is, she didn't even remember him. Holding his hand.

Truth is, she held so many hands. Back when she was perfect. Did everything. Gave everything. Perfectly. Perfect little Piper. She'd hold their hands. All their hands. She'd give her all. Always.

And sometimes. Sometimes. When it got too much. She'd take something to take the edge off.

But she kept it safe, responsible. Paced herself real well. She was an expert, after all. A professional. Not a junkie. No way. Not her. With her perfect grades and perfect smile and need to please, please, please everyone.

And now.

Well, now she'd be anyone.

Anyone she could get.

If it meant one more hit. Of that sweet, sweet taste. In a patch or a tablet or a lollipop, ground up and snorted or smoked in a pipe, who cared. As long as it kept coming. As long as it meant one more stretch of slow, sweet bliss. As long as it made the shame and the fear and the pins and needles in her brain, white light shooting across her vision, heart-in-her-throat fear fade. Away. Away . . . to that blank-slate place. That nothing zone. Where none of it mattered. And nobody cared.

Sure, it made her vomit. It made her itch. Made her fall asleep on her feet at work, which got her fired twenty times over until she couldn't get a job changing bedpans. But so worth it. Wasn't it?

Until.

Until.

Until her man disappeared.

Who knew where Denny went, but he was gone. Maybe he finally worked up enough cash to skip town. Enough to buy a condo in one of those armed quarantine-within-a-quarantine gated communities for the super-rich in Hout Bay or Simon's Town. Where everything was safe and Colgate happy and the supermarket shelves were stacked to the max with olive oil and Camembert and real coffee beans—not that chicory shit she'd been making do with for the last four years. Or maybe Denny had finally caught the Joke and laughed himself to death. Thing was, she didn't know. And it didn't matter anyhow. All she knew was that he wouldn't answer his phone, wasn't responding to her texts, and she was vomiting and itching and scratching herself raw and all she saw when she closed her eyes was that boy.

So she'd settled on plan B, gone around to see man number two, walked all the way to the top of blasted Kloof Street, because the guy didn't have a phone. Knocked her knuckles raw on his door to find out he wasn't home. She was sitting outside his flat now; it had been three hours, and she was still waiting for him. There was only one thing left that she could do. Man number three, plan C. But he wasn't answering his phone, either, and his place was all the way in Bantry Bay, and she didn't want to waste money on a taxi, so she'd have to walk. Because she couldn't sit here any longer, in this concrete hallway with its face-brick walls and slam-lock security doors, she just couldn't. She was desperate. She was nauseous. Her nose was a faucet, her joints were aching, her stomach was cramping up. She was shaking with chills. And all she could see when she closed her eyes was that boy. That boy. That boy. That screaming boy.

Worst of all, she was starting to realize. Starting to know. Who the kid really was.

The devil.

He was the devil.

In disguise.

Finally come to claim her soul for what she did. For what she was doing. And for what she was going to do.

For all of it.

40

SANS

A manhole cover.

He was standing in the middle of a dirt parking lot in the middle of the night, next to a crazy guy, staring down at a manhole cover. What had the fat man said about a nightmare?

Fred grinned at him. "How low can you go, hey, boet? Help me lift this, will you? My back isn't what it used to be. Old rugby injury."

The cover yielded beneath Sans's grip with a dull clunk. The sin-eater procured a small purple flashlight from inside his windbreaker. He laid the light on the ground and rolled up his pants legs. "Better do the same. It gets quite wet down there." He picked up the light again and gestured towards the hole with one palm.

"After you."

The walls of the tunnel were moving. At first Sans thought it was just another hallucination, but it wasn't. Roaches, hundreds of them, caked the cement like thick, live brushstrokes. Sans shifted his eyes to follow the sin-eater's hunched back, one foot in the water, the other on a dry patch of wall for balance. Above their heads a car swished past the open grate, making the discarded plastic bags blooming under the grate's belly sway like kelp.

"Piss. I'm walking in someone else's piss right now, aren't I?"

"Nope, boet. This isn't a sewer. You've been watching too many movies, haven't you? This here's water, just plain water. No piss. No evil clowns, either, hehe. This used to be a stream, you know, before the Dutch, homesick for Europe, converted it into a canal. It used to be the lifeblood of the city back in the day, before the bastards polluted it so much they had to cover it all up. Now it's nothing but a tar-covered trickle forgotten by history. As we all are eventually, I suppose."

The sin-eater turned his head to look back at Sans, as if expecting a response, but Sans wasn't in the mood; just kept his head down and his hands away from the crawling walls.

"This little stream might be innocent," continued the sin-eater, "but it killed a lot of people back in 1713. A group of the Dutch East India Company's slaves who were working as washerwomen washed a bunch of clothes from a Dutch ship infected with smallpox in a stream just above that parking lot you and I stood on. The virus trickled down here and infected the city. Ended up totally decimating the local Khoisan population—it's said that not even ten percent of them survived. Pretty hectic, hey, boet? Later, this stream here also played a role in spreading the bubonic plague. Funny to think a little stream could be so bloodthirsty; that something so small could alter the past in such a big way.

"Anyway, just to give you a heads-up," continued the sin-eater as he plunged ahead, "this oke we're about to see is a bit unusual."

"No kidding," muttered Sans as a tiny crab scuttled past along the bottom of the tunnel wall. His sneakers and the bottoms of his pants, even though he'd rolled them up, were sopping wet, and more than a few times he'd almost slipped.

Up ahead, the fat man had come to a halt. "Hey, what's wrong with your voet, boet?" he asked, while waiting for Sans to catch up.

"Huh?"

"Your leg, man, your leg."

"Long story." Sans sighed. "Roller-coaster accident. I was ten. My mom tried to sue the carnival, but it didn't stick—someone lost the incident report," he added, his hands drawing imaginary quotation marks around the word *lost*. They continued wading through the muck. His Nikes were getting seriously fucked.

The ceiling lifted and the tunnel became wider as they came to a fork, one end opening up into a roomy cavern. In the far corner, a shack, balancing on a makeshift stage, rested against the wall. "Helloo! Anybody home?" called the sin-eater, his voice reverberating as it bounced off the walls. "Mickey?"

Nothing at first. Then something. A sound, a kind of splutter, and the door to the shack creaked open. "That you, Fred, my man?" A scant, skinny, bald man squinted into the beam of the sin-eater's flashlight.

"Mickey!" said the fat man. "Long time, no see, neef. How are things in the data trade?"

"Never better, Fred, my man. Never better. Like my new pad?"

"Yes, sure, but why the move, neef?"

"Isn't it obvious?" Mickey lifted a finger towards the ceiling. "I moved because of what's up there, neef."

"What's up there?" asked Sans.

"Why, the castle, of course. Don't you guys know anything? This little den of mine is right beneath the Castle of Good Hope. Yes. I can see your little brains working it out now. We're currently sitting right in the heart of Sick City's military headquarters. The only place in the city with twenty-four-seven power, high-speed internet, and no censorship firewall. That's why I moved down here, built myself this fine abode, and persuaded one of the military engineers to jack me into their line. This way I can download like a boss and my customers get their fix on time without fail every week. Impressive, né?"

"You're him!" said Sans, as what he was hearing finally fell into place. "Mickey. The Mouse. You're Mickey Mouse! You're a legend, man! A total legend!"

"Pleased to meet you," said the Mouse, holding out one arm while stepping back into his shack. "Come in, come in. I'll brew us some tea and we can get down to business."

The Mouse wasn't much of a decorator. Inside there was a chair, a sofa, a few large plastic bins, and one trestle table with three computer towers on it with their innards showing. The sound of humming, spinning, whirring, and clicking. A few big screens. Piles of hard drives everywhere. A two-plate stove on an orange crate. In one corner, a half-dead potted plant. A pink-haired teenager in gumboots, with a skateboard lying at her feet, was sitting in one corner, stuffing hard drives into a backpack.

"Now, remember what I told you," Mickey said to the kid, while wagging one finger. "They're eggs, man, eggs. So no slamming the pack down on the ground or swinging it or accidentally bashing it against anything. You break another one and I'm docking your pay, you hear?"

"Yes, yes," said the kid.

"Here's the address list. Now scram."

The kid slung the backpack across her shoulders, picked up the skateboard, and made for the door.

The Mouse was floating around in the cramped space like Muhammad Ali. "Don't just stand there," he said. "Sit, people, sit."

The sin-eater slid his bulk onto the battered sofa and Sans opted for the chair while the bald man put a kettle on the two-plate stove and dialed the knob to the max.

"So how long have you been living down here, Mickey?" asked the sin-eater.

"A few months now, Fred, my man. Nice and quiet here. Nice and quiet. Only place I can hear myself think, you know? When the rain gets real bad, it floods and I have to move out for a few days, but mostly it's all good. I have these nifty waterproof plastic containers for all my equipment, so it works out."

The sin-eater turned towards Sans. "Mickey's my cousin, on my mother's side. He used to be in the family business. Was bleddie good at it, too, better than me, I daresay. But he gave it up for this fake med-pass and data running business. Heaven knows why."

"You still carrying a grudge about that, Fred, my man?"

"Ag, it's not that, neef. I just don't get it, is all."

"I've told you already. How many times have I told you? Having a direct line to every dead person from here to Nairobi just gets to be too much. I'm not an extrovert like you, Frederik. I need my space. And these buggers keep calling and calling and they don't leave voicemail, you know. It's just all day, every day, around-the-clock moaning—on and on it goes. When's a man supposed to get some sleep? No, I'd rather stay down here where it's nice and quiet—or quieter—than up there with all those nagging souls to contend with."

"Fair enough, neef. Fair enough."

"Anyway, moving on . . . What brings you down here, neef?"

"We need a new medpass, Mickey. A good one. Not like that rubbish you tried to load off on me last time."

"Hey! That was top of the line!"

"Just messing with you, neef. It wasn't bad."

"Always the comedian, aren't you? Do you have photos?"

Sans dug in his pocket and pulled out the envelope of ID photos the fat man had made him take before they went missioning through roaches and crabs and shit knew what else was hiding in the dark corners of this damn shack. Mickey might have been a legend, but if Sans had to be honest, this place was giving him the creeps.

"This one has to be a diamond, Mickey," the sin-eater said.

"Sho," said Mickey.

"What's a diamond?" said Sans.

"A diamond pass. You know, for the diamonds: the top of the top of the top of the crust. The inner circle inside the inner circle. They get issued these VIP medpasses so they don't have to bother with the daily postbox screenings—can just check in once a month. It's kind of an under-the-table thing. No one's supposed to know about it. If the public found out, they would be pretty pissed. Anyway, it helps okes like you who don't want to go for weekly checks."

"What happens when my month is up?"

"Then you're on your own, boet. But that's still weeks away, so cheer up."

The bald man reached for three mugs and lined them up next to the two-plate stove. He fished some tea bags from a tin, poured in the water. "There you go, son," he said, handing Sans a mug with YOU CAN'T SCARE ME, I SELL INSURANCE printed on the front.

"So. When do you need it by? The pass?" he continued, fondling his mug like a puppy.

"By the next med cannon."

"What?" he scowled. "Have you lost the plot?"

"Please, Mickey," said the sin-eater. "Call it a family favor."

The bald man's glare softened. "Well, I suppose I could—" Then his head cocked and his face flat-out flipped.

The mug dropped. Tea and shards of patterned porcelain painted the floor. "Hey! No passengers!"

"Neef?"

"There!" said Mickey, his trigger finger raking the air. "Right behind him! Out! Get it out of here!"

Sans spun around in the direction of the pointing digit. Behind him was nothing but furniture and thin air.

"Don't you see it? Don't you see it? Right there. A bloody passenger. Sitting on my favorite chair, nogal."

"Sorry, neef. Can't see it. What does it want?"

"Do I look like a donnerse fortune-teller? I think you guys should leave. All three of you. I need a lie-down."

"But what about the—" the fat man started. "Sans here . . ."

"I know where he lives. I know where everyone lives. One of my guys will deliver. Now please go."

"Sorry about this, neef," said the sin-eater, backing out of the door. "I really didn't know he had a passenger. Didn't see it myself, no."

"Yes, whatever. I need to lie down. Speak later. There's the door. And please, please, please . . . make sure the passenger goes with you."

They were stomping back through the wet tunnel the way they'd come, the sin-eater muttering under his breath, swinging the flashlight.

"Wait up," Sans said. "What the fuck just happened? What was that about a passenger?"

The fat man stopped. He leaned against the wall and Sans watched the roach paintline make a detour around his shoulders. Sans wanted to throw up. His head was pounding. What was he doing here, underground in a sewer, with this basket case?

"Sometimes, for some reason or another, the ancestors or some random lost soul who doesn't want to move on attaches itself to a breathing body—either just as a way of stealing breaths from them in an attempt to glow stronger or, other times, they stick around or come back from the dead, so to speak, to deliver a message. We call them passengers, in the business."

"But there was no one there." Sans tried to balance on one leg, scratching at the other with his sopping Nike, sure he'd felt something disgusting on his shin. "There was no one there, right?"

"Yes, well. Mickey sure thought he saw something."

"And you? What about you? You're supposed to be the damn ghost-buster, aren't you? Why didn't you see anything? Or did you? What's going on? Are you bullshitting me, because if you're bullshitting me—"

"I'm not. And I didn't see the passenger, per se. But that doesn't necessarily mean anything."

"What's that supposed to mean?"

"I don't know yet, boet. I'm guessing it's your girl he saw. But I'm not sure yet. I'll have to think. Sleep on it, maybe. Talk to some people."

The sin-eater pushed himself off the wall, sending roaches scuttling every which way, and started walking again. Sans could see the end of the tunnel. The light at the end of the tunnel—yeah, right. No light here. All he could make out in the distance was the ladder they'd climbed down, getting him precisely nowhere but deeper in the shit. "Hey. What about the money?"

"What money?"

"You said you could help me find my lost cash."

The sin-eater cleared his throat. The flashlight flickered, went out, then on again. "That part might have been a bit of an embellishment, if I have to be honest. I've been trying to branch out. Those new Ugandan healers have service lists the length of my arm. It's hard to compete."

"So it's a scam? You're a bloody scam artist." Sans felt very tired. He needed a drink.

"No, oh no. Well, not entirely. I did read this book recently."

Here we go again. "What book?"

"*Traditional Healing for Beginners* by Dr. S.C.H.J.K. Odoki."

"And what did it say?"

The sin-eater fumbled around in his jacket pocket and took out an egg-shaped envelope. "Here. Put this in a pot on your windowsill. Burn it. And your lost money will find its way back to you. Easy-peasy."

Later that night, as he was lying in bed, snatches of car guard Pavarotti drifting in through the open window where the stinking piece of bush the fat man had given him in the envelope stood burning on the sill, Sans thought about everything the guy had said. Which was a lot, and most of it probably bullshit. Had he turned into some kind of modern-day Nostradamus overnight? Someone who caught glimpses of the past and the present all rolled into one, everything overlapping in one confusing jumble, and got weird nonsensical messages from ghosts? Or was the answer simpler? Did the hallucinations come with being infected? Was he really infected?

Was the Laughter working away at turning his brain to mush?

That was what had happened to his mother in the end. The virus was like one big blender that liquefied everything. Turned her insides into a gloopy, watery soup that poured out of every orifice. Sans hadn't been there himself to see it happen; he'd stopped talking to her by then, but that's how the nurse with the messy ponytail had explained it afterwards. There he was, clutching a bunch of Blushing Brides to his chest—his mother's favorite—when the nurse told him. That he was too late. That his mother was already dead. Her bones disintegrated and her organs liquefied like a magician's trick. Maybe he should write a book: *The Disappearing Woman* or *The Vanishing Mother* or *The Prodigal Son Returns Too Late*.

If it were true. If the fat man was right. If he was sick. Then any decent human being would have given themselves up to the Veeps around about now. Rather than run the risk of going all Typhoid Mary, infecting people everywhere he went with every touch, every breath.

Sure, he'd never been Boy Scout material, but he'd also never had anyone's death on his hands. But the stories you heard about those places, the quarantine camps nobody ever seemed to come back from, scared him shitless. And besides, he was wearing protection, right? It's not like he was going about breathing naked air down people's necks, and touching them left, right, and center. Was he ready to be a martyr? Do the right thing? Probably not.

No. He'd wait a while, scope this thing out. Maybe he wasn't even sick. Just crazy. People went crazy all the time. Like his mother did, long before the sickness punched in her number. Stripping naked in airport waiting lounges, busting out Britney Spears's "Baby One More Time" to the gawping crowd like the whole world was nothing but a huge joke. Or ranting to anyone who wanted or didn't want to hear about how Sans was nothing but a throwaway runt. How she'd only ordered him from that place in Paarl because her ovaries had dried up. But no, that was his mother. Not him. Fuck that. He wasn't sick or crazy. He just wasn't. He'd rather be a psychic than a joke.

THURSDAY

41

THE DAILY TRUTH

SAY BOO?

By Lawyer Tshabalala

Is Sick City turning into Spook City? asks Lawyer Tshabalala

Seen any ghosts lately? You're not alone. Our lines at the *Truth* have been abuzz with people calling in to report sightings of the spectral kind.

"What we seem to be witnessing is some sort of unprecedented paranormal explosion. I don't quite know what to make of it," said Sick City sin-eater/ghostbuster Fred Mostert. "But by the looks of it, we are headed for a disaster of biblical proportions. Human sacrifice, dogs and cats living together, mass hysteria. Who knows what's coming next. Best lock your doors, be vigilant, and phone me at 078 555 5679 if you need any assistance of the spectral kind."

What's going on, folks? Is the Apocalypse on our doorstep? Is this some kind of Halloween flash mob or a practical joke? No, my dear readers, my guess is the answer is much simpler—that this whole ghost business is connected to the postbox med scandal I told you about earlier this week. Surprise, surprise: looks like it's not just figurative anymore, folks—the government is now also literally making us crazy. Don't know about you, but I'm inclined to think enough is enough. The guys up top have been lying to us for far too long. Let's step up and rise up, people. Put an end to the lies, the control, and the tyranny! Or we could just stay home and keep watching TV. Tough choice, I say, tough choice . . .

42

SANS

Sans was snoring. Until the phone rang, and spoilt a perfectly un-eventful blackout. Typical. The thing never seemed to have a signal unless he didn't want it to. He held his breath, squinted at the screen. The caller ID said it was Tiger, from the Forensic Pathology Lab in Salt River. He exhaled. Picked up.

"Howzit, broe."

"Tiger! Long time, no hear, man. Chopped some locks for me again, have you?"

"Nah, my broe, I'm not calling about ponies today."

"What, then?"

"*Jy sien*, Sans, *die ding staan*, so: I've got one of yours here on the slab. Was doing my rounds today and I recognized the laaitie."

"Which one?"

"Sorry to say, but it's little Lucky."

"Lucky? You sure?"

"Is true, my broe. *Ek spelie met iemand anders se ma se trane nie.* He's got that tjappie on his shoulder of that stukkie from *Dragon Ball Z*."

"Android 18."

"Ja, that's it. That's the one. Anyhow. He's been cold since Monday already. Shot in the head by some gangster in Bree Street. Nearby that therapy bar where they all mos wear fancy dress and moer each other to yesterday and back. Died instantly. Poor laaitie, couldn't have known what hit him."

Lucky? Lucky dead? So the little rat hadn't jumped ship.

"Then the dead collector's van that was supposed to bring him here got stolen by some muthi-jackers and the cops only managed to track down what was left of him now."

The money. What about the money.

"You there, broe?"

"I'm here. When they brought him in, did he have a backpack with him by any chance?"

"Not when he got to me, no. Just the clothes on his back, is all. Listen, I'm going to need you to come around to identify him. Just a formality. There's no one else, far as I know."

"Yeah, okay, okay. I'll come. But—"

"Anyway, broe. *Laat my hake vlam vat.* Salute."

43

LUCKY

The thing about death is you hardly ever see it coming. Lucky sure didn't. On the day his namesake ran out, Lucky was on his way to Bree Street to make the Monday drop. He was on the roof of this abandoned office block doing a quick check for bars on his cell (hoping for a text from this girl he was into) when he realized his backpack was half-zipped. A crisp R200 note was sticking out through the grinning zip like an orange mug-me flag. He tried to close it, but the zip was stuck. Lucky was pulling at it like a maniac when these two guys appeared at the top of the stairs. One of them had a brown paper bag in his hands. "Hand it over, Denny," said the other man. "No more screwing around." At first, this dude, Denny, looked like he was going to hand over the bag, but then he made a run for it.

Shouting. A scuffle. A shot.

Death was quick. A sweet release. So quick, in fact, that Lucky didn't feel a thing. One moment he was tugging at the zip, then the bag ripped wide open, and the next thing there was this light. This beautiful, beautiful blinding-white light. Lucky's whole being was begging him to walk towards it. And he almost did. But Lucky was a busy guy. He didn't have time for pretty lights. Major was waiting for the money at the convent and Sans would be heavy pissed if he didn't rock up. So he did what any sensible guy in his position would do and said screw you to the pretty light. Next thing he knew he was walking past that new therapy bar—the one he'd been dying to check out—then meeting Piper and smoking that pipe, remembering zero about any lights. Except for a nagging feeling at the back of his mind that something wasn't quite right.

He only figured it out later. Much later than most. And, by then, he was already totally toast.

- 44 -

FAITH

Faith stuck her hand in front of her mouth and stifled a yawn. The sun was still painting with pink, but the square was already a heaving quilt threaded with bodies and colors and square-shaped stalls. Ash was a Bicycle geisha, a fan of red-and-blue cards blotting out the bottom of his face.

Bicycle cards. She'd read an article about them once. During World War Two, the United States Playing Card Company made special 007-style ones that you could soak in water and peel in two. At the back of both halves there'd be a map. When you peeled and put together the whole pack, you'd have one helluva large map—of a top-secret escape route out of a German POW camp.

An escape route. She wouldn't mind one about now. Out of this city, out of this case, and out of the churning maelstrom that was her head.

She was leaning against the church wall, reading the *Truth*. Pony Boy was AWOL again. She wondered if he'd gotten his head troubles sorted out.

One of the card-playing dead collectors was moaning about his morning pickup: "We were picking up a grinner from this big-ass pad in Higgovale, right. The family had hired this pissy little death midwife to mop up their grief and she was totally getting in my face. Saying I was rushing the job, not showing enough respect. And I was thinking to myself—does this fancy bitch even know what a quota is? Let her try to do our job for a minute, and she'd totally freakin' freak, right?"

Faith thought about yesterday. The girl, Tomorrow. The kid was clearly in denial. And who could blame her; Faith, least of all. Denial was practically her middle name.

If Faith had been smart, if she'd been anyone else, she'd have told the girl no way, no thank you, and good luck. But she hadn't. She'd been an idiot yesterday. The kid had stood there, elbow-deep in dishwater, with her nose all red and fat from all the snot, and instead of being a grown-up and telling her the truth, Faith had just sat there, nodding her head and saying *No worries, we can fix this. We can fix this.* A lie and a stupid thing for anyone to say, let alone a truthologist.

The wind was doing a jig today. The *Truth* whipped and fought against Faith's hands, desperate to join in, to have this dance. In the end she gave in, rolled the paper up, pushed it into her bag. Yes. Truth was, the kid was in denial. There was no two ways about it. But the truth was a sticky thing. A thing that could stretch and shift and blow up and pop at the prick of a pin. Like gum. Who was she to force it down other people's throats?

If she were to treat Tomorrow right, treat the case right, she had to at least entertain the possibility in her own mind, for the girl's sake, that she was really looking for a missing ghost. She wouldn't be a good truth finder if she didn't. "Believe in everything until it's disproved," Lawyer would say. "Fairies, the myths, dragons, even ghosts . . ."

But she wouldn't be able to go it alone. What in heaven and on Earth and the great ethereal in-between did she, Faith September, driver for the Hanover Lazy Boys Corpse Collection Association, know about ghosts? It was dead bodies she ferried across the Liesbeek River, not souls.

45

SANS

Dead. He couldn't believe it. The kid was really dead. He was so sure the poor little bastard had jumped ship. So damn sure. And now he was lying here on this cold slab in this damn ugly son of a bitch of a morgue. Dead. Stone-cold dead. And all on his dead own, too. Not a mother or an aunt or a cherry to cry over his dearly departed soul.

But what was worse, much worse (if he had the guts to be entirely honest with himself), was that the bloody backpack was gone. Had upped and vanished, poof. Most probably nicked by some random hungry sucker with a hope and a dream and a wandering eye who zipped it open hoping for a sandwich or a warm sweater and found R50,000 staring back. Lucky bastard had probably been grinning like a Cheshire cat while bathing himself in the orange notes like a certain cartoon duck all week. Or maybe he'd spent it already, who knew.

After he had left the morgue, Sans walked around a while. Just walked. Every now and again he'd think he noticed a passerby staring.

He was sweating. Could they see? His hands kept going up to his face to wipe away the wet with the back of his gloves. Again. And again. And again. Until his skin felt red and raw. What was worse, he had this crazy urge to giggle. He could feel the Laughter building inside his throat like a bomb.

So he tried to keep his face taut. Pursed his lips so tight they hurt. Knotted his brows into a frown. And carried on. Carried on. Without a plan A or a plan B. No mission. No map. For the first time in his life, he didn't know what to do. He needed help, but from where? From whom? Should he phone the fat guy again? Nah. That guy was as crazy as they came. And his bush-burning hadn't gotten him anywhere, had it, now?

Maybe he should look higher.

Go right to the top.

The inside of the brown cathedral with the fancy windows on the edge of the Company's Garden was real pretty. With votive candles burning and the works. Right now it was empty, except for one solitary fart kneeling right at the front and a hot young thing with a crazy-long weave hovering around where the candles were.

Sans slid into one of the pews and sat there, not quite knowing what to do or how this was supposed to go. He'd never gone to Sunday School. His parents hadn't been religious much. Except if you counted their faith in science, logic, facts. Which was kind of the same thing, different jacket, according to some. Anyway, it felt quite peaceful, sitting there, staring at the stained-glass windows.

After a while, he tried to talk to God. But he had no clue what to say to the guy. So he tried to think back to what they did in the movies. Crossed himself. Went on his knees. Stayed like that a while. Lit a candle. Maybe if he tried praying . . . So he clasped his palms in front of his chest and told God about the fever and the money and his unicorn. Said he knew he wasn't exactly the choirboy type, but hey, it wasn't all his fault. Some of the dice were cast way before he had a say in the whole shebang. He didn't choose how they rolled. It wasn't first prize for him, either, to grow up under the glare of a staunch atheist with mental problems and a nihilist drunk. Maybe his real mother had been religious? Although he doubted it. If she had been, she would probably not have gotten her panties into such a fix in the first place.

He left the church when he ran out of things to say. It was drizzling now. At least the rain helped to mask the fever. He cut through the garden with its fat pigeons and the odd squirrel who hadn't made it onto a sosatie stick yet. Past the shit-stained statue of the serious-looking cherry with the beastly water spouts sprouting from underneath her toes. Into the street.

46

FAITH

There she was, slurping noodles for breakfast, waiting for the ghost-buster, cursing this new freelance gig. She got into this to help people. Probably, if she had to be honest, it was, like Lawyer kept telling her, because she couldn't manage to help herself. At first anyway. Back Then. When they locked up her someone and her little someone else in that place on the Flats and threw away the key and it felt like she'd killed them herself, that it was all her fault, because she hadn't done enough. Hadn't protected them hard enough.

She wasn't even allowed to say goodbye. She could still hear the puffed-up zombie marshmallow woman, her voice robotic inside the suit. "You want to what? No. Of course not. Hands at your sides. Keep your hands at your sides. Mouth, too. Cover it up. There's the door, ma'am. Please. Get out."

She had. Gotten out. Got out forever and then some. With a few extra miles for good luck. She'd never look back, she promised herself, as she stood lost and disorientated in that bloody mortality factory's parking lot that day, pressing the car's immobilizer on repeat. Trying to find the source of the beep.

Yes. She'd forget. And keep forgetting. Till she damn well croaked. From tomorrow on, she'd decided, standing there in that parking lot with the wind whipping at her clothes, spraying that fine white Flats sand into her eyes, today would be Today. Every day. And Yesterday? She'd keep that somewhere else.

But she was remembering now and it was hard to describe the feeling. A quiet was simmering in her guts, a vexing, numbing quiet. Like a pre-storm calm. It had visited her before, this squall-signifying quiet. Back Then. When it brewed and brewed and boiled and blew into a big damned rumbling bang that went off like a universe-sized cymbal at the center of her very being before her walls started caving in. Turning and turning in the widening gyre. Falling apart.

In the end, after everything, this freelance gig, the Society of the Down, along with Lawyer, was what had helped to patch up the wall between Then and Now. It had helped her to make sense. Of nothing. And everything. But was there a line? And how was she supposed to know when not to cross it?

Ghosts. Ghosts? *Really, Faith?* She hated the idea of ghosts. Hated, hated, hated it. As a rule, Faith's mind was open. Way open. More open than most. You had to be open to different angles if you wanted to see how the light reflected off them. But she'd rather believe in anything—be it the Loch Ness Monster, Bigfoot, Adamastor, aliens, giant unicorns, the hai-uru, the aigamuxa, the tokoloshe, or any other kind of mythical creature, tall tale, myth, or conspiracy theory—before she believed in ghosts. She was a patternologist, a puzzle solver. She needed one and one to make two, not the unholy trinity.

The real ugly thought, however, was that if ghosts were real, her own baby's soul could be out there drifting around somewhere, all alone, scared out of his wits, screaming for his mom. The thought was too awful to linger on, so she shoved it away as best she could.

She was sucking spilt soy sauce off the neckline of her white T-shirt, real classy, when a bell pinged, the door of the noodle bar swung open, and there he was. She watched as he stooped down to wash his gloved hands in the bowl of chlorine that waited on a pedestal by the door. Saw him hang up his windbreaker and look around for her. She waved. A smile clicked into place, and he walked her way.

"Mr. Mostert. Nice to see you again," she said as he squeezed his bulk into the booth. "Thanks for agreeing to see me on such short notice, and so early at that. How is the spirit trade treating you?"

"Good. Things are good. Death and taxes, you know what they say, there's always work in death and taxes."

"Just the thing I want to see you about," said Faith, laying down her chopsticks.

"Well, I'm not a tax collector, so I'm guessing it's the other kind of problem you need sorting out?"

"You guessed right."

The waitress arrived with a bowl of noodles. She slid it onto the table in front of Fred and teetered away on her green stilt-like heels. The sin-eater pulled the bowl closer, tucked a serviette into his collar, and chuckled at his own joke.

"I've never tried noodles, you know. For sin-eating. Snakes in a bowl. Don't you think they look like snakes coiled together in a bowl? Thin and slippery and easy to digest, come to think of it. Maybe the sins would slip down easier with noodles? Although I'd have to get a hang of these bleddie chopstick thingies first, wouldn't I?" He signaled the waitress for a fork and she brought it to him with a scowl. *Click-clack-clickety-clack* went her green heels on the tiled floor.

"So," said Fred, sticking the fork into the bowl. "Tell me what you need me to do."

Hair. The answer to everything was hair. Sitting in the Happy Happy Joy Noodle Bar, with her legs pulled sideways against the soft red padding of the booth, Faith had quizzed the sin-eater on how this whole ghost-hunting thing had to go. "A favorite toy, like a teddy, will do," he'd said, "to conjure up a spirit. It will give you a fifty-fifty chance. But the real meat is in the flesh-and-bone stuff. DNA. That is the ticket for cooking up some class-A ghost bait." But Elliot's DNA, Tomorrow had said, had been burnt to black, black smoke.

She left the sin-eater to slurp the last of his noodles in peace, and headed back to the Bo-Kaap, to see if there was a way to make a cold trail heat up.

So there she was again, knocking on the door of the candy-pink house, revisiting an image she had never wanted to have a cup of tea with in the first place. Black, black smoke, burning everything.

Actually, Tomorrow had said, no, not quite. There was this place she and Elliot had gone to, a few months before he got sick. She'd been worried. Had had a premonition of sorts. Couldn't sleep. So she slung Elliot across her hip and carted him off to this big old house in Sea Point. Not a sangoma, no, she wasn't into that. This was Sunday School stuff with a bit of a twist. Just a bit. Which meant it was way more legit. She'd heard about it from a friend of a friend of a friend's mother, who was real religious—knew her Bible front-to-back and to the front again. This woman had gone there, to this Holy House, and taken her kids with. And as a result, they were healthy as horses, and you could bless the holy sisters for that. That was what the woman had said anyway, and Tomorrow had seen her kids, running around and playing and kicking each other. Healthy as horses for sure. "Right?"

"Hmm," said Faith. The kitchen was spotless. No dishes in sight. Tomorrow must have done some serious industrial-type cleaning last night.

"So," continued the girl, off she and her baby brother had gone. To the Sisters of Godiva House of Holy Hair. There the sisters in their bruise-blue turbans sat on the ground in rows, wielding their clippers with pious absorption like electric rosary beads. She'd waited in line with the rest until their turn came and a pear-shaped sister, who had big round eyes and a hint of a Namakwa twang when she opened her throat, had shaved Elliot's wispy toddler locks and offered them heavenward. Most of his baby locks were for burial in the house's holy garden, with one lone lock to be kept apart and bottled and displayed with the rest of the many in the holy hall—"A what-do-you-call-it, a shrine, Faith, the size of a rugby field, true story, cross my heart, I swear—lined with candles. Can you imagine?"

"Hmm." Faith saw the rows of bottles in her mind, glinting in the darkness.

That was it, the sisters had told Tomorrow as she wiped the hair from Elliot's nose, pulled his beanie down over his shorn head, picked him up, and swayed him in the breeze to make him stop crying. Their duties to God were done. A whole head of hair like Elliot's could keep the Laughter at bay for months, years, if you were prepared to put some serious prayer power into it. So Tomorrow had gone home. And slept. For the first time in months.

- 47 -

PIPER

Piper unlocked the gate, shoved the key back in her pocket, and folded her arms. The wind was biting at her ears. She hugged herself to beat the breeze, and made her way through the overgrown garden. Along the winding path. Over the wet grass. Past the mossy vision of the Virgin growing on the wall. And the stone statue with its eyes downturned. Across the empty courtyard. To the wooden door.

She knocked and banged. Knocked some more. No one came. The caretaker was probably sleeping off a hangover somewhere. She'd seen him drinking on the sly before. Knew his type. Hell, she *was* his type.

Decision time. What to do? Wait for him to wake up or go off script?

She knew the rules: always go through Major first, never walk on the property unaccompanied, never knock on the old woman's door. *You're a no one, a nothing, remember that.* But she'd already broken all the rules, hadn't she, the rules that were supposed to count? Turned her back on the Hippocratic Oath. Why stop now? And the boy. The boy. She was seeing his face. He was haunting her. And it had to stop.

Had to stop.

Even a junkie knew that.

She scratched her cheek. When she withdrew her fingers they were red with blood, her blood. But never mind that.

She'd been to the office once or twice before. She was sure she would be able to find it again. Through the archway into the open hallway stacked with identical wooden doors. Right to the end, then turn right. Third door on the left. There. It was this one. She was sure of it. She came to a stop and knocked.

"Come in," called the voice on the other side.

The old woman was sitting at her desk, massaging her bare feet, her blue turban wrapped tightly around her head, her white kaftan slightly too long at the sleeves. She'd been a real nun once, Major had told her, pure old-school Catholic, no hippie bullshit. Then the Down Days happened and things got rough. So she branched out. Got a makeover. Glammed things up a bit. To attract more souls.

"You?" said the nun, looking up from her feet. "What are you doing here? I thought you were Sister Alice bringing the tea. Where is Sister Alice? Where's Major?"

"I'm here about the boy."

"The boy?"

"The one from yesterday. About twelve. Maybe thirteen. Manga tattoo on his shoulder. Had a real strong glow."

"Ah, yes, I remember," said the nun, lowering her naked feet to the floor. "Quite the soul. Lots of life in him."

"I want him back."

"You know it doesn't work like that. That's not the deal."

"Then I want to negotiate a new deal. I want the boy and I'm not leaving until I get him."

"More money," sighed the nun. "That's what this is about? You want more money?"

"No, it's not. I mean . . ." Piper paused for a moment, thinking of the possibilities. "No. All I want is the boy." Piper folded her arms and lifted her shoulders to her ears as the nun took her time to study her, the old woman's eyes trailing her up and down with a frown.

"I don't know what's gone into you this morning, young lady," said the nun finally. "This isn't you. You are polite. Well-mannered. A respectable young woman who has fallen on hard times, working her way up again. That's why I hired you. To help you to help yourself."

Polite. Well-mannered. Perfect little pushover. "You don't know me."

"You're right. I don't. But you don't know me, either. And you can't just barge into my office like this and trade the boy back like a baseball card. What's done is done. It's too late. His soul is in a better place now."

The door opened. It was Major. The old cow must have pressed some kind of panic button.

"Miss Jones was just leaving," said the nun.

"I was?"

"You can come back by appointment. As I said, I don't like people barging into my mornings like this. Where is Sister Alice with the tea? Major?"

"Mother," said Major, "I'll deal with the girl and I'm sure Sister Alice is on her way, but—"

"But what?"

"There is a woman at the gate. Wants to see you. Says it's about a missing boy."

"What missing boy?"

"She didn't say. She says she needs to get a sample of his hair."

"That doesn't sound good." The old woman stared through the caretaker and the open door into the empty hallway. "Doesn't sound good at all."

"She says the kid's almost two years old. Went missing Monday. At the museum market."

"Tell the woman at the gate I'll see her, but she'll have to wait. My feet are hurting and I'm not doing anything until I've had my darn tea."

"Yes, ma'am."

"And you." She turned to Piper. "We will discuss this again at a later stage. Next time you come by for a delivery. With Major. On appointment."

The caretaker held the door open. Piper could smell his breath on her neck as he escorted her down the chilly passage. She shivered, pulled her sleeves down over her itching arms, and scowled from behind her mask at a sweet-faced sister hurrying along with a tray.

48

MAJOR

Major woke up to a racket at the gate. He'd fallen asleep on the couch again last night. Through the window the sun was already sailing high on day juice. *Bang, bang, bang* went the gate, playing bongos on his pounding brain. His eyes were thick with drink—he'd been at that new therapy bar in Bree Street until the clock rewound last night. He rubbed at his eyes and headed towards the fuss.

The banger was a pert little skirt with arms you could ring with your fingers, a body so skinny it could snap in the breeze. But step closer, zoom in, and you noticed the muscle there beneath the skin. And the guts in the eyes. Like she was readying to bite.

"We're closed," said Major and cleared his throat. "Donations open at twelve on Thursdays. And I'm not sure you qualify, any case. Your hair's a bit blue, isn't it?"

"I'm not here for that," the skirt snapped and pushed something through a gap in the bars. A card. F. SEPTEMBER. TRUTHOLOGIST.

"Truthologist? What the hell is that?"

"It's, uh, kind of a fancy word for PI."

Shit, thought Major, *the sisters aren't going to like this one bit.* He squeezed his heavy eyes together, stretched them open again, and steeled himself. "Oh, right. I can never keep up with all these new politically correct terms. But you've got the wrong address, honey. No cases to be solved here."

"No honeys, either. But never mind that. I'm here about some hair. A boy's. I need it for a case I'm working on. The kid donated here a few months ago."

"Sorry. No can do. No takebacks. If you give it to us, it goes with God, and you can't steal from the Big Guy. Company policy."

"This is important. Kid's missing. Looks like a kidnapping. His sister believes he was snatched by a woman at the museum market last week. Name's Elliot. He's only two years old. His sister, his only living kin, is a wreck about it. We need some DNA evidence to follow a lead and she says you have some. So please. Cut me some slack."

The skirt was playing the sympathy card. Good move. He'd have to counter well. "That's a real tragedy. I'm sorry. But I don't think there's anything we can do to help. How are we supposed to know which locks are his? Do you have any idea how much hair we cut in a week? You can cover the whole blasted Island in it."

"See, I've done my research, brother. Turns out, to qualify for NGO status, you guys have to be approved by the Genetic Registry Service. This means perfect records of each strand donated, including serial numbers, the works."

Oh, heck. What now? Idiot card. Yes. He'd play that. "Oh, well. See, I just work here, miss. Sweep the floors. Pluck the weeds. Don't know anything about that GMC mumbo jumbo. You'll have to wait until my boss gets in, then. Don't know when that will be, though. Might be hours. Hell, it could be days. I can take your number and call you when she comes in? Or you can make an appointment."

"No. I'll wait."

Thought so. Little spitfire. Typical skirt. Charging into other people's mornings, ruining a perfectly good hangover. "That's fine, miss. I would let you wait inside, but my boss has the key, see."

"She just locks you in here at night?"

"Yes, well."

"Never mind. I get the picture."

The skirt folded her arms into a koeksister and performed a quick pirouette. Then she draped her back against the bars of the gate. Major headed inside, feeling like a puppy that had just been newspapered.

49

FAITH

Faith was getting restless. She'd been standing on the same spot for what felt like forever, but was probably closer to fifteen minutes, watching the butterflies playing tag in the overgrown garden behind the gate. Now and then a blue-turbaned sister would pass through the open courtyard in the distance. In one corner of the garden, underneath an old lemon tree, was a statue of the Virgin Mary. The Holy Mother cut a sorry figure, standing there all alone, eyes cast downwards, palms open at her sides, face disfigured by moss. Tiny blue flowers—Faith had no idea what kind—grew in clumps at her feet. Tall green stalks of something—weeds, probably—crept up against the cement folds of her skirt.

The weather was turning. The wind was brewing up a storm and the whole garden was beginning to dance to its beat. The branches of the tree were shedding their twirling leaves this way and that. Faith's arms were bare and the creeping cold was beginning to get to her. She shucked off the straps of her backpack and bent down towards the pavement. Undid the clasp and took out her coat. She put it on, did the buttons up. Tried to smooth out the wrinkles with her palms.

More minutes passed. Finally, footsteps. But it wasn't the man with the one lazy eye, the one she'd talked with before. A woman was walking towards her through the garden. Head tilted down, eyeing her feet as she walked. She didn't look like a nun. And judging by her long, bottle-red hair, she wasn't a donor, either. The woman was wearing scuffed pumps, a bloodred cardigan to match her hair, and a white wrinkled shift dress pocked with an army of tiny black grinning cats. Dark circles ringed her eyes and there was a bleeding scab on her cheek. One hand kept pulling at the sleeve of her cardigan as she walked.

"Hi," said Faith, as the woman reached the gate.

The woman didn't look up. Just mumbled something and squeezed past Faith into the street. The gate swung homeward with a drawn-out squeak. Faith slipped her hand in the shrinking gap, and pushed it open again. Slipped in.

"Hey, what the hell!" It was Lazy Eye, making his way down the path.

"That other woman, with the red hair, she let me in."

The man cleared his throat. "Damn junkies," he muttered to himself. Then to Faith, "Mother will see you now. But make it quick, please. She's a busy lady, you know."

She followed him up the garden path, through the courtyard, and down a long open corridor, lined with arches on the one side and rows and rows of doors on the other. All closed. Except for a set of arched double doors, a crack open. Faith could just make out the dim hall inside and caught a glimpse of candles and glass jars ("as big as a rugby field"). Tomorrow was counting on her.

No one other than the two of them seemed to be around and their footsteps echoed on the cement floor. Lazy Eye turned a corner, and came to a stop. He knocked on the wooden door in front of him. "Come in," called a voice from inside.

"Go on," he said. His arms were flecked with a string of tiny tattooed stars, woven together with bugs, webs, crowns, and a drawing of Casper the Friendly Ghost. "Go on," he said again. "I'll wait here."

Mother was a plump woman in her fifties with red splotches on her nose, forehead, and dimpled cheeks, as if someone had left her in a handbag with a leaking pen. Fierce black glasses hugged her uppity nose. She was staring up at Faith from behind a desk so big it almost filled the room. "Sit," she said, without bothering to introduce herself. She motioned to the only other chair in the room. "Major said something about you needing some hair?"

"Yes."

"Please explain."

"Well, I'm a private detective of sorts and I'm working on a case involving a missing boy. I need a DNA sample of him in order to follow a lead."

"Of sorts?"

"Yes."

"You do know I can't give you that without permission from next of kin?"

"I have a letter signed by his sister. Both parents are deceased."

"I see. Well, there are other issues, too. Each ponytail offered is not only an offering but also a form of confession and it would be highly unorthodox to share a confession with a third party."

"Surely this can be waived if the donor's safety is a concern? Especially in this particular case, where the donor is a minor and I have permission from his legal guardian?"

"That is debatable, Mrs.—"

"Miss. It's Miss. September."

"That is debatable, Miss September. But there is also the issue of numbers. Do you have any idea how many donations we receive every month? Hundreds. How do you expect us to keep track? The holy hall is filled with strands going back at least five years. How do you expect us to sift through all those jars and find the locks of one little boy?"

"I've done my research, ma'am. I know the law. It says you have to keep records in order to qualify for NGO status. You need to be GMC compliant. So the issue of records shouldn't be a problem. Provided everything you're doing here is aboveboard, of course."

Mother's throat made a sound. Somewhere between a snort and a sigh. "It seems you've thought of everything. I'll have a look through our files. It might take some time. Can you come back next week?"

"Sorry, but no. This is urgent, ma'am. A young boy's life may depend on this information."

The nun reached across the desk for a pen and a Post-it Note. "Do you have a phone number where I can reach you?"

As the woman fiddled with the pen, Faith noticed a pile of books on the corner of the desk. *Cryptography for Beginners*, by M. L. Steiner, was on the top.

"Interesting read?" she said to the nun, indicating the book with her chin.

"What? Oh, this." The woman wasn't wearing gloves. She stroked the cover of the book with one naked forefinger, picked it up casually, then set it down in front of her. Faith studied her cartographic hands with curiosity, then glanced back at the pile. *Vaccines, Sixth Edition* was the title of the next book. The nun saw her looking and she picked that one up, too, but this one she stowed away in a drawer underneath her desk. "Your contact number, Miss September?" The pen was poised above the Post-it Note.

The digits rolled off Faith's tongue and the nun caught them, one by one, with her pen. She pushed her sliding glasses back in place and looked up at Faith. "Thank you, Miss September. I will be in touch. Major will show you out now."

Outside in the corridor, the man called Major was standing a few meters to her left. He had his back to her and hadn't heard her come out. He was talking to a tall sister with piercing blue eyes in the same shade as her turban. Faith slipped away to the right, and made her way down to the far end of the corridor. Towards the arched double doors she'd noticed when she came in. The doors were still open a crack. Faith glanced up and down the corridor to check if anyone was looking and squeezed through the gap.

An ocean of glass jars glinted in the candlelight. Swaying votive flames glowed like star-struck fireflies. Stacks and stacks of bottles and candles wallpapered the room all the way to the ceiling or curved along the floor to form an intricate labyrinth of narrow pathways.

She stood there for a moment, in the dark, surrounded by all that hair. So many bottles. How was she supposed to find Elliot's hair in here? It would take a miracle.

Kneeling, she picked up the bottle closest to her. Held the little glass vial in front of her face to see it better in the gloom, inspecting the lock of brown hair inside. Turned the tiny bottle on its head. On the bottom, the letters *KL* and a four-digit number were written in permanent marker. She picked up another jar, which also had two letters and a number written on the bottom.

A sound. A shock. A voice against her neck, so close she could feel its owner breathing. "Found what you're looking for?" Her body twitched electric. The bottle almost dropped.

"Break one of those and they say you will condemn the donor's spirit for all eternity."

"I'm sorry. I—"

"I know, I know. You just couldn't help yourself. Nosy types like you never can," said the man with the lazy eye.

"Hey. That's not—"

"I think it's about time you left now, miss. Best not to overstay your welcome, don't you think?"

He led her to the gate, through the courtyard, where the sisters were starting to gather for lunchtime donations with their baskets and their shavers in hand. Down the garden path and past the frozen Madonna, who seemed even more demoralized when seen up close.

Faith stepped through the gate. The man shut it behind her without ceremony. It creaked on its hinges. Needed some oil. She was about to point this fact out to the caretaker but one look at his good eye told her not to.

MAJOR

The sound of the rusty gate screeching on its hinges didn't do his throbbing hangover any good, and the episode with that nosy visitor hadn't helped. He headed down the path rubbing his temples, wishing he could dig his fingers into his brain and pull the hurt right out. The self-righteous little skirt had upset the balance of his morning. He might not be brain surgeon material, but he was no idiot when it came to reading people, either. He could see the judgment burning in the skirt's eyes, smell it on her skin. He knew her type, the lucky type who'd never had to get her hands dirty, and now she went around judging other people's stained fingers like she knew what was right. Acting as if Mother were some kind of supervillain in a comic book where everything was black-and-white and she was there to save the day. The type who didn't understand a thing about real life.

Truth was, Mother was just doing what she needed to do to keep the convent safe. The old nun was a servant of God, yes, but she was more than that. She had responsibilities, a flock to protect. A sisterhood. Fifty girls, many of them with pasts that would make your palms sweat and your stomach do a flip just hearing about 'em. They needed someone to watch their backs. And to do that, you needed more than a leaking roof and a holy book. You had to have business sense. You had to have guts. And if your moral compass had a kink or two in it, well, let those who were so quick with the stone-throwing just try to manage half of what his boss had to do and see how far they got. They should take their outrage to Bree Street for some skop and donner, punch it the hell out. Leave Mother alone.

There was a time when Mother had been more holier-than-thou, though. But they'd gone through a rough patch a few years ago, living day to day, meal to meal. Morale was so low some of the sisters lost their faith and left. And without any marketable skills or street savvy, the real world came as quite a shock. (Major knew of at least one sister who ended up walking the streets at night in a very short skirt.) A plan needed to be made.

So the old nun sent Major to the city library and he took out all the business and marketing books he could get his hands on. For two weeks Mother did nothing but read, only to come to the conclusion that traditional religions just weren't selling in the current market. To make things work, they needed to do some rebranding. So she read some more. Looked to other countries, other cultures, other religions for inspiration. Came up with the idea of hair as penance. And got one of the sisters, an ex–fashion designer, to redesign their habits. Give them a more exotic flavor.

And it worked. Followers started streaming in. The convent had never seen so much traffic. But though the new changes were making the convent more popular, they still weren't making enough money from the donations alone. So they branched out. Started a recycling drive. Recycling was a moral gray area, but Major did some smooth talking, convinced Mother that God didn't deal in physical things. That the hair itself wasn't what was important. It was the offering it up that counted. What happened afterwards was moot. And if selling the hair meant they could put food on the table, how could it not be the right thing to do? Besides, recycling was an eco-friendly practice. Sustainable. So they were saving the planet, too.

Thanks to the recycling, the convent's troubles did a one-eighty. But there was a ceiling to this kind of success. And they were reaching it fast. This was a small city, and there was only so much hair going around. Supply was running out. They needed a backup plan.

So the nun did some more reading. Phoned some experts. Started talking about Laughter cures, saying she was convinced this whole sickness had a spiritual root. Then last month she came back from some spiritual convention sounding very chipper, rambling on about amakhosi gangs, saying something about a conversation she overheard between a sangoma and a sociologist who were arguing over whether it was a spiritual or social phenomenon.

Had he heard of them before? she'd asked. Amakhosi gangs?

No, he'd said.

Then she'd said something about a plan. It was too early to talk about it, she said, but it was good. Next thing he knew that junkie was borrowing Mother's van and turning up on Monday nights.

He still had no idea what the old bat was doing with the street rats. Not a clue. Except that it was all part of her new backup plan. Something promising, something that would change everything. So he left it at that. Major knew better than to pry too much. The whole reason he was still working here after all these years was because he was good at knowing when to keep his mouth shut. Take this journalist fellow, Lawyer somebody, from the *Truth* (the name didn't ring a bell, but then he only read the sports section and the classifieds), who had come snooping around yesterday, asking all sorts of questions about the junkie, only he called her a medic, which was odd.

Now this skirt was asking about lost boys. He wouldn't lie, he was getting worried. Helluva worried. It was all getting to be a bit much. But who was he to say anything? He had a good gig here. A nice paycheck. So he'd keep mum. Just keep doing what he was doing. Living his life with his eyes on the ground. Not wondering, not asking, not sticking his nose where it didn't belong. Keep mum.

- 51 -

SANS

There was a queue in front of the Long Street Baths. It was bleach day. Members of the Sanitation Church were lining up for their weekly ritual dip. For a second Sans considered joining them. Maybe the bleach actually helped? It would wash away his sins like they said and he would be reborn anew, sparkly clean and feverless? But what if someone saw the sweat dripping down the arch of his back while he undressed? Nah, bad idea. He'd rather sit that one out.

He was about to cross the road when the bang of the med cannon boomeranged through his gut like he'd been shot. Shit. It was time. A kid in gumboots had delivered his spanking-new medpass from Mickey Mouse first thing that morning. It looked real enough but he wasn't ready to find out if it was legit.

There was a postbox next to the laundry stall where this guy, Sailor, ironed clothes with a coal iron for fifty cents apiece. Sailor had a bad burn on his arm that wasn't pretty to look at, but he was a nice enough guy with some pretty solid ironing skills. Sans nodded at him as he passed.

"Hey, Sans, long time, no iron, bra. Have you found another guy? Is it that charlatan bastard in Loop Street who reads poetry and juggles while he irons? That guy is just a show-off, I tell you. You won't get quality like I do it from that backstabbing verraaier, bra. Nobody beats the things I can do with an unruly crease or a difficult pleat."

"I know. I've been busy, is all. I'll come around again next week."

Sans joined the queue in front of the postbox, his eyes scanning the street for Veeps. The queue petered out slowly. When his turn came, his hands were shaking so much that he almost dropped the card.

"Move along, man, I don't have all day," growled the fat sweaty suit behind him. Sans fiddled with the plastic rectangle, turning it around and around in his fingers like he'd never done this before, didn't know which way was up. Finally, by some kind of mother of a miracle, he calmed his hands enough to stick the thing into the slot. Thank God no Veeps were around, either, 'cause he was acting suspicious as fuck.

Sans shoved his hands into his pockets to keep them still. The machine gave a low drawn-out hum. The seconds ticked by. Finally, the humming stopped. "Diamond pass," flashed the letters on the screen. "No further corroboration needed for now." Sans swallowed down the rising bile. The world was spinning slightly, and he put his hands on the frame of the machine to steady himself. "A healthy city is a happy city," sang the voice before spitting out his card. Stilling an urge to kiss the plastic rectangle, he opted for sticking it into his pocket instead.

He was walking along, breathing easy for a change, when in the window of a shop selling secondhand clothes he noticed the reflection of the man again. Blue-sports-bag man. He'd first noticed the guy on Tuesday. Then standing next to a street pole, reading a copy of the *Truth*. This morning, as he was strolling down Long Street past the one-armed bleach seller with the patchy buzz cut and bushy brows, he saw the guy again, bending forward to tie a stray shoelace. He had that bag slung across his shoulder. Sans could only imagine what was waiting in there. Was the guy following him? Had the gangsters hired someone to take him out? Or was it the paranoia getting to him?

There was a betting shop down the street. He knew the dude who ran the place. Knew about the back door leading into the side alley, too, so he slipped in there hoping to lose his tail. It was a cardboard box of a place. Real small. With a couple of punters huddled around, placing bets. They had a dead pool going for local celebs. There was a list of names above the counter and, next to it, their odds of catching the Joke. Screw it. Sans took out his wallet and emptied the contents onto the counter. Bet his last R100 note on that soccer player with the smug mug. Who knew? Maybe the guy would kick the bucket for real and his money troubles would be sorted out.

"Aweh, brother," he said to the owner. "Busy day?"

"Always, man, always." The owner was a Zimbabwean, real friendly, named Choose. Apparently Choose's dad had made two cherries pregnant way back when Choose was nothing but a fertilized egg inside his mom's recently impregnated belly. Choose's mom was pretty pissed with the egg's soon-to-be dad and stressed to the nines to boot about how she was going to raise this kid on her own if Daddy Dearest decided to make a run for it. So she told him enough was enough, it was crunch time—time to choose between them and the other pregnant chick. His dad chose Choose, and his mom christened Choose accordingly. True story, or at least according to Choose.

"Mind if I slip out through the back?" asked Sans after placing his bet. "I have a new friend out front who's getting real clingy."

"Sure," said Choose, lifting up the hinged counter.

"Maita basa, brother."

"Hey, wait a second. Want to have a beer or two before you go? Catch up? I feel like closing up early."

Who was he to turn down a drink? He had sorrows to drown by the bucketload.

Four beers later—or was it five?—he slipped out the back door and walked to the square. The sun was sliding behind the mountain and most of the vendors had already packed up and gone. But he stuck around for a while. Hoping, as always, to catch a glimpse of his unicorn. He could have sworn he'd seen her here yesterday, fingering a string of crimson-colored beads, but when he got closer to talk to her, two street rats cornered him, hassling him for loose change. When he looked up again, she was gone. He'd gone up to the bead seller anyway, tried asking her about the girl, but the bead seller didn't speak any English or didn't want to, and he wasn't in the mood to play charades. So he gave up. Left.

Now he was back, but the bead seller wasn't. And there was no sign of his unicorn or the India ink strands of her hip-length hair that seemed to glow and change shade with the light—from blue black to purple black to midnight blue to charcoal, carbon black, gray black, jade black, jet black, grease black, oil black, crow black, ebony, onyx, liquorice, raven, sable, eggplant, obsidian, peacock, wine black, and back to midnight-blue black.

- 52 -

FAITH

The sea-green couch in the lobby of the Cosy Sleeps Hotel had stuffing flowering from its armrests. Tonight, just after eight, it was occupied by a trio of working girls. At least two of the girls were high as kites, their glassy eyes tuned in to another frequency. The third was hunched over her toenails, a bottle of nail polish in one hand.

Flickering oil lamps lined the windowsill. A little boy, sitting cross-legged on the floor, was conjuring shadow puppets onto the wall with his fingers. A bunny first. Then his stubby fingers readjusted themselves and the shadow became a big black dog. "Woof, woof," said the boy to the shadow. Then he pulled in his lips and growled.

At the front desk, Raul, the night manager, was reading a well-thumbed book on permaculture. "Hey, Faith," he said, closing the book. "Guess what? I got a new tattoo. Wanna see?"

"Yes, sure."

Raul rolled up his sleeve.

"Nice, Raul! Who's the girl?"

"It's Hecate."

"Huh?"

"She's a Greek goddess. She's real woke, man. Real woke. She's like a liminal goddess, so that means she holds sway over the in-between. You, know—crossroads, borders, doorways, city walls . . . all the liminal spaces between life and death. She helps ferry the dead to the afterlife and protects her followers from them. You know, from restless spirits."

Faith examined the image more closely. "Why does she have those big dogs on either side of her?"

"Oh, yeah. She has these two ghost dogs who follow her around all the time. Kind of like a calling card and her welcome party rolled into one. If she's around or expected to arrive somewhere soon, you're supposed to hear dogs howling and barking and kicking up a fuss. Cool, right?"

"Very."

Raul grinned at Faith. There was a window all along the reception desk, so he wasn't wearing his mask and she couldn't help staring at his mouth. The Cupid's bow, the deep dimples enfolding it in parentheses. His teeth, Colgate white.

He rolled down his sleeve and slid the keycard through the hole in the window. "Here you go. Room seventeen."

"Cheers, Raul."

"Sure thing, Faith. Later."

Faith made her way up the stairs and followed the elephants down the corridor. When she got to the last door on the left, she slid the keycard into the lock.

SANS

The only stick of furniture in the lobby of the seedy hotel was a puke-green couch. Three glassy-eyed hookers were sitting on it. One of the hookers was painting her toenails the same green as the couch while her bare, bruised knees kissed her chin.

"I'd like to get a room," Sans said to the night manager, a tall Rastafarian with a Moses beard and a leather top hat resting on his natty dreads.

"Any particular room?"

"Yeah. Room seventeen."

The manager felt around underneath the counter. He produced an electronic keycard. There was a number printed on it: 17. Below that was a drawing of a court jester, like the ones you get on playing cards, with black hole eyes and a wicked grin.

"Here" said the natty dread, handing Sans the card. "Remember to bring it back when you're done."

Sans nodded, glanced at the card again as he pocketed it—at the jester holding a stick in his palm with a little face on the tip that mirrored his own. Same hat. Same eyes. Same creepy grin.

He made his way up the stairs and down the dimly lit corridor. So dim, you could barely make out the army of happy elephants, lined up slurp to tail, marching along the skirting. (In a previous life, the place had been a day-care center.) His footsteps printed into the pliable shag carpet as he passed rows of cloned yellow doors. At number seventeen, he stopped and slid the card into the slot. Waited for the click.

Inside the candlelit room twenty-odd people sat huddled around a smattering of tables, laughing. None of them was wearing gloves or masks. On the stage in front, a comedian was well into his act, which for some reason involved a live chicken. The chicken was clucking across the stage and the comedian was pretending to corner it. The audience was tearing up big-time. Some almost frantically, desperately, like their lives depended on it.

Sans nodded to Konishiki, the manager, who tilted his triple chin back at Sans. He knew his regulars. Konishiki used to be a sumo wrestler in his youth, and he still had the body to prove it. His suit jacket clasped his stomach like a possessive lover, fabric zebra-striping across his waist, pulling at the buttons. Sans made his way to an empty table at the back. Took a seat.

When he was a student, he'd once read an article about how French aristocrats during the 1832 cholera epidemic had organized elaborate masquerade parties as a kind of big fat finger to death. They got dressed up as corpses and danced to cholera waltzes. Every once in a while, one of the revelers would rip off their mask and croak right there on the dance floor, mid-waltz. At the time, it seemed to him a weird thing to do (the dancing, not the dying), but now he finally got it—whoop whoop.

This place was kind of like that. Somewhere to laugh in the face of the Laughter. Now that laughing was considered a private act, done in the dark between consenting individuals only, places like these had had to move underground. This one had been around for about three months. Not exactly illegal, but bordering on it, the chance always there for a bust by the Veeps.

Probably not the best spot to be for someone in his condition, but he'd never been the kind of guy to do the right thing for the sake of self-preservation.

Even as a kid. The more he'd gotten into trouble, the more he'd seemed to want to steep himself deeper. Like a gaping cut you were itching to get your finger into, tear open further. As if the pain would make everything better. His mother used to tell him how he'd been a breech baby. Or so she'd heard. That he'd been upside down from the start. So, there was no helping it, this urge to sink himself deeper into whatever muck he'd caught himself up in. To screw himself until he was so tight in he couldn't untangle. It was all nature, no nurture, she'd said. A fault entirely of his own making. That they'd just have to learn to live with it, the two of them. Devil may care. That's what she called it. His damn devil-may-care streak.

He was sitting there, nursing a whiskey, straight, when he noticed the muscly guy with the crazy-ass scar at the table next to his. The guy was talking to a woman in tights and a short skirt. She had a hoodie pulled up over her head. That wasn't the interesting part, though. What caught his eye was the big-ass chain at the guy's feet. And attached to it, a damn hyena. Just lying there like a puppy, chewing on a rather large jawbone. A row of teeth lining the thing. He rubbed his eyes, in case it was another hallucination, but the scene stuck.

Actually, he'd seen the guy and his hyena around before—word was that the pair had recently started working security at the museum market—but never up close. Then the woman in the hoodie turned to signal a waiter and their faces met. It was the dead collector, Faith, the one who had sent him to that lunatic sin-eater.

"Pony Boy," she said, her lips seeming to force a smile. "How are things?"

"Great. Just great. You?"

"Yes, sure."

"Hey, nice hyena."

The dead collector bent down a notch and patted the creature's big blotchy head. "Pony Boy, meet Jamis. Jamis, meet Pony Boy."

The dead collector and the hyena man went back to their conversation and Sans ordered another whiskey. Better make it a double.

Fast-forward two hours and he'd ended up at their table. Had he invited himself over or did they offer him a seat? All he knew was that he was drunk. Real drunk. So drunk that he was breaking the rules. He was talking about her. His unicorn. And he couldn't get himself to stop. He was showing them the photos on his phone, the photos he'd taken of the girl on the wall of the Sad Facts Nights Café, the one who looked just like her.

"Wait a sec," the dead collector said. "I've seen that face before."

"Yeah?"

"Don't think it will help, though. It was just a painting. A portrait, really. But the woman in it looked exactly like her."

"You sure?"

"Well, I'd have to have another look, but I think so. Her hair was different, though. It was loose and long and way lusher."

"Where? Where did you see it? The painting, I mean?"

"It was hanging in the library."

Sans knew where the public library was. If he wasn't so drunk (and anyway, it would have been closed at this hour), he would have—

"No. Not the public library." The dead collector had read his thoughts. She looked shifty-eyed all of a sudden. "The library where I saw the painting isn't open to the public. It's kind of a members-only affair . . ."

Something in his voice or eyes must have worried her, because she gave this weird frown. *Don't come on too strong or desperate like a lunatic,* he chided himself. *She probably thinks you're a nut already. Just stay cool, stay calm. Dial down the crazy. Maybe make a joke. A joke, a joke . . .* "Nice skirt. Very bright, though. Pity I forgot my sunglasses." *Idiot.* Why did he just say that? *Not funny, Sans, you moron.*

"Me, too. I can barely see the stage through the glare of those Nikes."

He held a fist to his chest and groaned. "Ah. Right through the heart. Ching-ching-ching—you win. Anyway, so what kind of library is members only?"

"I can't really talk about it."

"Then how do I get in to see this painting of yours? Can you hook me up, at least?"

"I don't know. It's not really up to me. I'm kind of in the doghouse with these guys."

"Aw, come on, Faith, how long have we known each other?"

"Not very long, in fact."

"True-true. But you know I'm good for it, right?"

"Good for what, exactly?"

"Everything." He grinned.

"Smooth. But, I don't know . . ."

"Oh, come on."

"I suppose I know a guy I can call who might be able to help you. I'm not in his best books at the moment, but I'm willing to try. I need a favor, though. In exchange."

Of course. "You cockroaches are all the same, aren't you? Bunch of bloody hyenas."

"Nothing wrong with hyenas," said the guy with the crazy scar.

"But you just said—" said the dead collector.

"What exactly did I say? That I'm a good guy. Nothing more than that, I think."

"All right, Mr. Model Citizen, Good Samaritan, class-A guy," said the dead collector. "Just tell me one thing before you ride off into the sunset on your very high horse. What does the 'jack' stand for in ponyjacker again? Or should I rather call you Mr. Pony-please-can-I-cut-your-hair-with-this-sharp-and-friendly-knife-of-mine-and-sell-it-for-profit-if-you-don't-mind-madam-er?"

"Fine," Sans said, throwing his hands up like a flock of seagulls. "Spit it out, then. What do you need?"

"I need all the dirt you have on the Sisters of Godiva."

"The who?"

"Don't try playing dumb with me. Rumor is they don't just shave heads and offer the hair up for God knows what, which is a whole other type of scam, preying on the desperate. I heard they're in the hair trade, too. That they're selling the stuff. And if that's true, I'm guessing you would be the one to know."

What the . . . ? Something wet and weird and sickening was happening on his bare ankle. He jumped and peered down at the floor in the dim light. The hyena grinned up at him with his slobbery tongue sticking out. Jesus. He glared at the muscly mofo holding the leash, but the guy just shrugged. Then he turned his attention back to the dead collector, whose eyes were laughing now.

"Don't be such a diva. A little bit of hyena slobber never killed anyone."

"Yeah, right."

The creases around her eyes deepened. "So what about it, Pony Boy?"

54

PIPER

Funny how a person's whole life can change in the span of one cigarette. One second Piper's world was up and the next it was down. Only thing was, she thought it was down in the first place. But that was before she found out what down really meant.

So she'd managed to get this new freelance gig at the Bree Street therapy bar. Three nights a week. She still couldn't believe the manager had hired her. (It was pretty obvious that she wasn't the employable type.) But no matter, 'cause it turned out not a lot of folks wanted to patch up other people's bloody wounds these days. Too risky.

At first, Piper had thought about not going in tonight. Three days without a fix and she was ready to tear the skin off her face. But there was always a chance she could score if she pitched, that Denny would be there. Denny was a regular—she could always count on him to be there on a Thursday night (half-price moonshine and karaoke after twelve), and he was still not answering her calls. Why? What the hell? Maybe he'd lost his phone? Whatever it was, if he wasn't dead or dying or living it up in some upper-end quarantine zone in Hout Bay with a new sugar mommy, he'd be there tonight, she was sure of it.

When she got to the therapy bar, first thing she did was scour the crowd for Denny's face. She couldn't spot him, but the damn manager spotted her. Came over and made a scene, wanted to know where she'd been, why she wasn't in the booth patching up suits. So off she went with her tail between her legs. Obedient as always. Perfect little pushover.

She was sitting there when this guy, one of the fighters, came in wearing a Stormtrooper suit, blood pouring from a laceration to the face. She was stitching him up, doing a pretty decent job, considering the way her hands were shaking. But she was itching so much she could scarcely bear it. So she asked him if he'd mind if she took her mask off for a sec.

Lucky for her (or unlucky, take your pick), he didn't care one way or the other. He was that type, real macho, didn't give a rat's ass about the rules or the Laughter, thought he was invincible—always cracking up to show you how unfazed he was.

He offered her a cigarette and the two of them started talking while she stitched. He was cracking jokes and they were both giggling like two schoolgirls at a slumber party. It felt good to laugh without caring. So good. She couldn't remember when last she'd laughed out loud like this. Then he told her he had some smack—did she want to have a taste? 'Course she did.

So they shared a needle, and for the first time since Monday, the whole world righted itself again. Everything was A-OK.

FRIDAY

55

THE DAILY TRUTH

SPIRIT SOUP FOR THE SOUL

By Lawyer Tshabalala

Everyone's talking about the recent spate of spirit sightings sweeping the city. You know my view on the whole thing (read yesterday's column if you don't), but to mix it up I asked Dr. John Samson, a psychologist and author of two bestselling books on grief and trauma, for his take on it all.

Dr. Samson, rumors are rife that the postbox injections are inducing hallucinations in some, and that this is behind all the ghost sightings sweeping the city right now. Others say it is proof of the existence of the supernatural and the afterlife. Then there are the members of the public who believe it's a sign of the end times. But you have a different theory? Yes, I do. To understand what's behind this phenomenon we have to take into account that we are living in an unusual time in Sick City's history where death is a daily occurrence for most of us. We are a city in mourning. And this has to have certain repercussions for our psyches. A measure of post-traumatic stress during an epidemic like this is inevitable.

But how does post-traumatic stress tie in with ghost sightings? There are many documented examples of cases where people have claimed to see the spirits of their deceased loved ones after they have passed on. Most psychologists regard these kinds of hallucinations as a perfectly normal response to grief. A mechanism for dealing with the trauma of the situation. Visions of loved ones are often a great comfort to those who experience them.

But surely what we're experiencing right now is different? This isn't

just one granny seeing her dead husband brushing his teeth in the bathroom. The scale of the sightings we are experiencing is quite something. It is actually not that unusual. Mass hallucinations like these have been known to occur in the aftermath of traumatic events. We saw exactly the same kind of mass ghost sightings in Thailand after the 2004 tsunami. People are always eager to ascribe these kinds of psychological manifestations of grief as proof of the existence of the supernatural and the afterlife.

So, say I've been seeing weird things lately. My dead mother-in-law's head in the fridge between the mayonnaise and the cauliflower, for example. Does this mean I'm going crazy? Not at all. As I've explained earlier, visual hallucinations like these are normal manifestations of grief. One study found that 80 percent of elderly people were visited by a hallucination of their dead partner about a month after they had passed on. Other experts put the percentage of people experiencing some kind of grief hallucination after a loved one has passed on at 50 percent. So this is perfectly normal, and generally not a sign of psychosis.

Phew. Thanks, Dr. Samson. That's a relief.

Do you hear that, folks? We're not crazy. We're grieving. I'll leave you with that lovely thought for now. More to follow on all of this as soon as I have the scoop. Winter's icy teeth are beginning to bite early this year, so bundle up nice and tight, folks. Till tomorrow for another dose of cold, hard Truth. *Love you long time. Over and out.*

56

SANS

It was the same damn bar. And he was sitting at the same damn table ringed with the same galaxy of stains. But it was too early. Too bright. The place had just opened up and the emperor didn't have his clothes on yet, the air thick with broken dreams and empty promises. And that smell. That smell.

The ring-browed barman was polishing a row of glasses to "Girls Just Want to Have Fun" by Cyndi Lauper, shaking his bony hips and lip-synching while rubbing up a beer glass with a tartan dishcloth. In one corner, a janitor was cleaning up vomit in a hazmat suit. A lone roach was walking the line up the wall. There was nothing to bring you back to reality quite like an empty bar in daylight, the morning after a good time.

Sans had told the bow-tied waiter that he was here to see the librarian, just as the dead collector had told him to do. And now he was waiting, nursing a beer, staring up at the same graffiti-streaked painting of "Jan van Riebeeck." You could say what you wanted about him, but the guy had damn fine hair. And not a bad moustache, either.

Two beers later this old guy shuffled up to Sans, wearing a velvet jacket with the elbows worn out. Wispy white hair with a streak of black.

He was holding a creased A4 sheet, which he slammed down onto the table in front of Sans.

"That your girl?"

His eyes zoned in on the copy of the photo of the painting of his unicorn. "Where did you get this? Who is she? Wait—who are you?"

"Why I am the librarian, of course."

"Okay, fine. Just checking. And the girl?"

"This is Anna de Koningh. Founder and very first librarian of the Society of the Down."

"The society of the what?"

"Never mind that."

"So she's real. She's a real person."

The man gave Sans a dubious look. "Ye-e-es," he said. "A real person."

Sans studied the photocopy, holding it up to the light.

The librarian frowned. "You're not one of those krokodil addicts, are you?"

"Do you have her number?"

"Her number? My boy, they don't have phone numbers where she is right now. That woman's been worm food since 1720."

"I don't understand."

"She's dead, man. Dead. Has been for forever and a day." Sans's brain felt thick with fever. He could feel the sweat pooling at the back of his neck. He inched his back closer to the wall, praying that no one in the bar would notice him dripping like a broken tap. He rubbed his palm dry against his jeans, took another swig of beer while one hand wiped at his neck.

The man gave a slight frown. "Ow," Sans said quickly. "Damn neck. Hurts like hell. Must have slept in a funny position." The librarian nodded.

Sans rubbed his sweaty palms against his jeans again. He needed to think. He needed to process this. His unicorn was real. His unicorn was dead. Long dead. The fat man. Was that crazy charlatan onto something? Was he?

The fog of fever was making it harder and harder to think. There was a maze in his brain and he was trapped inside it—didn't know which way was out. He rubbed his fingers against his temples like he was thinking, which he was, but also to erase the sweat.

"Are you sure?" he asked the librarian. "That this woman in the painting is dead, I mean?"

"Are you serious?"

"Okay, okay. No need to get snarky. What's her story?"

"I'm a busy man, you know," said the librarian, drumming his hand against his leg like a tambourine. "I don't have time for chitchat."

"Fine." Sans sighed. "What if I buy you a drink?"

The old guy shrugged and slid his thin frame into the booth. "I am not impartial to a good gin and tonic. Hold the lime."

Sans lifted his hand to the waiter. "So, this Anna chick?"

"Well, she was a slave, for starters. Came to the Cape from Bangladesh—back then it was Bengal—as a child. But her fate turned around when she caught the eye of a Swedish captain, name of Oloff, who freed and married her. When he passed away, she inherited all his money and his land, including his farm, Groot Constantia. She was an interesting woman. Very unusual for her era. On top of starting the Society and its library with her inheritance, as a way to give voice to the voiceless, she was also a talented seer."

"A seer. Like telling fortunes? Visions and whatnot?" What the actual fuck? He rubbed his palms dry against his jeans again. Rubbed them until they burned. This was sounding more and more like what the fat man was on about. The maze inside his mind was growing corridors, with no exit in sight, fog swirling every which way like a goddamn smoke machine.

"Yes," continued the man, still drumming on his leg. "Legend has it she possessed the gift of the third eye."

"No shit." Sans couldn't believe his fucking ears. The fat fuck had actually been onto something.

"Yes, indeed. Although that was a big secret back then. The society ladies she associated with probably wouldn't have approved of anything that smacked of the occult. There were still lots of paranoia doing the rounds during that time about witchcraft and the powers of Malay witchdoctors or *Doekums*. The Dutch were always suspicious that the slaves would try to poison them or work their magic on them. The slaves far outnumbered the Europeans so they were constantly alert to uprising or rebellion of any form. All this was before the occult revival of the late 1800s, when being psychic became all the rage abroad."

"Yes, yes. Whatever. What kind of shit did she see?"

"Language, young man."

"What kind of *visions* did she have?"

"Beats me. Her diary containing her prophecies is supposed to be somewhere in the library collection, but I haven't been able to find it myself. Before I came along in '75, the catalogue system was a mess. Unfortunately, my predecessor had a habit of looking too far into the bottle instead of tending to the shelves, if you catch my drift. It's taken me years to organize the place."

"Wait. Back up. What library?"

The old man lifted his hand off the table. Whirled his fingers in the air like he was changing a lightbulb. "All this, of course."

"What are you talking about, old man? This is a bar."

"Yes. Po-tay-to, po-tah-to, as they say."

"Please. Just stop with the games. Always, everybody with the games! Library, my ass. Tell me, old man: is this Fuck with Me Friday? Or are you a fucking charlatan, too, like everybody else in this town? Who set you up to mess with my head? Was it the fat man?"

The librarian downed the last of his G-and-T and stood up slowly, one hand steadying himself against the table as he did so. "Fuckin' joints," he muttered to himself. "Always have to ruin my chances for a dramatic exit, don't you?"

"Language," muttered Sans under his breath.

"Ha! Tell the dead collector I am done doing her charity work," said the man. Then he drummed his palm against his leg—three quick taps, like Morse code or something—and gave one side of his head a quick two-fingered farewell tap.

"Wait a second," called Sans as the man swiveled around to go. "I'm sorry. Just one minute. Please."

"What?"

"Do you know what was inside it? The diary?"

The librarian turned back to face him, slowly. Sans watched as the old man looked him up and down like he was sizing him up and finding him wanting. "Wouldn't know." He sighed. "As I said, I've never seen it."

"Thank you. I'm . . . I'm . . ."

"But the story passed on by Society members is that the journal predicted the Laughter itself. And that it contained a cure. If that's true, it could be quite a find indeed."

57

FAITH

"No woman, no cry," crooned the busker with his eyes closed, one hand curled up in a fist, holding his imaginary mic. His friend on the guitar was smiling at the patchwork people threading in and out of the quilted square like he meant it, his skintight jeans rolled up to show off his skinny calves.

Faith was watching the two-man band doing their thing with the same buzz of joy and longing and regret that always burned through her when she heard this song. As she watched, a kind of chasm opened up in the sky, the clouds were drawn to the side like a curtain, and she could see the past rolled out like a reel of film or a red carpet, until it wasn't just two men standing before her singing this song but every single soul who had ever sung it. Then Bob himself joined the party, tilting his head back and shaking his chin while remembering that government yard in Trenchtown while his natty dreads twirled around the mic with a life of their own like some kind of mythical squid.

Bob was drying his tears now with one palm while a trio of angels were swinging their skirts and chorusing by his side.

"Hey, you, woman! Shit or get off the pot, please," a voice yelled from somewhere close, pulling the plug on Bob. It was Ash, and he looked pretty pissed.

"Fine, fine," said Faith and chucked a ration coupon into the pot on the boot of the car. The game continued, and Faith tried to keep up.

The buskers were doing "Redemption Song" now: "Old pirates, yes, they rob I, Sold I to the merchant ships . . ."

A blood hawker pushing a worn ice-cream tricycle made slow progress across the cobbled stones. "AB negative, some lovely ice-cold AB negative," he shouted to whoever would listen while ringing his bell. The Dairymaid ice-cream cooler on the back of the bike had seen better days. The paint was faded.

The wobbling cart scared a fat pigeon, which whipped itself into the sky like a pebble from a slingshot, bringing Faith back to earth. Her thoughts reversed back to the night before. She noticed that the ponyjacker with the limp was AWOL again, probably out hunting his dream girl somewhere. At least she wasn't the only one losing the plot. The poor kid was seriously losing it, too, along with a screw or two. She had felt sorry for him after listening to his blind-drunk ramblings in the comedy club. Having that kid Lucky run away with all his cash and then meeting and losing the love of his life all in one day sounded rough. But the guy wasn't exactly a Boy Scout, so the way she figured, he had it coming. And besides, everyone had crazy problems these days. She wasn't feeling particularly sane herself, what with hanging out with Parow Arrow psychics and planning séances with Casper the Friendly Ghost. Right now it felt like the only sane people in her life were Ateri and Jamis, and the latter wasn't even technically a person, so . . .

Faith tossed another card onto the pile. The wind was being a poltergeist. Her coat nipped at her knees. She scrunched up her shoulders and shoved her cold hands into its pockets. And felt something. There, inside her left pocket. The back of her hand brushing against something.

Smallish. Rectangular. Firm, but bendable. She closed her hand over it and pulled it out. It was a piece of paper, folded into a rectangle. Her fingers unmade the folds. Smoothed out the creased square. A flyer. Around A4 size. For the Bree Street therapy bar, the one where Lawyer liked to get beaten up for extra pocket money. At the bottom, someone had written a phone number with a red pen and the words, "I can help."

How had this note gotten into her pocket? She certainly hadn't picked up any flyers and she wouldn't have folded it up and put it in her coat pocket anyway. In fact, she knew her pockets were empty. When she was waiting for the caretaker at the convent's gate and her hands were freezing, she'd stuck them in her pockets to keep warm. They were empty. So someone had put it there—but who? She couldn't imagine the caretaker slipping her anything but the finger.

Wait. That woman with the red hair and the scratch on her face and the grinning cats on her dress. The one who had bumped into her at the convent's gate. She was the only one who had come close enough. Except for Ash.

"Hey, Ash?"

Ash looked up.

"Weird question, okay?"

"Okay, but make it quick. I'm in the zone. You're messing with my mojo here."

"Did you slip a flyer for the new therapy bar into my pocket for some reason?"

"A flyer? What are you talking about, woman?"

"This one." She held it up. "Bree Street."

"I know where Bree Street is. No. No way. Not me. Why would I do that?"

"You sure?"

"Yes, I'm sure. Now, shoo. I'm trying to win over here."

The first twelve times she phoned the number on the flyer it went straight to voicemail.

Lucky number thirteen.

"Denny?" said the voice on the other side of the line. "I've been trying to get a hold of you. What the hell?"

"No. Hi. I—"

"Who is this?" A splutter on the other end of the line. A *clang*, like something falling.

"I got your number in my coat pocket? You said to call."

Nothing.

"I'm sorry. I think maybe I have the wrong number."

Another strange splutter. A cough, perhaps? "Shit. Oh. It's you. No, no. I did. Put my number in your pocket. It was about the boy. You said you were looking for a boy?"

"How did you . . . ? Yes. Do you know something?"

Another *clang*. Another kind-of cough. "I'm late. I have to go. I don't know if I can help anymore."

"Please," Faith said quickly. "He has a sister. She's worried sick."

For a second Faith thought the line had gone dead. Then, "Okay. Meet me in the Company's Garden in an hour. But don't be late. I don't have much time left."

58

SANS

Blink, *blink, blink.* Bloody phone. All dressed up in disco mode, spitting out a Tourette's stream of strong words and lights. *Blink, blink, blink.* Most of the blinking things were from the Ones Who Shall Not Be Named, but those ones he had long stopped reading. Now it was Major who kept leaving messages, reminding him that his problems hadn't gone anywhere, that in fact they were piling up, one on top of another. Major was running out of angles to spin to his boss who wanted to know why this week's load of ponies hadn't been picked up yet. Please, please, please, could Sans at least come around for a drink and a chat and reassure Mother that he was not reneging on their little business deal?

So he went to see the old bag in her office that smelt like mothballs and rancid potpourri. Switched on the charm, did some smooth bargaining, and kept his tail between his legs. Begged for more time. *Please, sir, can I have some more* and all that. Maybe the nun was distracted by the pretty sister who was busy massaging her gnarly old feet, but she actually seemed less full of shit than the caretaker himself and eventually just waved him off. Afterwards he went to sit outside and watched Major paint a vision of the Virgin Mary onto the convent's garden wall, using a mixture of yogurt and moss that stood waiting in a bucket at his feet. Marian apparitions were a new thing the Sisters of the Holy Hair Cult were trying in order to attract more donations.

He was watching the caretaker do his thing, feeling thoroughly emasculated from his recent begging session, when a blue-turbaned sister came walking past, all pious with her eyes downturned, but with a smoking-hot body and generous ass that molded to her robes as she moved.

"Maybe I should get my hair shaved," he said to Major as he watched the girl disappear into the convent's new high-tech cafeteria. "As penance, I mean. I've stolen enough ponies in my life to rack up quite the black list with the Big Guy. Maybe it's time I gave some back to even the score."

"What are you talking about?" said Major, pausing to recoat the brush with mossy yogurt glop. "Which big guy?"

"You know, God, Allah, whatever."

The caretaker stepped back from the wall to survey his handiwork, then stooped to dip the brush into some water. "I thought you didn't believe in all that stuff? I mean, you know as good as I do that none of these ponies ends up with God. I'm sure some of the rich yuppies who eventually buy them have a God complex or two, but that isn't the same thing, now, is it?"

"Well, sure. It's not like we send it all up to heaven in a glass elevator or anything, but the intention must count for something, right? The fact that the hair meant something to the head that offered it? And that they gave it up in good faith, even though it might have been hard?"

The caretaker folded his tattooed arms and frowned. "What's up with you today, brother? Have you started smoking again? You know you shouldn't touch that stuff. It makes you all Eeyore. I've told you this."

"Nah, it's nothing like that. I just feel, I don't know, like all these ponies I've taken these last few years must have left a mark on me. Like the universe has been keeping track. And decided it's time I got my own back."

"I don't know what you're talking about, but if you ask me you're sounding like that naked guy who hung around on top of the Absa building last year saying if we all dropped trou the aliens would see it from space and come and rescue us. Ha! That guy was a piece of work. Remember him?"

"Yeah. Sure. He was hilarious. Wonder where he is now."

"Didn't you hear? He caught the Joke and succumbed."

"Fuck. Must have missed it. Makes sense, though."

"Hey. There you go looking all Eeyore again! When last did you have a bit of a stukkie, brother? Some tail? To keep you warm at night? You look like you're in need of a serious dose of womanly love, my friend."

"Ag, what's the point in getting a cherry, man? She'll only die anyway."

"Sho," said Major, dipping his brush into the water and sending a spray of it towards Sans sitting cross-legged on the grass. "Ray of sunshine alert!"

"Sorry."

"Listen, I don't know what's gotten into you all of a sudden. You said it yourself, it's just hair, right? You chop it off, it grows right back. It's not like you're jacking cars or mugging people for their hard-earned money, right? So I don't see what you have to feel oh-so-guilty about."

"Mmm."

"Know what?" said the caretaker, picking up his buckets and brushes. "I think the Virgin here is done for today. Let's leave her to simmer. Most of the sisters should be off shift already, too, so we can go to my office. I'll pour us some moonshine. The good strong stuff. Cures all ills. My nephew brews this one. The kid has real talent. What do you say?"

In the processing room here and there the odd sister was still at work, sorting ponies or threading them into weaves, but for the most part the hall was empty, quiet. Major led Sans to his office, a doorless enclave at the back of the hall. The caretaker had strung an old yellow curtain onto a plastic cord with clothes pegs to cordon it off. Inside this makeshift tented barracks was an old couch and a side table adorned with a blue cloth. A broom, a mop, a few empty plates, an enamel mug, and a smattering of other tools and personal effects were scattered around the space, along with one lone copy of the *Daily Truth*, open at the sports section.

"Your leg?" said Major as Sans bent down to sit. "It looks like it's really bothering you today. You keep grimacing."

"Nah, it's fine. No big deal. I'm okay."

"Hey, know what, brother? I've known you for so many years and I've never asked you what happened to it."

"Gunshot wound. Gang thing. Don't like to talk about it."

"Thought so. No sweat. I'm just popping out to the kitchen for an extra mug. Be right back. Make yourself at home so long, okay?"

59

FAITH

There was a protest boiling in the street at the edge of the Garden. Faith threaded her way through the bodies and placards and onto the green. She found the woman from the convent with the bottle-red hair next to that gnarly old last breath of a pear tree, the one that was crutched up with metal poles. Lawyer once told her that the tree was more than four centuries old. The oldest living thing in the whole bloody country. Still holding on. Still surviving. Still breathing.

The woman was scratching like the devil. First her cheek, then her arm, her thighs, and pacing about left, right, like a manic ping-pong ball. She was wearing the same white dress with the cats, and had a canvas duffel bag slung across her chest.

"You're late," she said.

"I'm sorry. There's protest action back there—"

"I've got to go. I've got to go now," said the woman, tugging at the sleeves of her cardigan.

"Just a sec. Please. You said you knew something about the boy? I need to make sure: Which boy were you talking about?"

"Take your pick," the woman said. "Take your pick. I'm talking about all of them."

"Sorry?"

"I'm the one who's sorry. So sodding sorry-sorry. But I have to go now."

"I don't understand."

"I really have to go . . . The convent. The old woman. She found this book. The thing is supposed to contain the cure for the Laughter, but it's written in code and she's only figured out parts of it. Or maybe none of it. I'm not sure. Anyway, something convinced her the Laughter has a spiritual basis, so she's been experimenting. Vaccinating some of the nuns with dead kids. She thinks their spirits can give the sick power, heal them or something. I don't know. It all sounds kind of cracked, if I say it out loud. I've been hallucinating some stuff, I think. Withdrawal. Must be the withdrawal. It's not common with opioid use but I've been using some other stuff, too, lately, before Denny ran off. But this is real, I promise, I'm not making it up. I mean, I'm pretty sure, I think, that I'm not."

This woman was off her rocker.

"You have to get them out," said the woman, waving her arms around like windmills. "The kids. You have to help them. Lucky. The one with the manga tattoo. You have to help that one. You need to get him out."

"I want to." Lucky. Where had she heard that name before?

"It's my fault. It's all my fault. I didn't even know what the hell it was all about at first, didn't know they were dead. I thought they were just normal kids. Mother says I see them better because the drugs make me liminal, that you lose your inhibitions when you're strung out. Sounded like bullshit to me, but she paid well and I needed the money and she promised she wouldn't hurt them, that she was helping them find the light. Like they do in the movies, you know? I believed her. I really did. I mean, how can you hurt someone who's already dead, right?"

"What about the caretaker? Could he see them? The kids?"

"Sometimes. Not every kid, every time. But when he'd been looking into the bottle, he seemed to notice them more."

"The kids. Are they at the convent?"

"Yes."

"Will you help me?"

"I can't. I can't. I really can't. I'll kill them. I'll kill you. This is as far as I go. I'm done. Done. I'm going up the mountain after this. You're my last stop."

She put her hand in front of her mask, bent over, and began to cough. No, it wasn't coughing, it was something else. Faith thought about reaching a hand out to her but stopped herself. "Slow down," she said. "I'm trying to understand, but you've got to explain."

"I'm dead. I'm as good as dead. I'm a walking skeleton. I've been spiking a fever since yesterday. I think I'm done for it. Done. It's time to pay up. Time for the reckoning. But I'd rather go up the mountain and die where there's a view, you know? Watching the clouds. It's beautiful up there. Have you been?" The woman bent down again, spluttered. "I've heard there's a death cult hiding up there in the old café on top of the table who does euthanasia rituals. So that's where I'm heading. I'd rather go on my own terms." Another spluttering fit. No, not spluttering—laughing. She was trying not to laugh, doubled over, clutching at her mask. "Sorry," she cackled. "That's not funny, not funny, I know, but I can't help it, I can't stop. Best keep back. Don't come too close, okay?"

Two men on horseback trotted up the path. Virus patrollers.

"Shit," said the woman. "I have to go. Here—"

She thrust something into Faith's open hand and Faith caught a glimpse of a tattoo on the inside of her wrist. A snake on a stick, Tomorrow had said. A serpent entwined around a staff. The rod of Asclepius.

"Stop!" she called. "Wait!"

But the woman who had taken Elliot had already vanished into the fray of the protest.

Faith opened her fist. Lying across her palm was a key. Big, solid, heavy. The kind you used to open a gate. She slid it into her coat pocket and followed the vanishing junkie out of the green and into the tar-black street.

When she got back into the van she looked at her phone. Five messages from Tomorrow. *Please call me.*

She thought about texting, but decided to try her luck. The phone picked up on the first ring. The girl must have been waiting at a signal sweet spot.

"Faith. Have anything? Please tell me you have something."

"I'm not sure. Maybe."

"Maybe what?"

"I'm working on a lead. But it's a long shot. No point in telling you yet."

"Just tell me. I'm dying over here."

"You know that hair cult? The one you took Elliot to?"

"Yes."

"There's a chance the head nun has been kidnapping kids, or the spirits of kids, to use in some kind of experiment. But I don't have any real evidence yet, and the more I think about it, it just sounds too over the top. So let's not get ahead of ourselves, okay?"

"But you'll follow up on it, won't you?"

"As we speak."

"When will you phone again? I'm going crazy in this house. Waiting. I can't stand it."

"Tomorrow morning. First thing, okay?"

"Cross your heart and hope to die?"

"Promise."

60

SANS

While waiting for Major to come back, Sans sat on the couch and thumbed through an old copy of the *Truth*. He couldn't believe how many people, Major included, spent money on this gossip rag. What were they thinking? Had the whole damn city lost its collective mind?

He thought he'd go into the hall to have a look at the day's fresh ponies, but the last trickle of sisters had packed up and left, and the long tables stood empty and smooth, hairless to the max.

He was on his way back into the garden, in the hopes of spotting a glimpse of the hot young sister with the pert but pious ass, when he spied movement out of the corner of his eye. Did Major's yellow curtain just move, or was he imagining things again? Wind probably, right? He looked towards the wall, checking for any open windows, but they were all shut tight.

He was about to turn back when he saw it moving again. The curtain. There was a sound, like shuffling footsteps, and a loud crashing *thud*. So he did what any idiot, shark-bait, horror novice who didn't know he was in a story would do—he went closer to have a look.

A flash of indigo, oil, charcoal, raven, ebony, midnight black. It was her. It had to be. He catapulted himself towards the curtain. It rippled and billowed. He grabbed at it, yanked it open. The yellow fabric tore off the pegs and dropped to the floor.

But behind it, nothing. Not a damn thing. The caretaker's office stood dead and empty like before.

Wait.

Something was different. The side table that had stood next to the couch was gone. The tablecloth lay tossed aside and the stacked books that he now saw had made up the base of the table were scattered all over the floor. Some of the books looked old. Really old. Like they could be worth something. He wondered where Major had found them. The caretaker wasn't the kind of guy who spent his weekends scouring the city for antique books. Hell, all Sans had ever seen the guy reading was the sports section of the *Daily Truth*.

He was picking up the books and shaping them into a table again when he noticed that one of them, a fat leather-bound thing that looked way older than his gran, had this weird glow about it. All around the edges. Kind of like a halo. What the hell? Was he hallucinating again? No. Enough of this. He scrunched up his eyelids until he saw stars. Opened them up again. And the glow was gone. Thank fuck. It was just a book. Old, certainly, but just a book. He looked for the title and realized that the writing on the cover was handwritten, the letters faded. *Ama*. No. Wait. *Anna*. A space. And a *D*-something. *D.U. Konh. De Kongh*? No. That wasn't it. *De Koningh? De Koningh*. The wheels in his brain rewound, back, forward, every which way. Could it be?

The diary? *The* diary? No fucking way. Not a chance. It had to be a setup. He wasn't one of those suckers who believed in signs and coincidences. The planets aligning and all that hippie mumbo jumbo. And his tenuous grip on reality had already been stretched to the max this week. He didn't want the last dregs of his sanity to snap like a twig. He wouldn't allow it. No. This had to be some kind of scam. A trick.

But he hadn't told the caretaker about his unicorn, had he? So who had he told? Who knew about all this? The dead collector knew some of it, along with her hyena-muzzling beefcake. That fat bloody faker. And the librarian, the guy who gave him the information about De Koningh in the first place. Maybe the trio was in cahoots and this whole thing was some kind of elaborate gaslight plot set up to make him crazy? But why?

Hold on. Who had told him about the charlatan sin-eater in the first place? And who had told him about that librarian? That blue-haired, fast-talking dead collector. And where had he met the unicorn first? When he was hanging out with Faith on the square, playing cards. What if she was behind all of this? No, it didn't add up. What was her motive? What kind of axe did she have to grind with him? He hadn't spoken more than ten, maybe twenty words to her before Monday, if you didn't count poker talk, that was. Was she working for someone else? His gangster chums, perhaps? Or was she some kind of undercover pony activist? She'd known about his job, yes. (All the dead collectors on the square did. It had come up while they were playing cards a few times. Some of the guys in the card ring sometimes brought him dead ponies on the side.) And she didn't approve. He could see it on her face. Chicks rarely did anyway. Except the gold-digger types who were hoping to score free weaves.

What if the dead collector was a pony activist and she was driving him crazy as some kind of whack revenge plot? That was why she'd cornered him in the comedy club, bought him drink after drink, and asked all those questions about the convent and what the security was like there. What had he told her, exactly? That evening was still hazy. All he could remember was the chicken on the stage and that grinning hyena licking his ankle. But the processing room was always locked, bolted, burglar-barred, and buttoned up like Pollsmoor and Alcatraz had gone and had a baby. Not even he could break in without help. So how would she have gotten in?

Maybe Major was in on the whole thing? Maybe she'd paid him off?

Nah. That couldn't be it. He'd known Major for years. The guy had his quirks, but he wouldn't throw him under the bus like that. Sans had helped him out many a time—getting that gig for his nephew, for example—and Major had hooked him up with the convent gig, without which he'd still be as broke as a joke on coke. Besides, it almost felt like he had been led behind that curtain, all the way to the book, by . . . well, her. His unicorn. Hallucination or not, he'd definitely seen her—caught a glimpse of her onyx hair when the books toppled down. He was almost sure of it. And the glow. That weird glow the book had given off. No way the dead collector could have engineered that.

Careful not to damage the antique paper, Sans opened up the book to a random page. And realized that he couldn't understand a thing. The diary wasn't in English. Hell, it wasn't in any language he'd ever seen. More like hieroglyphics. A mishmash of weird symbols, with a bunch of random numbers and alphabet soup thrown in for good measure.

If this really was Anna's diary, the one the librarian had told him about, and the librarian's story added up, then somewhere within these pages was a cure. A cure to cure all. Something like that would be worth a fortune. So although the whole scheme sounded totally mental, it was totally worth checking out.

But where was he going to find someone to decipher this lot?

Footsteps. Major was coming back. This would be one hell of a story to try to explain to the caretaker, and Sans wasn't sure it was worth the effort. And it wasn't like the guy knew what he had here, right? He'd been using the book to balance his moonshine on, for fuck's sake.

Yeah, he'd just borrow it.

Stuffing the book in his backpack required a bit of Tetris. The thing barely, just about, fit. But it did. Thank fuck. He clipped the top of the backpack shut. It wasn't stealing. He was just borrowing it. To find out if it was legit. He spread the blue cloth over the restacked books. Perfect. He was willing to bet Major wouldn't notice that his precious side table had shrunk a notch.

There was a slow creak as the door to the hall opened. Footsteps, then the curtain pulled back and Major's face appeared. "Hey," said the caretaker. "What's up?"

"Where were you? You were gone a month."

"Ja, sorry. Ran into this stukkie I'm trying to woo. One of the new girls. Damn fine piece of work."

"Good for you, brother, good for you. Let's drink to that."

"With my nephew's finest moonshine, yes." Major gestured to a shelf behind Sans's head. "Just grab it, will you? There behind the Handy Andy and the bleach."

Sans stood up and reached for the unlabeled bottle. Passed it to the caretaker, who poured them each two fingers of respite. Sans sloshed the liquid around in his cup. Inspected it. It was thick, syrupy, and smelt like it could kill. And the color was . . . unusual. Kind of like burnt umber.

"Hey, you're in a better mood, brother," said Major. "What happened? Get lucky while I was gone, too?"

"Nothing like that," Sans said. "Just gained some perspective on a few things, is all."

"Good. That's good." The caretaker raised his cup. "Let's drink to that."

"Cheers," said Sans. The liquid burned like hellfire as it reached his throat, but it hit the spot.

61

FAITH

Twelve a.m. The moon was the top of a fingernail dancing on a pin.

"Have I mentioned I'm charging extra for this?" said the sin-eater, while Faith rummaged in her bag for the key. "Breaking and entering. It's not exactly cricket, you know."

"Yes, yes. Send me the bill." She wasn't too keen on him being here, either, but if the junkie's crazy ramblings had even one nanobyte of truth in them, she was going to need a good ghostbuster when she got inside. Ghosts . . . what did she know about ghosts? She didn't even believe in them. Even if they were real, she was pretty sure she wouldn't be able to see them. Not everyone could, the sin-eater had said. You had to be sensitive to the spiritual realm and whatnot. You had to have the knack.

So she'd brought Fred with her, for spiritual backup. But the way he was standing there whispering louder than a freight train in that flaming-orange bull's-eye of a windbreaker, she was starting to regret the decision.

She pushed the key she'd gotten from the junkie into the key-shaped groove. It slid in like it fit. She held her breath, turned.

Nothing.

It was stuck.

She jiggled it this way and that, but no luck. She pulled it out again.

"Let me try," said the sin-eater.

She handed him the key. He slid it into the lock, fiddled with it with his stubby fingers, but it still didn't move.

Idiot, Faith chided herself. *I'm an idiot. Coming all this way. For this. For nothing.* She was about to tell him to stop trying when—

Hold on.

The key was turning. Actually turning. Almost.

"It's a little stubborn," said the sin-eater, "but I think, it just might . . . if I put my wrist into it . . ." The key caved and did a full swing.

The gate pivoted on its hinges with a throaty *schweee*. Faith winced at the sound. They slipped in through the gap and pushed it shut.

Through the convent's garden they skulked. Up the path and over the grass. They were walking past the ghostly Virgin whose stone eyes still trailed the ground when Faith had a flashback. A Then one. She saw herself walking ahead, with her everything in tow.

He was dragging his feet, with his forehead scrunched up in a scowl. "Why do we have to come here?"

"I'm your mother. I have to do everything to keep you safe. Even if it seems crazy and far-out. So let's just do this. Get it over with quick."

"But Dad says it's nonsense. Just superstitious nonsense. That you can't keep the Laughter at bay with an electric shaver and some half-baked faith."

"Your dad's probably right, but what have we got to lose? Just some hair, right? So let's turn that scowl upside down and get it over with, quick."

The sin-eater had stopped. He looked back at where she was standing. "What's the problem? Cold feet? If you keep walking, they'll warm up." He giggled at his own joke and Faith snapped back to reality.

"Shush," she said. "Nothing's funny here."

"Nothing's funny anywhere anymore," said Fred.

When they reached the courtyard, they stopped.

"Which way now?" asked the sin-eater.

"This way." She led him down the open corridor. Predictably, the holy hall was locked.

"The doorframe," said Faith. "Up top."

The sin-eater stood on his toes, felt around, found the key. Just where the ponyjacker had said it would be. Pony Boy hadn't been very forthcoming about the convent, but he was quite drunk when he talked to Faith at the comedy club, and after some gentle prodding, and a few more shots, he had let something slip about the caretaker being too lazy to carry around a big bunch of keys all the time, and leaving spares above doorframes.

The big, dark hall gave her the jumps. All those bottles. All that hair. All those candles burning through the night.

"This is such a bleddie fire hazard," said the sin-eater. "What are they thinking, leaving them burning like this?"

Faith didn't say anything at first. Just stared. At the orbs. Those crazy dancing disco orbs. Everywhere.

"The orbs. All those orbs. What are they? Some kind of trick of the light?"

"What are you talking about? What orbs?"

"The lights. All those lights. Don't you see them?"

"You mean the candlelight?"

"No."

He couldn't see them. But she could. She couldn't see anything else. Semitransparent, the blobs of light were mostly silvery white, but also blue, orange, black, red, and green, each floating above its own bottle (though some bottles were without). They were swaying slightly, suspended in midair like helium balloons or stunned fireflies.

Why didn't Fred see them? Was she hallucinating? Going crazy?

What was worse, what was totally worse, was that she had this feeling. This weird feeling. That the orbs were trying to talk to her. Hundreds of them all vying for her attention, calling out. Like a radio switching channels or something.

Faith closed her eyes. Tried her best to concentrate on the feeling, focus it, channel it, align it with her mind and her body. Call it one of her hunches (or desperation, maybe), but she knew she had to do this.

"Elliot," she whispered, "I know your hair is here. I can feel it."

Nothing at first. Then a sound. Like a rumbling. Or a drone. Like the sound a washing machine makes, but with more jumps. A halt-and-flow sound. Like the first practice notes of an orchestra. Then it got louder. Much louder. So loud it started to hurt her ears. A huge cacophonous drone. As if a hundred voices were talking—screaming—at once.

"Please," she tried again. "I don't understand. You've got to help me."

There. On her left. Close to the door. Was it her imagination, or was one of the orbs glowing brighter, the light pulsing, contracting and expanding in a slow waltz? No, she wasn't dreaming. This was real.

She made her way towards the orb, intending to scoop up the tiny vial underneath it, but before she got to it, something happened. As if a channel were switched, the orbs changed.

Defined.

Sharpened.

Came into focus.

She was wrong. She could see that now.

They weren't orbs. They were faces. Hundreds of them.

62

SANS

S ans opened his eyes. There were tendrils on the bed. Black tendrils snaking from his feet across his stomach to his neck, touching his skin.

No, not tendrils—strands. So many strands. And not just black anymore, either. Blond, white, brown, auburn, strawberry blond, copper, red . . . Thick strands, thin strands, straight strands, curly strands. A thousand different ponies, all slithering and snaking up to his neck, twisting around his throat. Around. And around. A necklace of hair. Coiling tighter. Tighter.

Choking. Choking. Choking. Him.

Try . . .

. . . ing

to . . .

. . . breathe.

He woke up, for real this time. Curled over in a coughing fit. It was 3:00 a.m. The devil's hour. He scrambled out of bed, lit a candle, poured himself a glass of water. Sat down at the desk next to his bed.

His apartment was a blank space. Bare but solid. Safe. His own small patch of terra firma in this wild, sick, dark-as-damn-dark but also light-as-a-puff-of-dandelion-fluff city. No dragons here.

Sure, he could have upgraded. Moved to squat in some abandoned mansion against the mountain in Higgovale with an Olympic-sized swimming pool and a sauna and tennis court. But he liked it here.

What the apartment lacked in size it made up for in being his. Fair and square. He'd bought it a decade ago with the money he got from the Road Accident Fund. That was back when there still was a Road Accident Fund. There had been an accident. It had been raining. The road was wet. The rain was one of the few things he could still remember from that night. Or at least he thought he did. Maybe someone had told him afterwards, or his mind had embellished that bit. Wasn't it always raining in stories about car accidents? Wasn't that how it went? Hey, maybe his was the first one. The first cliché to set up all the rest and point the way in the curved trajectory of his whole damn cliché-ridden life, causing a kind of follow-on domino effect. Who knew? What he did know was that the truck driver who came too fast around the bend and lost control of the wheel was drunk.

He'd waited in the crumpled origami heap for six hours before someone came upon the wreck and called the ambulance who brought the Jaws of Life to cut him and his mom out. He was sixteen years old. The accident fucked up his leg, killed his father, and opened the door to all the crazy in his mom's head. (This was before that guy walked into her office and shot himself and the crazy just started to spill out with nothing to plug the leak anymore.) While this was all true and factual for sure, it had also gotten him this flat. And it was a good flat. Small but functional. Nice.

All this was when property ownership still meant something, before the clock reset and turned the city into one giant free-for-all. Now the title deed was just a piece of paper. A dead tree. But who cared. It was his dead tree. His own patch of blank space. Flag planted. Fair and square and solid. No foul play required.

The couch was comfortable, the bed wasn't small, the mattress soft but firm. There was a computer on a desk in his bedroom next to his bed. Not a laptop, but a big fat old-school monstrosity dressed up all in black. He liked to play games on it, liked the way the games made his mind go blank. He preferred vintage shoot-'em-ups, but he'd play anything he could get, provided it shut up his brain for a sec.

Now he sat at the desk, holding a candle to the book, wishing his apartment had solar panels on the roof. He could barely make out a thing in this light and he had no idea when the power would be back on. Fucking electricity. The government was apparently working on a new plan to use the grinners and the ash factories on the Flats to power parts of the city. But they'd hit a few snags: a few grieving morons were protesting, saying it was disrespectful to use the dead to power toasters or some such sanctimonious rubbish. Idiots.

Earlier Sans had gone up to the roof. There was a chick there who had a satellite dish, some batteries, and some solar panels. She knew stuff about computers and had one stashed in a wooden garden shed on the roof. Anyway, the chick had internet, most of the time, a lot of the time, so he'd gone and asked her if she could look something up for him. She had a hair thing going. A self-professed diva, always changing her look. So he'd promised her a fresh pony in return.

The website was a kind of conspiracy-theory site about the Laughter. It was over the top, sensationalist, but it was the only reference she could find that mentioned the diary. And it basically confirmed the librarian's story. Running his fingers down the spine of the book now, he thought about his unicorn. He'd seen her today in the processing room. He was sure of it.

He thought about a book by Stephen Hawking he'd read once. Hawking said the afterlife was a fairy story for people who were afraid of the dark. Sans was inclined to agree with him. That's why he didn't think his unicorn was a ghost. But a seer seeing across time, somehow making her shape known to him to get some kind of message across— now, that was a thing he could maybe get his head around if he tried. He also remembered reading an article in which Hawking talked about wormholes and how you could travel across time through them, but you could only go forward, not backwards. There were some other caveats, but Sans couldn't remember them; he hadn't exactly been taking notes. But that was then. And this was now. And now he was cursing himself for not paying more attention.

Anyway, what if that was what was happening here? That this freed slave librarian chick with her perfect, perfect unicorn hair was reaching across time to talk to him? To tell him about her diary? To tell him that the thing held the cure?

Maybe.

Maybe not.

Maybe it was all bull and he was just drinking too much.

Or was he just going crazy, turning into his mother? Was that what this was all about?

He tried to focus on the book again. The script was tiny. He went through it, page by page, hoping for something written in English, or maybe a drawing or something at least halfway legible or digestible, but no luck.

What had he been thinking, stealing—borrowing—this moth-eaten thing? It was useless. Useless. He was no better off than before, only now he was a guy who'd stolen from someone who could, argu-ably, be called his best friend. Being a thief was fine, but a thief who stole from his own—that was a problem. A line. One of the few he hadn't yet crossed.

A low hum. The power was back on. Sans opened his cupboard, took out an old T-shirt and wrapped the book up in it, placed it in his backpack, and then switched his computer on. His package for the week had arrived courtesy of one of Mickey's gumbooted, skate-boarded couriers that afternoon.

He scrolled though the content, clicked on yesterday's edition of an online newspaper he read when he was feeling like he gave a shit. There was an article on the postbox riots sweeping the city. How anger was brewing after an article in the *Daily Truth* claimed the postbox meds were inducing hallucinations.

Halle-fucking-lujah. This was it! The answer he'd been looking for! Screw that fat bastard with his bullshit theories, screw his bloody beau-tiful unicorn. He wasn't crazy, he wasn't sick, he wasn't seeing dead people—he was just going postal with the best of them! Thank the fucking government for bad meds! Everything was going to be A-OK.

But wait.

That wouldn't explain the book, would it? That thing was real. There was no denying it.

- 63 -

FAITH

Hundreds of faces. Hundreds. And one of the faces was glowing so brightly it seared. Faith was burning. Melting. Cracking. Falling apart. It was him. Her everything. Right there in front of her unbelieving eyes was the face of her everything.

The space around Faith's heart was a wall. So solid, so impenetrable that it would take a thousand armies a hundred years to crack one brick. But now the whole damn thing was crumbling, and she with it. With not a single army in sight. Just the husk of one small boy. One single soul. Glowing so brightly that her whole damn being was going nuclear for it.

She was drowning. Gasping for air, her body caving in on itself, crumpling to the floor in a heap. She'd heard stories about sailors lost at sea who said they saw the Virgin Mary while drowning. (Although she wondered how they could have told anyone about that if they'd drowned. Maybe it was those who survived to tell the tale?) Apparently the brain does something strange when it gets deprived of oxygen. People start to see things. Like mermaids. Or ghosts.

Or ghosts . . .

She was reaching out her hand to him, her ghost, her everything, when she heard a crash and a scuffle behind her. Shouts, too. And swearing.

Self-preservation told her to turn around, but her body couldn't obey. It was locked in on her son's face. His beautiful perfect face.

More shouting. It was scaring him away. His face, which was also her face, and the others, the other orb faces, they all disappeared.

And reality came gushing in.

Faith stared. Blinked. Closed her eyes and opened them again. The hall was just a hall. No blobs of light and color. No dancing fireflies. She could hear noise, but it wasn't the same noise. It sounded more like a scuffle. She turned around. Shit!

The caretaker with the lazy eye was in a pink dressing gown holding a baseball bat. He had the sin-eater pinned to the floor.

"Stop," Faith tried saying, but no sound came out. "Stop, please," she tried again. "We're not here to fight! We just want the hair. Call the cops on us if you have to, but just drop the bat. Please."

The caretaker lifted up the bat, pulling away from Fred. He was panting hard. "You. The skirt from the gate. Not just a detective but a thief, too, I see."

Faith saw his body relax and his shoulders slump. "I'm not going to call the cops. Open up that can of worms—are you crazy? Besides, what are the chances they'll come? No. It's better if you guys just get out. Let's pretend none of this happened and move on. Okay?"

"Works for me," said the sin-eater, his face a lobster, his back against the floor.

Faith had watched a documentary once called *The World's Most Dangerous Volcanoes*, and one of the volcanoes was Mount Vesuvius. One hell of a lethal lump of rock, best known for its AD 79 eruption that buried the ancient Roman city of Pompeii twenty-five meters deep in ash while emitting a hundred thousand times the thermal energy released by the Hiroshima and Nagasaki bombings.

They were walking back to the van, their feet stomping an out-of-sync rhythm onto the tar. Her cheeks were red as lava, hotter than hell.

"You okay there?" said Fred. "You haven't said a thing since we—"

Vesuvius. She was Mount Vesuvius. Last major eruption, 1944. Next expected eruption, right about now.

A grumbling, a rumbling, a curse, a cuss. A furious bang. "You didn't see a bloody thing, did you?" The words spewing out.

The street was empty except for a couple of teenagers making out through their masks in front of the gate of an ugly face-brick apartment block. They stopped kissing to stare. Faith glared at them.

"See what exactly, now?" said the sin-eater.

"Those glowing orbs. The faces. The ghosts."

"No, well . . . not really."

"Not really? What does *not really* mean? You're supposed to be a spirit medium, the best in the business, and you didn't see a thing? I'd call that more than a little suspect."

"What are you implying?"

"I'm implying exactly what I'm saying."

"And what's that?"

"That the way things look now it sounds to me like you're a complete bloody fake."

"Now, before you start bashing away at my professional credibility, have you stopped for a second to consider the very real possibility that the problem isn't with me?"

Faith glared at him. She could feel the lava building behind her eyeballs. "Come again?"

"You know as well as I do what they're saying about the postbox meds. Maybe you were hallucinating the whole business? I mean, it would make sense."

"Bullshit. That back there was the realest thing I've seen in years. It was no hallucination, that's for sure. I've never been so sure of anything in my life." Okay, that wasn't quite true. Faith had her doubts. But she was on a roll and picking up speed and finding it difficult to slam on the brakes. "The truth is, you're a big bloody charlatan. The sin-eating, the spirit channeling . . . It's all just one hell of an act, isn't it? Making money off the desperate and all that. Ghostbuster, my ass. I can't believe I trusted you."

"Sho. That's a bit harsh now, isn't it?"

"Is it?" She stopped walking, folded her arms, and gave him her death stare.

Fred's head did one of its little wobbles. A hand came up and tugged at the moustache end sticking out of the mask. He sighed a long, drawn-out sigh. "I, well, see, the truth is—"

"The truth is what?"

"Please just hear me out, darling. I can explain."

"Firstly, I'm nobody's darling, darling. Secondly, the writing is on the wall. I really don't see how you can dig yourself out of this one, you charlatan cocksucker."

"Allow me to try. Please."

"Fine. Whatever. Shoot."

"Truth is I really do have a connection to the other side. Well, I did. Or at least I thought I did, as I suppose one can never be sure, hey. But then I went out and got these pills, see. To tune the voices out."

"Why the hell would you go and do that?"

"Well, thing is, before the Down Days I worked for the South African Police Force for a few years. Occult Crimes Unit. Do you know about them?"

The Occult Crimes Unit was a favorite topic of Lawyer's, but Faith was feeling contrary. "Doesn't ring a bell," she said.

"Well, they were kind of like Mulder and Scully for the rainbow nation—investigating all sorts of weird supernatural and unexplainable phenomena. Witchcraft, zombies, muthi murders—that kind of stuff. Anyway. I was headhunted by them, 'cause of my special skill set. The unit was struggling to close cases and I suppose the guys upstairs thought it takes a thief to catch a thief, if you get my drift. So, long story short, the stuff I saw while on that beat would make your skull explode, darling."

"Here we go again. I'm not your damn darling. Let's get that for damn straight, right?"

"Yes. Sorry. Old habits and all that. Anyway, moving on. I saw some seriously messed-up stuff. Kind of made me doubt my ancestral trade. I was going off the rails a bit, drinking too much, that kind of thing, so they said I had to go see a psychiatrist, who said I was suffering from PTSD-induced psychosis. Prescribed these little pills. So I took them—I mean, why not, thought it could be nice to quiet down the cacophony of voices always clamoring for attention in my head for a change. And as the little pills started working their magic, for the first time in my life I felt great. Nice and boring and normal. And I liked it."

"Let me guess." Faith rolled her eyes. "You continued making a living in the spirit trade?"

"Ja, well, that was afterwards. When the city turned all topsy-turvy and the whole bleddie system went kaput. I was working as a plumber. No one was wanting their pipes fixed anymore. Money was getting tight. And I thought to myself, You know what? An oke's got to eat."

"Fine. Whatever. So nice for you that you're feeling so sane these days. But it also means you're totally useless to me. So what the hell do I do now? Spy that in your fake crystal ball somewhere, do you?"

"Well, I do know someone. Whose connection to her ancestors is the real deal, class-A stuff."

"Just like you were supposed to be, huh?"

"What can I say, except," the sin-eater shrugged, "trust me?"

- 64 -

FRED

If he had to give himself a label, it would be *Fred Mostert—Hopesmith*. There were a lot of fancy words on his business card and he knew he might have exaggerated his skills in his ads, but if you cut right down to it, he was a hawker of hope. That was the family trade.

His dad called it a calling. A gift. The doctors, on the other hand—in Valkenberg and Lentegeur and the slew of other madhouses he had been committed to (involuntarily) throughout his life, with their cold floors and quaint phrases like "We comfort, we care, we heal" adorning the walls of the visitors' rooms—called it something else. Schizophrenia. Never mind the Laughter, Fred's entire family was a laugh. His dad, his grandfather, his uncle, the lot. His cousin Mickey was so far into the family way that he'd run away from the real world. Because what kind of nutter took himself off to live in a shack in an old tunnel under a castle and made like it was a business decision? On days when it rained, the moron had to pack up all his worldly possessions into plastic buckets and tie them to the ceiling. What a chump.

All things considered, though, Fred was good at what he did. On any given day he had customers lining up around the block. You didn't have to believe in something in order to be an expert in it. Didn't even have to be particularly talented. What was that thing they said about ten thousand hours? He'd heard it on a chat show on TV once, some guy saying it took roughly ten thousand hours to achieve mastery in any field. Fred had put in that many and then some. He'd been accompanying his dad on callouts since he was a laaitie. Seen a lot of crazy shit. Heard the voices, too, sure, but he was on medication for that now, and Dr. Botha had explained a lot of things to him. Said there were no such things as ghosts. That it was all in his head. An imbalance in the complex interrelated chemical reactions of his brain. Of course Fred wanted to believe him. He didn't want to end up like his dad. *Maller as 'n haas, was his oubaas.* Crazier than a cat in a crack house. Drove his mom to the bottom of the bottle and back again.

So, the little blue-and-yellow capsules Dr. Botha kept prescribing were the first things he took every day with his morning coffee and they did the trick. They kept the voices at bay. He'd made the mistake of reading the folded pamphlet inside the pack and it made his head spin. Paragraph after paragraph of risks: "Irreversible tardive dyskinesia, potentially fatal neuroleptic malignant syndrome, leukopenia, neutropenia, and agranulocytosis. Extrapyramidal symptoms, such as pseudoparkinsonism, akathisia, and dystonia. Persistent tardive dyskinesia, tachycardia, hypotension, light-headedness, and syncope . . ." He hadn't understood half of it, except for the words *fatal* and *irreversible*. But what wasn't fatal and irreversible in this city? So he'd stopped reading and threw the pamphlet in the bin. He was a hopesmith, after all, and so was Dr. Botha.

And if there was one thing he had found in his line of business, it was that hope wasn't free. It always came at a cost.

When his dad passed away and Fred took over the family business, the first couple of years were rough. It was the lying that got to him. He knew the script. His dad had been grooming him since before he could talk. He just had trouble with saying it all with a straight face. Didn't believe in what he was selling.

Then a friend gave him tickets to a play. Some kind of Shakespeare thing. *Midsummer Night's* whatever. As he watched the actors prance across the stage in their silly tights and frilly tops spouting all that old-fashioned gibberish, and all the while looking like the cat that got the cream or however that saying went, he figured it out. It's a role. The whole thing was a role. He'd already learnt his lines. Now he just had to learn how to act out the script. So he watched a few more plays and a whole bunch of old movies, and started channeling his favorite stars: Robert De Niro, "You talkin' to me?"; Sean Connery, "Shaken not stirred"; and, more appropriately, Bill Murray in *Ghostbusters*: "This city is headed for a disaster of biblical proportions . . . Human sacrifice, dogs and cats living together . . . mass hysteria!" It took the edge off that way. And the job got easier. He didn't feel like such a skollie anymore. Nope. He was one of the good guys. Hope. Fred Mostert gave people hope.

That's what Faith needed right now, and he was going to give it to her; come hell or high water, he wasn't going to give up. Fred might not have been in top supernatural form lately thanks to Dr. Botha and those little blue-and-yellow pills, but he knew someone who was. Someone who was the real deal—a young gun supernatural maverick with balls to match, who was right at the very top of the city's spiritual pops. If she couldn't figure out this whole damn drama-rama, no one could.

SATURDAY

65

THE DAILY TRUTH

POSSESSED POPOS ON THE LOOSE IN SICK CITY?

By Lawyer Tshabalala

Possession is nine-tenths of the law. For real now, writes Lawyer Tshabalala

So you guys remember how I wrote about amakhosi possession a few weeks ago? Missed it? Let's do a quick recap, then. *But, Lawyer,* you say, *these amakhosi whatsamathingies, what are they again?* Seriously, I can't take you guys anywhere. This amakhosi thing has been around forever and a day. Have you guys been living under a rock? Let me spell it out for you again: schoolkids are mixing brandy, milk stout, and muthi to channel the spirits of older, stronger ancestors. The possessed teens then go around in gangs getting up to all sorts of mischief. Starting fights, robbing little old ladies, stealing stuff, or just climbing walls, standing up to bullies, running around like vigilante superheroes, and winning soccer games.

Last time I wrote to you, my dear readers, I was telling you about this crazy Cuban doctor who is claiming he might have a cure for the Laughter by way of using amakhosi muthi. By substituting young spirits for ancient ones. Sounds kind of Stikland, but wouldn't that be a kwaai experiment if it works, hey?

The latest news from behind the hyena curtain is that our dear Mr. President is in on the amakhosi action again. Some of you will know, he's been shipping gangs of amakhosi kids out to war zones across the world for years—as rent-a-soldiers in exchange for fat wads of cash. But amidst the recent increase in border breaches, he is apparently planning to beef up security by enlisting some of these returned ex-mercenaries into the Veeps. Now, isn't that a bunch of nightmare fuel for thought? That's all we need, folks, a bunch of possessed kids with PTSD running our police force. Happy days.

66

SANS

The bird looked down onto the quilted square shouldered by noir-ish *Batman* high-rises. It was an ordinary bird. Just your average, run-of-the-mill domestic pigeon. Nothing special about it. And like most pigeons, it didn't give a flying coo about Art Deco architecture or comic strips. (Although it was quite partial to a good Gothic gargoyle. As partial as the next bird, it supposed.) So it wasn't the noirish architecture that piqued its interest down below in the square today. Nor was it the patchwork of colorful interconnected stalls.

It was a cap. A bright red, peaked cap. Its wearer standing motion-less. Talking. Waiting. Just for him. Next to that pointy, sticky-out sky perch. Next to that white vrooming box thing.

The bird loved red. It was its favorite color. Birds can see colors; they aren't dogs, thank you very much.

The bird stretched its wings and aimed. Ah. Presto. *Better. Much better*, it thought to itself before flapping off in search of a perch.

"Shit," said Sans. "Shit, shit!"

"It's good luck," said the dead collector, one hand stuck in the pocket of her coat. Her voice sounded dull and numb, like she was talking through a cardboard tube.

"Luck," snorted Sans, flicking the bird shit off with his fingers. "There you go again with your mystical hippie hoo-ha. There's no such thing as luck. Or fate. Or choosing your own reality in seven different colors and sizes with free shipping via Amazon or whatever. But hey. I guess you just can't help yourself, can you?"

"That's what I've been told," said the dead collector in a weird high-pitched half whisper that gave him the heebie-jeebies. No jibes. No quick comebacks. Her eyes blank, defeated. Like he'd gone and broken her high score or something.

Shit. "I'm sorry. I'm being an ass again, aren't I?" What? What was he saying? This wasn't like him. "You look like you're having a rough week. Can I buy you a coffee?" Argh. Why did he just do that? He didn't want to go for a coffee with this chick! He had way more important things to do today. Like finding a way to translate that damn book. *Shut up, Sans. Get ahold of yourself. Shut up!*

She was going to say no. He could see it on her face. What a relief.

But somehow, some-why, he couldn't help himself. It was like someone else was talking through him. As if he was possessed or something. "No strings," he said, his mouth going AWOL again. "Just caffeine. It's a sin to say no to a free cup of coffee—didn't your mother ever tell you that? Gift horse in the mouth and all that." What was wrong with him? Was this some kind of John Malkovich thing?

Her mouth was closed but she moved her jaw. She was thinking about it.

"If you want, I can lace it with something," Sans continued. "You look like you might need some extra kick. Spirits for the spirit, as my uncle used to say."

"Fine," said the dead collector, not looking too happy about it. "Fine."

"Fine," said Sans.

Fine.

They were sitting in that sad army face place. The one with the photo of Anna on the wall. The waiter brought the coffee and walked away, leaving a great big southern right whale of a silence behind that was threatening to swallow Sans whole if he didn't fill it with something. Anything. "So," he said, "what do you do for fun?" *What do you do for fun!* Seriously, he had to get ahold of himself. He was sounding like a cheese ad.

The dead collector glared at him, like he'd just asked for her bra size or something. Then her face thawed.

"Puzzles. I like solving puzzles."

"What kind of puzzles?"

"Any kind, really. The more difficult, the better."

"Hey. That's a weird coincidence. A stroke of luck, even, if you want to call it that. Turns out I have a puzzle of my own to solve right now. Maybe you can help?"

"The puzzle of how not to be such a huge asshat all the time? Sorry, guy, you're on your own on that one. I don't think that one's solvable. Some weeds can't be pruned, my gran used to say. Their roots run too deep."

"Ha, ha. Always the comedian, aren't you?"

"Yup," said the dead collector, but her eyes weren't laughing.

"Come on. Aren't you curious? Aren't you? Just a bit?"

"Fine."

"Fine." He took his phone out of his pocket. Showed her the pics he'd taken of the first two pages of the diary.

"What's this?" she asked, her eyes coming alive.

"Never mind that." If the book really held a cure, it was valuable as fuck. The fewer people he told about a cash cow like that, the better. "Can you read it?"

She glared at him. Looked at the image on the screen. Frowned.

```
⌐⌐⌐⊡⌐>⌐⌐⌐⌐⌐⌐⌐⌐⌐⊡⌐⌐⌐
⌐⌐⌐⊡⌐⌐⊡⌐⌐⌐⊡⌐⌐⌐⊡⌐⌐>
⌐⊡⌐>⌐⌐⌐⌐⌐⌐>⊡⌐⌐⊡⌐⊡⌐⊡
⌐⌐⊡⊡⌐⊡⌐⌐⌐⌐⌐⊡⌐⌐⌐⌐⌐⌐
⊡⌐⌐⌐⌐>⌐⌐⌐⌐⌐⌐⌐⌐⌐⌐⌐⌐⌐
⌐⌐⊡⌐>⌐⌐⌐⌐⌐⌐⌐⌐>⌐⌐⊡⌐⌐
⊡⌐⌐⊡⌐⌐⌐⊡⌐⌐⌐⌐⌐⌐⌐⌐⊡⌐⌐
⌐⌐⌐>⌐⌐⌐⊡>⌐⌐<⌐⌐⌐>⌐⌐⌐⌐
⌐>⌐⌐⌐⌐>⌐<>⌐⌐⌐⌐⌐⌐⌐
```

The dead collector took her hand out of her pocket and stroked the symbols on the screen with her fingers. "Well, the first pic is easy. It looks like a simple pigpen cipher. You just substitute each letter of the alphabet for a symbol."

"Cool. Great. What does it say?"

"Do you have something to write with?"

He signaled the waiter to ask for a pen. He appeared promptly with a black ballpoint.

"Let's see," she said, smoothing out a serviette. She stuck the back of the pen under her mask, as if to bite on it, pulled it out again.

"Stop that," she said.

"Stop what?"

"You keep tapping your nails against the table. I can't concentrate."

"Fine. I'll stop," said Sans, lifting his hand and putting it on his leg.

"Say, what happened to it anyway, if I may ask? Your leg, I mean. Why the limp?"

"Nothing. I mean, it was a long time ago."

"You don't have to tell me if you don't want to."

"No. It's fine. No big deal. I was bitten by a Rottweiler when I was three."

"Sorry."

"No worries."

The dead collector's coffee grew cold as she worked. He was looking out the window, watching the OCD bleach vendor across the street stack and unstack his wares into perfect pyramids when she put the pen down and looked up: "All nature is merely a cipher and a secret writing."

"Say what?"

"The cipher. I've cracked it. It reads: 'All nature is merely a cipher and a secret writing. The great name and essence of God and His wonders—the very deeds, projects, words, actions, and demeanor of mankind—what are they, for the most part, but a cipher?' It's a quote by Blaise de Vigenère. My dad told me about him. He was a sixteenth-century French cryptographer."

He was so happy he could kiss her. Maybe things were finally coming together. Maybe he was going to be all right. "Great," he said. Feigning nonchalance. "Show me how to do the rest and I'll get out of your hair."

"Not so fast. After this, the cipher changes."

He swore under his breath, sighed. "Can you decipher it?"

"Yes. I think so."

"There's more."

"More what?"

"More messages. A whole book of them."

The dead collector sighed, stuck her hand back into the pocket of her coat. She'd been sticking that damn hand in and out of that pocket like it was a jack-in-the-box all morning. A nervous tic?

"I thought you liked puzzles?" he tried. "Come on. It'll be fun."

"Where's the book?" she said, sighing again. This time louder.

"I'd rather keep it with me, thanks. It's got . . . sentimental value. Can't I just text you all the images?"

"My phone's out of juice. And the reception at my house sucks. What time is it? I have to get to work."

"Fine," he said, folding his arms like the cliché he was. "Will you copy the first two pages from my phone at least? I'll give you the rest tomorrow at the square."

"Fine," said the dead collector. She gulped down the dregs of her tepid coffee and reached into her bag for a notebook, while Sans wondered why the hell she hadn't taken the thing out in the first place instead of bothering with the flimsy serviette. "But you owe me for this, Pony Boy. You know that, don't you?"

- 67 -

FAITH

"Flowers for the dead, flowers for the living, a ruiker to meet your maker, a bouquet to make your day. Flowers for the dead, flowers for the living . . ."

Outside the station in Adderley Street, the flower sellers were punting their wares to mourners boarding the trains in black dresses and suits. The monochromatic funeral-wear struck an odd contrast with the bright blooms, like someone had scanned in an old photograph and gone to town on it with a Paint Bucket tool. A portrait in black, white, and gray, interspersed with bright spots of rose red, chrysanthemum pink, gerbera yellow, carnation white, and creamy red streaks of Double Delight.

The flower sellers sat hunched over plastic crates that served as makeshift tables on which they sorted the blooms into bunches or wove wreaths. A large tarp was spun over the stalls to keep out the rain, the poles of this makeshift tent stuck into plastic jerry cans filled with sand.

"A rose is a beautiful thing, lady." The vendor had one of those faces kneaded so heavily by time it looked like it was folding in on itself. "Don't you want to buy one to brighten your day? Three lovely proteas, a few daisies, some baby's breath. Bunch it all up together, put it in a vase, and it'll take the blues right away, I promise you."

"No thanks," said Faith. "Not today." Her hand strayed back to the vial in the pocket of her coat. She gripped it tight and stroked it with her thumb. Then pulled it out to stare at it again. Hoping.

There was a funeral procession crossing the street up ahead. They were singing: *Amazing grace, how sweet the sound . . .*

Porters in station suits ran up to the van with squeaking trolleys. Ash unlocked the back and together they lifted the grinners out, one by one, packing the body bags onto the trolleys. The grinners all had tickets on this morning's mortuary train. They were on their way to Death City—a huge neighborhood of ash factories, cemeteries, funeral parlors, coroners' offices, and sanatoriums on the Cape Flats. Before the Laughter, the Group Areas Act and gentrification meant the rich moved into the inner city and almost everyone who wasn't lily white and moneyed was booted out, but the Down Days switched things up again. When most of the rich fled or died a lot of people living on the outskirts moved into the city center (including those whose families had previously been forced out by the Group Areas Act). As a result one of the world's most segregated cities finally became a bit more integrated again (call it a silver lining if you will).

Most of the outlying hoods became wastelands. Until some bright star in government got the idea to use these empty areas as burial and quarantine space. And Death City was built. A weird place. Faith had only been there once, and she hoped she wouldn't have to visit again.

Next door to Death City was the seaside suburb of Muizenberg, where a necklace of Art Deco death hotels hugged the shoreline. This was where the more affluent mourners could sleep over, should they want to make a weekend of saying goodbye. With a funeral director on call so you could plan the whole thing from the comfort of your room. Room-service menus for picking out flowers, preachers, urns, hymns, and videography packages for Facebook mourners. (Not really Facebook, of course, what with the firewall and all. The government had come up with their own version. Trying to be cute, they'd called it *Fact*book, but most people still called it Facebook—old habits and all that.)

She was sitting in the van, waiting for Ash, with the pages Sans had let her copy spread out on the steering wheel, one hand glued to her coat pocket. She'd been thinking about those orbs all night, sitting awake, staring at the little glass bottle she'd stolen from the convent until the sun came up, turning it around, examining it from every angle until it felt like both her brain and heart were going to burst. The same went for this morning. Every second of every minute of every hexed hour. She couldn't stop.

She'd taken the pages out of her bag as a last resort. As a way of shutting down her spiraling thoughts.

The first page had been easy. Almost as if the person who wrote it wanted it to be read. Page two started off easy, too. On the top of the second page, she found a line of seemingly random letters: L DP D FKLOG RI IDLWK. She started with the two single-letter words, tried A, I, and O (the only one-letter words in the English language), and after that the rest came easily. A simple Caesar cipher with each letter of the alphabet removed thrice, so that the L became A and so on until you got to *I am a child of faith.*

Than a paragraph break followed by what looked to be a much more complex cipher. A Vigenère, if she had to hazard a guess.

She tapped the pencil against her thigh, wondering about the juxtaposition of the two pieces of code. Maybe the first cipher was some kind of riddle? A clue to the key for the next cipher? She stopped tapping and stuck the pencil underneath her mask, biting into the soft wooden shell.

I am a child of faith. I am a child of faith . . .

The head porter came up to the window and held out the book for her to sign. The singing mourners were passing by behind him now. She was taking the pen from his hand when she saw the back of the boy. And the world stopped spinning.

Everything froze. Nothing moved. Nothing existed. The whole universe was a station she couldn't tune in to. Like she was turning the knob of her consciousness, trying to connect. But all her brain could focus on was the boy.

The porter. She knew he was talking to her. She could see his lips moving but she couldn't hear the words coming out.

The boy.

The boy was walking in the heart of the singing crowd. His gait. His hair, the way he held his head cocked to the left. It was him. It had to be. Had to be . . .

The one who gave her her stripes.

The one who pushed himself into her world without asking, stretching her womb and her heart. Making it too big to bear. Then left her on her own with this monstrous bleeding pulsing thing. A pumping canticle of joy and hurt. Joy and hurt.

But mostly hurt.

Her boy. Her son.

Her everything.

It was him. She was sure of it. Whether he was real or a ghost or a postbox hallucination, she didn't care.

The crowd was entering the station. "Hey!" shouted the porter as she slammed the van door into his stomach, knocking the wind out of him and sending the book flying.

But Faith was already too far away for her to hear him.

The big white ticket hall was a looking glass. Beneath the glossy white floor was an upside-down world where people did upside-down things while thinking upside-down thoughts. But Faith's eyes didn't have time for this universe below. She was concentrating all her thoughts and steps and breaths on reaching the boy in the crowd.

The mourners had already passed through the turnstile. Faith waved her pass at the security guard. She ran along the platform towards the singing throng. Above her head, white fluorescent tube lights shone in a row like arrows to the afterlife.

The mourners in their Sunday best were boarding now, their voices swelling and falling as they sang: "Yea, when this flesh and heart shall fail, and mortal life shall cease, I shall possess, within the veil, a life of joy and peace. The world shall soon dissolve like snow, the sun refuse to shine, but God, who called me here below, shall be forever mine."

"Jacob!" she screamed. "Jacob!" But the singing crowd drowned out the sound.

She was almost there now. A few more steps and she would be able to touch him. Within the folds of the crowd, the boy's feet crossed the yellow line and he climbed onto and into the train. Before the doors encased the singing crowd, he turned around. His brown eyes locked onto hers. But his face was the face of a stranger.

- 68 -

SANS

The busker with the bull ring and the black lines tracing his brown eyes strummed the blues, his fingers weaving a web across the strings like a spider on caffeine. Sans leaned against the cold wall and watched the web grow.

The song stopped, the busker flexed his fingers and picked up a bottle lying next to him on the tar. "Hey, man," said the busker, inching down his mask for a quick swig. "Long time."

They bumped elbows and the busker made a passing jab at the wind—how it was being a real howler today or something like that. Sans couldn't quite catch it, but agreed anyway. The busker put the bottle down and narrowed his eyes. "Enough about the weather. I'm guessing this isn't a social call?"

Sans nodded, stepped closer, sat on the pavement. "You still in the business, Beno?"

"How long's a piece of string, man?" The busker grinned and pushed up to stand. "Just a minute," he said, and he sauntered over to the coal-iron stall, poking his head behind the curtain of dancing shirts to stow his guitar, then beckoned for Sans to follow him.

The doorbell of the Happy Happy Joy Noodle Bar spluttered as they entered. Beno stooped down to soak his hands in the plastic bucket of chlorine at the door. Sans sucked in his breath, hunched over, followed suit. No matter how many times he had to reenact this same ritual, he could never get used to the smell. He unfurled his spine and followed the busker, past the rows of pleather booths and through the swinging door into the kitchen with its clatter and sizzle of pots and pans, the *tut, tut, tut* of chopping knives and the shouts and yelps and background radio drones in a mangle of languages and dialects. Beno led him through this choreographed dance to another door at the back, unlocking it with a key he wore around his neck.

Once inside, he knitted his body through the maze of cardboard stalagmites stacked every which way to a dark mahogany antique desk at the back. He switched on an expensive-looking brass desk lamp and slid into a plush leather chair like some kind of don.

Like Sans, Beno was a self-made man. A kind of modern-day pirate. Back when the Down Days first swept the city into a whirl, Beno cashed in on the chaos by raiding the mansions of fleeing foreigners and selling the loot, mostly paintings and antiques, to overseas collectors. That was before the borders snapped shut and the wall went up. Nowadays he traded in anything hard to come by—if it was difficult to find and you needed it, Beno was your man. The guy had an encyclopedic knowledge of arcane objects and their worth. The busking was a cover and a passion rolled into one. The blues was his baby.

When he got drunk, he'd always swear he sold his soul to play like that. At a crossroads in the dunes somewhere out in the Flats, close to Macassar, when he was a kid. Said the devil had yellow fingers and smoke billowing from his nostrils, and in his hands he carried a big black pipe.

"So how about these protests we've been having?" said Beno. "Do you think there's any truth to it?"

"To what?"

"To the rumors that the meds inside the postboxes are making some people hallucinate."

"Uh. No. I mean . . . have you been seeing anything? Hallucinating, I mean?"

"Nah, man. You?"

"No. 'Course not."

Beno folded his hands in front of his face and tucked both thumbs underneath his chin. Above his head hung a big-ass framed drawing of a hyena. The beast was standing atop an abandoned car in a winding city street crammed with abandoned vehicles, empty of all life except for this scavenging beast who was glaring at the viewer, its eyes piercing the glass of the frame accusingly. As the third act in a triptych by William Kentridge—*The Conservationists Ball*—the drawing was worth a mint, but Beno had grown a liking to it and refused to sell.

"So, what's up, brother? Are you here to buy, sell, or barter?" asked Beno.

"Sell."

"I'm listening."

"I know you have a thing for Laughter objects. Magical objects and rare items that are supposedly Laughter cures?"

"I thought you didn't believe in all that stuff. That you were a skeptic through and through. *I only believe in what I can feel and touch*, wasn't that what you told me once? That you're a man of logic and reason and truth and facts?" The pirate gave an Olympic grin—and for the first time, Sans noticed the symbol tattooed on one of his capped canines, a maze-type thing. Where had he seen that before? "Science. A crock of rubbish, if you ask me, just another colonial belief system, another lie we tell ourselves to sleep at night. But to each his own. I'm all for freedom of religion and all of that."

Sans remembered why he hadn't been here in such a long time. The guy was an idiot. But never mind. He was the idiot he needed right now. "It's a book. I've got sources saying it was written by a seventeeth-century seer, Anna de Koningh. And that it contains a cure."

Beno raised his tattooed eyebrows. "The mythical diary of Anna de Koningh. You must be kidding me. Are you sure? Have you read it?"

"No. It's written in some kind of code. But I have someone on it. Someone who has already deciphered parts of it. She says she thinks she can crack the whole thing. That it's only a matter of time."

"Can I see it?"

He was about to say yes, but his gut told him to hold back. "If I'm right about this thing, it's valuable as fuck. Do you think I'd be stupid enough to carry a thing like that in my backpack?"

"How about a few photos, then? Can I at least have that?"

"All right."

"Let me pass the photos around, line up a few buyers, get a bidding war going, then I'll phone you tomorrow to arrange a viewing, okay?"

FAITH

She met the sin-eater in Woodstock, the city's edgy enclave for designers and artists, where a grungy forgotten factory now housed sexy glass-fronted apartments for moneyed hipsters. A bald doorman was sitting behind a sleek stainless-steel counter.

"We're here to see Pinky," said Fred.

They signed in. The doorman picked up the phone and did his thing. "Tenth floor," he said. "Good luck."

There was a lift, but it didn't make sense to take it, what with all the power cuts, so up and up the stairs they went to the tenth bloody floor, and down a corridor to the thirteenth door. It was open. Fred stepped over the threshold and Faith followed suit.

Pinky was a pixie of a thing, twentysomething, wearing high-top sneakers and a yellow dress streaked with neon lightning bolts. The only sign of her profession was the goatskin bracelet she wore around her wrist and the string of white-and-red beads circling her throat.

Her apartment was an IKEA catalogue, all clean lines and Scandi design. In one corner of the slick screed floor was a worn red Persian carpet. Pinky was sitting on it, cross-legged, the carpet's intricate flowers curling out in cursive rays from underneath her bare brown knees. The cords of white earphones dangled from her ears, one end connected to a skinny laptop. Behind her back was a floor-to-ceiling shelf, stocked to the brim with a curious collection of jars all labeled in black-inked letters.

"Have a seat, please," said the sangoma in a throaty voice that rose and fell like a song. She motioned towards a couch in an adjoining room. "I'll be just a sec. Just finishing up an online consultation."

"This new generation of healers are quite high-tech," said Fred as the pair of them waited on the sleek gray couch. "It's all Factbook and SwipeRight and all that social media hocus-pocus. That's why she lives so high up. The internet is better here. Me, I prefer to kick it old school, thank you very much. Keep things face-to-face. But Pinky is incredible. You'll see. Talk about hearing voices, though—I've got nothing on that girl. The kid's brain is as crowded as they come, with her, her dead mom, her grandmother, and her uncle all vying for space in there and helping with the work. Talk about keeping it in the family. Don't know how she does it, hey. I can't even bear to share a house with my family, never mind a brain."

The sin-eater picked up a glossy tome from the plywood coffee table and thumbed through it, while Pinky murmured to the screen in the next room and Faith studied the print on the wall: a woman was sitting in a red car next to a man in a suit. The man was watching the woman with shady eyes, but the woman just stared straight ahead. The collar of her fur coat was pulled up, the tip of it grazing her pearled ears. Faith was certain she'd seen the print before, but she wasn't sure where.

Fifteen minutes ticked by before Pinky popped her head in through the doorway. "All done," she said. "Good to see you again. Come, sit."

The big man heaved his bulk onto the carpet and Faith plopped down beside him. "How are your knees, Fred?" asked Pinky.

"Much better, thanks, Pinky darling. That stuff you gave me helped a bunch."

"Glad to hear it. So, what brings you here?"

"Ag, Pinky dear, Faith here has a spirit problem. And it seems to be above my current level of expertise. So I thought I'd better call in the big guns."

"I see." Pinky took a yellow candle from the shelf behind her and lit the wick. She clutched a tangle of a dead bush and dried yellow flowers above the dancing flame. Smoke spiraled up towards the ceiling.

"Impepho," said the sin-eater. "Holy incense."

"Right," she said. "First I'll respectfully invite my ancestors and other spirit mediums into the room. Then I'll introduce them to you. Okay?" Faith nodded.

The syllables rolled from Pinky's songbird tongue as she held out her muthi bag. "Please blow," she told Faith.

Faith blew. Pinky tipped the bag. Bones and stones and shells and dice and dominoes scattered on the mat. Her fingers sifted through them. She looked up. There was a weird look on her face. Like she was in pain or something. Then her face went blank.

Faith was so focused on the scattered bones, and on Pinky herself, that she almost missed it at first, but something was moving on the wall, right behind the sangoma's back. Her shadow. While Pinky herself was sitting rock still, almost catatonic, her shadow was doing something else. Was Faith imagining it—was it a trick of the light—or was the black shape against the wall growing, stretching, spreading out, transforming, into four distinct humanoid shadows that danced on the wall, bucking and swaying and bowing silently to the rhythm of their own silent beat, before slowly shrinking back into one, much smaller, singular shape again? Faith shivered.

"The boy," said Pinky, finally. "The ghost. He's just a manifestation. Nothing but cold, hard grief. But you know that."

"But the girl," said Faith. "She's so sure her brother's ghost is real. She's not going to believe me when I tell her that."

"No. Not the baby. The other one. The boy."

It was like she was hearing a song, but her brain couldn't make out the lyrics. Didn't want to. *No. Not the baby. The other one. The boy.*

"You know what I mean," continued Pinky. "You've been hiding from the hurt for too long. It's consuming you. You should let him go before it's too late. Before it kills you. Or worse."

"I don't think I can," said Faith, her face a mask.

"Huh?" said Fred. "The baby's not real. Case closed. So why the drama? The Nile-long face? All this talk about killing? Am I missing something here?"

"No," said Pinky, still looking at Faith. "The baby is real. Or at least I think so."

"Huh?"

"Is he at the convent?"

"I think so."

"Is there a way to help him?" asked Faith.

"The baby?" asked Fred.

"Yes."

"I'm asking my ancestors, but I'm not getting a clear answer. They say you will find him if you let him go."

"Well, that's really useful. Thanks a lot."

"I know you're angry. And I might not have all the answers for you. I can only tell you what my ancestors are telling me. And they're telling me that you need to hand over that bottle in your pocket before it consumes you."

"What bottle?"

"The one in your pocket you've been stroking this whole time that we've been sitting here talking. The one that you took from the convent while Fred here was feeling up the cross-eyed caretaker."

Her heart was banging against her ribs, rearing to run. Her throat was crammed with words she couldn't get out. Mount Vesuvius was stirring again. Jacob, she'd seen him at the train station—she wasn't imagining things! If ghosts were real, if Tomorrow's brother really was dead and at the convent and there was a way to find his ghost, then why not her Jacob? Why couldn't she get him back, too? Why did she see his face? The orb? No, no, no.

No.

She just couldn't bear to believe what she was hearing. Just couldn't even start to try to consider it. The sangoma had to be lying to her. People lied all the time, right? For all sorts of reasons. People spread all sorts of alternative facts . . . There had, *there just had to be*, a way to get Jacob back. "This is . . . this is all bullshit," she screamed at them both. "This whole damn thing is bullshit. You! Fat man! This is all your fault. I can't believe you talked me into coming here! Sangomas. Real ghosts, fake ghosts! What a crock of shit! I'm getting out of here. I've had enough. Enough! I'm letting myself out!"

The sin-eater opened his mouth as if to say something. Then he seemed to catch himself.

Faith jumped up. Running to the door, her hip hit a side table, and a white vase printed with pale blue flowers crashed, spitting out shards onto the cement floor.

"I guess it's true what they're saying about those postboxes making folks crazy," she heard the sin-eater tell the sangoma before she fled.

SUNDAY

70

THE DAILY TRUTH

THE MAYORS OF CRAZY TOWN

By Lawyer Tshabalala

I don't know about you guys, but it seems to me the whole bleddie city is going crazy. This is crazy town, folks, and we are all its mayors. The way things are going, we're all going to be walking around wearing tinfoil hats soon, I tell you.

Starting with the postbox riots, Sick City was plunged into chaos yesterday afternoon when hundreds took to the streets to protest what they believe is the government's plot to drive us mad (either intentionally or because of corner-cutting, depending on who you ask) via the postbox meds.

While many are blaming the government-mandated postbox meds for the spate of spirit sightings or hallucinatory visions sweeping the city, some have other ideas.

Laughter denialists stand fast that this is just another example of mass hysteria or *folie à plusieurs* (that's "madness of many" in French, folks).

Others are saying it's a plot by the government or the West or some other nebulous force to gaslight us. To those of you not familiar with the term, gaslighting, according to the Merriam-Webster dictionary, is: "to attempt to make (someone) believe that he or she is going insane (as by subjecting that person to a series of experiences that have no rational explanation)."

Sick City sin-eater Fred Mostert says the spate of spooks is a sign that strange times are afoot. That the Down Days have upset the balance of things. "The lines between the living and the dead seem to be thinning. And the dead are circling the drains like rats abandoning a sinking ship. Or maybe the living are the rats? Anyway, I digress—the result is that the city is becoming a liminal, in-between place, where normal rules of reality don't apply anymore." Mostert believes things are only going to get worse, and that the living and the dead will just have to learn to live together to make things work.

Some would call this the beginning of the apocalypse, but Mostert is a fairly pragmatic man for a sin-eating ghostbuster, who, in contrast to his comments to the *Truth* earlier this week, now says he doesn't really believe in "all that apocalyptic hoodoo any more than I believe in vegans or the tooth fairy."

John Pistorius, spokesperson for the Church of the Four Horsemen, offered a different slant: "It's a sign of the apocalypse. It says so right there in the book. Isaiah 26, verses 19–20: 'Your dead shall live; their bodies shall rise. You who dwell in the dust, awake and sing for joy! For your dew is a dew of light, and the earth will give birth to the dead. Come, my people, enter your chambers, and shut your doors behind you; hide yourselves for a little while until the fury has passed by.'"

Let's hope the postbox protesters are right, folks, otherwise we might soon have dead folks selling us insurance, teaching our kids interdimensional post-terrestrial geography, and asking for equal rights and seats in parliament. Now wouldn't that be a gemors?

71

FAITH

Faith stood in the hallway, locking her front door. Her phone felt heavy in her pocket. Its blinking screen was weighing her down. All those messages. From Ash, asking where she was, why she didn't pick him up for work this morning. From Tomorrow, wanting to know why she wasn't hearing anything from her about the case.

Faith left the blinking phone there to marinate. She'd get to it eventually. But not right now. She was having a sick day. A break day. A think day. The messages would have to wait.

Her hand brushed against her pocket. There was another thing in there, weighing her down. She took the vial out, rubbed the glass with her thumb for the millionth time, tried to concentrate, tried to make it glow. Hoping to see Jacob's face again. Nothing happened. So she stowed it back in her pocket and turned around. Saw Ateri and Jamis floating above the Porsches, probably getting back from the hyena's morning walk.

"Hi, Faith. Guess what?"

"What?"

"I got the job! That freelance job I told you about. I'm starting today. Looking forward to it, actually. Will be nice to get some fresh air for a change. And I think Jamis will enjoy all the space to roam. Might as well take him off the chain, let him stretch his legs properly for once. He's generally more of a city mutt. Prefers the feel of tar under his paws. But I think a change of scenery could do us both some good. Things have been mad around here of late."

"That's great, Ateri. I'm happy for you."

"Thanks. Hey, Faith."

"Yup?"

"You got any sunscreen on you I could borrow, perhaps?"

72

SANS

Purgatory. This was purgatory. Pacing up and down on a windy roof. Holding out his cell like a dowsing rod. Waiting, hoping, half praying for a signal. With not a single damn bar in sight. (Talking about bars, he needed a drink.)

The roof was deserted. But it wasn't empty. Almost every available space was lined with plastic crates planted with vegetables. In one corner stood two rabbit coops and a chicken coop. Sans looked at the puffs of rabbit fluff huddled against each other in their coops. His stomach was growling. He hadn't had breakfast yet. He had some rabbit meat in the fridge at home that he could fry up in the pan when he got back, but nothing much else. He wasn't a fan of rabbit meat at the best of times—too many tiny bones—but he was flat-out broke and beggars couldn't be choosers.

Two hours before the morning signal rush. The sun had barely reared its head and the mountain was undercover, going full vigilante in a smoking gray cape. The urban farming collective who tended the animals and crops were still fast asleep. So, it was just him, a down-and-out one-man show without a cent in his pocket. Just the clothes on his back, his phone, a dusty old book, an urge, and a hope. The urge? The same damn urge he always got when he stood on rooftops, clifftops, balconies, bridges (and on airplanes, too, back when). That urge, almost uncontrollable, to jump. Not a suicidal urge. (Sans didn't

have a suicidal bone in his body.) This was something else. More like
he was drawn to the edge like a moth to a lightbulb. Drawn to fly. The
French had a phrase for it—this instinctive urge to jump from high
places. *L'appel du vide. The call of the void.*

He was standing on the edge. Hearing the call. His toes against
the low parapet wall. Looking out. At the ant colony below. When he
heard something behind him. A rustle. A click.

Not again, he thought. *Not again. Damn visions. Damn unicorn.
Damn crazy fucked-up fever bullshit.* He was about to turn. To face her.
To tell her and her holy hair to fuck off once and for all. When he felt
a hand on his shoulder. Gripping, pulling, tearing at him. Shoving him
to the ground.

A struggle. His back kissed concrete and his face came face-to-face
with another face. So close he couldn't make out its features, just cratered
cheeks, stubble, and teeth. Then the head pushed back and the face came
into focus. The blue-bag man. Pushing him down onto the cement. His
eyes were throwing knives, but his breath smelt like strawberries.

"What do you want?"

"The money. I'm here for the money," Blue Bag said. "My bosses.
You're not answering their calls. They're tired of waiting. It's time to
pay up."

"I don't have it. I lost it."

"Ever wondered what it would feel like to fly?" said Blue Bag, gripping his throat.

Not anymore, thought Sans. But he kept his mouth shut.

Blue grabbed him by the collar. Lifted him up, like he was nothing.
"You see all those horsebacked Veeps down there? Thanks to yesterday's
postbox protests, the city is swarming with them this morning. They're
coming out of the woodwork like cockroaches on a sinking ship. Which
isn't so great for you, is it? See, I've been watching you, ponyjacker. Since
Tuesday. Saw you sweating up a storm. Saw that girl with the gumboots
knock on your door. She wasn't knocking on package day, so I'm guessing it's not the latest Netflix show she had in that envelope she gave you.
Saw your pathetic postbox panic attack later that same day. So it wasn't
that difficult to put two and two together. Hand it over."

"Hand what over?"

"Don't play coy with me. This isn't a blind date. Your wallet."

Sans pulled his wallet from his pocket, handed it to Blue, who opened it up. Took out his fake medpass. "I'm pretty sure if I take this card down to those two guys below, ask them to have a look—I mean really look—they're not going to be too impressed. Should we do it? Go down? Have a little chat with them? What do you say? If you don't feel like taking the stairs, we can take the short way down."

"I don't have the money. I've told you."

"What a pity." Sans felt his feet leave concrete again.

"Wait. I have something else. Five minutes. Give me five minutes to explain."

The grip against his Adam's apple slackened. "Okay. Five minutes. But if I don't like what you tell me—" Blue's arms let go of Sans's shirt. Then he lifted them up to form a cross. He was swinging them around now like a kid playing fighter jets. "It's liftoff."

73

FAITH

She was falling. No. Wait. She was walking. No plan. No aim. No inkling. She needed to think. And she did her best thinking on her feet. So she let them carry her along. Braiding them through the tide of bodies and breaths, getting lost in the crowd. The street was covered in trash from yesterday's protests. Bins were lying on their sides, their contents strewn everywhere. As she walked, she passed quite a few boarded-up shop windows and the smoking remains of at least two petrol-bombed postboxes. She noticed there weren't a lot of stalls trading this morning, either; the traders were probably worried about all the action.

Down the street she spotted one lone ironing stall. The vendor was filling his iron with coals. He lifted his hand to her as she passed. She'd helped him with a case once—someone kept breaking into his chicken coop at night. She'd caught the kid and in return he now ironed her clothes for free each week.

Next to him a busker was crooning the blues on his beat-up guitar. The busker recrossed his beaded ankles and winked at her, rippling the rail-track line of tattoos that traced the edges of his eyes like a superhero mask. She could do with a good caped crusader right now. She could do with a good saving. Not a knight, though. No shining armor, thanks. And no horses, either—they made her think of virus patrollers.

What's wrong with you, Faith? she chided herself. Not only was she hanging out with schizophrenic ghostbusters and hipster sangomas, but she was seeing things, crazy things, unbearable things, that according to said ghostbuster and sangoma weren't real. Even though it felt real. Unbearably real. And to make matters worse, now she was making lame jokes about superheroes? *No. No more. Pull yourself together. Get a handle on things.*

She stroked the little vial in her pocket with her thumb. Thing was, it all started with the case, didn't it? This case. It was driving her crazy. It was too close to home. Too close to Then. It was breaking down her walls. Time to brick them up again. Time to see the girl.

She arrived at the pink row house. Pressed her knuckles against the rotten door. The groove was still there. But she didn't wonder about it anymore. She didn't care. Her own skinny groove had worn away. Time for her had folded back in on itself. She didn't know anymore where Now began and Then ended. And whether that even mattered much.

Tomorrow opened the door. "Where have you been? I've been calling you, texting you."

"Yes. I'm sorry. I've been busy."

"With what? Did you find Elliot?"

"I'm sorry, Tomorrow. That's what I've came to tell you. I can't work on your case anymore."

The girl looked like she was about to throw up. "What do you mean? Why not?"

"I just can't."

"You still think I made the whole thing up, don't you? What about the convent? The nun? You said she was kidnapping kids. You said you were following a lead."

"I was."

A woman was approaching the gate. Her body bent, her jowls elastic, her head shaking slightly as she walked. "Tomorrow! How are you, my angel?"

"Good, auntie. I'm great. Do you need something?"

"A cup of milk, man. Please."

"Sure. Give me a minute." Tomorrow turned, disappearing behind the rotten door. The woman stayed put. One veined arm leaning against the gate.

"Nice weather," said Faith as the old woman speared her eyes with hers.

"I know who you are. I've seen you," said the woman.

"I'm sorry?"

"You're the one who comes for us. When it's our time to go, you come to take us to the other side. But not me, you hear? Not me. I'm not going, no sirree. So, don't come knocking on my door when the times comes, 'cause I won't go, okay?"

Tomorrow appeared at the door holding a jam jar filled with milk. "Here you go, auntie."

"Thanks, my angel. You take care now." The old woman placed the jar inside the cloth bag tied to her crutch, then turned to face Faith again. "And you. Don't you even think about it, Grim," she said, wagging one bony, liver-specked finger. "When it's time, my Alfie has promised to burn me up on the braai and scatter my ashes beneath the floorboards. There's no way you Grims are taking me back to the Flats. I'm never going back there, you hear me? Never. Over my dead body." Then she hobbled across the road.

Tomorrow sat on the candy-pink steps. Faith followed suit.

"I'm sorry. The whole thing is crazy. You know it is. Deep down. I mean, ghost trafficking?"

"You don't believe me."

"It's not that. You've seen what they're saying in the paper, on the radio—it's the postboxes making us all crazy. There are no such things as ghosts. Only grief." A moth was crawling over the step. For a moment, its soft gray body quivered and shook, as if someone had just walked over its tiny moth-sized grave. Then it righted itself and, as if nothing had happened, continued on.

"You don't really believe that, do you?"

"No. Maybe not. But this case, it's eating me up. I'm not the right person to help you right now—help anyone—I've got my own ghosts to deal with. If it helps at all, I went to this sangoma whose ancestors seem to say that Elliot's ghost is at the hair cult. I don't know if it's true or if she was conning me, but if you want to go that route, I can give you the number of a guy, a ghostbuster, who knows about the case and might be able to help. But I think . . . I mean, whichever way you cut it, Elliot's already dead, right? And you're not. You're still ticking. Grief . . . it holds you back, Tomorrow. Even if he's real and not just something your head made up to get a handle on things, even if you find him—he's going to hold you back. Don't do that to yourself. Don't choose that road. 'Cause you're not going to like what you find at the end of it. Trust me, I know."

The moth was playing dead now. The girl studied the tiny gray beast for a moment, then said: "Thanks for the fancy speech." Just that.

There was a pebble stuck inside Faith's sneaker and she was fishing it out with her car keys, so her back was bent beneath the wheel when she heard a knock on the window. Tomorrow. Her face flat. All the emotion she'd seen there, minutes earlier, smoothed out.

"Ask you a favor?"

"I guess."

"Can I get a lift to the market? I'm out of kerosene."

"Yes. Hop in."

"Thanks. You should check your back tire, though. I'm no expert but it looks kind of flat."

"Dammit. Okay. Be right back." She checked the left side first—the side facing Tomorrow's house. But the tire seemed fine. "I don't see anything," she called out to the girl, who had already climbed into the passenger side. "Other side," the girl called back.

She walked around, checked that side, too—nothing.

"Looks good to me," she said when she got back into the van.

"My mistake, sorry. I told you I'm no expert. It just looked weird, is all."

"No problem." Faith started the engine and they drove on without talking. The quiet unnerved her. She'd never been good with uncomfortable silences. Especially not this one. There was too much unsaid between them and it was digging a chasm between their seats. Faith was teetering on the edge of it, in danger of tipping in. A person could get lost in chasms like these. Lose your mind, even.

"So, is Tomorrow your real name?"

"What's it to you?"

"Just making conversation."

"It's not. It's a nickname. I mean, who goes by their real name these days? It's Persephone, before you ask. Persephone Pretorius. Daughter of Zeus, queen of the underworld and all that. My parents weren't really into all that Greek stuff, they just thought it sounded cool or something. Anyway, can we just drive, please? I don't feel like talking."

So Faith put the radio on and tuned the channel to Cape Chat. The DJ was talking about all the postboxes that had been blown up. That the whole city was going up in smoke. All these people started calling in, cashing in their two cents: "What's up with this Lawyer guy and his gossip rag stirring up these rumors, all this trouble?" one caller was saying. "Why can't he just keep his mouth shut and let us get on with our lives? This isn't a TV show. It's real life. Things just happen. There's no grand conspiracy under every bliksemse rock and there's no point in thinking like that if you want to survive. Thanks to him we've now got hooligans running around burning down the whole bleddie city. And to what end, I say? To what end?"

Faith reached for the radio, switched it off, and focused on the road instead. Next to her, Persephone Pretorius, the queen of the underworld, crossed her arms and twisted her head to lean against the rolled-up window.

74

SANS

The two men were walking arm in arm. Just two lovers enjoying a morning stroll through this sick, sick city, nothing to see here, folks.

But what if someone looked closer? Would they notice the stiff gait of the man on the left, the one with the limp, and the way he kept clenching his fists? Or the revolver-shaped bulge where the second man had his hand tucked underneath the first man's jacket?

A convoy of trees were waving their arms in the air like they just didn't care on either side of the skinny lane through which the two walked—a line of ancient sentries sent as seeds on ships when the city was still virginal, and left here to shoot up into these tall tales. Leftovers from history, a tunnel to funnel the lonely on their way to everywhere.

Up ahead of our pseudo-lovers a protest was brewing. The crowd was a wave, thick and full and angry. Sans skimmed the placards floating above the tsunami roaring their way. "No more going postal." "My body, my choice." "Stop the shots." "No more lies!" "Postboxes are toxic!" "Say no to medical tyranny!" "Stop driving us mad!" "Citizens should call the shots." He was biding his time, readying himself to make a run for it into the swell. But Blue must have been brighter than he looked.

"Don't even think about it," he said, tightening the grip on Sans's arm. "This isn't some B-grade Hollywood thriller. I have a real gun pointed at your back with real bullets in it."

The man adjusted the shoulder strap of the sports bag, which now held the book, gripped Sans's arm tighter, and ruddered him to the outer edges of the crowd. "So, this book. I'm not buying it. You got any way to prove it's the real deal? That the cure part is not some story? Some bullshit fairy tale?"

"Not exactly, but . . ."

"But what?"

"I looked it up online."

"And?"

"There's a website. On the deep web. A kind of online version of *The Truth*. Anyway, there's this whole section about supposed cures. The book is one of them."

"That doesn't prove a thing."

"Yes. But there's a lot of people in this city who buy into it, who treat the *Truth* like it's fact. And many of these same people would spend a mad amount of cash to get their hands on that book."

As the protest washed over them, Blue increased his grip on Sans, digging the gun deeper into the small of his back, and for a few minutes, things got so loud Blue's voice was drowned out completely. The roar was everything. It was all there was. The roar was the word. And the word was *truth*. Then the flow ebbed and the roar subsided and the world became quiet again. And all that was left was the trees and the road and one man plugging a gun into another man's back like a docked cable trying to charge.

"This whole thing better not be some kind of escape ploy, son," said Blue, quickening his pace.

"It's not."

"For your sake, I hope that's the truth."

They reached Blue's car, a rusted, busted, yellow Volkswagen Golf. Blue ordered Sans to get in, got in himself, and then tossed the backpack onto the backseat. Then he stuck the key into the ignition and flicked his wrist. The engine spluttered, spluttered, groaned.

Sans shifted in his seat, turned his head to eye the backpack. If he stuck his arm behind him he could just about reach the bag. He thought about grabbing it and making a lunge for it before the car picked up too much speed, then decided against it. Better to wait it out for now. Wait for Blue to relax his guard, then jump out at a stop sign, grab the backpack, make a run for it. So he bided his time, kept his eye on the road.

Blue cricked his neck, took his mask off, tossing it onto the backseat.

"Say," said Sans. "Aren't you afraid I'm going to infect you? I mean, you know about the fake medpass. It doesn't faze you one bit?"

"No."

"Why not?"

"Don't believe in it."

"Believe in what?"

"The Laughter, of course. The whole thing is just a big old population control experiment by Western imperialists who are lining the pockets of our government to turn a blind eye."

"That's crazy. Don't you see what's happening all around you? What about the deaths? The bodies? How do you explain those away? Wait, let me guess: the postboxes. You're one of those sickos who think the postboxes are the cause of the whole damn epidemic?"

"Don't act like you don't believe it. The evidence is all there, son. You did the right thing getting that fake pass. It might extend your life a bit. That is, if I don't kill you first," said Blue, tapping his gun against the steering wheel.

Sans kept his mouth shut. Watched the road. All along the pavement trash cans had been upturned, all sorts of crap littering the road, some of the shop windows were smashed—the protesters had already been this way today.

Time had spun a cracked web across the windshield, fracturing the scene outside into a million splintered pieces. Maybe it was the adrenaline playing tricks with his brain, but it seemed like the cracked glass was a kaleidoscope reflecting an endless variety of patterns and actualities. Hope. It gave him hope.

He was studying the cracked windshield like it was some kind of oracle, like the glass could see his future, tell him tales, when something moved in the corner of his vision. A white flag was blowing across the black tar, as if the road itself was surrendering to the yellow Golf. The blue of the sky made the white of the flag appear even whiter. Blindingly white.

No. Hold on.

Not a flag.

A person, a woman, running across the tar—red hair (bad dye job), bare legs, white billowing dress. Two Veeps on horseback charging after.

The flag turned her neck back, her red hair whipped across her face. The horses were almost on top of her now. On top of them. Blue slammed on the brakes. The car spun and spun and screeched, narrowly missing one of the horses as it came to a stop with a jolt and a shudder. Blue's head hit the steering wheel with a thud. The horse reared upwards, shucking its rider off onto the car, his helmet plowing through the windshield. Sans pushed his arm back; he could feel the bag on the seat behind him. He pulled it towards him. Then his fingers found the door handle.

Later, he would lie awake, wondering about the girl in the white dress. What her story was. But at that precise moment he was only thinking one thing. One single word was blasting across his brain in red neon strobing lights. *Run.*

75

FAITH

After dropping Tomorrow at the market, she sat in the van, just watching the world go by. There was another protest marching past. But this crowd was angrier, more alive. Placards and fists were bobbing up and down like pistons in a big breathing, steaming machine—some kind of organic automaton of rage. For a second, she thought she caught a glimpse of Sans, limping along through the pulsating mass.

She waited for the protesters to pass, got out of the car, and stepped through the gate that led into the Company's Garden. Maybe it was the time of day, or maybe it was the protests that had scared everyone off, but the grand old garden was strangely quiet. Near the old pear tree, a smattering of geese were pecking for worms. She bent down beside them and sat on the soft grass. Her thoughts lingered back to Tomorrow. The wall. She'd felt like a real jerk, leaving the girl in the lurch like that, but sometimes you had to look after yourself, too. She pulled her hand out of her pocket, looked at the little glass bottle nestled in her palm, all covered in dirty, sweaty thumbprints. The bottle would have to go. She would have to let it go. But not now. Not yet. She had other things to do right now. Other things like . . .

She took the notebook out of her bag to take a crack at the code again. She was sure about the first line: *I am a child of faith.* But the rest was still gibberish:

WCBOEPOWRPEGDLGGVGDIRRMQVIRDIPDSWYYGXX
FOKPOEROWRYJAYRDSHCXGCISSWEWXSRURMGQ
CLYRSOLYAKEGFKFMEXWYYCXSSQLRYILDVSCXWYY
USXFGLYDMZOPGOZCDSZOQWQVCKXCCXYXHKYWR
SQNYVRKRRVMDOWUYVIGLYDJMVPMGWFOVCYR
RRIQOTYQIQSWKIVCMSPNXMISSOZCBCRRMLQQW
FMQSSLCLYFIPOZCKPCNXMWIYLSSDXFOPYEKFDIPS
LMZIRRMQNMYBCUSPJLIQEJDSGGORRDSCHTJKM
LDSWYYKIZGCMMXWMXXFSWNYMLDELNAFKXGLI
JSITOXFOCAYYJNQCKRDYVWYYPGSPVHRYQWQVCKX
POKPOXWYYKEWRERBOVQDELNXFKXGMELXSRKX
ROWRPSPOZCBCQSREVIDKGRGVGDXCXHMGRFO
VCKWWYYWYYPCIJPAGVPMPGMEVQOYLNIPCXYXHR
RIMZEOEILKXSBIMPELIZGCMMXELNXFKXGKQYDX
FOQCBGWYJCKGFCMERXYXHAKRMXPWRETOJYSXF
DLYDAFKXGCICSWPSKFDFSDMRBYQDXFKXGDAGVP
FOPNNSUSXFSXURERISSGMJVYQOMRKWWYYRRMLU
FCCXZEXNBEWLIDYVCISSNIASTFOVRRIPOWRISSRE
TOXMDEIOEKYQCXXRYLCVTWYYPCIJPXFOCMEREVE
BITCBWCZLMXIGCCMEVYXGFYVWYYPGEWLEAUC
MERCOHFOVFOPNSRERIPGMJVLCVTWYYRYVCWIKLIP
GLMISSBIYVPWKVCLCRRIRSQCISSBIYNXFSWQRIUS
PJRETOEJBIYNCMZILOHNKRBYVYCFMHWMZPCKW
CPSPKPJYYPCEIOWKKOCREQDIUSXFKPJWCFOEPDELX
EBOOMXMLQL

The line at the top of the page was the key to the rest of the text. She could feel it. But it didn't work if you used it as is. It had to be some kind of riddle. *I am a child of faith.*

She stuck the sharp end of her pencil into the soft grass where it rested like a flag, stretched her legs out, and rolled her neck. *Think, Faith, think . . .*

A young mother walked past, pushing her baby in a yellow pram, singing while she walked. "Utata uJacob, Utata uJacob, Usalele, Usalele . . ."

Father Jacob, Father Jacob . . . She used to sing like that to Jacob when he was little. It was the only way she could get him to go to sleep.

I am a child of faith. I am a child of Faith.

Jacob. A silly idea, but it niggled, and it grew. Until it was all she could think about. It wouldn't work. Of course it wouldn't. She was just projecting again. Her wall was crumbling, making it hard for her to think straight. But she wasn't ready to text Ash and apologize for pulling a disappearing act, wasn't ready to step back into real life. Wasn't ready to let go. She gripped the little glass bottle tighter. She'd stay here a little longer. On this patch of quiet, soft earth. This little oasis in the eye of her storm. *Jacob.* She'd try the cipher key. She'd try it first. Then, maybe after that, she'd try to let go.

Time ticked on, while her shadow shortened. And under the nib of her pencil, the cipher transformed—first into letters, then into words. Until she had a whole page of sentences, strung along like a road. A map into someone else's brain. But even though the words were written in English, the map didn't make any sense:

My dearest Faith,

I write this letter to you in the greatest of confidence. You may not know me, but I know much about you. Enough to entrust you with what I believe to be my greatest and most important life's work. What follows here on these pages is my record to you—everything my visions have revealed to me about the Laughter. I hope this diary will be sufficient to explain to you my visions on this point and what I believe they could mean for your world. To my great regret, you must understand that I cannot attest for every single fact written down here (as you yourself will of course understand the opaque nature of any vision, and that I am at the mercy of each sight and can only have faith that what I see is right)—but I trust that it will help.

Do with it what you will, use it as you think best. But pray, before you decipher the rest, you have to take a moment to help yourself. The young lady, Persephone, is your anchor, your way back. You need her. Helping her will help you to remember who you really are.

By the time you read this, she will have already opened Pandora's box. So please, for all our sakes, make haste.

With all my heart,
Anna de Koningh

Anna de Koningh. *The* Anna de Koningh. Faith had been searching for this book off and on for years. It was the Holy Grail of puzzle books. And she wasn't only holding a passage from it in her hands, but it was addressed to her. How could this be?

Back in the van, she stowed the vial under the seat. The words in the letter coiled through her mind in a loop. The Laughter. A cure? Tomorrow. And Pandora's box? Was the whole thing some kind of elaborate setup?

She was putting the keys in the ignition when she noticed the glove compartment. The unclipped latch. She reached over and lifted the flap.

The gun.

The little rat had stolen her gun.

She should have known something was up when the kid had come begging for a lift as if nothing had happened between them, then asked her to check the tires, all sweet. It was all so obvious, looking back.

But why? Why did she steal it? To sell? No. The kid wasn't the type to commit suicide, either, at least not with a gun. That left only the convent. The nun.

76

MAJOR

The world was going tits-up crazy and Major needed a drink. Someone had sent one of the sisters video footage of the protests happening in Roeland Street. So many people. Who knew the city even had that many living, breathing souls left? Everyone and their mother seemed to be on the streets. The crowds were going crazy. Breaking windows, throwing things, burning tires. *Laughing.*

One of the mobs was passing the convent now. Major had seen more than his fair share of protests in his day, but nothing like this. The crowd wasn't shouting and chanting slogans. They weren't waving placards about. They were cracking up. Laughing hysterically. Every single one of them. What the hell? Had the whole damn city caught the bug? Some of the sisters were freaking out. Talking about the apocalypse. If Major was religious at all, even just an ounce, he'd agree with them. He'd say the mob was possessed.

Some of the cackling protesters were throwing petrol bombs. A flaming petrol comet landed in the garden, setting fire to the grass. One of the younger, less bright sisters had tried pouring water over it, which naturally made the blaze worse. Major had shouted at them all to go inside; wait this thing out in the convent's dining hall. He was putting the fire out with a blanket when he saw the girl at the gate. She was an adorable little runt, about the age of his niece, with freckles and puppy eyes.

"Please, oom," said the tyke with tears in her puppy eyes. "Please help. It's really scary out here. Can I come in, just for a while, until things quiet down?"

Now, Major wasn't the bleeding-heart type. Not even close. But what kind of monster would he be if he left the tyke outside? It was the end times out there. Besides, Sans's little tirade about karma on Friday had touched a nerve or two. So, after taking her temperature to make sure she wasn't about to go all giggly on him, he let the kid in.

He was picking up the charred blanket from the grass, rolling it up, his back to her, when she pulled it out. It was dark and hard to see properly, but he could swear it was a gun. Yes. My God. The little rat was holding a gun to his chest. And not a toy one, either. No, he was pretty sure it was the real deal. He'd been a bit of a skollie in his day; he knew a thing or two about guns.

"The matron," said the little tyke holding the gun. "Take me to the matron."

"Huh?" said Major. Not smooth, sure, but what the hell, the kid had caught him off guard.

"The head nun."

"Or what? You won't shoot me, kid. You don't have the balls."

"You'd bet your life on that?" It was her eyes that did it. That look. It spooked him even more than the cackling crowd outside. Cold. Hard. Not an ounce of hesitation in sight. The tyke would pull that trigger, wouldn't even blink. He was sure of it.

So he walked her to Mother's office. What else could he do?

- 77 -

SANS

He was pulling at the door handle, his fingers numb and useless with shock. It was stuck. The fucking door was stuck. He could hear Blue groaning in the seat beside him. But he didn't look back. Just focused all his energy on the handle; put his shoulder into it. The door flew open with a start, catching him off guard, and his body rolled out of the car and onto the tar, one arm pulling the blue backpack behind him. His shoulder ached from the impact but he brushed the pain aside. Run. He had to run. Which way? Right—into Oranjezicht. Suburbia offered better camouflage than the open streets. Lots of gardens and trees and walls to hide behind.

He was pulling himself up from the tar when he felt something brush his arm. Soft, gentle. Like the feel of perfect Pantene hair on skin. He jolted. *Not now, Sans, not now. Don't start hallucinating now. You have to run, for fuck's sake.* He brushed the vision away with his head, with his hands. But when he touched the spot on his arms that the vision had brushed, his fingers caught hold of something real, something firm. And whatever it was, it was grabbing him right back. At first he thought it was Blue, but thank fuck, it wasn't. It was *her*.

"Sans," his unicorn said, in that sweet, perfect voice. "Sans." He could see her now. Her face framed with indigo black.

"No."

"I can help you," she said again. "Please. Listen."

He stuck his fingers in his ears like a two-year-old. He didn't have time for this. He had to go. He had to run.

"Sans. Just listen. You've got to listen."

"No. *You* listen. I don't know what the hell you are—whether I'm sick and hallucinating or crazy or you're some long-dead psychic slave with a sick sense of humor—but I'm tired of all this hocus-pocus. My life has been one big crazy crapshoot since you came along. And I'm done with it. I'm out."

"I can help you," his unicorn said again. "Follow me."

"Why should I trust you?" He was pulling the bag onto his back when he saw the driver's-side door open. Someone climbed out. Blue's forehead was a river of red. *Fuck.*

"Why not?" said his unicorn. *Why not.* "There is a price, though."

"There always is."

"Hold on to my hair," she said. "Now!" What more did he have to lose? He grabbed hold of a clump of inky strands, and it moved and writhed like a hundred skinny snakes and began to coil around his fist. Then his unicorn's face and body melted into a soft mist, until all that was left was a trail of moving, floating, dipping, diving hair, tugging at his wrist like some kind of possessed GPS.

He followed his vision. One hand leashed to her ropy indigo hair, deeper and deeper into the depths of suburbia. Every now and again he'd glance back to see Blue still following. His lungs were on fire. His leg, too. He didn't know how long he could keep going like this.

There was a white wall to his left. Low, no electric fence in sight, with a garden the size of fucking Kirstenbosch. All cut grass and fancy flowers. The hair was trailing over the wall now, tugging him to follow. It seemed like a bad idea. What if the rich yuppie fucks who owned the place still lived there, what if they hadn't flown the coop?

But Blue was slowly gaining on him, his blasted bum leg hurt like a mother, and he didn't have any better ideas.

So he jumped. Followed the strands over the wall.

On the other side, his feet planted into the wet grass—he could see trees, a wooden guard house to the left, and to the right, an empty swimming pool. Then he heard something snarl. And a giant thing of a dog appeared out of nowhere like magic, so out of left field that he almost slammed into it. Wait, not a dog. Fuck. The hyena. From the comedy club. And his handler. There was a gun slung over the man's shoulder. The beast at his legs was whooping and growling, tugging at its chain, baring its fangs, while the tall man held it back.

"You're Faith's friend," said Sans, blowing out panicked air in relief. "We met the other night."

The hyena was still growling. The tall man patted it on the head like a puppy. "Down, boy," he said. And the beast backed off. "You're not supposed to be here. This is private property. You're lucky my boss isn't here. He'd probably want me to shoot you."

Sans looked from the man to the beast to the gun, and back to the gun. "There's a man back there. He's going to kill me. Please."

The hyena man looked. Saw Blue Bag man approaching down the street, on the other side of the wall. His face tightened; he seemed to be considering what to do. Then he curled his lips inwards to meet his teeth, and reached for his gun. "Run," he said. "There's a gate at the back. That way. Go. I'll hold him off."

So Sans did. He ran. Kept running. At some point he thought he heard screaming. And gunshots. But he didn't stop. Not yet. When he got to Buitenkant Street, he sank to his knees, panting. The rope of magical unicorn hair that had wound itself around his fist was tugging him hard, but Sans didn't budge.

"You've got to keep going," he heard her voice at the back of his mind.

"Why? He's not following me anymore. Hasn't been for a while now."

"You need to go on. I told you before. There's a price."

"Listen here, whoever you are. I've been running forever. I need to rest. My leg's killing me. It's busted, or haven't you noticed yet? And before you ask—skiing accident."

"It's Anna. My name's Anna. And I told you there would be a price."

"Yes. How could I forget? So say I don't pay it? This price of yours . . ."

The voice in his mind seemed to be sighing. "You heard what the librarian said. This book. It holds answers. It could be the cure. It could heal this city. Don't you care?"

"Please. This city can't be healed. Everyone knows that. It's fucked. Broken from the get-go. From the day that first fucking fruit tree was planted in that garden back there. And besides, why would I want it all fixed anyway? I liked the way things were. I'd grown used to its fearful fucking symmetry. Well, that's before you showed up, that is, and started fucking everything up."

The voice was quiet now. The strands hung in his hand, limply, like wet spaghetti.

"You haven't even asked me yet," the voice whispered. "What it is I want you to do. Aren't you even curious? After everything." The strands around his fist spun tighter again.

"No! Yes . . . Okay. Fine. I'm listening."

"Find Faith."

"What? Like God or something? I tried, but that's not really my thing."

"No. The dead collector. Faith. Find her. Give her the book." The magic hair gave a quick pull to the left, towards Roeland Street. Sans watched it tugging in the wind like a horde of possessed balloon strings. Ridiculous. To think this morning when he woke up, he'd thought his life couldn't get any weirder. And all this because of a book. He stuck his empty fist in his mouth and bit back the giggle brewing in his throat.

"That's it?" he told the voice, his own voice sounding almost hysterical by now. "That's all? Ha! Sure. Fine. That doesn't sound too hard, I guess. Just let me go home and take a nap, okay? Change out of these sweaty clothes. Have a drink. Or three. I'll sort this whole thing out for you tomorrow. Give the damn dead collector your musty old book."

The strands gave another yank, harder this time, much harder, the magic hair cutting red rivulets into the skin of his fist. "No. Now," urged the voice. "It has to be now."

"Of course it does. Listen here, you crazy Anna whatever you are. Stop pulling me along with your magic hair like I'm some kind of puppet. I'm nobody's fucking Pinocchio. I'll dangle my own damn strings, thank you."

"This isn't about you," the voice was getting louder now, begging, desperate, almost screaming at him. "It's much bigger than that."

"Oh, really."

"Stop. Stop pretending that you don't care about anything. Your leg. The car accident. Your father. Your mother. You think it was your fault. You've let your grief shape your memories; twisted them all up. Now you go around pretending that nothing matters. That you don't feel. But you do."

"Hey! Whatever you think you know, lady, you don't."

"I know you want to help her."

The hair was hurting him now. His fist burning from the pressure. His bum leg burned and he was tired. So fucking tired. "Fine. Let's say I do this. Will you stop haunting me?"

"Didn't you listen to the sin-eater? I'm not a spirit."

"Ghost, seer, mind-fuck . . . who cares. I do this, you stop torturing me?"

"Yes."

"Let's get it over with, then."

78

FAITH

Outside the gate to the Company's Garden, the crowd was a beast, baying for blood, carrying her along like a current.

Smoke everywhere. Black smoke. Bodies. Sweating bodies. Angry bodies.

A row of armored Casspirs was blocking the road to St. John's Street, where her car was parked. Police in riot gear were forming a human chain, to cordon off the street. Four men and a woman. All of them not a day older than twenty. She could see their faces behind their helmets. They looked scared. She had to go that way, she had to get out.

She had to find a way to get to them, show them her medpass, tell them she was a dead collector, that she needed to get to her van immediately. Maybe they'd listen. She had to try. Get out of here, to the convent, to Tomorrow.

Her hands felt in her coat pockets for the little plastic rectangle. Shit. Nothing in her pockets. Her pass? Did it somehow fall out? Was it in the car? It had to be in the car. Her car behind the human chain. What now? Tomorrow. She had to get to Tomorrow. Before . . .

Something was happening. The crowd heaved. Like it was sighing. Like it was breathing. One last big breath before . . . She was sure the others felt it, too. Everyone. That moment. Before a pot boils over. Before a dam cracks. A quiet. The calm before . . . Then it happened. Something burst.

Laughter. Horrible laughter. Hysterical laughter. So much laughter. Everywhere. Everyone.

Shots ringing out. (Rubber bullets. *Please, God, let it just be rubber bullets.*) Screaming, running. Police, protesters, bystanders, one gigantic human soup. A tall man in a red hoodie to her left throwing a fist at a Veep. The Veep swinging his baton. The man falling, sinking into the crowd, holding one hand out like he was drowning. More fists. More shots. People running. Trying to run. She was running, too. Almost tripping. Something beneath her feet. A discarded shoe? A backpack? No. A hand. A leg. A stomach. A head. Oh, God, bodies. Bodies lying on the street, curled up like babies, cackling hysterically. Bleeding. So much blood. *Don't fall, Faith. Don't let the wave drag you down. Don't drown. Keep running.*

Running.

A hand on her back. Pulling at her. *No. Let me go, you motherfuck—*

A voice above the roar. "Faith!"

Hope.

Hope.

She turned towards the hand. *Pony Boy.* It was Pony Boy.

Follow me, Pony Boy mouthed, stretching out his open hand.

She grabbed it. Gripped with all her might. *Don't let go*, his lips mimed above the roar. *Don't.*

Then the whole world went up in smoke. Her eyes were on fire, her nose was streaming with snot, her throat was burning, closing up. She was blind. She couldn't stop coughing. She tightened her grip on the ponyjacker's hand, and followed him blindly, stumbling, tripping, running away, coughing, coughing, tears streaming down her teargassed face. They were running up a side street on the edge of the crowd, heading towards the mountain, when her eyes started seeing again.

"No!" She coughed. "Wrong way! We have to go down! I need to get to Sea Point! I need to—"

Pony Boy stopped, bent down, vomited onto the road. "Won't work," he said after wiping his mouth with his sleeve. "There's no way we can make it through that crowd."

Her lungs were still burning from the gas and the words struggled to come out. "Have to! I have to—"

"I know. Get to Sea Point. I've been told. I can help. Trust me."

"Trust you?"

"Unless you have a better idea."

A manhole cover; he was bending down, pulling at a manhole cover. Had he lost the plot?

"Just trust me, okay? And if you can't trust me, trust Anna."

Anna.

They were inside a tunnel. Water was trickling beneath, soaking her shoes and ankles. Pony Boy spread his legs wide, one on each side of the stream, waddling like a penguin. She followed his lead, pressing one hand against the wall for balance.

"I wouldn't do that if I were you," he said, turning his head back to look at her.

"Why?"

He pulled out his cell phone, lit up the screen, and shone the light on the walls. Cockroaches—the walls were covered in cockroaches. She pulled back her hands, fought the urge to scream.

"What is this place?" she asked instead. "Where does it lead?"

"All the way to Strand Street. This used to be an open canal. The Dutch built these babies to channel water from the freshwater springs in the mountain all the way to the harbor. Then the fuckers polluted the water in the canals so badly that they just built over it. Forgot about it. Now most of this water just ends up running into the ocean. What a waste. Pretty fucked up, isn't it?"

"Strand Street. There isn't enough time . . ."

"What?"

"Strand Street isn't far enough. We still have to get all the way to Sea Point, on foot, before . . . If we had a car . . ."

"Don't worry about that. It's all sorted. I phoned a friend."

SANS

They came to a fork in the dark. "Left, we're going left," he said. His Nikes squelched as he walked. (Poor babies were having one hell of a rough week.) At the end of the tunnel, there was a small wooden door. "This is it," he said. "We're here."

He pulled at the door. For a moment, the light blinded him. He blinked the white light away, opened his eyes again, almost couldn't believe them. There, next to the road, waving at them through the rolled-down window of a white Toyota Hilux, was the sin-eater. Thank fuck.

"You came," said Sans.

"Of course, boet. Of course," said the sin-eater. "Come on, then. Don't just stand there. Get in!"

ATERI

Ateri was digging. Jamis was lying next to him, chewing and licking and slobbering on a big fat leather shoe. *Thud, thud, thud* went the shovel as it hit the dirt. Down, down, down spiraled Ateri's thoughts as the hole sank deeper and the mound of brown earth beside him piled higher. Sweat stung his eyes. A jarful of curse words clogged his throat.

Done.

The shovel struck soil again.

He was done with being a muscle. He missed the family trade he was born into. Show business. The rush you get from a rapt crowd. He was a performer—always had been, always will be—not an enforcer.

Maybe it was time to go back to all that. But not street circus tricks this time. No. Something else. Ateri had never said this out loud to anyone, but he'd always thought he'd make a good comedian. He could be quite funny if he tried. And he loved coming up with new jokes. He was practicing his lines on Jamis all the time.

Maybe he'd talk to Konishiki. Ask him to hire him and Jamis at the comedy club. He could bartend or clean or help with bouncing when he wasn't busy on stage. And when he was, Jamis could get in on the act, too. They could be a team. A comedy duo.

Ateri took the dead man by the arms and lowered him into the hole. He wrestled the chewed shoe from Jamis and chucked that in, too. The hyena gave a halfhearted growl, then slunk away to find something else to do.

As he shoveled dirt onto the dead man's face, a plan took shape. It could work. He'd try. He'd really try this time. It was time.

81

SANS

They found them in the holy hall, just like Anna said they would. The street rat was holding the gun, pointing it at the nun, her hands shaking violently. "I want my brother back!" she cried.

"I'm sorry," said the nun, shaking her head, "but the dead aren't meant to be kept as pets. It's not right. They need to move on."

"Pets!" screamed the rat. "How can you say that? My brother isn't a pet!"

"I didn't mean it like that. It doesn't even hurt, the procedure. We only use a tiny spark of spiritual energy. Their spirits don't even register it. There's a faint whiff, like the smell a photocopier emits, then we send them right back where they belong."

The girl's head was swaying, her crazy hair doing this crazy jig to the tune of her whipping neck and her shaking hands. "You're crazy. You're a crazy old woman."

"Don't you realize this is all your fault?" It was the sin-eater, his eyes locked on the nun. "The riots. The souls. It's all on you. You're hoarding them. In these bottles. Tying them to this plane. They can't move on."

The nun turned her head. Noticed the three of them crowding the door. "Sans. Who is this man? What is he doing here? What is he talking about?"

"You really don't know, do you?" said the fat man.

Then the old nun said something else, but Sans couldn't hear it. He was watching the street rat now. There was this look in the kid's eyes.

Resolve. Her hands, which had been rattling earlier, were still. The dead collector had noticed it, too—she took a step forwards, holding her palms up in front of her. "This isn't the way to fix things, Tomorrow. You know that. Give me the gun."

"I thought you didn't care," said the rat.

"I do care," pleaded the dead collector. "Please, give me the gun. There are other ways to fix this."

Silent tears were streaming down the girl's cheeks and the candles made the wet salt glitter like dew. "It's too late for that," she said softly.

"Please, kid," Sans tried. "You can't fight fire with fire. Take it from me." *What a stupid thing to say*, he chided himself silently. But it was all he had.

"I don't care. I don't care anymore," said the little rat. "Elliot. None of it matters without him. You don't know what it's like. To have no one . . ."

I do, kid, I do, Sans wanted to say. But he didn't.

"She's evil. She has to pay. Someone has to pay. For all of it." The rat changed her grip on the gun. Her eyes spat brimstone now.

"Not now!" shouted the sin-eater. "Wait!"

The trigger clicked.

The girl looked down at the gun.

Then at Faith, her eyes a question mark.

The dead collector sighed. "Did you really think I'd leave a loaded gun in my glove compartment?"

FAITH

"Did you really think I'd leave a loaded gun in my glove compartment?" Faith said, sucking in a breath of relief. *Thank God, thank God, thank God Ash didn't leave a loaded gun in my glove compartment.*

Tomorrow's whole body slumped. "I—I don't know what else to do. I don't know where Elliot is."

Faith turned her attention to the burning orbs. There were hundreds of them. Hundreds. She was thinking of Jacob's face, his burning, glowing face. She couldn't see it anywhere. She couldn't see Elliot, either. She remembered the sangoma's words: *You will find him if you let him go.*

Then something in her mind clicked. "Forget about her. I know where Elliot is," she told the girl, reaching out her hand. "Just give me the gun."

FRED

"She's evil . . ." said the girl, but Fred didn't hear the rest. Didn't even hear the trigger click. All those glowing orbs. So many faces. He hadn't been taking his little blue-and-yellow pills since Thursday. (That whole damn fight with Faith on Friday, it had unsettled him. Made him think. He couldn't take the little pills after that.) And now the convent's holy hall, that had previously just been a drab dark room with bleddie baie bottles and candles to him, was lit up like a soccer game at night, with lights in his eyes and spectators crowding the stands. So many spectators, all shouting to be heard, all screaming at him, trying to get his attention. Making it really bleddie hard to keep his eye on the ball.

"Not now!" he shouted at the orbs. "Wait!" *Eye on the ball, boet, eye on the ball,* he told himself. *You used to be a cop jou donner—keep your eye on the ball, assess the scene, focus on what's important. Focus. Drown out the voices, the faces, focus. Focus on the threats. The caretaker. The girl. The nun . . .*

The nun. Something in the old woman's eyes; she was looking at the caretaker, a flick of her wrist, and Fred knew what was to come. But it didn't make a difference. The caretaker was too fast and Fred was too out of shape. The caretaker launched himself towards the girl and the gun. The gun clattered, skidded across the wood.

The girl fell, her body locked under the caretaker's bulk.

TOMORROW

The fall knocked the breath right out of her. The world went dark. She couldn't breathe, couldn't move, couldn't see. Her head hurt. The smell of alcohol and sweat filled her nostrils until she wanted to choke. She could hear Faith shouting, but she couldn't hear what.

The caretaker was pulling at her arms, trying to pin them behind her back. The claustrophobia, the weight of him, she needed to breathe, needed to get up, get out. She screamed until her lungs burned and pulled with everything she had until one arm wedged free. Clawing at his hair, his ears, tearing at anything she could get a grip on. "Elliot!" she screamed. "What did you do with my brother, you bastard!"

A crash, and Tomorrow blacked out.

MAJOR

Major screamed in pain and let go of the kid. As he let go, he fell against the candle-lit shelf. A kaleidoscope of fire and glass lit up the dark as the long shelf toppled over and a hundred candles tumbled down, their flaming tips kissing the wooden floor. He scrambled to his feet, pulling off his jacket. Saw Sans doing the same. Together they tried to choke the flames. But it didn't help. The flames couldn't be tamed. They were spreading too fast.

Smoke filled up the hall, blanking out the light. He looked around for Mother, but he couldn't see her—the smoke was disorientating him. He didn't know his left from his right.

"We have to go," said Sans, pulling at his arm. "We have to get out of here. We have to go now!" But Major wasn't going anywhere without Mother. He found her at the back of the hall, next to the tipped-over shelf. She was lying on her back. "Come!" he yelled, holding out his hand towards her. "Come."

"No," she answered. "I can't. My leg. It's caught underneath the shelf."

"Help!" he called to Sans. Together they heaved at the shelf until their sweat turned to steam and their eyes were blind with smoke.

"It's stuck," said Mother. "It's no use. Just go." The roof was popping and crackling. Angry black waves rolled across the ceiling.

"We'll go get help," coughed Major. There were knives in his chest, so many knives. He had his shirt pulled up over his mouth, and so did Sans, but it wasn't helping anymore.

"Go," said Mother again, before exploding into a coughing fit. "The sisters. You have to warn the girls. The bell. In the garden. Go ring it. Wake them up."

SANS

The flames were rolling across the ceiling like a freight train without brakes. "The bell! You've got to find the bell!" he shouted to Faith. She nodded, and sprinted towards the garden, the bell. The fat man followed her, holding the girl in his arms.

Three quick bangs rang through the corridors. "Gunshots," shouted Sans. The virus patrol!

"Not gunshots," wheezed Major. "It's the windows exploding."

They started running. Down the open corridor. Towards the convent's sleeping quarters. Panicked sisters were starting to stream out the doors. "Go, go, go!" the caretaker shouted at them. "To the garden! Out!"

Sans was helping the caretaker pull open the big double doors to the dining hall when he realized his back was feeling strangely light. And there was this weird pulling feeling against his wrist, like something was tugging him in the other direction. Fuck. The backpack. The strap must have broken in the shuffle. He'd lost it. The bag. The bloody book.

"I know, I know!" he screamed at the pull on his wrist. "I'm going back, fuck it, I'm going back!"

FAITH

Crawling along the floor on their hands and knees towards the door, they left the smoke, and the flames and the orbs that glowed like the world was going to burst. The sin-eater was carrying the girl, who was sobbing quietly into his shoulder, covered in soot, a large red gash spitting blood from the back of her head.

"Is she going to be okay?" said Faith, eyes on the blood.

"She'll be fine."

"Where's Sans?"

"I haven't seen him since we reached the hallway; I think he's with that tattooed guy with the wonky eye, trying to see if any of the sisters need help getting out. Come, we need to find the bell."

"Elliot," murmured the girl. "Elliot . . . we need to get Elliot . . ."

"He's okay. He's here." Faith pulled the bottle out of her coat pocket and shoved it into the sin-eater's palm. "Do you know how to get him out?" she asked him.

"Are you sure it's the baby boy?" said the sin-eater. "It could be anyone in here. You don't want to give her false hope."

"I think so. Just tell me you know what to do? To get him out?"

"I'll phone Pinky. We'll figure it out."

At the bottom of the garden, they found the bell. Next to Mary with her eyes downturned.

Fred covered the girl with his jacket, and laid her down on the grass.

The sound of the ringing bell bled into the dark, seeking out the last of the slumbering nuns, who swirled outside in twos and threes, clutching at their robes and coughing in fits as the smoke spiraled and the sulphurous smell of burnt hair clawed at their noses and throats.

But Faith didn't hear it. Her brain had tuned the world on silent, and all she could see was her pulling arms on the bell cord, while her tongue tasted soot, her throat burned, and her brain sang the same childhood song on repeat:

Oranges and lemons,
say the bells of St. Clement's.
You owe me five farthings,
say the bells of St. Martin's.
When will you pay me?
say the bells of Old Bailey.
When I grow rich,
say the bells of Shoreditch.
When will that be?
say the bells of Stepney.
I do not know,
says the great bell of Bow.

Here comes a candle to light you to bed,
Here comes a chopper to chop off your head!
Chip chop chip chop—the last man's dead.

TOMORROW

The fat Afrikaans man gave her the bottle filled with Elliot's beautiful brown locks. "Your brother's in here," he whispered. "We're going to get him out." He wasn't wearing his mask and his moustache moved as he talked. But she trusted him. She couldn't see Faith anywhere, and when she tried to move her neck it hurt, but she could hear the dead collector's voice, over the noise of the fireworks. *Fireworks?* Was she starting to hallucinate? Why fireworks? Then the bell started ringing. And something came flying through the convent's window, and landed a few meters away on the grass. A backpack.

"Elliot," she whispered, gripping the bottle tight. "I did it. I found you. It's going to be all right."

SANS

He was lying in the holy hall next to the window while the flames leapt higher and the smoke turned the world black. He wasn't alone. Someone was sitting next to him on the floor, her hair glowing black, blue, indigo in the orange light.

"Hey, I thought you said you were going to leave me alone now," he coughed.

His unicorn, Anna, smiled at him, and he smiled back.

"You did it, you saved the book," she said.

"But I didn't manage to save myself, did I? The door is blocked. Fucking roof beam or something."

"Yes."

"I'm not going to make it out of here, am I?"

"No. Not this time, kid."

"Oh," he said. "I guess I'm fine with that."

Anna held out her hand and he took it. Was he imagining it, or was her indigo hair growing? Reaching out? No, it wasn't a trick of the light, the strands were stretching towards him, snaking over his hands, his arms, his legs, his feet, his stomach, covering him like a blanket, a beautiful black cocoon. Enveloping him.

"Where am I going?"

"I don't know," she murmured. "It's different for everyone."

"Say," he coughed as the strands started snaking over his eyes, his cheeks, his lips, his face. "Why the hell didn't you just tell me who you were from the start? What you wanted from me? Why the charades?"

He could feel the strands streaking through his hair now. His mother used to stroke his hair like that. "Would you have listened?" she asked.

She grinned at him, her teeth a Cheshire crescent, a white moon of incisors blinking at him in the dark, and he wanted to laugh. He stifled the urge out of habit, before he realized he didn't need to anymore. "Probably not." He cackled. "Probably not."

90

PIPER

After fleeing the crash that saved her life, Piper kept running. Up, up, into the fynbos folds of the mountain. Higher, higher. When she was finally certain she was alone, that no one was following her, she stopped and pulled her mask off. Drank in the beauty of the fynbos. Allowed herself to feel the sun on her lips. Then the corners of her mouth stretched outward. Until she was just teeth and no lips. Her body began to shake, but she didn't have to keep it in anymore. Alone among the fynbos, she could finally laugh without fear—she didn't have to pretend anymore. She gave in to the laughter, and her body shook with violent giggles. She let it all out, expunged it, until her muscles ached, but she could breathe again.

Feeling sober again, she pushed on. The plan was simple. Head up to the mountain's table, find the death cult living up there, inside the old tourist café on top of the mountain. She'd heard they performed this ritual, before they injected you, a ritual to improve your chances of reincarnation. Piper had always liked the idea of reincarnation. A fresh start. A chance to try again. She'd read about a research professor of psychiatry at the University of Virginia, a Dr. Ian Stevenson, who'd done some incredible research on the topic, and it had given her hope.

Hope. It was all going according to plan, until the wind started up and a thick white mist erased the scenery. The world disappeared. And it became cold. So cold. Unimaginably cold.

The world was so white that she couldn't see the trail anymore. And she was so, so cold.

She remembered reading stories in the newspaper as a kid about tourists climbing the mountain who'd strayed from the marked paths wearing the wrong gear only to fall off cliffs or get lost and die of hypothermia. "Stupid tourists, don't they have any sense?" her dad would say while she munched on her cereal, playing with whatever toy she'd been taken with that month.

Now she'd gone and done the same. Was she going to die here? Was she already dead? She pulled her coat tighter across her body, folded her arms across her chest, and trudged on.

After what seemed like hours, she found a cave. She almost hadn't noticed it because of the mist.

There was firewood inside. Cooking utensils. A can of baked beans. A lighter. Someone had lived here once.

She didn't remember falling asleep. But she must have. Because she remembered the dream.

The dream was a weird one. Even for her. She was lying on the floor of the cave, while two old men sat hunched over her dreaming body. Both had pipes clamped to their yellowed lips. One of the men was wearing a hat, and the other a purple coat, with horns growing out of his forehead.

"Is she dead?" asked the first man, the one wearing the hat.

"Depends on how you look at it, I guess, but no, not quite," said the second, while filling up the bowl of his pipe and tamping it with his yellow fingers.

"Decent ears," said the first man. "You can tell a lot about a person from the shape of their ears, I always say."

"Yes. You've told me," said the second man, and Piper thought she saw him rolling his eyes. He struck a match against one horn and waited for a few seconds for the sulphur to burn away before firing up the pipe.

"Do you think she's going to make it?" asked the first man, who was now packing his own pipe, his bony old fingers shaking from the effort.

"They never do, do they, Van Hunks?" said the horned man, drawing in the nicotine with obvious pleasure.

"There you go again," said the one called Van Hunks, pinching some tobacco between his fingers. "Always focusing on the negative."

"Hmph!" said the second. "How many years have we been sitting up here now? Watching?"

"A long time."

"How long?"

"I don't know. Centuries."

"Yes. And nothing ever really changes, does it? It's like reading the same book on repeat. Don't you get tired of it?" He was blowing smoke rings now. The puffs of smoke making strange shadows on the wall of the cave. The shadows danced and writhed and morphed into images that played before Piper's eyes like moving pictures—images of war and plague and smallpox and polio and AIDS and TB and malaria and the Spanish flu and scurvy. And other kinds of death, too. And horror and depravity. And armies of mythical beasts with fangs and claws and horns and batlike wings. And things. Many more things. Things she didn't have the words for but recognized deep down at the very base of her being.

"We could always do something," said the first man. "Interfere. Try changing things for once."

"Hmmm . . ." said the second man. "Shut up and smoke."

The night wore on, breathing and pupating in its chrysalis, while the old men sat like the ancient sentries they were, watching over and over and over and always. Always sucking, sucking, sucking in the smoke from their pipes, always watching, always waiting, always almost breathing, while the shadows danced and Piper slept, slept, slept the sleep of the dead. Until the dark broke free from its chrysalis and split into dawn without ceremony. And just like yesterday and the day before that and the week before that and the month before that and the year before and the decade and the century . . . it was morning.

MONDAY

91

THE DAILY TRUTH

NO MORE PRICK FIXES

By Lawyer Tshabalala

We told them where to stick it. And they listened!

Yesterday was a scorcher, with protests and burning postboxes across the city. Amidst all the chaos, everybody's favorite hair cult, the Sisters of Godiva, was set on fire, with conflicting reports on whether the fire was set by protesters. Nearby residents and business owners say the smell of burning hair was still fouling the air late last night, seeing more than one bystander bent over in a fit of vomiting. By evening, things had quieted down across the city after the protesters and the government had reached an agreement.

Amidst all the violence and unrest, the president is in talks to scrap the mandatory meds (with some theorizing that they were nothing more than a placebo to calm and control the anxious public to begin with).

To tell you the truth, I still don't know what to make of all this, my friends. Maybe it was ghosts all along? Maybe there's truth to the reports from spiritual camps that Sick City is turning into some kind of limbo on earth? Wasn't it Dante who said that purgatory is located on a mountain in the Southern Hemisphere? On it, next to it, it's all semantics, isn't it?

Or maybe there was no grand conspiracy to begin with and we've been making ourselves crazy. Mass hysteria or whatnot . . . Could be we were all crazy to begin with, and sometimes when things get too much, the crazy just boils over a little bit. Who knows?

Till the next. Love you long time. Over and out.

SEVEN
MONTHS
LATER

THE DAILY TRUTH

A RUMBLE IN THE JUNGLE

By Megan Moosa

Things are gonna get rof tonight at the Bree Street therapy bar when retired heavyweight champ Ebrahim Baadjies steps into the ring with Limbo City's favorite Easter Bunny and Daily Truth *reporter, Lawyer Tshabalala, for a skop and donner rumble in the Cape jungle.*

When the *Truth* caught up with Baadjies earlier this week at his house in Tamboerskloof, he hadn't yet decided which suit he was going to zip up for the momentous occasion. "You know, there's this laaitie from the therapy bar coming by later today with a selection of costumes. So, I'll have a look and we'll see from there. But I've always had a thing for the Joker, you know, from *Batman*. Otherwise, maybe I can be a corpse cockroach or a ghost or a fat-cat cop."

So, come, people. This is going to be a jol for the ages. Catch the match at 7:00 p.m. sharp. Just R30 for breathers and the dead pay half price.

She was in the lobby of the Cosy Sleeps Hotel. One lone working girl was sitting on the velvet couch. Tomorrow checked in with Raul at the front desk. He was reading a big fat book about plants. "Hey, Tomorrow," he said, closing the book. "Guess what? I got another tattoo. Wanna see it?"

"Yes, sure."

Raul rolled up his sleeve.

"Ooh. Nice. Who's the girl?"

"Not a girl. Another goddess. Persephone."

"Queen of the underworld."

"Impressive! You know your Greek goddesses?"

"Only this one. It's really cool, Raul. It looks like a painting."

"Right again. It *is* a painting. A painting by this famous dead brother, Frederic Leighton, called *The Return of Persephone*. I found it in the library."

"I thought the public library had closed down."

"Not that library. Another one. A secret library." Raul gave a weird little wink.

"Secret, huh?"

"Yup. Maybe I'll take you there someday."

"That would be awesome, Raul. I'd love that."

Raul grinned at Tomorrow. He rolled his sleeve back down and slid the keycard through the hole in the window. "Here you go," he said.

"Cheers, Raul. See you later."

"Sure. Later."

Tomorrow made her way up the stairs and through the gloomy corridor. Her gumboots squelched as she walked. When she got to the last red door on the left, she slid the keycard into the lock.

The comedy club was packed tonight. She'd never seen it like this before. The air was so thick with smoke and sweat that she was struggling to breathe. On the stage, the security guard from the museum market was talking to his hyena. The guy was telling the hyena jokes and the hyena would either laugh, lie down and put one paw over its eyes, or roll over and pretend to be dead. The audience was loving it—they were pissing themselves like they were about to keel over. Lock-you-up-and-throw-away-the-key kind of stuff.

All that howling, open laughter made her uneasy, but she tried her best to shrug it off. Feeling like a right prude, she cricked her neck and waved at Konishiki, who gave her a nod, then turned back to the stage where the hyena was rolling over onto his back now, laughing maniacally.

She fiddled with her mask for a sec, making sure it was properly secured, then chided herself for being so paranoid. She knew that things were different now, that masks didn't really matter anymore, now that being dead wasn't such a death sentence. But old habits die hard.

Molding her hips through the snug nest of tables—trying to act cool and unfazed, but still careful not to touch anyone—she headed to the office at the back to drop off this week's packet: a hard drive full of the latest international movies, music, TV shows, antivirus software, and newspapers, courtesy of her new employer, Mickey. It was a good job. A million times better than cleaning other people's blood off walls, for one. With some bonus perks, too, like getting her own packet for free each week.

So many things had happened in the last few months. They were living with Faith now, in this ginormous mansion by the sea. Tomorrow couldn't believe that Elliot had been in Faith's pocket all that time.

Luckily the dead collector had figured it out, and with the help of that fat Afrikaans guy and a real woke sangoma, they'd managed to get Elliot out.

After the night of the fire, when the dust and ash had cleared up and the city had come out of its haze to find that the truth couldn't be explained away so easily and that the postbox meds had nothing to do with the spate of spirit sightings sweeping the streets, Faith had set to work decoding the book. (The one in the blue backpack that Sans had rescued from the fire.)

For four months, the dead collector hardly slept, only ate when Tomorrow cooked for her. The book became her obsession—an obsession Tomorrow guessed had less to do with finding the cure than a last-ditch hope that her son, whom she still didn't really want to talk about, wasn't totally gone. That some part of him still existed somewhere. Hope. Tomorrow knew all about hope.

Eventually, Faith had managed to decode every single page. But it didn't give the answers any of them were expecting. There were other answers, though. Strange ones. Crazy ones. About how to live in this weird new world.

It had been seven months since the fire, and the whole The Dead Are People, Too movement was gaining traction and the city was getting used to this weird state of liminal limbo where mouthbreathers and soulbreathers lived side by side and jostled for the same dreams, the same rights.

The world was becoming crazier by the minute, or maybe saner, she wasn't sure, but there was one thing she did know: she, Tomorrow Persephone Pretorius, was doing fine.

GLOSSARY

ag: Afrikaans equivalent of "oh," as in "oh well" or "oh please."

aweh: informal greeting or term of acknowledgment.

baie: Afrikaans for "a lot."

bandiete: bandits.

bergie: homeless person.

bleddie: alternative version of "bloody."

blerrie mal: Afrikaans slang for "bloody crazy."

bliksemse: slang expletive similar to "bloody."

boere: farmer in Afrikaans, but used here as a slang term for the South African Police Service.

boerewors: a type of sausage that is a popular South African delicacy.

boerie rolls: boerewors rolls, like a hot dog, but substituting the wiener or frankfurter with boerewors (see above).

boet: brother.

braai: South African wood fire barbeque.

broe: slang for "brother."

broekie lace: intricate wrought ironwork resembling the lace trimmings on panties or "broekies" that adorns Victorian buildings.

doek: headscarf.

donner: slang insult. Often used in frustration. Similar to "fucker" or "asshole." (From the Afrikaans word for thunder.)

donnerse: slang expletive. Similar to "bloody" or "damned," as in "the damned thing is broken."

dop: alcoholic drink.

eish: exclamation for expressing a variety of emotions, including surprise, horror, excitement, resignation.

ek sê: I say.

Ek spelie met iemand anders se ma se trane nie: I don't play with someone else's mother's tears.

entjie: Cape slang for cigarette.

fokken piemp: insult. Cape slang for "fucking informer."

fynbos: a unique type of local vegetation famous for its enormous diversity of species.

Gadawan Kura: hyena handler (Hausa; rough translation).

gemors: mess.

guardjie: aka sliding door operator or sliding doorman. Responsible for opening and closing the door of a minibus taxi and collecting passengers' fares.

hayi wena: exclamation. Used as an expression of disappointment / anger / indignation / dismissal. Variations include "suka wena," "hayi wena."

impepho: Sacred incense. Indigenous South African plant that is dried and then burnt as an offering to the ancestors.

ja: Afrikaans for "yes."

jirre: exclamation.

jissis: exclamation. Slang for "Jesus."

jol: party.

jou: you.

kasi: township / informal settlement (used in this context to refer to a style of music, kasi rap (a mashup of hip-hop and kwaito).

koeksister: South African delicacy. Plaited, crunchy sticks of dough deep fried and dipped in syrup. (Not to be confused with koesister, which is similar to a donut, but with ground spices such as ginger, cinnamon, aniseed, cardamom, and tangerine peel added to the dough, before being fried, boiled in syrup, and rolled in dessicated coconut.)

kwaai: From Afrikaans for bad-tempered (person), severe (storm), or vicious (dog). Used in this instance as slang for "cool."

laaitie: kid.

laat my hake vlam vat: let my heels catch fire.

lekker getrek: slang for being drunk.

maita basa: thank you (Shona).

maller as 'n haas: crazier than a rabbit (Afrikaans).

meisiekind: girl/daughter.

moer: impolite term used in this instance to mean "beat up."

mos: implies whatever has been said is self-evident. Closest English equivalent is the term "of course" or "(as) you know."

motjie: Cape slang for a wife or steady partner.

muthi: aka muti. Traditional medicine.

my laanie: slang term of address for a well-to-do person.

naira: Nigerian currency.

né: right?

neef: cousin.

nogal: rather. As in "It's rather warm today."

okes: slang for "guys."

oom: uncle (Afrikaans term of respect for a man who is older than you).

oubaas: father.

Parow Arrow: Derogatory nickname (similar to the term "white trash") for an Afrikaans person from the Northern Suburbs of Cape Town. (Parow is the name of a Cape Town suburb.)

rand: South African currency.

rof: rough.

ruiker: bouquet.

sangoma: traditional healer.

shambok: a long, stiff whip, originally made from animal hide.

sho: exclamation.

sisi: sister (respectful way of addressing a woman in Xhosa and Zulu).

sjambokking: flogging of someone with a shambok.

skollie: a hooligan or hoodlum.

skop: kick.

sommer: just because.

sosatie: popular South African delicacy of marinated cubes of meat threaded on a skewer and cooked on an open fire (similar to a kebab).

stukkie: a small piece. Cape slang for a woman, especially a girlfriend or sexual conquest. Similar to "piece of ass."

tackies: sneakers or trainers.

tik: South African street name for crystal meth.

tjappie: Cape slang for a tattoo (most commonly used when referring to prison tattoos, although used more generally here).

tokoloshe: mythical (although still very real for some) mischievous evil spirit in South African (Xhosa/Zulu) culture. Said to be hairy, short in stature and extremely libidinous.

tsotsis: informal term for gangsters/criminals.

Usalele?: Are you still sleeping? (Xhosa)

Utata uJacob: Xhosa for "Father Jacob," a popular South African lullaby. (Aka Vader Jakob in Afrikaans, Frère Jacques in French, and Brother John in English.)

verraaier: traitor.

voet: foot.

ACKNOWLEDGMENTS

Truth is often stranger than fiction, and many ideas in this novel were inspired by real events and people, including (but not limited to) the South African Occult Crimes Unit, the Tanganyika Laughter Epidemic, and the phenomenon of social panic around amakhosi possession. Many of the responses of Sick City inhabitants to the Laughter were also based on reactions to real epidemics throughout history. A variety of sources were unendingly helpful in writing this book, but the seed that laid the groundwork was *Plague, Pox and Pandemics: A Jacana Pocket History of Epidemics in South Africa*, by Howard Phillips (Jacana 2012).

I am deeply indebted to my agent, Stacia Decker. Thank you for believing in me and going above and beyond to get this book into the world.

To my superhero of an editor, Mike Braff, for taking a chance on this crazy book and helping me to make it even better.

To Nathan Burton and Andres Juarez. Thank you so much guys; the cover rocks!

To Linda Sawicki for her eagle eyes and for teaching me what a pot plant is. Everyone else at Skybound and Simon & Schuster without whose hard work behind the scenes this book wouldn't have happened: Kate Caudill, Joe Monti, Madison Penico, Alexandre Su, Lauren Jackson, and Shauna Wynne.

A big thank you to Alison Lowry, for her generous advice and unending patience.

The following people also kindly offered their time to read drafts and/or give advice: Dr. Ralph Goodman, Stephanie Van Gelderen, Annette Klinger, Nadia Kamies, Anette Hugo, Nobukho Nqaba, Imraan Coovadia, David Cornwell, Lucia Saks. (I didn't always listen, though, so any faults, blunders, factual inconsistencies, and all the other sucky bits in this text are entirely of my own making.)

To the National Research Foundation, who awarded me with the necessary financial assistance to complete the first draft.

To Daniel, my rock, my muse.

To my children, Kai and Maia, of whom I am incredibly proud.

To my mom, who gave me the best gift in the world—a lifelong love of reading—and without whose belief and constant cheerleading this book would never have seen the light of day. And to my dad, who gave me the next best gift—a sense of humor.

And to Evermore Chaka: Your patience, kindness, and never-ending optimism is an inspiration. Thank you for keeping me sane.